Includes Bonus Story of
A Love so Tender
by Tracey V. Bateman

The Carpenter's Inheritance

LAURIE ALICE EAKES

BARBOUR BOOKS
An Imprint of Barbour Publishing, Inc.

The Carpenter's Inheritance ©2012 by Laurie Alice Eakes
A Love so Tender ©2005 by Tracey V. Bateman

Print ISBN 978-1-60742-580-9

eBook Editions:
Adobe Digital Edition (.epub) 978-1-63409-727-7
Kindle and MobiPocket Edition (.prc) 978-1-63409-728-4

Published by Barbour Books, an imprint of Barbour Publishing, Inc., P.O. Box 719, Uhrichsville, OH 44683, www.barbourbooks.com

Our mission is to publish and distribute inspirational products offering exceptional value and biblical encouragement to the masses.

 Member of the
Evangelical Christian
Publishers Association

Printed in the United States of America.

One

Miss Trudy Perry, Attorney at Law, would not, after all, be joining Miss Lucinda Bell, Attorney at Law, in practice in Loveland, Massachusetts. She had decided to follow her brother to San Francisco and practice law out on the West Coast.

"Follow her brother indeed." Lucinda folded the flimsy yellow telegram and glanced around her office. "Follow her heart is more like it."

And who could blame her? California was friendlier to lady lawyers than Trudy's home state of South Carolina.

"Just like Virginia." Lucinda stuffed Trudy's telegram into a folder marked PERSONAL CORRESPONDENCES, where it joined another wired message that had shattered her hopes of practicing law alongside her father, as he had practiced alongside his, and his father had done before that. . . .

WE LOST *Stop* SUPREME COURT SAYS VIRGINIA CAN PREVENT WOMEN FROM PRACTICING LAW *Stop*

That telegram from Belva Lockwood had sent Lucinda, freshly graduated from the University of Michigan Law School, hundreds of miles from the Virginia mountains she loved to an unfamiliar and, thus far, unfriendly town in Massachusetts, where becoming a lawyer as a female wasn't considered wrong.

At least the state bar didn't consider it wrong. She had yet to learn about the citizenry.

She glanced around the second-floor office she'd acquired with the help of one of her father's numerous friends and colleagues in the law. His son had started there in the small town on the Connecticut border. He had long since moved back to Boston but said the county was in need of another lawyer. He gave her suggestions, advice, and names of people to befriend.

He hadn't told her the law office had become a storage room for the saddle and harness shop on the first floor in the year the premises had been empty. All shelving had been removed, apparent from the brackets left behind without their boards, and hooks installed. Massive hooks so high on the wall, Lucinda couldn't so much as fling her hat atop one. All that remained of any use was the desk. Though scarred, it was solid oak, wide and deep, with lots of drawers.

"I need a carpenter." She supposed she spoke to the spiders likely hiding in the corners. Talking aloud was better than the silence. "Where do I find a carpenter?"

"*Ask Gertie,*" Daddy's friend had advised her when talking about the town. "*That woman knows everyone.*"

Lucinda hadn't met her yet. She had walked into the office thirty minutes earlier, found Trudy's telegram waiting for her, and simply sat staring at it the whole time.

Useless where she sat, Lucinda rose, found her hat hanging from a bent bookshelf bracket, and perched it on her head at a more or less reasonable angle. Gertie could be found at the café across Main Street, and down two blocks. The Love Knot Café, not the Loveland Café. That belonged to Selma Dickerson, who didn't approve of ladies doing anything but entering her premises for tea and scones, if they weren't home being wives and mothers. Or so Lucinda had been warned.

She exited her office and poised on the landing to jiggle the key in the lock until she heard the tumblers fall home. The telegrams were the only thing in the office to steal, but a good habit was a good habit. Once she had client files in there, she must keep matters secure.

The steps led down the outside of the building. Still, the smell of leather and mink oil turned her stomach before she reached the pavement. As soon as she could manage it, she would have to move her office somewhere more appealing to female clientele. At least Lucinda hoped she would draw female clientele. She wouldn't turn down men, of course, but the ladies' plights appealed to her, from collecting pensions long denied them, to helping them make out their own wills, to. . .whatever anyone needed. She wasn't about to be choosy at this stage of the game, though she preferred not to handle criminal matters.

Once away from the harness shop, the sharp sweetness of dried leaves crunching underfoot freshened the crisp autumn air. Overhead, those still clinging to their branches blazed red on the maples and golden on the oaks lining the streets. A few wood fires burned in the distance, perfuming the air with fragrant smoke, masking the less pleasant aromas of the oil or coal stoves. In the middle of the afternoon, few pedestrians strolled the business area of town. A handful of ladies in frothy taffeta gowns and befeathered hats entered the Loveland Café, a block from Lucinda's office. Each woman gave her a bold glance from her black felt hat with its one feather to her black serge skirt and her jacket over a white blouse trimmed with only a narrow band of lace. She wasn't unfashionably dressed, just looked more like she attended to business than wore her finery for tea with friends. She smiled at the ladies. Only one returned her smile, a woman about Lucinda's age with coppery curls bouncing beneath her leghorn straw hat. The other ladies either did not or pretended not to see

Lucinda, as they turned their backs on her and entered the tea shop. She suspected the latter. It wasn't the first time in the three days she'd been in town that ladies had pretended the female lawyer didn't exist.

"But I am a lawyer," Lucinda murmured to herself. "I am a member of the bar."

And without having to go awfully far from home, though she was farther north than she wanted to be. She likely would wish she had taken Trudy's path and gone to California instead, regardless of the distance from Virginia.

Lucinda turned her back on the Loveland Café then trotted past the bank, a dress emporium, and a jewelry store. Across the street from the library, a free public library at that, the Love Knot Café rested, its blue-and-white-striped awning cheerful, the gaslights inside bright even on this sunny autumn day. Encouraged, she opened the door. Warmth, light, and the aromas of hearty, wholesome food like apple pie and roasting chicken surrounded her. So did silence. The instant the bell above the door chimed her arrival, everyone in the oak-paneled room ceased talking, ceased eating, seemingly ceased breathing. They didn't cease moving, at least not their heads and eyes. Every head that needed to swiveled in her direction. Every pair of eyes fastened on her.

They all belonged to men. Not the soft-handed, suited kind of men with whom Lucinda usually associated. Men in rugged flannel shirts, denim pants, and boots; men with bronzed hands, whose faces needed the attention of a razor.

As if those eyes were darts, Lucinda slammed back against the glass window in the door. Its coolness penetrated through her jacket and shirt. The rest of her heated as though she slaved over the stove, cooking the delicious food scenting the air. Her face flamed like one of the gas jets on the wall. Mouth dry, she tried to think of something to say, how to ask the men for Gertie, or simply how to flee with grace and a smidgen of her dignity left.

She groped behind her for the door handle. If she got the door open, she could spin on her heel and rush away, let the men think she'd simply stumbled into the café instead of—of the hardware store next door. Her fingers felt cold metal, grasped it.

And it turned. The whole door moved, flying outward. So did Lucinda. One minute the support of the portal lay behind her; the next she fell back against something else, something solid, with a thud hard enough to drive the wind from her lungs. In front of her, the room erupted in laughter. Behind her, two hands grasped her waist, steadying her. A man exclaimed, "I am so sorry, miss, wasn't paying attention. Are you all right?"

All right? With his hands nearly spanning her waist and his chest still against her back? All right with that café full of men— well, half a dozen or so of them—laughing at her?

No, not at her. With her breathing and balance restored, she caught their remarks.

"Dreaming of Samantha Howard again?"

"I was dreaming of Gertie's beef stew." The gentleman released Lucinda. "Were you coming or going, miss?"

"Going." Lucinda turned toward the street.

A mistake. It brought her nearly face to chest with the man. Because she wanted to drop her gaze to the pavement and scuttle away, but needed practice looking men in the eye, she raised her gaze to his face. A young face, not much older than hers. A clean-shaven face surrounded by unruly waves the gloss and color of polished mahogany. Eyes the rich golden brown of amber smiled down at her.

"I believe the ladies' aid society is meeting at the other café," he said.

"I'm not a member. That is—" Lucinda licked her parchment lips and sought for the right answer.

Her downfall as a lawyer. She got nervous when speaking aloud to strangers.

She tried again, though speaking too quickly: "I came to see Gertie about finding me a carpenter."

The café erupted in laughter again. "Looks like you got yourself one, miss."

If the man hadn't blocked her way still, Lucinda would have fled down the street, possibly all the way to the train station. Surely being a lawyer in her own right wasn't worth this kind of humiliation.

"Ignore them." The man they'd called Matt tucked one big hand beneath her elbow and guided her inside the café. "We'll see what's keeping Gertie from helping protect you from these oafs."

"We're the oafs?" a man shouted. "You're the one nearly knocked her down."

"And got to hold her up," another man pointed out. "Always did have the luck with the—"

For the second time in the past ten minutes, the room fell silent as though a door had slammed on everyone's mouth. A woman, with a massive bosom heaving above a miniscule waist, swept through a swinging door in the back, brandishing a coffee-pot in one hand and a basket of rolls in the other, like they were a sword and a cutlass. "What's going on out here?" she demanded in a voice as deep as most men's. "Can't I get the bread out of the oven and set a new batch rising without having you all causing— What you got there, Matthew Templin?"

"Looks like a lady." He pulled the door shut behind him and Lucinda. "Says she's come to ask you to recommend her a carpenter. Think you can do that?" He grinned.

Lucinda caught it from the corner of her eye, and her stomach performed a somersault. Hunger. She was hungry, and the smell of the fresh bread made her mouth water.

"Stop teasing the poor girl." Gertie plunked the coffee and bread onto a table before a grizzled man with more hair on his face than his head. "You pour the coffee, Ned, while I help this young lady." She bustled forward, black bombazine skirt swirling around her, and clasped Lucinda's hands. "What fool sent you in here without warning you?"

"M—Mr. Smithfield." Lucinda's face heated again at her slight stammer.

Behind her, Matthew Templin jerked as though she'd shoved her elbow into his middle.

"Smith—aha." Gertie enveloped Lucinda in a fragrant hug. "You're the new lady lawyer come to take his place. Well, why didn't you say so straight off? These men might have shown you some respect. Matthew, you pull out a chair for her and get that coffee away from Ned. Have you had lunch, child? You don't look like it. Come sit. Ain't no one with you?"

"No, my father had to get home for a trial." Lucinda made the explanation so no one would think poorly of Thomas Bell, Esquire.

Hmm, if male attorneys were esquires, were female attorneys esquires, too?

She was delirious with hunger, fatigue, maybe a little apprehension, to judge from the shaking of her knees and flips still going on in her middle, not to mention absurd thoughts like signing her name Lucinda B. Bell, Esq.

She dropped onto the chair Mr. Templin pulled out at one side of the room, the side away from the men and not beneath one of the gaslights. Pooled in darkness and in a corner on her own, she would be unnoticeable enough for the men to forget her presence—she hoped.

A cup and saucer appeared in front of her. Rich, dark coffee jetted into it, the aroma itself heartening.

"Cream, Miss Bell?"

She jumped. Matthew Templin had served her, not Gertie. That lady had vanished through the swinging door.

"Yes, thank you." She made herself look up at him. Way up. She wasn't a short woman, but he was a tall man.

He produced a cream pitcher and set it on the table, then seated himself across from her. She opened her mouth to object to this bold behavior, but he raised a staying hand as though knowing her intentions. "You said you need a carpenter. What all do you need done?"

"You know a carpenter?" She eyed his woolen coat and blue flannel shirt. "I mean—a good one?"

"I'm the best in at least three counties. Just ask anyone here." He said it with such matter-of-fact calm, the words held no arrogance or braggadocio—only simple truth. Confidence. And in a man no older than twenty-five or twenty-six.

She wrapped her fingers around her thick, warm coffee mug, looked into his face, started at that weird tumbling in her middle, and busied herself pouring too much cream into her coffee. "I need help straightaway. If you're that good, you're likely not available straightaway."

"Depends on what you need. I— Ah, Gertie, is that your venison stew?" He flashed the buxom middle-aged woman his heart-melting smile.

She batted her eyelashes back at him. "It is. Saved you a bowl."

"Only one." He sounded genuinely disappointed.

"Two, but you'll have to share with Miss Bell, here." Gertie set two wide soup plates on the table.

Lucinda shook her head. "No, I couldn't."

"Refuse Gertie? No." Templin gave the thick pottage, smelling of garlic and thyme, a longing glance. "And if you don't eat, then neither can I."

"I'll bring you some more bread." Gertie bustled off.

Reluctantly, Lucinda picked up her spoon and took a mouthful. Then she took another, and another. The bowl had dropped to half full when she realized she'd been eating like a starving person rather than a lady.

"I'm so sorry." She stared at the succulent bits of stewed meat, potatoes, and carrots floating in savory gravy before her. "I didn't realize what I was doing."

"You mean eating?" Matthew Templin laughed. It sounded rich and a little hollow in the empty café.

Lucinda realized the café had emptied save for them—probably not good for her reputation.

"I thought you were hungry. Ready to talk about your office? You're above Shannon's Harness, aren't you?"

"Yes." She wasn't at all surprised that he knew its location. "I think they used it for storage while it sat empty. It's. . .bleak. No shelving, no paneling, nothing left."

"So what do you want?" He set down his spoon, his bowl empty, and leaned back in his chair. "More shelves? You have books, I presume?"

"Yes, quite a lot of them. And I need shelves in the other room, my living quarters."

"That's not an office, too? We thought two of you were coming."

"Two were. One"—Lucinda sighed—"went to California with her brother."

"And left you on your own. That was unkind." The gentleness in his golden gaze suggested he could never be unkind. "I can do all that in a day at the most. I'll work it into my schedule. Tomorrow?"

"Well, yes, if you can." She fumbled with her coffee cup. "And will you tell me how I can get furniture? I mean, where? I need chairs. I need something for my clients to sit on in the office

He stared at her, not moving, not speaking. He simply leveled that bright gaze at her for at least a minute. A clatter of metal pans in the kitchen seemed to shake him from his paralysis, and he leaned forward, reaching out to her without touching her. "Do you think that wise, Miss Bell? That is, well. . .a young woman on your own and all."

Lucinda stiffened. "I have been on my own for six years, Mr. Templin. I am a full member of the Massachusetts Bar and am perfectly capable of taking care of myself."

"Except for putting up shelving."

"That, sir, is why I pay a carpenter." She pushed back her chair and surged to her feet. "I will expect you at eight o'clock tomorrow morning." She fumbled with her purse for the money to pay Gertie for the delicious lunch, better than the apples, bread, and cheese on which Lucinda had been living since Daddy left. She found the silver, laid it on the table, and headed for the door.

Behind her, Matthew Templin murmured something she didn't catch. She didn't care. He was merely a hired handyman coming to make her office look respectable. She would find furniture on her own. Someone in town would have it or tell her where to get it. He had no right to admonish her about living on her own in the room above her office. It was perfectly respectable. She had a private stairway, even a bathroom and an icebox. She simply couldn't cook hot food, other than make coffee or tea over a spirit lamp. But it was enough for now. Once established, she could find a better place to live—a little house—as she had planned to do with Trudy, until her friend scampered off to California.

If people were friendlier out there than they had been thus

far in Loveland, Massachusetts, perhaps Lucinda should follow Trudy. Still too annoyed with a near stranger questioning her living arrangements to pay attention to whether anyone so much as tipped a hat to her, Lucinda stalked the two blocks to her office. Now that her stomach wasn't rubbing against her spine, the leather odor from the harness shop smelled pleasant, a reminder of the Virginia countryside with its abundance of horses. She climbed the steps, paused to pull her key from her purse, and stared at her door.

It was open, the lock broken. Scrawled on the door, in what appeared to be a child's coloring pencil, were the words LAWYER, GO HOME.

Two

Matthew Templin cast a last longing glance at the remains of Miss Bell's stew and pushed back his chair. If he was so concerned about her living on her own, he should be concerned enough not to let her walk home alone, even in broad daylight. His mother had, after all, raised him to have some manners. Even if Lucinda Bell had dismissed him like the hired help. Even if one glance from her crystal-blue eyes had sent his insides twisting like a sailor's knot.

He laid his own silver on the table and headed for the door.

"Where you going, Matthew?" Gertie called from the kitchen doorway.

"Back to work"—he snatched his hat from the hat tree by the door and dropped it onto his head—"by way of the lady lawyer's office."

"Uh-huh." Gertie sailed into the dining room and began to clear off tables. "Pretty, ain't she?"

"I suppose I'd be a liar if I said I didn't notice."

Gertie chuckled. "I'd say you shouldn't be handling a saw if you didn't notice. Like as not, you'd cut off a few fingers." She made a shooing motion toward the door. "Go after her. She's too pretty to be strolling about on her own."

"Or living on her own." Matt opened the door then closed it again. "She's living in that office of hers."

"We wondered where she was staying. Gotta get her out of there. Good people in this town. No one will hurt her. But they won't think she's a good woman, living on her own like that." Gertie scooped plates onto a tray with a rattle and crash of crockery and flatware.

"Mrs. Woodcocks already has some reservations." Matt grimaced over the name of the mayor's wife.

Gertie paused on her way to the kitchen. "And how would you be knowing that?"

"I'm repairing the paneling in their library. The wall is a bit thin between it and some sort of sitting room. And I should get to work on it, if I'm going to take a day off to fix up Miss Bell's office."

"You just walk past her place then. Tell her to come here for supper."

"You're not open for supper." Matt grinned at her.

"Get going." Gertie shoved the kitchen door open with her hip.

Matt departed through the front door, inhaling deeply of the crisp autumn air. Winter wasn't far off. Frost, snow, warm fires— alone. One of these winters, he'd stop sharing his fire with someone other than his dog and cat and a good book. A wife would be a nice start, and a few children down the road.

Unbidden, the image of Lucinda Bell flashed through his mind—slightly above medium height and fairly slender, though it was hard to say with the way women cinched themselves up and wore puffy sleeves. Blond hair so pale it was almost silver, like moonlight. And eyes the clear crystal blue of a northern lake, all dressing for features strong enough to draw the eye, delicate enough to give her feminine beauty. Patrician beauty. Along with her soft, southern drawl, Matt knew what that meant—a lady far above the touch of a mere carpenter. So what if he was the best in the trade in at least three counties and at only twenty-six. She made it clear she thought he wasn't good enough to carry a conversation with, let alone further an acquaintance with except on business terms. So he shouldn't bother walking two blocks out of his way to make certain she had gotten home safely. Of course she had. This was Loveland, not Boston, and two o'clock in the afternoon, not two o'clock in the morning. Still, she might have encountered Mrs. Woodcocks along the route, a force not to be taken lightly.

In the middle of the afternoon on a chilly day, the sidewalk proved nearly empty. He spotted the librarian ducking out for a breath of fresh air and tipped his hat to her. She'd been his teacher in grammar school and told him to go to college. As if a Templin would ever have the money for that. Still, she encouraged his reading. He would have to introduce her to the lady lawyer, who must read a great deal, too.

He shouldn't think about the lady lawyer in any capacity except for work. Yet there she was before him. Above him, actually. She was poised on the edge of her landing as though about to raise her arms and take flight. Her face was ashen, and the door of her office home stood open.

Matt took the steps two at a time and caught her by the shoulders. "What happened? Are you hurt?"

"Yes. No, I mean—" She gestured behind her. "A mean, nasty trick. Nothing more. But—" Her voice broke. Her face twisted.

"Wait here." Matt slipped past her, approached the door. The words glared at him. A nasty trick indeed, and unusual. He didn't know when something like this had ever happened in Loveland. "I'm going inside." He glanced at her. "Have you been in to see if anything's disturbed?"

She shook her head. "I didn't know if someone might be there, waiting." She hugged her arms across her middle and shivered as though the temperature were fifteen degrees instead of fifty. "I mean, it's so nasty, so—"

"Unkind." Matt reached out his hand but withdrew it before touching her cheek as he'd intended. He didn't know her. He was the hired help, not some scion of a fine family. "I expect no one's there. People who play nasty games like this don't usually wait around in broad daylight."

And how had someone managed it in broad daylight?

On the threshold, he glanced up and down the street—or what he could see of it. Not that much. The stairway, railing, and overhang of the roof sheltered the landing from a street view. More important than *who* remained *why*.

Mind completely blank on that score, Matt entered the office. If Lucinda hadn't told him in Gertie's that the place had been neglected, he would have thought she'd been vandalized. Only a scarred but high-quality oak desk remained of the furnishings he knew had once been simple but elegant. He would need more than a day to set the place to rights to his satisfaction.

Scanning the chamber from floor to ceiling, wall to wall, he continued to the back of the room. As in front, a grimy window lent the place light, along with two gas sconces on the walls. The front showed the street; the back showed the alley and the tree-shaded side yard belonging to Roger Stagpole, the town's other attorney. An interesting choice for a legal office, and not accidental on the part of Lucinda's predecessor, he'd bet, were he inclined to do such a thing. Easily, she could watch who entered and exited her competition's house. With curtains at that window, he wouldn't be able to do likewise unless the client came up the rear steps.

Those steps rose beneath the window, but the door must enter the other chamber. That room's door was closed and appeared to have no lock on it. Matt didn't want to enter it, if Miss Bell lived there.

He started to turn, to call out to her to enter, but a light fragrance, something sweet and floral he had missed in the café, touched his nostrils, warning him she had come in on quiet feet and must be near. He glanced back, feeling the impact of her clear gaze as he had in Gertie's—like someone seizing his innards in an iron fist.

"I see everything's all right in here." She let out a soft, humorless laugh. "Not that they could have done much damage."

"No, but you'd better look at your room." Matt gestured to the other door without looking at her again. "If the outside door enters there, it's possible. . ." He didn't say what was possible. She would know.

"There are two rooms, actually. A kind of storage room, and then mine. I suppose that will help keep the cold out in the winter."

"Yes, which makes me think we should do something about this office. I see a radiator, so you should have plenty of heat from the steam, but cold air will come right through that door."

She glided past him to the other door and twisted the glass knob. "What could you do?"

"Turn the landing into a foyer."

"Truly?" She stood before him, gazing at him with those wide, bright eyes, and his mouth went dry. "Would the owner let you?"

"I expect he would. It would make this more valuable space for an office."

"Expensive?" Some of the light dimmed from her eyes.

To bring it back, Matt said, "No, I can use leftover materials from other jobs and work on my off times."

For you.

"That's such a kind thought, except—" Abruptly, she turned toward the door and shoved it open.

Her floral fragrance drifted to Matt's face, stronger, as though she'd sprinkled more on the carpet than on her person. It made him think of warm summer days in a garden. Miss Bell glided into that garden, in this case, a rug—strewn with faded pink flowers, woven with some kind of green vine—her skirt sweeping the nap with a gentle whisper.

Like her, it was a neat room, a sitting room—not a bedchamber—with a sofa beneath the window, a small table and two chairs, a tall cupboard, and a smaller chest. She'd mentioned an icebox. It must be in the storage room where getting the ice to it would be easy. She also had a bathroom. Matt knew. He'd helped install it when he was an apprentice. At some time, the building's owner thought to rent the space as an apartment, but then renting it as an office had proved more lucrative.

While Matt perused the room, Lucinda Bell inspected drawers and cupboards—the latter apparently holding clothing—then the back room. Matt wanted to follow her but didn't feel right about stepping into her living quarters uninvited.

She reappeared in a moment. "All is well. Not so much as a chunk of ice disturbed."

"We can assume mischief makers only, then," Matt said, his smile cheerful. "I expect some boys thought it would be fun to frighten the newest lady in town. Still"—he sobered—"you can't stay here until that lock is fixed."

"I suppose there's a locksmith?" She knit her delicate brows. "Or something like that."

"There is, but the door is damaged." Matt retraced his steps to the front door and examined the latch.

Indeed, someone seemed to have given it a good, hard kick.

"A locksmith won't fix this. This is cracked right through the panels."

A swish of fabric on boards, the encircling fragrance—Lucinda, close beside him. "I'll pay extra if you fix it today."

Of course she would. Society ladies always thought they could have what they wanted with money. So did the men, for that matter. They'd demanded, through money, his mother into her grave. Matt swore he wouldn't let money rule him, wouldn't allow it to kill him. But he did like his little cottage and garden, small though they were, and the woman who cooked and cleaned for him liked payment.

"I can get a new door and locks on here tonight." He turned to look down at her. "No extra pay necessary. Call it my welcome-to-Loveland gift."

"I couldn't. That is, you're too generous. Surely your family wants you home." Her cheeks glowed, not quite a blush, but a heightened pink pearlescence beneath her skin.

"No family." Matt shrugged off the twinge in his heart over no family. "Just a cat and dog. Now, if you'll fetch some things, I'll help you take them down to Gertie's. She'll find you a good place to stay for the night."

And hopefully keep Miss Bell there, especially if town vandals thought the young woman made a fine target.

She hesitated a moment, then nodded and retreated to the sitting room. Matt walked down the steps and slipped into the harness shop to ask the owner if he'd noticed anyone going up the steps. He hadn't. No windows in the shop looked out on the side or rear steps. By the time Matt returned, Miss Bell had packed her valise and carpetbag. From its weight, Matt decided the latter held nothing but books.

"Let's go down the alley," he suggested. "Gertie won't have the front open any longer, and you're less likely to encounter the ladies' aid society."

"Is that what I saw going into the little tea shop?" She trotted alongside him with athletic vigor and speed, as though she was used to long, brisk walks. "What looked like ten or so grand dames sailing along beneath their feathers?"

Matt laughed aloud. "An apt description, but I'd think you'd want to be there."

"I wasn't invited."

"You sound rather cheerful about that."

"Of course." Her footfalls crunched in companionable rhythm with his on the gravel alleyway. "They're having tea and scones and discussing—what? The next town festival? While I am wondering who dislikes lady lawyers enough to vandalize my office. Which would you prefer?"

He glanced at her, caught a sparkle in her blue eyes, and laughed. "I believe I see what you mean. Here's Gertie's."

With a sense of regret that lent itself to a sense of relief, he reached the back door to the Love Knot Café. It stood open to a cloud of steam smelling of carbolic acid. Gertie and her obsession with cleanliness, not that anyone complained. No one got sick eating at her establishment, unlike other places. He called to her, not wanting to drag Miss Bell inside with the caustic fumes.

"Who wants me?" Gertie appeared in the doorway, face and hands damp and red. "Matthew, what's— Ah, Miss Bell, decided you don't want to stay alone up there after all? No trouble. I have more than enough room upstairs."

"It's more than that." Matt glanced at Lucinda. "Someone broke the lock on her door and left a rude message behind."

"Get out of here." Gertie's face grew even redder. "Who would do a thing like that? Wait, never you mind. Come on in, child. How distressing for you. You're going to fix it for her, aren't you, Matthew?"

"Yes ma'am." Matt headed for Gertie's outside stairway. "I'll just carry these up so I can get to work. The Woodcockses aren't paying me to play bellman, so I have to get a bit more work in there." At the foot of the steps, he paused, unable to resist, and set the bags down so he could return and hold out his hand to Miss Bell. "I'll see you in the morning, bright and early."

She slipped her hand, soft enough to belong to any lady at the tea shop, into his as he'd hoped she would, her handshake firm.

"Thank you." And she smiled.

That smile turned her eyes from ice-blue to aquamarine—a smile holding enough warmth to go right through him and nearly make his jacket unnecessary on the chilly autumn day. A smile that made his step light all the way to the mayor's mansion. It hadn't been condescending in the least, but kind, appreciative, beautiful—as she was kind, appreciative, beautiful.

She was also educated and came from people who owned a lot of land. Above his touch, his mother would say. *"She's above your touch, Mattie."*

What female in town wasn't? Unless he pursued the girls who worked as maids to get enough money to run off to the city to be actresses or shopgirls or maids in bigger houses, where the excitement ran. He was an artisan, not a businessman. Young women wanted to marry wealthy men, or men with the potential to be wealthy. He would be comfortable all his life, he expected, but never wealthy. His hands were calloused and scarred.

And he'd held Lucinda Bell's hand for just that moment, so soft a hand he'd probably scraped it with his own rough paw.

Even a lady lawyer would want a man of means, or would gain enough means of her own to not want a husband who settled for perfection of his craft over wealth. So he should stop the nonsense of this giddy, schoolboy crush. In so many ways, she wasn't for the likes of him.

He slipped into the Woodcockses' through the back door, nodded to their cook at work on dinner, and made his way to the library, a room in desperate need of repair. Someone—the mayor's seventeen-year-old stepson, the story went about town—had fallen asleep while smoking and caught the paneling on fire. An alert housekeeper had caught it and extinguished it before more than a few books had been destroyed, but the floor and paneling on one wall needed complete replacement. Because the house was old and the paneling ornate, Matt needed to inlay each piece of flooring and wall covering with care and precision, just the sort of work he loved. Completing it would take him weeks, as he was still in the process of removing the ruined wood without damaging the plasterwork above. Another two hours should finish this first part of the job. Darkness would fall before he finished, but Miss Bell's office possessed enough lights to work after dark.

He didn't want the rooms open and unoccupied for the night. Yes, he could presume senseless vandalism caused the damage, a mean prank, nothing more. And even senseless vandals returned for worse damage.

If only he believed in those senseless vandals. If only he hadn't overheard that conversation between the mayor and his wife the day before, saying they would make Miss Bell's life as uncomfortable as possible until she left town. If only the paneling in the library lay against a solid wall instead of merely more paneling to the next room, allowing sound to carry through like a partially open window.

Matt crouched on the smoke-dulled floor and ran his hands over the next panel, seeking the miniscule nails beneath the varnish now black from the fire, trying not to feel a twinge of guilt.

He should tell Miss Bell what he knew. Except, he knew nothing for certain. He'd heard a mere snippet of a conversation and could draw a number of conclusions from it. No sense in making trouble where none might be intended. If worse occurred, then he would tell her. And nothing worse than a scare or two would happen. Matt didn't like the mayor and his wife, but he didn't have to like them to believe them not capable of a potential crime.

His mind more at peace, he worked the panel free, then another, then another. He settled into the rhythm of the work, accompanied by the light hiss of the gaslights a maid entered to light so he could work better in the fading afternoon, the aromas of wood and paint perfumes to his soul. He stroked every sliver of wood, inspecting it for damp or vermin infestation, for worse damage than smoke. None of the former, too much of the latter. A filthy, dangerous habit, smoking. Fire destroyed so much beautiful wood.

Someone entered the room beyond, a heavy tread, a male cough. Paper rustled. Matt expected to find a hole in the wall for the rustling paper to come through that clearly. He began to inspect more thoroughly than even before. He used his hands and eyes—no, no holes—just a sheaf of papers, yellowed, edges curled, ink fading, still legible.

Shockingly legible.

Three

S hoe heels clicked on the wooden treads of the front steps. A sharp counterpoint to the thud, thud, thuding of Matthew Templin's hammer against the office wall. Lucinda wouldn't have heard the approaching new arrivals if she hadn't just reached the landing herself and paused on the threshold to admire the carpenter's handiwork with the door.

It wasn't a new door. A few nicks and scratches marred the varnish, but it was finely paneled and hung more snugly than the previous door. The locks—two, she noted—gleamed with brass brilliance that would need regular polishing. Well, Lucinda wasn't afraid of hard work if it kept her safe.

Odd to think *safe* in a small town where she'd been assured she wouldn't find herself asked to practice criminal law. Loveland didn't have much in the way of violence, and only a few petty crimes. Vandalism, on the other hand. . .unruly boys' tricks was all. Gertie had assured Lucinda of that, while trying to get her to eat too much rich and wholesome food, and tucking her into a bed far more comfortable than the sofa Lucinda slept on in her solitary room. The temptation to remain with the restaurant owner ran strong, but Lucinda didn't want to spend any more money than necessary until she started making money.

Slowly Lucinda turned to face the newcomers and blinked. If she'd hit her head recently, she would have thought she was seeing double. Both ladies were petite, nearly a head shorter than Lucinda, and as fragile-boned as birds. They wore yellow straw hats adorned with orange bows, set at the exact angle atop nearly black hair. Their skirts and jackets were of the same rich brown, and each lady wore a gold cat pin affixed to her left lapel.

"We're Hope and Hester Floyd," one of the ladies said, holding out her hand in a yellow kid glove.

"Twins," the other said, quite unnecessarily.

"Don't worry about which of us is which." The first one's handshake was firm and warm, even through the leather. "I'm Hester and talk a little more than Hope, but even our own mother couldn't tell us apart after she stopped changing our diapers."

"I have a birthmark," Hope announced.

Lucinda didn't know whether to laugh, run, or blush. She decided to laugh. The way identical dark brown eyes twinkled at her, she knew that had been the right response.

"I'm Lucinda Bell." She shook Hope's hand, which wasn't quite as strong or warm as Hester's. "My office is rather at sixes and sevens right now, but if you can step carefully through the dust, I'll give you tea in my room."

The hammering had ceased.

"Are you having work done?" Hester asked. "That looks like a new door and lock. You do have Matthew working here, don't you? I wouldn't let anyone else work on my house except for him. Will Flint—that's who he apprenticed with—does good work, but Matthew is an artist. Hello, dear boy."

He stood behind Lucinda. She caught a whiff of freshly cut wood and something clean, like soap. No bay rum or Macassar oil. His hair would be springing up in those crisp waves, not slicked down. And no doubt dust and wood shavings would coat his clothes, instead of a gentleman's pristine smoothness.

As though it mattered. He was her handyman at present, no matter that his face had remained in her mind, a face that was really too attractive for a lady's comfort.

Lucinda led the Floyd sisters past Mr. Templin.

"Good morning, ladies." He spoke in that deep voice that also was too nice for comfort. "If you give me just a minute, I'll sweep a path clear for you."

"That's so kind of you, dear boy." Hope Floyd positively simpered, though she was at least three times Matthew's age. "And I'm so pleased to see you helping out Miss Bell. She needs a strong man around, being a lady on her own."

"Not that we ever needed one," Hester said.

"We have each other, Sister."

Lucinda kept herself from stiffening at the implication she needed a man around. She was paying Matthew Templin, not taking favors from him. Except for his working on the door the night before of course. That had been above and beyond the work of a hired man. It had been sheer kindness.

And your father helped you get this practice.

Cringing at the reminder that she was being hypocritical, Lucinda led the Floyd sisters along the path Matthew swept through the dust on the floor. "I have a spirit lamp and can make you tea, but I'm afraid I don't have any cake or cookies to offer."

"We brought some for you." Hope lifted a large handbag, as though she expected Lucinda to see the contents behind the soft brown leather. "We made them ourselves."

"Lemon drops," Hester added. "It's Mother's recipe, God rest her soul. Oh, isn't this charming. Such a nice place to receive female clients, rather than an office with a desk and all. So masculine and cold."

Lucinda closed the door behind the sisters to keep in the room's warmth so it didn't flow out to where Matthew worked with the front door open. The hammering resumed, perhaps with more vigor. Lucinda hoped she would be able to hear the sisters over the racket.

"If you make yourselves comfortable, ladies, and give me just a few minutes, I'll have some tea made." Lucinda busied herself with lighting the spirit lamp beneath the copper kettle that had gotten her through many late nights, reading and writing her way through law school.

"Earl Grey tea or orange pekoe?" she asked, a little too loudly to be heard over the hammering.

"Orange pekoe, if you have some milk." One of the sisters joined Lucinda at the table and set down a cloth-wrapped parcel that smelled of lemon and anise seed. "If you tell me where you keep your plates and cups, I can help."

"And I'll fetch the milk. Do you have an icebox?"

"I'll get it." Lucinda ducked into the storage room, cold enough that her ice barely melted, and retrieved a bottle of milk. She hadn't been in there since arriving a half hour earlier, and noticed that the back door bore a shiny new lock, too. The sight sent a curl of apprehension twisting through her middle. Mr. Templin claimed the incident the day before stemmed from mindless vandalism, and yet he'd taken the trouble of installing a new lock on this door, too, likely working late into the night.

Her hand icy around the milk bottle, Lucinda returned to the light and warmth of the sitting room and the Floyd twins. The water had come to a boil, and one of the ladies poured it into the teapot, Lucinda's mother's teapot of blue Wedgwood from England. It matched the delicate cups, saucers, and biscuit plates. When the sisters glanced her way, their identical gazes held respect.

"We'll have to let that snob Charity Woodcocks know you have fine china," one twin said. "She thinks you must come from the dregs of society to be a lady practicing something so indelicate as the law."

"Of course, I think doctoring would be more indelicate." The other twin shuddered. Hope. Her hand trembled just a little on her cup, and her voice shook, if one listened carefully.

"So why did you go to law school, child?" Hester asked. "Mind you, my sister and I both went to college."

"It wasn't very common in those days," Hope added. "Not that many girls do now, but more and more, and we like the notion of women getting educated. Harder for men to deny us the vote if we get ourselves educated."

"Which is why we cheered—yes, my dear, we cheered and clapped our hands—when we heard a lady lawyer had come to town. Roger Stagpole has everything his way, and that's not right."

"And Charity Woodcocks thinks women have no business doing anything but serving the interests of the community over a teacup." Hester laughed over her teacup. "She thinks we don't know she really runs this town. Her husband doesn't have two thoughts to rub together. But she pretends her place is only in her home, unless it's planning how to raise money for the poor."

"Not that that isn't worthy. Jesus would approve of charitable works." Hope dabbed at her lips with a napkin. "Delicious tea, Miss Bell. Goes well with the cookies."

"It does." Lucinda spoke the truth. The lemon drops melted on her tongue with buttery sweetness.

"What was I saying? Oh yes." Hope took another cookie. "I do approve of raising money for worthy causes, but we prefer our cause to be voting rights for women."

"Wait, Sister." Hester held up her hand. "First, Miss Bell, so we don't frighten you off, we want to know why you're here instead of in Virginia."

"To answer my calling to practice law." Silence had fallen in the next room, and her voice sounded too loud to her ears. She swallowed and began again. "My father is a lawyer, as was his father before him, and way back. I used to help him in his practice. I liked it so much I went to law school. But the court won't let women practice in Virginia unless the Virginia Bar says we can, and right now they say we can't because we're too delicate." She curled her lip on the last word.

The twins went off into peals of laughter.

A board clattered in the adjacent room. Good, he was working, not listening.

"But Massachusetts isn't so narrow-minded, so my father contacted a friend in Boston, who suggested Loveland. It's—well, I prefer a smaller town to the big city, to be honest."

"Ah yes, Mr. Smithfield." Hester nodded, orange bow bobbing. "His son was most welcome here to counter Roger Stagpole's work, since we all know he and the judge golf together with the mayor and things run as they like, not always as they ought. But the boy married some society girl from Boston and joined her father's practice there. You won't do anything like that, will you?"

"Of course she won't. She is obviously a lady of principles to move all this way to follow the Lord's calling on her life." Hope narrowed her eyes. "That is what you mean, isn't it, dear? You will be coming to church?"

"Most definitely." Lucinda smiled. "Contrary to what many people think, many lawyers have a deep faith in the Lord."

Not even when she'd been staggering with fatigue from studying or writing during law school had she missed finding her way to a church. The singing, the prayer, the sermons never failed to wash away her fatigue and send her back to her books with renewed purpose to bring justice to the world.

"And I was told I'm needed here," she managed to say.

"Of course you are, which is why we're here." Hope reached out her hand as though to draw Lucinda close. "We need our wills made."

"Both of you?" Lucinda glanced from one smiling, gently lined face to the other. They had to be seventy if they were a day, despite the black hair, which was probably dyed to be absent of gray. "You haven't had wills made before?"

"We have," Hester admitted, "when Mr. Smithfield began here, but we have changed our minds about one or two bequests."

"We have a different ladies' suffrage movement to support."

"I want nothing to go to that charity of Charity's."

"And we'd like to endow a scholarship for females at our alma mater."

Lucinda's eyes widened. The ladies looked well off enough. The quality of their wool jackets and skirts spoke to that, but how well off they must be to endow scholarships!

"You can do that, can you not?"

The hammer recommenced at that moment, drowning Lucinda's voice. She simply nodded and raised her teacup to her lips. Instead of the rich aroma of strong orange pekoe, she caught a whiff of wood stain. *Ah, that was why he'd been quiet, not because he'd been eavesdropping.* Shame on her for thinking so. The hammering ceased. "I can do whatever you like, though I'd prefer to meet with you individually." Did they do anything individually?

They nodded in unison. "Of course. We may disagree on a few bequests, and it's best not to argue in front of you." Hester finished her tea and rose. "Here is our direction. Send someone around with a message when you're ready to take appointments." She laid a cream-colored card with gold lettering on the table. "Now we're off to rescue cats."

"Rescue cats?" On her feet also, Lucinda couldn't help but stare at them.

The ladies trilled out their identical laughs. "Don't look so surprised, my dear," Hope said. "Someone must protect the poor things from being drowned or otherwise done away with. We find homes for them instead. Would you like one?"

"I don't think—" Lucinda began.

"That's a splendid idea." Hester nodded toward the window.

"It can watch the birds from that window all day. Nothing makes a cat happier than a window. We'll have you out to the house so you can see what we have."

Lucinda struggled for appropriate words as she slipped past the ladies to open the door. The instant she did so, the reek of varnish smacked her in the face. She gasped and fanned her hand before her face, as though that would do any good. Then she saw Matthew Templin and gasped again.

As though it weighed no more than one of the Floyd ladies' hats, he lifted a five-foot-long shelf into place with one hand. Muscles in his arm bulged beneath the sleeve of his shirt. His other hand held an apple from which several bites had been taken.

"He is a handsome thing, isn't he?" Hester asked in a stage whisper. "He'd be a fine catch if he weren't—"

"Hush, Sister, that's gossip. He'll hear you."

He already had. At least the fingers gripping the apple tightened enough to bruise it, and the shelf slammed onto its brackets instead of sliding into place.

If he weren't what? Just a carpenter? Or something truly awful enough to be titillating gossip? She could scarcely ask. Gossip was wrong. And it would come to her, regardless. Word always did in a small town.

Thanking the ladies for their call, Lucinda strolled back inside to admire the work accomplished already. "You work quickly."

"So do the Floyd sisters. Let me guess—lemon drop cookies." He flashed her his grin, a grown man grin, and a little dangerous to a girl's heart for it.

"Yes," Lucinda affirmed when her breathing was normal again. "They're delicious." She headed back to her room and more tea.

More hot tea, while he worked in the cold of the open doors and windows to keep the fume smells down, partly for her sake, not just his own.

She paused in the doorway. "Do you want a cup of hot tea?"

"No, thank you. I don't do well with those dainty cups of yours." He didn't look at her, and the back of his neck grew a bit ruddy.

Of course the English china wouldn't do well for him. He wouldn't be the sort to sip tea, and the cups were smaller than his hand. And maybe he didn't even like tea. He'd drunk coffee at Gertie's.

"A cup of coffee?" she offered, and wondered why she tried. She'd never offered refreshment to people working on her father's house. "I have something less froufrou you can drink out of."

He continued to work on the shelf without looking at her. "Thank you. You don't need to bother yourself."

"Of course I don't," Lucinda snapped. "I have fifteen people in line waiting to see me and six rooms to clean. Now, do you want a cup of coffee or not?"

"Well, if you put it that way." He set down the rag with which he'd been rubbing the shelf and faced her, eyes twinkling, grin in place. "Thank you. It's a bit chilly in here."

"It's as cold as the Arctic in here. You closed the radiator."

"Not good with the varnish."

"Then come into my sitting room in a few minutes."

"Your carpet. I'm covered in sawdust."

"Brush off the worst of it." She left him to return to his work.

In her room, she exchanged the teakettle for a coffeepot and the Wedgwood for two thick mugs she preferred for coffee or hot cocoa, when she indulged in that treat. They kept the drink warmer longer. The Floyd twins had brought her at least four dozen cookies. She set the whole plate on the table. Only when she went to the door to tell Mr. Templin the coffee was ready did she wonder about the propriety of having him in her room, alone. But surely no one would think anything of it. The curtains were open, and surely many ladies in town allowed him in their homes when they were alone and he was working on something. Besides, eventually she would have male clients she would see alone—she hoped.

She opened the door. "It's ready."

He nodded then brushed off his trousers and shoes. The back of his shirt looked as if he had stood beneath a shower of wood dust. She reached out as though she would have the nerve to sweep it away. Perhaps if he had worn a jacket she might have, but a shirt only?

Her face warm, she tucked her hands behind her and retreated to the table, beginning to talk before he entered. "You seem to know the Floyd ladies well. They're charming ladies. Does the town consider them eccentric?"

"Yes, yes, and yes." Footsteps lagging, he entered her room and perched on the edge of a chair. "No milk, thank you. Black and strong is the only way to drink coffee."

"That's what my father says." Lucinda poured milk into her own coffee. "I figure it's like chocolate—you don't drink it without milk."

"I don't drink it at all." He picked up his cup, sipped, and twisted it between his hands, staring into the dark liquid as though it were a crystal ball. "Miss Bell, may I ask you a question?"

"I. . .think so." Her hands suddenly cold at the seriousness of his face and tone, Lucinda wrapped her fingers around her mug of hot coffee. "I suppose you can always ask and I can refuse to answer."

"Yes, you can. Of course." He cleared his throat. He shuffled his feet beneath the table; then he set his cup down and looked at her. "I suppose if this is legal advice, I should pay you."

"The first consultation is free, Mr. Templin. You may not need advice or legal services."

"Maybe not." He drummed his long fingers on the edge of the table and stared past her, out the window. "How much proof does a body need to prove he is who he says he is?"

Lucinda's eyes widened. "I beg your pardon? I mean, that depends on the state and the circumstances. Usually a birth certificate is enough."

"And if he doesn't have one?"

"That gets more complicated." Lucinda leaned forward, trying to catch his eye. "Mr. Templin, do you have need of proof of your identity?"

"I don't know." He picked up his mug and hid his expression behind the thick crockery. "I may." He drew his brows together. "You may as well know this from me, as you'll hear it anyway, but my mother was. . . Well, she didn't know who my father was."

"And so?"

"I'm not much accepted in this town, except for my work."

Lucinda laughed. "That makes two of us, minus the work part for me."

Four

Matt clamped down on his interest in Miss Bell, heightened by the companionable laughter. He must not care about her, a lady. She would never accept him, unless he proved what he'd found in those papers.

Those papers. Surely someone's idea of a joke, giving him hope just when he met Miss Bell.

He set down his half-full cup. "I should get back to work."

"Finish your coffee, Mr. Templin. You're going to get chilblains on your hands if you don't warm them a few more minutes."

"Chilblains?" Matt laughed. "Miss Bell, this is only October. Wait until December."

"I know." She rubbed her own soft, white hands together. "I lived in Michigan."

"Did you?" He leaned slightly forward. "Why?"

She smiled. "First I went to college at Hillsdale, then to the University of Michigan for law school. They seem to like to educate females there right alongside males, which is why I didn't go to Vassar. I wanted to go to classes and hear the male perspective. I was so used to it from my father."

"I would have been happy to go to college anywhere." The words slipped out without his realizing that he even thought them, let alone that he would admit to such a thing. His face grew hot, and he opened his mouth to apologize.

She laid her hand over his on the edge of the table, her smooth fingers warm and gentle, and slamming something like a fist right into his chest. "You don't need to go to college to be smart or well read, Mr. Templin. Once I have those books unpacked, you're welcome to borrow them anytime. That is, if I have something the library doesn't have."

"Thank you." His mouth dry, he drained his coffee and rose. "I'd better get that shelving done so you can unpack your books. Thank you for the coffee." He exited with as much speed as he could without being rude and recommenced his work, making as much racket as possible—so she wouldn't be tempted to come out and talk to him. If she did, he'd likely do something ridiculous, like ask her to go walking in the woods with him to see the beautiful autumn colors. She'd be too cold anyway, and he'd have to hold her hand to warm it up. Or be tempted to do so.

Just because his hearthside seemed lonelier each winter was no reason to succumb to the charms of every new female in town, especially those far above him. Oh yes, preachers and politicians alike could speak of equality of all. Matthew knew that one day he could make a great deal of money, have the financial equality of many and more than most, but he also knew he could be as wealthy as Andrew Carnegie or any of the other steel magnates, and yet the circumstances of his birth would shame him.

Unless those papers he'd found between the wall panels proved true. Or he could prove them to be true. Doubtful. No one would believe anything against Charity Woodcocks. She was the town matriarch, living up to her name with all her good works.

He wanted to look up inheritance laws in Lucinda's books before he talked to a lawyer. So kind of her to offer. So gracious. The lady of the manor bestowing largesse upon the serf.

Except for that touch on his hand.

The ham-sized fist slammed into his chest again at the memory. He couldn't breathe. For a moment, all he could see was her face, so delicate, so feminine, so intelligent. She'd been to not just one college, but two, more education than most men enjoyed. And he'd only read half the books in the lending library. He wasn't simply not good enough for her; he wasn't smart enough for her.

But he had his work, and he knew he was good at it. Better than good. Bless the Floyd ladies for recognizing it. Their generosity and appreciation of his craftsmanship had enabled him to buy a house. Every time he thought of the ladies of Loveland entering the Floyd parlor and sitting on those chairs, he smiled. Eventually, someone would ask who had made them. He was certainly good enough for the town ladies to patronize his work.

And Lucinda needed chairs for her office and for her room, if she insisted on living there. He could take her to his workshop.

A plan forming in his head, he finished varnishing the last shelf and stepped back to admire his work by the fading afternoon light. The wood gleamed a rich, golden brown in the final ray of sunlight. With a couple of chairs, a rug, and a table beneath the shelving, the office would look downright elegant. He was finished for now and could go home.

He knocked on Lucinda's door to tell her he was leaving. She didn't respond. Beyond the panel, the room seemed too still, too quiet. He dared not open the door for fear she was changing her dress or something, but he didn't want to leave without saying good-bye. No, to be honest, he wanted to see her, to offer to show her furniture on Sunday. All the way to Sunday. And if she was inside and ignoring him, she didn't want to see him. If she wasn't inside, she must have departed through the back door, and that could also mean she didn't want to see him. Or maybe she just didn't want sawdust on her clothes before she went out.

Out in the evening, when someone had vandalized her office out of deliberate spite or a senseless prank.

Matt locked the front door then realized he needed to find her. He hadn't given her the keys. She couldn't get into her office without them. He headed for Gertie's. Nothing would be open this late; therefore, Lucinda would return there. More than likely,

Gertie had invited Lucinda to dinner.

He knocked on Gertie's kitchen door, and there she was, Lucinda Bell, perched on a stool at the tall work counter, drinking from a steaming, thick white mug and eyeing a plate of fried ham and eggs, her brow furrowed. A yard away, Gertie stood with her hands on her broad hips. She spun around at his knock and motioned for him to enter.

"You tell this girl to eat," Gertie greeted him.

"I doubt Miss Bell will listen to the hired help, Gertie." He strode forward and took the plate away from Lucinda. "But I'll eat it. Can't let good food go to waste." Without invitation, he perched on a stool, picked up a fork, and cut off a mouthful of egg. "Do you expect coq au vin, mademoiselle?" He didn't try to keep the hint of sarcasm from his tone.

Her face turned the glowing pink rose color he'd noticed before, faint, but a definite blush.

Gertie gasped. "Matthew, that was unkind."

"So is not eating food you prepared." He ate the mouthful of eggs. They were perfect, of course, and he was starving, having skipped lunch.

"I didn't. . .I never intended. . ." Lucinda's lower lip quivered as though she were about to weep.

Matt's conscience pricked him, but he kept eating.

"I just—" She heaved a deep sigh that fluttered the ruffle at her neckline. "I don't like eggs fixed that way is all."

"Well, why didn't you say so, girl?" Gertie stomped over to the stove. "Scrambled? An omelet?"

"Don't go to any trouble for me, please." Lucinda slid off of her stool. "I should get home. I just came for my things, now that Mr. Templin has my new locks on."

"And how do you plan to get in?" Matt grinned at her and held up the keys.

Her eyes widened, and her hand flew to her cheek. "I didn't think. I came down the back way so as not to disturb your work. . . ."

"Put those away and make her stay for a decent meal," Gertie directed. "If this is all the better you take care of yourself, how did you survive on your own all those years?"

"I had friends." Lucinda ducked her head.

"You have friends here." Gertie cracked eggs into a bowl then began to whisk with vigor. "Doesn't she, Matthew?"

Matt took a bite of ham so he wouldn't have to answer.

"Matthew Templin, where are your manners?" Gertie demanded.

He set down his fork. "With my full stomach. I didn't eat lunch so I could get those shelves done today."

"Thank you." Lucinda looked at the keys he had laid on the table, at Gertie standing over the stove, at the canisters of flour, sugar, and the like above Matt's head, anywhere but right at him. "Let me know how much I owe you and I'll pay you straight off."

Put firmly in his place.

Appetite gone, Matt picked up his plate and carried it to the bin where Gertie dumped uneaten food. She kept a few pigs on a little land outside town, and the scraps never went to waste.

"I should be home. My cat and dog will be wondering where their dinner is." He nodded to both ladies and walked out. And maybe the door closed behind him a little harder than necessary.

Nice to him, while he did her work for her quickly, as a favor to a newcomer, to a pretty lady on her own in a strange place. Once the work was done, he was no more than someone to pay and dismiss, not call friend. He shouldn't care. He shouldn't let himself fall for females because they were bright and intelligent. They wanted more than he could offer—soft hands and fine suits; top hats, not a simple cap.

But his dog, Growler, and his cat, Purrcilla, loved him. They greeted him in his cottage's small, fenced yard as though he were the most perfect human in the world. Neither of any breed, just the appropriate four paws, floppy ears for the dog, pointed ones for the cat, and the needy love of pets. Growler never barked. From puppyhood, he had merely growled when happy, when angry, when warning of a stranger's approach. Purrcilla did her share of meowing, as she did racing ahead of him to the back door. But she purred a great deal, too, snuggling on his lap or on a pillow, expressing her appreciation for warmth and shelter, and for rescuing her from boys who had intended to drown her in a stream. Matt had found Growler wandering about in the woods, so young he shouldn't have been weaned yet. The three of them enjoyed a familial life together, three creatures without kin to speak of and no recognizable ancestry.

Except for those papers.

Once he had fed the animals and made himself a cup of coffee then built a fire, he settled before the blaze with the cat on one side of him, the dog on the other, and pulled the papers from behind the cushion where he'd stuffed them. He should find a better hiding place for them, perhaps in his workshop, in the event they were real.

But they couldn't be. Someone was playing a nasty trick on him. For what reason he didn't know, but people did things like that. Maybe John Paul Daggett, the mayor's stepson, wasn't as quiet and nice as everyone thought him, though Matt found believing otherwise difficult. A more polite youth, Matt didn't know.

But the papers lay on his knees, yellowed around the edges, ink slightly faded—a birth certificate and a baptismal certificate for a baby boy born on October 10, 1867, in Virginia City, Nevada. Matt's birthday. The birthday of lots of people, but lots of people named Matthew Templin?

Five

The office still looked empty. Matthew Templin's shelves added a touch of elegance and formality to the room, especially once Lucinda stacked them with her books—law books to hand, and others higher and farther from where clients would sit, once she found chairs. So far, though she had found a rug in the back of the hardware store, a carpet in rich, deep reds and greens, no one seemed to sell furniture, and she hadn't dared return to Gertie's to ask her where chairs could be furnished.

Lucinda had offended Mr. Templin, and thus Gertie, apparently. She hadn't meant to. But he was the carpenter, a workman who had done good work and quickly, above and beyond quickly with the door and new locks. She thought he would want his pay straight off. He had bills to pay, food to buy, a dog and cat to feed.

A dog and a cat. Somehow that knowledge left her feeling rather warm in the middle, as she visualized him seated by the fire, a dog and cat curled up at his feet. She loved her father's dogs, had been around them all her life except when she was away at school. Then, as now, she felt the lack, the emptiness so easily filled by a furry body and bright eyes that said "I love you" no matter the circumstances.

If Trudy hadn't reneged on her promise to come practice, too, they could have had a little house, a garden, a cat at the least.

Now all that came into her office was a bill from the carpenter and an invitation to a "tea." Apparently, one of Mrs. Woodcocks's ways to raise money for a children's home. The cost was outrageous for the entertainment of some local lady poets reading their work, a handful of sandwiches and cakes, and cups of what Lucinda suspected would be weak, tepid tea. But she would pay the fee and look at it as a business expense. An excellent way to meet the town's ladies, potential clients like the Floyds, now that laws had changed and married women could control most of their own money and make their own wills, independent of their husbands.

Not that she didn't meet people at church. The pastor and his wife were warm and friendly. They invited her for Sunday dinner. The Floyd sisters introduced her to everyone they could. Most looked at her as though she were some odd species of insect and hurried on.

As though she were beneath them.

It stung. She wanted friends in the town, too. She liked luncheons and dinners and talking about books she'd read with others. She didn't like being treated like—

The hired help.

If only they would hire her. She couldn't build a successful practice on wills for only ladies. But if she did well, the men would come. She needed other cases, the lucrative ones, like lawsuits.

For now, she began work on the Floyd sisters' wills, not easy work. They were shockingly wealthy with numerous holdings, both joint and individual. They enjoyed various activities and organizations, which they liked to support, mostly those promoting women's rights: the right to vote; to be educated alongside men; and if married, to have the same rights as their husbands. Women like Hester and Hope were why Lucinda could prepare these wills and outline their trusts. They had gone before her and paved the way for her ability to be educated as well as men, and then to practice law.

"Except in Virginia, where it's warm." She shivered in the draft creeping beneath her door. The day was dark and threatening rain, but no one had fired up the boiler, so no steam heat reached her room. She would have to make peace with Matthew Templin to persuade him to build that foyer to keep out the drafts, if the owner of her building intended to be parsimonious with the heat.

She stopped unfolding his bill and listened to her thoughts. Make peace to get more from him? That made her sound self-centered. She should make peace with him because. . .well, she wouldn't go so far as to say she liked him.

Or maybe she should.

She enjoyed so little conversation over the next weeks, she even looked forward to the tea, to meet people who weren't hurrying in and out of church. She dressed with care, eschewing her severe suits for a flowing chiffon skirt in deep blue and a white silk blouse, trimmed with lace and matching blue ribbons. For warmth, she wore a short, red velvet cape and perched a tiny hat atop her carefully piled hair. Fortunately, none of the ladies would be embracing her and so wouldn't figure out that, even in more formal dress, she wore the new corsets with elastic insets instead of boning that ladies wore for playing tennis or bicycling.

How she would love to do either. She missed rigorous exercise but hadn't dared indulge herself in one of her brisk walks. She'd given the town enough to gossip about with just arriving, let alone setting out on the road to the wooded countryside on her own. Perhaps she would meet someone with a like mind. From the look of them, aged as they were, Hope and Hester Floyd enjoyed brisk walks.

Heart racing somewhere closer to her throat than her chest, Lucinda set out for the church indicated on the invitation. The tea would be held in the parlor, suggesting no more than twenty ladies or so. Not too intimidating. Her mouth shouldn't be dry, blood roaring in her ears. She mustn't be a chicken. Must not. Must not.

She climbed the steps of a church that looked as old as the American Revolution, but well maintained, with its red brick and white trim. Inside the foyer, a woman with a face as pale as sifted flour and hair so fine and light it seemed to float over her head instead of spring from it, stood behind a podium on which lay a thick book. "Your name?" she queried in a voice as deep as a man's.

Lucinda jumped, having expected something wispy and frail to issue from the woman's lips. "L–Lucinda Bell."

She gritted her teeth at her stammer, the stammer a law professor warned her would destroy her in court if she didn't conquer it.

At the sound of her voice, nearly as wispy as she'd expected the gate guardian's to be, two women behind the receptionist stopped talking and stared. Ladies farther down the corridor fell silent in waves that turned to the rising wind rustle of silk and chiffon skirts, lace petticoats, heels on carpet, as they shifted forward to get a good look at the newcomer.

Lucinda made herself meet the eyes of every female she could reach. She smiled. She willed herself not to blush. She willed herself not to turn and run. If she could conquer this bevy of females, a judge would be nothing to worry about in comparison. But who made the first move to break the stalemate of stillness?

Behind her, the church doors burst open on a wave of chilly air. "There you are," the Floyd sisters chorused. "We were afraid you were too busy to come, after all. Ladies, this is our attorney, Lucinda Bell."

For another full measure of beats, no one moved. Then a young woman, perhaps a year or two older than Lucinda, wove her way through the crowd on a cloud of pink taffeta that went well with her rich, auburn hair and sparkling green eyes. She held out her hand. "Miss Bell, Samantha Howard. I have so been wanting to meet you."

Samantha, the young woman who had smiled at Lucinda the day she saw all the ladies going into the tea shop. Lucinda wanted to hug her. She shook the gloved hand instead.

"Pleased to meet you."

She was ecstatic to meet a female her age.

"Perfect." Hope Floyd clasped her hands together and looked about to bounce up and down on her high-buttoned shoes. "I just know you two will be fast friends. Miss Bell, Samantha's father is the best doctor in the commonwealth of Massachusetts."

Samantha laughed. "He'd be honored to hear you say that, Miss Hope, but he'll settle for the best one in the county."

Or three counties like Matthew Templin's carpentry?

Ridiculous thought to pop into her head now.

"And Miss Bell can tell which of us is which," Hester Floyd put in. "Smartest lady in at least this county, and probably more."

"No, no." Lucinda ducked her head.

Miss Howard laughed. "Come along." Still gripping Lucinda's hand, she drew her to the corridor. "I'll introduce you to everyone so Miss Hope and Miss Hester can get their wraps off. And you, too. Here, let me have your cape."

Lucinda barely managed to unclasp the silver clip at her neck before Miss Howard whisked the wrap away and carried it to a rack of other garments. Several ladies approached Lucinda and introduced themselves, elderly and middle-aged ladies, some with wedding rings, most without. One thing they bore in common—they all said the Floyds had been talking about Lucinda.

"I'm going to come talk to you about my will tomorrow," one lady whispered.

Three more ladies of the Floyd sisters' ilk murmured something similar throughout the afternoon. Lucinda's heart lightened with each confidential pronouncement. Gradually, the milling crowd migrated to the parlor to collect eggshell-thin cups of tea, which didn't look weak in the least, and an abundant supply of cakes, sandwiches, and hothouse strawberries.

"Take lots of food," Samantha advised. "Once Mrs. Woodcocks starts talking, you'll need to eat to stay awake."

Lucinda laughed. "I haven't yet met the mayor's wife."

A not-so-subtle hint.

"I know." Samantha's rosebud mouth pursed, and her eyes shifted to one side of Lucinda's face. "I'm not certain you will. She and her cronies don't approve of you." She leaned forward so that her lips practically grazed Lucinda's pearl earring. "She didn't want you to come to the tea, but the Floyds are too rich for her to deny them anything."

Lucinda laughed, then sobered and responded, "Will it hurt you to talk to me?"

"No, my mother is too rich, too."

They both laughed, earning censorious glances from several ladies. Lucinda didn't care. She hadn't laughed with another female her age since leaving law school.

"We'll talk more later," Samantha whispered. "Come to my house for lunch. I'll send the buggy."

The rest of the tea passed with little conversation but many talks and reports from the charity, messages to assure the women they were not wasting their money. By the time she returned to her office home, Lucinda knew she hadn't. She had three appointments for Monday and lunch with Samantha the next day.

Which dawned bright and cold. Lucinda dressed in wool, shivering, but happy to note that the boiler had been turned on for more than hot water. Her radiators clanged and banged and produced glorious warmth to counteract the frost riming the windowpanes. She hoped Samantha's buggy would be closed and would have a hot brick.

It did. When the coachman, an older man in a black coat and trousers, handed her into the buggy, she found the top up and the interior delightfully warm. The ride proved short, just to the other end of town, where the houses grew larger and the lawns sweeping, tree lined, even walled. Telephone lines ran to a few houses, and a longing started in her heart. How wonderful if she could have a telephone in her office. It would save so much time for clients and the lawyer. Of course, with the operator able to listen in, confidentiality would be a problem. Still, even to make an appointment would be helpful. . . .

The buggy turned between open iron gates and tooled up a long driveway. The house rose three stories with gingerbread trim dripping from the eaves, and ancient oak trees standing sentinel on either side. Although nothing like her father's hundred-year-old house, a stronger longing than telephone lines to her office ached through Lucinda's heart.

She wanted a house, a home, something with tall windows and lots of light, carved paneling and photographs of family on the walls. She wanted to be married, have a family, a husband to love her. But she wanted a career, too, wanted to practice law, was called to practice law. Pensive, she disembarked from the buggy with the aid of the driver and headed up a path paved with flagstones, to the front door. It opened before she reached it, and Samantha appeared, pretty and feminine in pink ruffles.

"Do come in. Mama is dying to meet you. We've never met a lady lawyer before, you understand, and now we're wondering why I didn't go to school."

"So the ladies of the town will all speak to you?" Lucinda suggested.

Samantha laughed. "No, so I could marry and produce lots of grandchildren. And here I am, twenty-four, and still a spinster." Samantha led the way across a marble-floored foyer, which rose all three stories, and into a small sitting room in the rear of the house.

Sunshine streamed through windows overlooking a manicured lawn edged in maple trees with scarlet leaves. Framed in one long glass pane stood a gazebo at the back of the yard, where the woods nearly encroached save for the chest-high wall. The other window illuminated a woman, a faded version of Samantha, elegant and fragile, in a wheelchair.

"I told Samantha to bring you today even if we had to kidnap you." Mrs. Howard's smile put the warmth of the sun to shame. "You must be the most interesting female to move to Loveland since the Floyd sisters settled here. We need more like you."

"Thank you." Lucinda took the proffered hand, afraid it would break if she did more than touch the slender fingers. "I like the Misses Floyd."

"And they like you," Mrs. Howard said.

"They'll want you to join their women's suffrage movement," Samantha added. "Do sit down."

Lucinda smiled. "I think I'll wait. As much as I'd like to have a say, I prefer to keep quiet about politics so as not to offend my clients."

"I understand obtaining clients is why you moved here." Mrs. Howard lifted a silver bell from the table beside her chair and rang it. "Virginia won't let you practice law?"

"No." Lucinda bit her lip against a stab of pain.

Before she could say more, a maid arrived. "Lunch is ready, yes, ma'am."

Samantha pushed her mother's chair across the hall to a dining room as beautifully sunlit as the sitting room. Three places had been set at one end of a long table and dishes placed on a sideboard. Unlike the day before, this was a full meal with three courses. Aromas of spicy soup, roasted chicken, and saffron rice permeated the room.

Lucinda's stomach growled. "I–I'm so sorry."

The Howard ladies laughed. "I was going to ask you a million questions," Mrs. Howard said, "but I'll let you eat first."

In the end, they compromised. After a bowl of soup and some bread, Lucinda offered to answer questions. But apparently her admission of hunger had set the ladies on a different mission.

"Are you really living in your office?" Mrs. Howard asked. "How can you possibly eat well?"

"I can't cook." Face warm from more than sunlight and soup, Lucinda dropped her gaze to the bread roll she had just crumbled on her plate. "I hope to be able to get a little house or flat soon though."

"Sooner than later." Samantha patted a stomach that was flat from either tight lacings or nature. "I'd die without hot food every meal, especially in the winter. We'll see what we can do to help."

Send her paying clients.

"Thank you. Eventually. . ." Lucinda shrugged. These ladies didn't understand living on little in order to save money.

"Right now," she said firmly, "I need to purchase furniture for my office."

"Do you?" Samantha's eyes glowed like sunlight behind green glass. "I know where you can find the nicest things without going to Boston. We can look—"

"The Floyd ladies will be happy to take you." Mrs. Howard's voice rose enough to drown her daughter's voice.

"But Momma—" Samantha suddenly paled.

Mrs. Howard set her spoon on her plate, a chime of silver against china. "We will not discuss your tendre for Matthew Templin in front of a guest."

"I don't have a *tendre* for him," Samantha protested. "That was over many years ago."

"Of course it was," her mother snapped. "Associating with

him would have made you unacceptable."

Lucinda ducked her head so she didn't have to stare at her hostess. She needed the good graces of women like Mrs. Howard, women with money to pay an attorney, but the snobbery destroyed Lucinda's appetite. Matthew Templin seemed like a fine man and certainly didn't deserve such treatment because of a parentage he couldn't help. She would like to know him better.

Except, associating with him might destroy her chances of success.

Six

The crunch of wheels on the gravel drive drew Matt out of his workshop and into the Saturday afternoon drizzle. He couldn't imagine who would come to see him on a day better spent beside a warm fire. But there it was, the heavy and ancient barouche belonging to the Floyd twins.

A smile tugged at his lips and he waved to the driver, indicating he would assist the ladies down. "I should think," he said, opening the door, "you ladies have more than enough furniture for your—"

Sight of the third passenger in the carriage robbed him of speech.

"Surprised you, didn't we, dear boy?" Miss Hope held out her shaky hand to him.

He clasped it and helped her to the ground. "Yes ma'am, you did."

They'd surprised him enough for his heart to perform somersaults, like an acrobat exuberant about his next performance. He should know better after their last encounter, but there it was—an unwelcome joy in seeing Lucinda Bell again, and at his house.

"Did you bring her here for furniture?" he managed to ask, his tone cool as the damp afternoon.

"They did." She held out her hand for his assistance to the ground. "You should have told me you made furniture."

"Why?" He held her gaze and her hand for a moment longer than polite.

She didn't break the contact. "I'd have come sooner."

"We didn't know she wanted chairs for the outer office," Miss

Hope Floyd said, as she, too, stepped to the ground with Matt's assistance. "We thought she would take everyone into that lovely little back room of hers and serve them coffee or tea, but I suppose she can't do that with male clients."

"Which I'm unlikely to have," Lucinda said.

Unless he hired her.

"I'd best get you ladies out of the damp so you can see what I have." Matt strode off to the workshop, an outbuilding nearly the size of his house. Smoke swirled from the chimney, sharp with the tang of burning pine. "It'll be humid inside. I have the steam box going."

"Steam box?" Lucinda caught up with him, her skirt swishing as though she wore a taffeta petticoat, her face shiny in the moisture. "What's that?"

"I put the wood in there when I need to make it curve for a back or seat."

"Oh, I thought wood was carved that way."

Matt laughed. "Were I that skilled. This makes it smoother, fewer marks from the tools." He pushed open the door.

Aromas of steam and damp wood billowed out, perfume to his nose. He glanced at Lucinda to see her reaction. Of course she would wrinkle that pert appendage, turn up its tip at the wood shavings on the floor, the odors of varnish and paint.

But she didn't. She glanced around with eyes wide and lips parted, as though she intended to ask a question at any moment. He braced himself for something rude.

"It's cozy in here." She strode forward and ran her hand over the curved back of a rocking chair. "There's a chair like this at home. My great-grandmother brought it with her from England. May I?" She moved to sit.

"Of course."

The sight of her settled in one of his creations shouldn't

please him so much, but his chest felt as though his heart had dropped into the steam box. The chair's dark cherrywood framed her pale hair and face in perfect portraiture. He wanted to see her there often, daily, seated beside his fire with Purrcilla on her knees, or maybe—

He drew his thoughts up straight. "I have a chair that might work for a visitor's chair in the office. You'll want to get a seam-stress to make you cushions."

"But she looks so comfortable in that one." The Floyd sisters burst through the doorway, and Matt realized he hadn't noticed their absence. Moisture dripped from their felt hats, and they grinned as they glanced from him to Lucinda and back again. They'd left him alone with the lady lawyer on purpose.

With ears hot beneath hair that needed to be cut, he spun on his heel and stalked to the far side of his workshop. The oak chair was heavy, but he lifted it with one hand and lugged it to set before her royal highness, who couldn't be bothered to stand. Or maybe she was just tired. Dark circles made her eyes look huge and shadowed, probably stemming from fatigue. More trouble she wasn't sharing? He wanted to ask her.

"I only have the one, but can make you a second one," he said instead.

She leaned forward, her face intent, her lips pursed in con-centration. She ran a hand over the wood, stroking it like a pet. She stood and examined every joint and seam, touching, peering, treating it like a hundred-dollar horse she intended to buy, rather than a five-dollar chair. His heart began to thud. Surely she would find it too imperfect, flawed, a joint loose, the turned legs uneven.

She faced him. "Mr. Templin," she said in a hushed tone, "you're not an artisan; you're an artist."

Her words were a gift; he wished he could hold them, put them carefully away, take them out for later inspection and warmth on cold, lonely nights.

He ducked his head. "Thank you. I enjoy it."

"That's obvious." She glanced at the Floyds, quiet for once, and watching them. "Why has no one ever mentioned that Mr. Templin does such beautiful work? He should have a shop in town, a room to show these things off."

"We agree," Hester said. "But some people—"

"Are ignorant," Hope finished. "How soon can you have a second chair for her, Matthew? I know a woman who can make cushions."

"I'm afraid it will be too expensive for me," Lucinda interjected. "These are too beautiful for my budget. I can order something from a catalog."

"Nonsense. Matthew doesn't charge nearly enough for his work." Hope wavered forward. "Matthew, how much?"

"I can let you have the one for five dollars or both for eight, if you pay in advance."

Her eyes widened again, lips parting. Shock over the price from a simple village carpenter? Or had she expected to pay more? She didn't indicate either impression by words, simply drew out her purse and extracted several bills. "You'll deliver them?"

"Of course." He took the money and tucked it into his pocket, as though his profit wouldn't go a long way toward finding a lawyer.

A lawyer, but not her. He needed a real lawyer, one with experience.

"I'll get to work on the second chair straightaway," he concluded.

"Not too soon, dear boy." Hester joined her sister beside him. "We'd love a cup of coffee or tea, whichever you have, before we go back into this damp. I need fortification before the ride home in this drizzle."

"But the sun will shine tomorrow." Hope winked. "A good day to ride through the country and enjoy the colored leaves before they all turn brown and fall."

If he owned a horse and buggy, he'd offer to take Lucinda with him. So good thing he didn't. No lady went driving with a carpenter from whom she had just ordered simple office chairs. Samantha's mother had taught him that.

"I do miss going for long walks." Miss Lucinda sighed. "I used to walk all the time in Virginia, but it's too cold here now, like it was in Michigan."

"Nonsense. It's not too cold for a brisk walk if the good company keeps you warm." Hester frowned at Matt. "Well, that tea?"

"I have coffee." His gaze remained on Lucinda. "But there's just the kitchen fire going, and the animals are in there. Miss Bell might not like animals."

"I'm a country girl, born and raised, Mr. Templin. I like animals." She flashed him a smile. "As long as it's a cat or dog in the kitchen, and not a pig."

Matt laughed. "After you, ladies." He closed the workshop and strode up the gravel drive to the back door of the house. He wished he had flagstones like the finer houses. He wished he had a fire going in his parlor. He wished he had reason to use that parlor for guests on Sunday afternoons, or a wife. . .

True to form, the Floyd sisters opened his back door and trotted into the kitchen. Growler emitted his throaty rumble, while his body wagged from shoulders to stubby tail. Purrcilla strode to the doorway and stared up at Miss Lucinda Bell.

She hesitated on the threshold, her head half tilted in his direction. The one eyebrow he could see, arched in a golden-brown question mark.

"The dog is friendly." Matt smiled at her. "He just doesn't bark. And the cat won't bite unless you're a rodent."

"I'm not afraid of your animals." Her chin stiffened. "I simply didn't think it polite to enter your house without you."

At her side now, he touched his forefinger to that firm chin, finding the skin smooth and a little moist from the damp air. "So you think the Floyds are rude? Tut-tut."

"I suppose I did say that." She tucked her head.

Purrcilla rose on her back legs and pawed at Lucinda's skirt.

She jumped and glanced down. "Your cat thinks she's a dog?"

"Something like that." Matt stooped and lifted the cat onto his shoulder. "This is Purrcilla."

"You don't mean Priscilla?"

"Nope." He stroked the feline's soft black, orange, and white fur. "She purrs constantly, thus the name."

"So I hear."

The feline rumbled nearly as loudly as Growler greeted two of his favorite people—probably because they usually brought him some sort of food treat.

"I like cats." Shyness tinged Lucinda's voice, and she looked at Purrcilla, not him.

Without a word, he held the calico out to Lucinda. She took the cat and nestled her beneath her chin. Purrcilla draped her paws over Lucinda's shoulder and settled down like she intended to stay as long as she could get away with it. Her cheek against the soft fur, Lucinda smiled, a faraway look in her eyes.

She looked happy. Happy holding his quite ordinary calico cat. For the same reason he found joy in the warm, furry body nestled on his shoulder? Loneliness, an otherwise empty pair of arms.

Careful, he warned himself.

She wasn't for him. She was an educated woman, probably the most educated woman he'd ever meet. He was a carpenter, at best; a man of all work, at the least. With his background—or lack of it—she would do better for herself. Unless those papers were real, meant something he could prove if he ever had the money, which was unlikely.

But of course the warning ran unheeded by his heart. As Lucinda stepped over his threshold, perfectly comfortable holding his cat and settling with the Floyd sisters on his simple furniture before the fire, his heart ignored his head and tumbled hard for another female who would have nothing more to do with him than his business, just like Samantha Howard.

He waited for the pain to strike of that youthful infatuation pulled asunder. While he set about preparing a pot of coffee for the ladies, he felt nothing beyond the warmth, the glow, of having Lucinda Bell seated at his fire.

Perhaps that was the insanity that prompted him to ask her to walk with him the next day.

Coffee was served. The Floyd twins appeared sleepy, nodding before the blaze; Growler curled up on their feet, tiny feet shod in neat, black shoes so high the tops disappeared beneath the old ladies' frothy skirts. Lucinda took the other seat on the old-fashioned settee, Purrcilla on her lap, and a thick earthenware mug between both her hands, hands too small for such a clumsy mug. She sipped daintily as though drinking from one of her English bone china cups, as delicate as eggshells.

With nowhere else to sit, except one of the two chairs at the kitchen table away from the women, away from the fire, Matt propped his shoulders against the mantel and gazed down at the top of Lucinda's hat. Of gray felt, it sported a jaunty feather, curling over the brim to caress her cheek. If a man could envy a feather, Matt did. The feather was red; a red nothing in nature would produce, not nearly as pretty as the crimson maple leaves. So he blurted out, "If you'd like to see the leaves' turned color, I'll be happy to walk with you tomorrow."

The Floyd ladies' heads jerked upright. Growler lifted his head. Lucinda kept her gaze on the cat, her coffee, something besides him. He couldn't tell, with the brim of her silly hat shielding her face.

Nausea clawed at Matt's middle. She was going to say no. Well, she was likely to say no thank you, perfectly polite. She had gone to lunch at the Howards'. She wouldn't want to be seen with him, and he'd just made a fool of himself to a potentially lucrative customer.

He opened his mouth to retract the offer, give her a way to gracefully turn him down.

Then she raised her head, looked him in the eye for so brief a moment he barely caught their rich color, and nodded. "Thank you. I believe I'd like a walk, provided the sun is shining."

"Oh, it will, my dear," one of the Floyds said.

Matt didn't look to see which one. He kept his gaze focused on Lucinda in the event she looked him full in the face again.

"Tomorrow at one o'clock, after church, then." He hoped the pounding of his heart didn't reach his voice. "That's the warmest time of day, and late enough for the ground to have dried out a bit. And I'll bring the chair now. I can load it into my wagon."

Needing the chilly air outside, he headed for the door.

"That's not—" Lucinda began to say something, but the door had already closed behind him.

He took several long, deep breaths of cold, damp air, felt himself steady, and paced to his workshop for the chair, then the barn, little larger than a shed, to load the chair into the wagon. He wrapped the wood in an old quilt and tossed a tarpaulin over it, then hitched his horse to the rig and led him into the yard, where the Floyds' driver had just returned from walking their horses.

"I believe the ladies are ready to go," Matt told the older man.

"Ay-yup, and bringing cat and dog hair with them to get all over the seats."

Matt laughed. "I expect so, but then, you're used to cat hair on the cushions, I expect. How many deliveries this week?"

"Six cats picked up from some farmer ready to drown the lot," the driver said. "Keeps me busy keeping all that fur away, and then the claw marks I have to repair." He shook his grizzled head. "Wish they'd take up something else."

"You'd be bored without all that cleaning." Matt patted his draft horse that had cost him a year's worth of earnings, but proved necessary when hauling heavy furniture and lumber about. "Will you be so kind as to— Never mind. Here they come."

Led by Lucinda, the three ladies emerged from the house, Growler and Purrcilla following. All five approached him.

"Thank you for the coffee, Matthew, dear boy." Miss Hester patted his cheek.

"We've decided we need to find a cat for Miss Bell," Hope added. "We didn't know she liked cats so much."

"Or that they would like her." Miss Hope winked.

The tips of Matt's ears warmed, and he was thankful for his overly long hair. Nor could he figure out why her remark would embarrass him.

"I'll, um, just follow your carriage," Matt said.

Lucinda nodded to him, the gracious lady of the manor, and climbed into the barouche without a direct glance.

But she said she would go walking with him. That thought kept him warm on the damp drive into town. First, the carriage paused at the Floyd ladies' mansion on the edge of town. Likely, they were weary and cold and Lucinda would have insisted on it. They were her clients, after all, and she was polite.

Matt continued to follow the vehicle until they reached her office and home on Main Street. The carriage stopped in front of the harness shop then drew forward before stopping again. Lucinda, being gracious again, gave him the space in front of the steps so he would carry the chair a shorter distance.

"She's a true lady," he muttered. "It means nothing. Remember how she was at Gertie's."

But she'd been tired and hungry then.

No, no excuses for her rudeness, her condescension. He must remember that.

He leaped from the wagon seat and hitched his horse to the post. If the Floyd coachman were younger, Matt would ask him for help lugging the chair up the steps. But he couldn't ask it of the man, who was nearly as old as his employers.

He unwrapped the tarpaulin from the chair and tossed the former into the wagon bed. He could lift the chair without any trouble, but keeping the blanket over it, so he didn't bang the smooth wood against the railing or a step and mar it, proved impossible the instant he drew the chair to the edge. For a moment, he stood motionless, frowning.

"Let me help." A small hand in a gray leather glove reached past him and gripped the edge of the quilt. "I'm stronger than I look."

"But this is heavy." He couldn't stop from grinning down at her.

She said nothing.

"All right, but if you drop it, it's your chair."

"Of course it's my chair. That's why I'll help, so nothing happens to it." She flashed him a sidelong glance.

Flirting with him? No, never.

"Please, I had a time of it convincing that ancient coachman not to come back here."

"All right. Just keep the blanket in place."

"Yes sir." Too solemn. Teasing?

He didn't care. She was near him, smelling of flowers and rain.

Springtime in late October.

"You go first, then," Matt directed her.

He needed her a little farther away so he could concentrate.

She followed his directions, holding the quilt in place until the chair slid free of the wagon bed. Then she held the front of the furniture, her hands curled around the arms and over the quilt. Matt still took most of the weight, especially once they started up the steps, but she was indeed stronger than she looked. Perhaps she liked to ride horses or play something like tennis. Probably tennis. All the society girls played tennis nowadays, running around the courts in their shortened skirts or even bloomers. Oh, he'd gone to watch as a younger man. He'd met Samantha there. . . .

At the top of the steps, they set the chair down on the landing. Lucinda took out her keys and unlocked the door. Chilled through his wool coat and flannel shirt, he anticipated warmth flowing from the opening. But the air was as frigid as that outside.

"Is something wrong with your heat?" He set the chair down in front of the desk and headed for the radiator.

"Nothing more wrong than that Mr. Shannon won't leave it on when his shop is closed." She dabbed her forefinger on her nose, where the tiniest bead of perspiration glistened. "But the inner room remains fairly warm. And it keeps the ice frozen in the icebox longer."

"Before long, you won't need an icebox." Matt puffed out a sigh of exasperation. His breath hung white in the cold for just a moment, and a moment too long. "Why don't you use your law-yering skills to make him leave the heat on?"

"Because. . . Because. . ." She swung away and stalked across the room to the back window. A curtain of soft, dark fabric hung there, likely helping with the drafts. Her shoulders slumped as though she were fatigued or carrying a burden too heavy for her, she pushed aside the curtain.

And her shoulders stiffened. Her head snapped up. Then she darted toward her room.

"What is it?" In three strides Matt reached her side as she fumbled with her door. "Miss Lucinda?"

"Someone's been here." She yanked open the door.

Matt followed her across the flowery carpet and into the storage room. "How do you know?"

"There's mud on my back steps." She rested her gloved hand on the glass knob of the back door, and the latch rattled with the shaking of her hand. "There are muddy footprints on my back steps."

Seven

Lucinda wrapped her arms across her middle and pressed her fingers into her upper arms. Still she trembled, from cold, from mortification, from the intensity of her reaction to seeing muddy footprints on steps that had been clean before she left.

"No one should have been here." She didn't know how many times she'd said that since looking out the window. "No one was inspecting anything. No one—"

"Shh." Matthew Templin dropped one of his broad, calloused, yet gentle hands upon her shoulder. "It's all right."

She should have pushed him away for having the temerity to touch her so familiarly. She should snap at him that he had no idea whether anything was all right. She was alone in a town whose leaders didn't particularly want her there. And, good grief, she had promised to go for a walk with this carpenter the next day. What had she been thinking?

That she didn't want to be alone another day, especially if it proved to be sunny and fine, and nature bore a cloak of autumn glory to show off. But now she knew she shouldn't do that, shouldn't have even considered that Matthew Templin was attractive, let alone agreed to a walk with him. She would tell him to go now, explaining that she couldn't take a walk with him after all.

She uncrossed her arms and stepped to one side, out from beneath that all-too-comforting hand. "I'm being silly. Please forgive me."

"Considering someone has broken your locks, I think it's reasonable for you to be upset." Matthew opened the back door and frowned down at the steps. "These are too large to be any female's I've seen about town."

"Why would a female come to my back door?" Lucinda glared at Matthew's broad back.

He shrugged. "Maybe some lady didn't want anyone seeing her calling on the lady lawyer. Sam–an–tha Howard, for example."

"But Samantha—" Lucinda stopped, catching the hesitation in Matthew's voice when speaking the young woman's name, remembering how Mrs. Howard objected to Samantha suggesting she would take Lucinda out to Matthew Templin's workshop for furniture.

So he wasn't heart-free either. Perhaps that would make going for a walk with him easier. If the weather cooperated. A cold blast of wind suggested no one would want to be outside from now until next April.

"These are male footprints," Lucinda said. "And it's possible, I suppose, that someone wants to talk to an attorney without anyone knowing. Strange, though, with the other lawyer's property right behind that wall. From an upper floor, he can see anyone coming or going from this door."

"Maybe it was him." Matthew turned, grinned at her, and closed the door.

He had such a nice grin, open and warm.

Lucinda took a step backward. "In other words, I'm being a fool to get upset, even though someone broke my locks when I arrived."

"No ma'am, not a fool, but maybe more nervous than you should be. You know Gertie will take you in. It might be better than you living alone here."

"Yes, I expect you're right, but one needs money to rent an extra room, and until my clients pay—" She slapped her hand over her mouth. "Forget I said that," she added behind her glove.

Instead, he laughed, a throaty snort. "I understand how that is. People can be slow to pay around here. But they will pay, I promise you."

"And meanwhile, I have to watch my pennies."

And find a way to stay warm in the evenings.

Involuntarily, she shivered.

"I think all is well here," Matthew said. "So let me go ask Shannon to turn on your heat. He can shut off the valves for his store if he thinks he's using too much oil."

"That isn't necessary. You're right. I should use my lawyering skills on him. It's just. . ." She ducked her head. "It's just that I don't want to make an enemy of him."

"Shannon may be stingy, Miss Bell, but he's not unkind. His house is on the way to mine. I'll put a flea in his ear." He held out his hand. "And see you tomorrow around one o'clock."

If he was going to get her heat turned on, she couldn't very well renege on her agreement to go walking with him.

"All right. Thank you." She walked with him to the door, then closed and locked the portal behind him. She didn't hear his footfalls retreat down the steps until the last tumbler clicked into place.

What a kind man.

Shivering, Lucinda retreated to her living quarters and lit the spirit lamp to make tea to accompany her bread, cheese, and apple supper. On a Saturday evening, neither of the cafés was open. As a single woman, she couldn't go into the hotel dining room.

Which gave her the impulse to do so. She was an attorney at law in the Commonwealth of Massachusetts, yet she couldn't eat dinner alone in a restaurant. Ridiculous.

On her way to fetch the cheese and apples from the storage room, Lucinda returned to her now-boiling water and turned off the spirit lamp. She suddenly felt unwell. Perhaps she would be too unwell to go for that walk she shouldn't go on the next day. Or perhaps she was just cold.

She began to pace up and down her narrow room to drive some warmth into her feet and hands. Matthew Templin was right. She should have confronted Mr. Shannon about turning the heat either off or down so far no steam reached her chambers. She couldn't survive the night like this, let alone the winter. She should know where Mr. Shannon lived so she could go to his house now and get him to return and make the place warmer. Or she could go to Gertie's for hot food, too, and kindness, if she went with a humble countenance over her display of snobbery before.

Still wearing her coat and gloves, she pulled a valise from the back room and placed some personal items in it. She would go to Gertie's. This cold was ridiculous for only October. Michigan was as bad or worse, but she hadn't been forced to endure it without heat in her boardinghouse.

She tucked her toothbrush into the valise and began to close it. A clang and a bang startled her. The case's lid slammed down on her hand. She cried out and raised the injured fingers to her face, nursing them to her cheek while stopping tears of pain.

A trickle of heat seeped past her. The clang and bang came from the radiator. Either Mr. Shannon realized he'd been inconsiderate, at best, in turning off the heat, or Matthew Templin had shamed the man into returning. Whatever the answer, it didn't matter.

Lucinda charged to the radiator and held her hands over the heat, breathing in the warmth like perfume. She wouldn't have to go to Gertie's, after all. She could remain in her own room with her tea and apples, and books.

And quiet.

Too much quiet. All the novels and law books in the world couldn't diminish the fact that she was alone. She would have to get a cat. If she talked to a cat, no one, including herself, would think her talking aloud odd.

"Why didn't you come, Trudy, or invite me west?" She slammed down her book and made up her bed. "I'd have gone had you told me."

She shoved the next thought aside and pondered pending work for her clients, then fell asleep composing a letter to her father. She slept until the church bells woke her, a pleasant alarm, background to her coffee and bread, carefully toasted over the spirit lamp flame. Breakfast eaten, she hastened to dress so she wouldn't be late for the service.

The day was, in truth, beautiful; cold, but sunny with a clear sky. She dawdled down the street to church, and arrived mere seconds before the organ slipped into the first hymn. A few people glanced at her with disapproval as she tucked herself into a rear pew, but others smiled with genuine warmth.

"I didn't think the lady lawyer would go to church," one woman whispered. "But she's here every week."

Lucinda's lips twitched. Going all the way back at least to Shakespeare, people thought lawyers some kind of evil beings. They weren't. Well, not all of them. She intended to do good, help women, especially, protect their property for their children, gain pensions so far denied them, get the vote. It was what God wanted her to do with her life.

So why had He denied her the right to practice where she wanted?

She didn't have an answer to that. The sermon was on loving one's neighbor as oneself, so when Matt approached her outside the church, she didn't turn him down.

"Good afternoon, Miss Bell," Matthew Templin said.

"Good. . .afternoon." Shyness swept over Lucinda. "I must don country garb before our walk."

"You're still planning to go?" He sounded surprised.

She glanced up at him. "Of course. I said I would."

"If you'd rather not. . ."

She would rather not. A few people were giving her disapproving glances. She looked back with her own disapproval of their behavior then smiled at Matthew Templin. "Just let me put on something warmer and sturdier than this." She plucked at the soft merino of her skirt.

"Then I'll fetch my wagon." He touched his hat brim and turned down a side street.

Lucinda hastened to her rooms to change into a serge skirt and find a pair of stout leather boots made for walking. Hooking the buttons took twice as long as she intended, for the faster she hurried, the slower she seemed to move. The button hook slipped from her hand twice, sliding across the floor, and then the leather loops eluded her grip. If she lost a button. . .

She didn't; at last the boots fit snugly on her feet. She tugged on the jacket that matched her skirt and skewered a small felt hat to her head. Without knowing the temperature outside for certain, she brought her cape along as extra warmth, though she hoped they could walk fast enough she would be plenty warm in the sunshine.

Matthew had just reached the front of the harness store when Lucinda descended the steps. People headed down the street, on their way to dinner, slowed to look. Lucinda ducked her head, but everyone would know who she was, would tell others they'd seen her climbing into Matthew Templin's wagon on a Sunday afternoon. This was why she regretted accepting his invitation. Being with him could hurt her business, if other women like Mrs. Howard disapproved of associating closely with him. Unlike the Floyd sisters, Lucinda didn't have the family and monetary connections to protect her. Too late now to think of leaving earlier, while everyone was still home or at church. She may as well enjoy herself.

"I'm looking forward to a walk," she said with complete truth. "I feel odd walking in town. People might think I'm too bold if I don't have an escort."

"They might." Matthew guided the draft horse down a side street. "This route will take a little longer but will keep us out of the crowd on Main Street."

Lucinda said nothing, as thank you seemed rude.

"Did you get your heat back last night?" Matthew asked.

"I did, thank you." She smiled at him from beneath the narrow brim of her hat. "Did it take much persuasion?"

To her surprise, Matthew said nothing as they drove past shops that grew poorer-looking with each block, then melded into small but mostly neat and well-maintained houses. Lucinda shifted on the bench, feeling each jolt of the broad wheels over the brick street, feeling the tautness of the man beside her.

"You didn't get him to turn on my heat?" she ventured.

Perhaps he was embarrassed that she'd thanked him when he'd done nothing.

"I did." He frowned, perhaps thinking of that encounter, perhaps because of a sudden rise and turn in the road, and the need to concentrate to maneuver the wagon around and up the hill.

Once he had, the view drove thoughts of heat out of her mind. Spread out at the base of the hill like an oriental carpet, the reds of maple, golds of oak, and greens of fir spread to the horizon, a crystal-blue horizon. The sharp sweetness of dry leaves perfumed the air, along with occasional whiffs of an apple-wood fire.

"Oooh," Lucinda said, her voice breathy through half-parted lips.

"I arranged this just for you." He flashed his toe-curling grin and started the horse again, taking them down the hill with care. "We'll leave this nag in my pasture and walk from there. That is— um, you needn't come into the house. I'll just be a minute or two."

"Of course." Despite the briskness, though not chill, in the air, Lucinda's cheeks felt hot. "Will Growler and Purrcilla be out?"

"Yes. They'll be happy to see you."

They were. While Matthew took care of the draft horse, his dog and cat swarmed around Lucinda's skirts—the former growling in his throaty, affectionate way that was nearly a purr; the latter trying to climb her skirt. To save the serge from claw snags, Lucinda picked up the feline and cuddled her close.

"You're fat, madame. Is that an insult to a cat?"

"Probably not." Quiet-footed, even on the gravel, Matthew appeared from around a small barn and bent to pat Growler's head. "She'll be fatter soon, I'm afraid."

"How do you— Oh." Lucinda's cheeks felt as fiery as the woods appeared when she realized Purrcilla was going to have kittens.

"Should we go?" Matthew took Purrcilla from Lucinda's arms and set her on the other side of a fenced yard. "She can probably climb this, but I like to think she doesn't."

He did the same with Growler then offered Lucinda his arm.

She took it reflexively. It was a fine arm for holding on to while one strode along a country lane. It was the kind of arm that would hold a woman upright if she stumbled, quite unlike the elegantly slim arms of other men who had escorted her on outings.

"Are you warm enough?" For the briefest moment, Matthew pressed his free hand over her fingers that rested on his arm. "It will get a little chilly beneath the trees."

"No, I'm quite all right." Lucinda bit her lip then admitted, "I was thinking about all the parties I'd have to attend if I were back in Virginia."

"You don't like parties?"

"Do you think I'd have gone to law school if that's what I like?" She slanted a sidelong glance at him. "Lady lawyers aren't invited to many places."

"Neither are carpenters who—" He broke off, cleared his throat. "You will be with the Floyd twins on your side. If they want you invited to something, you'll be invited. And if you make friends with Samantha Howard, she will give you the right introductions, too."

He'd said the name without a hitch today.

"Not if the mayor's wife doesn't like me."

"Is it the mayor's wife, or the mayor telling his wife not to like you?"

Lucinda stopped beneath the canopy of an oak that had to be at least two hundred years old; its trunk and crown rose so broad and high. "Do you know something you're not telling me, Mr. Templin?"

"I expect I know a great deal I'm not telling you." He touched her hand again; then he turned beneath the enormous oak and led them onto a path wending its way through the trees like a tunnel with a sun-dappled roof.

Lucinda pressed the tips of her fingers into his arm. "You know what I mean."

"I expect I do." He said nothing for at least half a mile, or perhaps only half of that, and then paused in a clearing with fragrant dry grass baking beneath the brilliant autumn sunshine. "Miss Lucinda." He turned to her but held her hand against his side. "Shannon told me something that concerns me."

"Something to do with me?" A shiver ran up Lucinda's spine and out through her limbs.

Matthew released her hand and held it between his, engulfing it. "Yes, about you. He said he's been turning off your heat because the mayor suggested it's a good idea to make you uncomfortable with staying here."

Eight

The stricken look on Lucinda's face encouraged Matt to keep holding on to her hand, maybe both of her hands. But he placed her fingers on his forearm and resumed walking instead.

"I know you're going to ask why when you can think again." He tried to keep his tone light. "I wish I knew the answer."

"It can't be just that I'm a lady lawyer and he doesn't like ladies or lawyers, and especially not the two together." She, too, sounded as though she were keeping her tone lighter than the subject. "It simply makes no sense to me, Mr. Templin. I've never even met the mayor."

"I grew up in Loveland, or I wouldn't know him much either."

She stumbled, gripping his arm hard to keep her balance. "Will associating with me make him discharge you, if he has taken me in dislike?"

"It could." Matt felt kind of queasy at the idea. He needed the money. "But it's not likely. The work's only half finished, and there's no one close who can finish what I've started."

That remark sure sounded arrogant.

"I didn't mean to sound so—what is that word? Egotistical?"

She laughed, a true, bubbling sparkle of sound. "Yes, that's the word, but I don't think you sounded full of yourself, just confident in the quality of your work compared to that of other carpenters around here."

"Thank you."

"No thanks necessary." She strode beside him in silence for a few minutes, their heels crunching on leaves that had fallen that morning, silent on ones that had already created a loamy carpet along the path. Then she paused to pluck a particularly large and bright red leaf from a low-hanging limb and, as she stuck it into the shiny band of ribbon around the crown of her hat, looked up at him. "Why did you become a carpenter?"

"Someone was willing to teach me, and I figured out I was good at it and liked it."

"Did you want to do anything else? I mean, you seem to have gotten this by accident or coincidence, not because you chose it."

Matt walked along, his gaze on the trees—most turning to plain brown deeper in the woods—and pondered his words.

Lucinda's fingers tightened on his arm. "I'm sorry. That was rude of me to say."

"Maybe, but it's all right. I didn't choose it." He hesitated. With the way he felt about her, his insides leaping and twisting at her voice, her laugh, the light touch of her hand, he may as well be honest about himself. She would never come walking with him again, and his heart would be safe from another blow. "I wanted to be a teacher, but I couldn't pay for more schooling."

"I'm sorry to hear that. You should be able to get an education if you want one. And do the work you want to do." She plucked another leaf, curled and brown, ready to fall, and then crunched it between her fingers. "I love that smell of dried leaves."

"It's one of the nicest things about fall."

"Yes. But about your schooling. Weren't there scholarships available?"

"Not for me." He heard the edge in his tone and strove to soften it. "Not because I wasn't good in my studies. I was. But. . .Miss Lucinda, you may as well know now. My mother was not a nice woman, and no one knows who my father is, including her."

"That must have made your childhood difficult." Her voice, her face, held none of the contempt he expected. She even tightened her hold on his arm as she paused and looked at him, her big eyes full of compassion. "I don't understand why the child is punished for what the parents did."

"Something about carrying the taint in our blood." He summarized the words he'd heard directed at him all his life, yet they meant nothing when he looked at her. His voice sounded like someone else's, far away and disinterested. All his interest focused on her pretty face, her shining eyes, her soft mouth.

And the way his heart tumbled over and over and over. He'd just slipped the rest of the way down the slippery slope he'd tried to avoid since meeting Miss Lucinda Bell, and fallen head over heels in love with her.

"That's nonsense." Her voice came as clearly and strongly to him as Sunday morning church bells. "I see no logic in that kind of thinking and never have. You are who you make yourself, and you seem to be doing well."

"Thank you." His chest felt so tight he couldn't think of anything else to say, so he set off on a trot through the trees that had her laughing and gasping alongside him.

"Are you going to a fire?"

"I'm sorry." He slowed his pace. "I was thinking."

"About what, may I ask?"

About her voice, her face, her acceptance of his past.

"You can ask," he answered. "But the answer probably makes no sense."

Or too much sense for her comfort. Or his. He must not forget that while she might not hold his parentage against him, that didn't mean she could care about him, too. Compassion wasn't a relationship. She still didn't want him sitting in his wagon in front of her quarters. She came out with him only because it was away from town, and maybe his company was better than nobody's. She might care about him as a person, but she would never respect him enough to love him.

"Ask me why I became a lawyer, if you want answers that make no sense."

He asked. She told him about her father's work, how she enjoyed his books and papers, and the importance of the work. They walked and talked about that work, about her books, and finally, about books they'd both read and enjoyed. By the time the path led them back to the road, Matt's tension had eased. Their dialogue flowed freely, and he thought, maybe, if she could get past his being an uneducated carpenter, she might accept him as a friend.

The sun was dropping rapidly in the western hills as he hitched the horse to the wagon and then helped Lucinda onto the seat. She glanced at the sunset with a worried frown.

"We'll be back before dark, won't we?" she asked.

"We have more than an hour of daylight, never fear." He climbed up beside her and gathered the reins.

Her stomach growled. She clapped a hand to her middle and her cheeks grew pink.

"Have you eaten today?" He clucked to the horse, which started obediently as ever.

She ducked her head. "I had some coffee and toast this morning. Only the hotel restaurant is open on Sunday, but people have invited me to dinner."

"I'm glad to hear that." He gazed out across the fields and trees. "I probably shouldn't admit to this, but much of the time in the winter, I work on my chairs on Sundays. In spring and summer, I work in the garden."

"You can grow things? I can't."

"Vegetables and herbs. Gertie uses what I can't eat myself."

"Ah, is that why she's always willing to feed you?"

"Gertie likes feeding people. You should take advantage of that."

"I haven't seen her."

"I know. She's hurt."

"I thought she was offended."

"No, not Gertie. She'll speak her mind then be done with it."

"Well, perhaps tomorrow."

"Or tonight. There's something I've been wanting to ask you, and I'd trust her hearing it, too."

"What do you want to ask me that you can't now?" She hesitated between each word, cautious, a little cooler than before.

"This is work related—for you, that is, and I didn't think it right to bring it up today on your outing."

"Thank you." She rubbed her arms. "It's getting cold."

"I was afraid of that."

Did she use the excuse of pulling on her cape to edge away from him?

"I shouldn't have mentioned that I wanted to speak with you about a legal matter."

"It's all right. If it's personal, though, you should only discuss it in my office, not even in front of Gertie."

"But Gertie doesn't gossip, if you tell her something is private."

"Mr. Templin, that doesn't matter. If it's something that could end up in court, she could be forced to disclose what you said under oath. No confidentiality rules apply to her."

He swallowed, feeling stupid, seeing the gulf of knowledge and education between them. She was a professional woman, a professional person. He was a worker, a laborer.

"All right, then, I'll come to your office during working hours."

"Anytime. Just leave a note, and I'll tell you when I'm available. Clients are lining up down the block, you know, so it may be a week or two."

He laughed at her attempt at humor, and they slipped back into the comfort with one another that they'd enjoyed on the walk. The drive wasn't long, and the sun still hovered well above the horizon as they reached her doorsteps in time to see someone descending them, a gloved hand resting on the railing, long, fluffy skirts trailing the treads.

"Good evening, Miss Bell, Mat–Mr. Templin," Samantha Howard greeted them.

Matt gazed at her for a moment, expecting, waiting for, the pain of lost and youthful love he'd experienced every time he'd seen her for the past four years, not that those times had been often. Nothing happened. That part of his heart was clear, free of an entanglement with her and well past time. Matthew Templin didn't belong with a Howard of Massachusetts.

Any more than he belonged with a Bell of Virginia.

He wished he'd just find a nice farm girl. Meanwhile, caught between the old love and the new, he leaped from the wagon, hitched the horse, and then assisted Lucinda to the ground. She barely noticed his aid as she talked to Samantha, light social banter that came so easily to some people.

"Did you come calling on me?"

"I did. Mama wants me to invite you to dinner."

"So sorry I wasn't here. I'm not anywhere near dressed enough for dinner at your house."

"I can wait. The coachman is driving the carriage around so the horses won't have to stand." Samantha looked at Matt. "Horses shouldn't stand long, should they?"

"Not hitched." Matt took her meaning. He faced Lucinda. "Thank you for the walk, Miss Lucinda. I'll be on my way so you can get yourself ready for the Howards."

"But—" She bit her lip, glanced at Samantha, and then looked back to him.

His breath snagged in his throat. She wouldn't dare turn down an invitation from Samantha Howard in favor of going to

Gertie's with him. Never would she risk her social standing and work prospects like that.

She turned to Samantha, a smile pasted on her lips. "I truly am honored by the invitation, Miss Howard, but I already promised Mr. Templin I'd go over to Gertie's with him."

Matt's breath whooshed out as though he'd been punched in the middle. Relief. Joy. Apprehension for her sake.

She had dared.

Nine

Lucinda set down her fountain pen and flexed her fingers. Perhaps one day she could afford a typewriter. That would make writing so much easier. And when one wasn't being paid for all this work, the work seemed even more onerous.

"Dear Daddy, how do I get people to pay their bills?" She'd written to her father the night before, upon returning from Gertie's.

Gertie's, where she had enjoyed an affable evening with two kind and generous people, not to mention an excellent bowl of chicken and dumplings, perfect for the chilly autumn evening. The warmth of Gertie's stove, hot food for once, and fresh air from the outing made Lucinda so sleepy that Matthew teased her about having to carry her home with Gertie following to tuck her into bed. Yet once she climbed the steps to her solitary chambers, sleep eluded her. Gertie had mentioned that her cousin had difficulty obtaining the settlement and pension to which she was entitled.

"Her husband was killed in a tunnel collapse, and the government hasn't paid her one cent," Gertie explained.

"Have her contact me and I'll be happy to review the case." The prospect of taking on the Commonwealth of Massachusetts sent a thrill of pleasure up Lucinda's spine. If she won this case, she would be taken seriously as a lawyer anywhere.

She dropped her head into her hand. She'd been a fool to turn down Samantha Howard's invitation in favor of going to Gertie's for supper. Yet such anguish had tightened the skin around Matthew's eyes, she hadn't been able to go back on her acceptance of his invitation. She hadn't thought of anything but making up for her earlier snobbishness after he had given her such an enjoyable day walking in the fresh country air.

Samantha hadn't appeared upset or offended. She merely smiled her sweet curve of lips, patted Lucinda's hand, and said she would call soon.

Lucinda doubted she would. She had allied herself with the wrong sort of people. Yet she couldn't help herself. Matthew, she admitted when she couldn't concentrate on her letter to her father, attracted her. A look, a touch, a smile left her insides aquiver like she was a schoolgirl.

So when he came to her office on Tuesday and asked if she would like to have lunch with him at Gertie's, Lucinda went. All the way down the street, she told herself she shouldn't. With Matthew beside her, tall and strong and quiet, she was glad she had said yes.

Yet as they sat at the table facing one another across bowls of stew and plates of warm, fresh bread, her tongue tied in knots, she couldn't think of a thing to say. That people stared at them didn't help. A few not-so-quiet remarks brought blushes to her cheeks.

"So Templin gets the second prettiest girl in town this time."

"Helps when he's the best-looking man in town," the man's wife responded.

Not unkind remarks, but affectionate comments. These people, those who worked hard for their livings, liked and respected Matthew.

Lucinda liked and respected Matthew. He was kinder and more thoughtful than most of the "gentlemen" who had escorted her to parties and balls, to church and picnics over the years.

She should be able to talk freely to him. She toyed with her spoon, setting it in her bowl and taking it out to lie on her plate. Then she picked up her coffee spoon and stirred the cream into the liquid, until Matthew's hand curved around her wrist.

"I think it's stirred, Miss Lucinda." He smiled at her, and suddenly warmth flowed through her, thawing her discomfort.

"I'm sorry. I—I haven't spent much time with men in several years. I mean, learning beside them, yes, but socially. . ."

"Me either—with females, that is." He removed his hand from her arm.

Her skin felt cold.

"I think we communicate—" He glanced out of the front window. "It's going to snow soon."

"I'm afraid of that. In spite of all the time I spent in Michigan, I can't get used to snow."

"I like it. Sledding, skating, snowball fights."

Lucinda shivered.

Matt laughed. Their eyes met, and Lucinda's insides somersaulted.

Oh dear. Oh dear, oh dear, oh dear. She hadn't felt like this since her last year in college, when she thought she wouldn't go to law school but pursue a fellow student instead. He hadn't returned her affections, and she had decided God had other plans for her.

Surely, He had plans for her other than this man.

At that moment, and many, many more to follow, she wasn't convinced of that. They could talk all of a sudden. Matt was reading Charles Dickens's *Hard Times*. Lucinda had read it, but recalled thinking it was only sad, not pondering the depth of the social injustice it illustrated. They discussed it until the café emptied and they realized they needed to get back to their work.

"It's getting too cold for walks," he said at the foot of her office steps. "But Gertie said we can meet in the café in the evenings. She'll play chaperone."

Chaperone, like they were courting. He'd asked Gertie ahead of time, like he thought she might be willing, or at least hoped she would be.

"I'd like to talk more about books. I haven't had anyone to talk about them with since my mother died."

"Your mother?" Lucinda wished she hadn't sounded so surprised.

Matt's mouth tightened at the corners. "When we were reunited and moved here to work for the Woodcockses, she had given her life to the Lord and taken to reading. She gave me my love for books."

Lucinda blinked. "Reunited? I think there's a story here I need to hear. You haven't lived here all your life?"

"No. I was born in a mining town in Nevada." He touched her cheek with his fingertips. "It's a long story. Will you be free on Saturday afternoon?"

"Yes."

With her cheek tingling from his touch, she would make certain she was free.

"If the weather is fine, we can go walking. If it isn't, we'll go to Gertie's."

Hand to her cheek, Lucinda climbed the steps to her office to plunge herself into work to make the time pass quickly until Saturday. She was lonely, that was all; a single woman in a town that wasn't particularly friendly. Clients trickled in, mostly the wives of farmers and workingmen, and the occasional man who had learned she would work out payment arrangements, as Roger Stagpole would not. Lucinda even accepted baskets of eggs and, once, a whole chicken roasted to a turn in lieu of payment for reading a deceased parent's will and explaining how to transfer the ownership of some land.

Although people like the Howards spoke to her at church, they didn't linger at her side and didn't extend invitations. They certainly didn't bring their legal business to her. They took that to her competitor, who did not attend church.

This sense of isolation, of having few people to talk to other than the occasional visit from the Floyd sisters, led to her interest in Matthew Templin. That was all.

A fine explanation that didn't account for the way that being near him made her heart flutter and the slightest of touches turned her insides to the consistency of jelly.

Saturday took too long to come. When it did, sunshine and crisp air promised a fine walk. They strolled through the woods beneath nearly barren trees. Leaves crackled underfoot, releasing the sweet, sharp scent of fallen leaves.

"So tell me about Nevada," she urged. "It sounds so much more exciting than my life."

"I think it might have been exciting," he began, speaking slowly as though choosing each word with care, "but I don't remember most of it. You see"—he paused, then took her hand and tucked it into the crook of his elbow—"I was trapped in a mine when I was five. I don't remember, but I've been told I wandered down there while my mother was working. They were digging deep for the silver by then, and I followed some men down. There was a cave-in, and we were trapped for days. When we were rescued, I didn't remember a thing."

"How horrible for you." Lucinda hugged his arm to her side, realized what she was doing, and jumped away.

Matt smiled down at her and took her hand in his. "From what I've been told, it's probably nothing I'd want to remember. I grew up on the streets of the mining town until my mother met Vincent Woodcocks and he offered her work back east. She'd reformed by this time, so she was the Woodcockses' housekeeper until she died ten years ago."

"I expect after nearly losing you, she was just as glad to leave the West."

"That's what she said. She said it was right to leave her old life behind and give me a better life and home than what I would have had."

"So you grew up with John Paul Daggett."

Matthew snorted. "Of course I knew him, but growing up together was hardly how it happened. We weren't allowed to speak to one another, and we are eight years apart. He, of course, went away to school."

"But the Woodcocks were good to you?"

"They were. They got me the apprenticeship when Mrs. Woodcocks found me repairing a banister on the stairway. I'd been doing things like that for years. I like working with my hands."

And such nice hands they were—calloused and scarred, but strong and gentle.

Oh, she was getting lost indeed.

Instinct told her to stay away from him, protect her heart for the sake of her work. Protect her heart for the sake of her heart. Yet as November turned colder and wetter, she found herself in Matthew's company more and more, from the occasional meal at the noon hour, to Saturday afternoon walks or conversations in Gertie's cozy parlor, to sitting beside him in church. The more time she spent with him, the more she liked him.

The more time she spent with Matthew, the less certain people spoke to her. Samantha Howard, for example, didn't contact her until a blustery day the week after Thanksgiving.

Lucinda paced her office, trying to think how best to respond to a letter regarding Gertie's cousin, Parthina Carr. The Commonwealth wanted proof she'd already given them, and she couldn't think how to say so without offending the recipient.

A knock on the door caught her in midstride. She spun, snatched her jacket off the back of her chair, and was buttoning it when the door opened.

"Good afternoon, Lucinda." Samantha Howard stepped over the threshold, a covered platter in her hands. "If you'll make the tea, I'll supply the food."

"That actually doesn't sound fair." Lucinda closed the door behind Samantha and led the way to her living quarters. "But I'm not going to turn down more of your mother's delicacies."

Samantha laughed. "You mean the cook's delicacies. Mama hasn't cooked a thing in her life."

"Well, um, yes." Lucinda began to prepare the tea. "I don't think my mama cooked either, but don't remember that much. I insisted that I know how."

"I tried to learn, but my parents wouldn't allow it." Samantha removed the cloth from the platter.

An array of scones, tartlets, and cookies bloomed with golden-brown crusts and deep red berry filling. The aroma set Lucinda's mouth watering so much she feared she might drool.

She hadn't eaten, again.

With tiny china plates and cups before them, Lucinda and Samantha faced one another across the table, sipping tea and nibbling delicacies, but not speaking. The street noise, carriage wheels and a man shouting at a cat, rose unnaturally loud. Then a wave of raindrops splashed against the window, and Samantha jumped. Her face lost its dazed expression, and she folded her hands on the edge of the table.

"Now that you and Matthew are courting, I suppose I should tell you about us."

Lucinda curled her fingers around her cup. "I've heard talk, of course, but what do you mean by 'us'? I mean, you and Matthew?"

Samantha sighed, and color tinged her cheekbones. "I met

Matthew six years ago. I was eighteen and he was twenty. He was an apprentice carpenter and came to the house to do some work. I was bored here, out of school in Boston, and. . . Well, you've seen him. I was susceptible to his looks and kindness and skill. He's more artist than artisan, you've noticed, I'm sure."

Lucinda nodded and glanced to the outer room, where one of his chairs presided in turned, wooden splendor.

"So we started talking when he came to the house," Samantha continued, her eyes downcast. "Then we started meeting at other times, going for walks, having picnics. Mama was showing signs of her illness then and wasn't paying much attention to me. Daddy was so worried about her, he didn't either. And I was too old for a governess, and no one has a companion around here, not even the Floyd ladies, who could probably use one." Her sweet smile flashed. "If I become more of a spinster, I may have to apply for the position."

"You're so pretty and kind. I can't see why someone hasn't snatched you up."

"They don't want to be saddled with an invalid mother-in-law, and, well, my courtship with Matthew rather tarnished my reputation here."

"Oh?" Lucinda arched her brows. "Why?"

"Because of his mother." Samantha shot Lucinda a sidelong glance. "Do you know about his mother?"

"Yes. I think people are ignorant and narrow-minded to care who his parents were or were not, and I know it's society's way. I barely passed muster for society back in Virginia."

"But I thought all lawyers were from good families."

"Most are, yes, but not necessarily women." Lucinda emitted a humorless bark of laughter. "In fact, most good families won't let their daughters attend something as vulgar as law school, while encouraging their sons to go. Does that make sense to you?"

"Not particularly." Samantha laughed, sounding amused. "No wonder the Floyd twins took a liking to you. You're a rabble-rouser like them."

Lucinda shook her head. "Not at all. I just want to quietly practice law." And someone in Loveland didn't want her to. "But no more about me. What happened with you and Matthew?"

"Young love. I think there's a rather vulgar term for it. My crush."

Samantha's refined voice speaking the slang term brought a smile to Lucinda's lips, and the meaning of her words brought a ridiculous pang to her middle. Or perhaps that was just hunger, not jealousy.

She took up a jam tartlet and nibbled the edge of the crust. "So what happened? Did you end it and break his heart?"

"My father caught us holding hands and sent me away to stay with my aunts in Maine for the rest of the summer." Samantha picked up a scone, which promptly crumbled between her fingers making a mess on her plate. "I don't know what was said to Matthew, but when I got back, he suddenly owned a few acres of land outside town and wouldn't even look at me."

Lucinda stared at her. "You mean, your father bought him off?"

"Apparently so. I tried to see him again, tried to talk to him." Samantha blushed fully this time. "I even went to his rooms one evening. He only said he wouldn't break his word."

"And what about his word to you?"

"What word?" Samantha picked up her plate. "Do you have some place for waste?"

Lucinda took the plate from Samantha and carried it into the storage room, where a metal canister held the scraps she'd promised to save for Gertie's pig. Rain pounded on the tin roof and against the door. The wind had picked up and now moaned around the corner of the building, making the steps creak.

She should have Mr. Shannon look at those steps, make sure they were stable. They shouldn't creak in the wind, unless nails had loosened.

Brows knit in thought, she returned to the living quarters and found Samantha calmly chewing a macaroon.

"Matthew never made me promises," Samantha continued. "He wasn't in a financial position to have a wife then, and we both knew it. That all has changed, you know."

"I can guess. But I'm not thinking of marriage to him or anyone else. We— Well, I like his company." And the way he looked at her, the way his touch on her cheek or her hand warmed her, the way he smelled of fresh-cut wood and fresh air. . .

Samantha sighed. "Matthew Templin deserves a kind and loving wife. He deserves someone who doesn't care about his background, and whose family doesn't care about it. I was hoping that person was you."

"It's too soon, Miss Howard." Lucinda plucked at the edge of the tablecloth. "No, that's not right. I mean, it is too soon, as we've only known one another for two months. And I doubt we can ever be more than friends with my needing to build my practice, and the people here—" She sighed and met Samantha's gaze directly. "I may as well say it, even though it doesn't sound nice. If people here won't accept him, except for his work, how can I form an attachment with him?"

Samantha frowned. "In other words, your career comes first."

"I've sacrificed a great deal to get it, including leaving my home, my father, and other family I love. I can't throw it away for something as frivolous as my heart."

"Then do tell Matthew." Samantha's tone was cold. "He doesn't need to be hurt again, and I think he's quite smitten with you."

"I don't want him to be smitten." Lucinda realized how calculating her words had sounded, and covered her face with her hands. "He's been so kind to me. I like him a great deal. How can you not like a man who names his cat Purrcilla? And he's been such a friend to me."

"Ah." Samantha emitted a low laugh and touched Lucinda's arm. "I think it will be all right. You keep being a friend to him, then. You're one of the few people in Loveland who's probably well read enough to keep up with him. He doesn't have much formal education, but he reads everything. And with all your education, you can probably give him a run for his money in the philosophy and literature area."

"He is well read and has a deep understanding of what he reads." Lucinda heaved a silent sigh of relief that the moment of crisis had passed. "I enjoy talking about something other than the law."

Samantha's sigh wasn't silent. "I wanted to go to college but couldn't, not with Mama ill and Daddy disapproving of educated females—educated beyond the basic reading, writing, and arithmetic, of course. Not to mention deportment. I must know how to walk across a room with a book on my head."

Lucinda laughed. "I got that, too, then said 'Enough' and left for Michigan." She rose to pour their now-cold tea down the sink and then refilled their cups from the still-warm pot before continuing. "You could go to college still."

"I can't leave Mama before—" Her throat worked. "The doctors say she won't live long. She gets weaker and weaker, and no one knows why. Maybe after she's gone, I'll do something special. I'd rather do that than settle for the kind of husband my father wants for me."

"A man who is handsome, debonair, wealthy, and dull?"

"Precisely." They shared a giggle. Then Samantha sobered. "Meanwhile, how do we keep Matthew from falling head over heels for you—if it's not too late already?"

"I don't know. I mean, I don't have many friends here and would miss seeing him."

"And not talking to him would hurt him again. Hmm." Samantha tapped her forefinger on her lower lip. "I suppose you could be honest with him."

"Or offer him free legal advice. Then we couldn't have a relationship, if I were his lawyer. He seems amenable to—" Lucinda clamped her teeth together, realizing what she was saying.

"Ah yes, the land deal. Well, I suppose it should annoy me that he'd trade my affections for a parcel of acres, but to be honest, it's for the best for us both. I couldn't be poor, and my father would certainly not have given me money if I'd eloped."

"I suppose that's true. We were never wealthy. Landed, yes, but poor by the old standards, since the War Bet—"

The back steps creaked loudly enough for her to hear in her living room.

She sprang to her feet. "I need to look into that. If those steps are going to fall down, I need to notify Mr. Shannon immediately."

She darted into the rear room and flung open the door.

A bedraggled, sodden youth toppled over her threshold and into her arms.

Ten

Lucinda gasped and leaped back. The young man staggered, caught his balance with a hand on the wall, and righted himself.

"John Paul Daggett, what are you doing sneaking in the back door and scaring Miss Bell half to death?" Samantha cried from the doorway of the living room.

"You. . .know him?" Lucinda asked. Her heart slowed and her breathing returned to normal.

The youth nodded. "Yes, she knows me." He didn't look at either Samantha or Lucinda. "I didn't think you'd have company on such a rainy day."

"I'm open for business." Now that her fright had been shown unfounded, Lucinda's pulse increased again, from anger this time. "You could have come through the front door and into the office."

"Not and risk someone seeing me." He glanced at Samantha. "Forget you saw me here."

"Why should she—" His name finally struck Lucinda with the force of a sledge to the brow. "You're related to the mayor, aren't you? I think Mr. Templin mentioned you once."

"He's the mayor's stepson." Samantha's voice sounded cold. "And he's been raised with better manners."

"So have I." Lucinda took in the boy's sodden blond hair hanging in his face, and his drenched coat. Likely his leather shoes had soaked through to his skin, too. "I'll make you some tea—" She stopped. "No, you'd probably prefer hot chocolate."

"I drink tea if I must. And something hot would be nice.

Do you have a radiator?"

"I do." Lucinda led him to the living room and stopped on the threshold. "Take off your shoes and coat first. This isn't a fine rug, but I'd rather keep it clean."

"I don't know if you want to let him in," Samantha cautioned. "This doesn't look right."

"You can stay and play chaperone, but I have to be alone with male clients. I don't see what's wrong with finding out why he sneaked in my back door."

"He sneaked in your back door. That's what's wrong." Samantha's mouth pursed.

"I couldn't come to the office. Everyone would see me." Teeth chattering, John Paul pulled off his coat and handed it to Lucinda, as though he expected her to take it like a servant.

She was tempted to let it drop on the floor. But she was raised better than that, so she took it and hung it on a hook over the radiator. The entire room would smell like steaming, wet wool soon, but she couldn't stop that. She couldn't be responsible for the boy catching a lung fever. That would be the end of her future in Loveland.

If she had a future in Loveland. If. . .

She retreated to the storage room to pull her small bottle of milk from the icebox. With the cold weather, she rarely needed to replenish the ice. The milk stayed fresh for days.

Lucinda returned to her living quarters, replaced the teakettle with a small pan, and poured in a generous amount of milk. Behind her, Samantha spoke to John Paul in quiet but indignant tones. She sounded like a scolding mother.

She should be a mother at twenty-four, as pretty and kind as she was. Of course, Lucinda thought Samantha should get the education she wanted, too, but if she couldn't do that, being a wife and mother was still good. Lucinda wanted to be a wife and mother. Many said that was impossible if she still wanted to practice law, but other women did it. If her husband loved her and supported her work. . .

As she stirred grated chocolate into the milk, she imagined doing the same over a real stove for a husband. It would be nice, on a cold night, to curl up before the fire with the man she loved, a warm fire, a good book. But that dream never had a face. Of all the men she'd met in school, none took her seriously enough to put a face to her daydreams.

Except, as the chocolate began to steam, Matthew Templin's face drifted before her mind's eye.

With a jerky twist she turned off the flame and poured the sweet, rich liquid into one of the sturdy mugs she used when she didn't have company. Or when she had Matthew for company. Then she carried the drink to John Paul. "Now that your lips aren't blue anymore," she told him, "do tell me why you came to my back door—why you stood out there awhile."

"I was waiting for Miss Howard to leave." He glanced at Samantha as though expecting her to disappear right then.

She held her ground. "I'm not leaving Lucinda alone with you. It wouldn't be right."

"Samantha," Lucinda reproved, "I see clients in here. This is my place of business."

"That's all right when you have the Floyd twins or other ladies, but it's not all right when you have a male here. A young male, especially." Samantha's lips thinned so much she resembled a governess sucking lemon drops. "You need a secretary, a permanent chaperone."

"I'll hire one as soon as I have the money. Meanwhile—" Lucinda fixed her gaze on John Paul. "What is it?"

"Can't." He shook his head. "Not in front of Miss Howard. She may tell her mother, who may tell mine, who may—"

"How old are you?" Lucinda realized she should have asked him immediately.

He dropped his gaze. "Eighteen, as of yesterday."

"Hmm." Lucinda ran through the laws she knew. "You haven't reached your majority yet. I don't think I can help you at all."

"You must." Alarm darkened his pale blue eyes. "There's no one else."

"Another lawyer in town." Samantha sounded downright hostile.

"No." John Paul gave his head an emphatic shake.

"Another lawyer couldn't help him either," Lucinda said. "He's too young."

"But you have to listen to me," John Paul protested.

"I don't have to listen to a minor." Lucinda touched his arm, damp and warming from the radiator heat. "Yet I will. But as Samantha said, she'd better stay."

"I'd rather—" He broke off on a sigh. "Do you have pencil and paper?"

"Of course."

"Then I'll write everything down if you'll burn it as soon as you read it."

Lucinda nodded and led him into her office. She pulled out the chair from behind the desk, indicating he should sit, then found clean paper and pencils. Once he was scribbling away on the page before him, Lucinda returned to her living quarters.

She closed the door behind her. "What do you know of this?"

"More than you want to." Samantha was making fresh tea. "He and his stepfather don't get along. John Paul is a nice young man. But Mayor Woodcocks has been known to cuff him around the head, even in public."

Lucinda gasped. "And they still elect the man?"

"You surely know that most people think a man has a right to treat his child that way."

"Not most decent people." Lucinda frowned at the village, still shrouded behind a facade of now-misty rain. Perhaps she didn't want a future here, if people made no noise about a lad getting his head smacked in a disagreement.

Stomach unsettled, she strode to the window and frowned at Main Street. Two carriages trundled by, their occupants invisible behind curtains, drawn, no doubt, to keep out the damp chill. Behind them, a wagon rumbled and rattled over the brick pavement. She recognized the figure on the seat. No one else was quite so brawny. But not unattractive, far from it. Her pulse skipped a beat. She needed to turn away, talk to Samantha more about John Paul, or go see if he was coming along all right with his writing.

She remained at the window watching Matthew drive past, until she would have to move to keep him in sight. A silly, school-girl thing to do.

"What about that empty street has you so fascinated?" Samantha asked from behind Lucinda.

She jumped then shrugged. "Nothing much of interest."

And she was such a liar.

"This is a quiet place," Samantha mused. "Not much interesting occurs here except for this time of year. We have the Christmas ball in four weeks."

"Is Christmas that soon?" Lucinda shivered. "No wonder it's so cold out."

"Yes, we'll get snow any day. Will you come to the ball? It's ever so much fun. Before it, we have a festival that includes everyone in town. We have games and music in the street for two days. Lots of food." Samantha stretched out her arms. "This street will be loud and crowded, but it's on Friday and Saturday, so shouldn't disturb your work."

If Samantha only knew that Saturdays were workdays, too.

"It sounds like a nice way to spend a couple of days," Lucinda murmured as she tiptoed to the office door and peeked in on John Paul.

He sat bent over the desk, pencil rasping across the paper. His drying hair had begun to spring up in curls around his head, making him look far younger than eighteen.

She closed the door without allowing the latch to click and faced Samantha again. "Where do they have the ball?"

"At our house." She grimaced. "Yes, we actually have a ballroom. Isn't that ridiculous? My grandfather had notions of grandeur after he bought land down here and built the house. So we host the ball every year. Mama takes great delight in planning it. I, of course, do all the running around to pick flowers and order this and that. It gives me something to do between summer and Christmas."

"Sounds lovely." Lucinda knew she sounded anything but interested. Her concentration lay in the other room with the boy and whatever missive he was writing to her.

And what was she going to do with it and him if he had some legitimate legal issue? He was a minor. Surely that could be trouble for her. She needed to read more law. Good. That would give her something to do into the evening to while away her time.

"So I'd like you to come to the ball," Samantha announced.

Lucinda snapped her head around to look fully at Samantha. "What? Me at the ball? I'm not in the society crowd."

"It's not a society crowd." Samantha's lips tightened with a sign of exasperation. "It's for everyone who can afford the ticket, and the prices are low, so more people can afford tickets. The proceeds go to support whatever good cause Mrs. Woodcocks wants us to support. This year it's the orphanage. The mayor's wife has a great fondness for helping children without parents."

"It sounds worthy." Lucinda could be sincere in this.

"Then you'll come?"

"No."

"Why not?" Samantha tilted her head and gave Lucinda a sidelong glance. "Matthew always comes."

"And I'm certain he must be quite popular with the young women." Lucinda smiled, wondering how he looked in a suit. Fine, she expected. "But I have nothing suitable to wear."

"Are you telling me that Lucinda Bell of Sweet Magnolia Plantation doesn't have a ball gown?"

"Of—" Lucinda stared at Samantha. "How do you know the name of my father's home?"

"Do you think we wouldn't have looked into your background, Miss Bell?" Samantha smiled. "We needed to make sure you are the proper sort, so the Floyd twins had someone look into your family history."

"Good heavens!" Lucinda's face felt hot. "Then why is Mrs. Woodcocks so against me? I mean, it's not the War Between the St—the Civil War, that is."

"No, and that's the odd thing about it." Samantha tapped her finger on her lower lip and paced around the tiny room. "It puzzles me. But perhaps he"—she gestured to the outer office—"will shed some light on this. If he doesn't make things worse for you."

"I know. That concerns me." Lucinda slipped to the door and looked out. John Paul was writing slowly, laboriously, as though writing didn't come easily to him. She closed the door and shook her head to Samantha's raised eyebrows.

"So about a gown. Are you certain you don't have a ball gown?"

"I have a few, yes, but not here."

"Ah, I knew it couldn't be true that you didn't have one." Samantha sat on the sofa and propped her chin in her hand. "Could you telegraph your father and ask him to send one up?"

"All right, I will."

Floorboards creaked in the adjacent room. Lucinda strode to the office door and opened it. "Mr. Daggett?"

"Yes." He handed her a sheaf of papers, a sheepish smile on his face. "My spelling and handwriting aren't very good. But I think it's legible."

"It is." Lucinda stared at his first few lines of large, schoolboy-like handwriting. Her mouth went dry, and her stomach dropped to the pit of her middle with a nauseating speed that should have thumped aloud in the silent room.

I am writing this letter to Miss Bell, attorney, because I need to do something about my stepfather, Mayor Woodcocks. He is robbing me of my inheritance.

She folded the papers in the event Samantha could read upside down and then looked at the young man. "Come back at ten o'clock."

"Lucinda," Samantha protested, "you cannot see male clients that late at night. He can come back in the morning."

"I can see them when I need to." She looked sternly at Samantha. "And don't go telling anyone. Mr. Daggett is only eighteen, for goodness' sake."

John Paul finished his hot chocolate in one long pull then set the cup on the table. He headed to the door. "I'll be back, Miss Bell."

Lucinda and Samantha remained silent while he pulled on his shoes and crept down the back steps. When locking the door,

LAURIE ALICE EAKES

Lucinda spotted the muddy footprints and knew where the others came from. This wasn't the first time Mr. Daggett had come to see her.

"Why do you do this?" Samantha asked, not sounding critical, just curious.

Lucinda smiled. "I love the law. It's my calling, my service to God and people. The law is what keeps people from settling disputes with their fists, or worse."

"But to go to court? That seems so. . .vulgar."

"A good lawyer doesn't go to court, really. We settle things before they go that far. At least, we try. It's rather more difficult with criminal matters, and I don't intend to take criminal cases if I can avoid it. It's one reason why I settled on an abandoned practice here."

"Still, you're so pretty and have a good family. Why would you give all that up for. . .this?" Samantha swept her arm in a semicircle, taking in the shabby rooms.

"As I said, it's my calling," Lucinda said with complete conviction. "Bells have practiced law since the commonwealths of Virginia and Massachusetts were colonies."

"Your calling, or your inheritance?"

Lucinda blinked. "What do you mean?"

"Do you do this because you love it or because you think you have a duty to do it?"

"Why do they have to be different?"

"Well, I don't know." Samantha's lower lip quivered and she glanced away. "I never had a calling, unless it was to be a wife and mother, perhaps, but that was denied me when Matt chose land over elopement."

Lucinda flinched. "That sounds ignoble of him."

"It does, without all the facts. But I know he was thinking of what was best for me. I don't know how to be poor. And Mother needs me." Samantha sighed. "Perhaps one day the Lord will provide me with someone else to love."

"He will."

Samantha still held feelings for Matthew, whatever she claimed. Another reason for Lucinda not to form an attachment to him—she didn't want him coming between her and her friendship with Samantha.

"I know He will. And don't go thinking I still care for Matthew. Not that way, anyway." She strode to the window. "The rain has stopped. I should be going." She gathered her coat, hat, and gloves and departed to where her carriage waited for her.

Lucinda sat on her sofa and read through John Paul's story. Though badly spelled, and with poor sentence structure, the meaning was clear. John Paul had reason to believe his stepfather and guardian, Mayor Vincent Woodcocks, was systematically embezzling from the boy's inheritance, left him by his father. He wanted help getting control of his fortune before it was gone.

Before the youth returned, Lucinda delved into her law books until she had an answer for him.

"I can help you," she told John Paul. "We need to petition for you to be emancipated from your guardian."

"Like a slave?"

"Something like that. You don't have many more rights than slaves did, not until you're twenty-one. That he strikes you about the face and head, and with proof of his embezzlement, we can get that done and perhaps even get some of your money back, provided he hasn't spent it. There's just one problem, and that's more for me than you."

"I know." John Paul's face slackened. "My parents already despise you."

"Why?" She may as well ask.

"I think they're afraid. They know that I could never go to Roger Stagpole, and they ran the other one out of town—the man who had an office before you. But you won't go, no matter how they try to frighten you off."

"In other words," Lucinda said, feeling more than a little queasy, "I'm a threat."

Eleven

The last person Matt expected to see enter his workshop was Samantha Howard. Yet as he rubbed the final coat of oil into Lucinda's second office chair, a knock sounded on the door, and Samantha strode in as though she was used to doing so on a regular basis.

"You aren't supposed to talk to me," he said reflexively.

"*You're* not supposed to talk to me." Sarah dropped her coat onto a new piece for him—a sofa for two just awaiting cushions on the seat and back to make it comfortable. "Isn't that what you traded for land?"

"We had no future, Miss Howard. It would have ended eventually, so I took the land your father was willing to buy me."

Samantha laughed. "Mercenary, aren't we?"

Matt shrugged. "I like to think of it as wise."

"It's one reason why I found you so refreshing. But now you have found someone else, and I'm happy for you."

"No, I haven't found someone else." Matt moved his cloth in regular swirls along the rich maple grain, making the wood glow as though it contained an inner fire. He didn't look at Samantha. "I am happy I can be friends with Miss Lucinda, but I know I'm not good enough for her."

"Of course you are."

"She's like you—family and land and a history. Her kind don't marry my kind."

"She's not like that, you know." Samantha approached the settee and ran her hand across its sleigh back. "She wouldn't be a lady lawyer here if she thought the way society thinks. She's more like

103

the Floyd ladies—thinking women should be equal with men."

"So probably doesn't want a husband at all."

"Which is why she went to dinner with you last Sunday night instead of going home with me."

That memory still sent a thrill through him, but he responded, "Yes, she's lonely. I expect I flatter the female side of her."

"Oh Matt." Samantha sighed, paused behind him, and touched his shoulder.

Once upon a time, that light brush of her fingers would have dissolved his insides like varnish under turpentine. Now he merely experienced the comfort of knowing Samantha was still a friend, as she had been when they were young and didn't think they were in love.

Which, of course, they weren't. He'd been infatuated with her poise, her beauty, her attention to the poor carpenter's apprentice. If he'd truly loved her, he would have said forget it to her father's bribe and asked for land far from Loveland and the humiliation of everyone there knowing his history.

If everyone knew his history correctly.

Those papers, now safely hidden behind a loose brick in his kitchen fireplace, still puzzled him, but he hesitated before asking for Lucinda's assistance. Helping him could ruin her chances for success.

"Lucinda likes you a great deal," Samantha continued as she made a circuit of the workshop. "She talks about you with such warmth, it nearly makes me blush."

Matt made a wordless noise in the back of his throat.

Samantha stomped her foot in its leather shoe, sweeping her skirt's lacy ruffles, completely inappropriate for a carpentry shop. She would gather sawdust and have to explain it to her mother. Her mother would guess where the particles had originated.

"Have a care," Matt said. "You're getting your skirt dirty."

Samantha glanced down, lifted her gown, and shook it. "It doesn't matter. I'm more than old enough to make my own decisions in whom I speak to. And so is Lucinda. If she wants to spend her time with you, she will. But only if you give her the opportunity."

"Ah, I sense you're ready to tell me why you're here." He glanced up, polishing ceased.

"I am." Samantha faced him, her hands folded together at her tiny waist. "She needs an escort to the Christmas ball."

"No."

"Matthew—"

"I'm not going to do that to her, walk in with her on my arm and have her lowered to my lev—"

"It's not lowering, Matthew. That's what I'm trying to tell you." Samantha sighed. "If you don't take her, she will be home alone during the festivities, and she spends enough time alone."

He pictured her seated behind her desk, head bent over a heavy law book or a paper of some sort. She might have a cup of tea at her side, but none of the cafés or restaurants would be open for her to find a hot meal. The hot food would be at the festival, and then the ball. She would nibble on what she had in the house. She'd be pretty hungry, not to mention lonely.

He knew loneliness.

"All right." He stood and gazed down at Samantha. "I'll see if I can persuade her to go."

"Thank you." She touched his face with her fingertips, gathered her coat, and swept out the door.

So how to persuade her?

Matt pondered the question as he finished a settle for a farmer and then left for work at the mayor's house. When he arrived, Mrs. Woodcocks stood in the kitchen consulting with the cook.

He took a good look at her, examining her features for anything familiar, but saw only one possibility—the set of her chin. It was unusually square for a female, making her handsome rather than pretty.

He had a square chin that fit much better on a male face.

And her hair glowed a rich chocolate brown, though she was in her midforties at the least. Only the merest hint of gray touched a few threads in her glossy coiffure, accenting the deep brown rather than detracting from it.

His hair was that dark and shiny.

But so were many other people's, too. He needed to work, not speculate.

He excused himself and lugged his tools through the house to the library. Today was likely to be his last day on the job. Today, he merely needed to inspect the paneling for any flaws in the finish and carving.

"Very nice work, Mr. Templin." Mrs. Woodcocks sailed into the library behind him. "We're quite amazed and pleased. Maybe I'll have you replace the paneling in the dining room next. It seems dark for a room that never gets sunlight."

"I'd be happy to do that for you, ma'am." He didn't rise from where he crouched on the floor, so he wouldn't tower over her.

"How much do we owe you? I'll get your pay immediately."

"Thank you." He named his fee.

Without a fuss, she nodded and left the room. A few minutes later, she arrived with an envelope, thanked him again, and swept away on a cloud of some flowery scent.

She was so kind and generous, he didn't understand why she'd taken such a hostile attitude toward Lucinda. It didn't make sense. She wasn't hostile toward the Floyd ladies. Of course, they were of an old family with lots of money, but Lucinda was from an old family, too.

Baffled, he looked in the envelope and saw how generous she'd been. His entire fee had been paid, along with a sizable bonus. And she wanted him to do more work. Did she truly want more changes to her house, or was it guilt work? Even after two months of pondering those papers, he couldn't believe they were real. Surely no one could keep up a lie like that for nearly twenty years.

Time to stop contemplating and take action.

He arrived at Lucinda's office the following day to ask if he could do just that. He hadn't seen her for nearly a week and took the steps two at a time. He raised his hand to knock, but heard voices beyond the door, female voices, their words indistinct. One sounded agitated, even weepy. Not Lucinda. Her tones soothed— calm, gentle, and kind. The voices faded. He pictured her taking the other woman back to her quarters and serving her tea.

When he no longer heard the voices, he knocked and then stepped into the office. It was deserted, but now he heard the murmur from beyond the inner door, an unfamiliar female voice, calmer but still broken. A bell lay on the corner of the desk, and he rang it.

Lucinda emerged at once. "Matt." She closed the door behind her and offered him a shy smile. "I'm sorry I didn't hear you come in."

"It's good to see you." He cleared his throat and ran his gaze over her face, trying to remember why he was there.

Her cheeks grew a becoming pink. "You, too. It's been awhile."

"I haven't been in town, and the days are so short now, coming in at night is difficult." The ten feet or so between them felt like a mile. He took a step toward her. "I, um, you have someone here."

"It's all right. She's resting." She closed the distance between them and held out her hands. "To what do I owe a visit today?"

"I needed to see you." He took her hands in his, and his heart lurched. Inside his coat, papers crackled, papers he'd brought just in case. "Are you warm enough here?"

"Mostly. There is a draft."

"Draft? From the door. Of course. That's another reason why I'm here." He strode to the door. "I want to measure for building your vestibule. Mr. Shannon says it's all right."

"So you really came here to work." Disappointment pouted her lips.

Her mouth, something he shouldn't look at for long, as it gave him ideas it shouldn't. He shifted his gaze to her face, but her cheeks were growing pinker. Heat stole up his neck, too. "I thought maybe I could borrow one of your law books."

"Of course you may borrow a book." She trotted to the row of shelves. "What sort of law book would you like to read?"

"Do you have anything about inheritance law?"

"Ye–es." Her dark gold eyebrows arched in a question.

He shrugged. "Just curious." The papers crackled in his pocket, giving the lie to what he said. He removed them from his coat's inner pocket to lay them on the desk. "No, I have a specific question. Will you read these for me? I—I can pay you."

"You'd better not. That would make you a client, and then you couldn't, we couldn't. . . I suppose it's all right amongst friends."

Friends? Did she honestly believe they were only friends? He must convince her otherwise.

He reached for the papers. "Never mind it. It'll make trouble for you here."

Her head shot up. "Trouble?"

"Yes."

"Why? How? I mean, the mayor's wife has reason to dislike me already."

Matt started. "You know why she does?"

"I do, but it was told me in confidence by a client, so I can't say."

"Then you want nothing to do with this. I was afraid of that, but Stagpole isn't trustworthy in this, and I'd rather not travel elsewhere to find an attorney, who, for all I know, will be part of Stagpole's crowd. I thought you, being a lady lawyer. . ."

She laughed, the sound like a clear note among discordant tones. "You figure a lady lawyer wouldn't be welcome, golfing or smoking cigars."

"Exactly."

"You're right. So let me have a look at those." She held out her hand. "And now, I'm very sorry, but I need to get back to my client."

Matt placed the papers in her hand. She reached for them. When their fingers touched, Matt curled his fingers around hers, held her hand, held her gaze.

"Just friends?" he murmured.

"Matt, I—"

He released her hand and grazed her cheek with his knuckle. "We'll talk later, when you don't have a client. I'll be in town all day."

She cradled her hand in the other. "When will I see you to work on the vestibule?"

"Tomorrow. Unless you come to Gertie's tonight."

"I may do that. It's awfully cold. Some hot soup would be fine before I turn in for the night." With a nod and a rustle of her skirts, she swept into the inner room.

Matt watched her go, then turned and departed just as the first flakes of snow began to fall.

Twelve

Lucinda stared from the door, picturing Matt's broad back as he descended the steps, each footfall firm and echoing on the wooden treads. Around her, the room felt empty, cold. She felt empty, cold.

She glanced at the papers he'd left behind, entrusted to her. Her fingers twitched with a nearly irrepressible urge to pick up the sheaf of vellum and read each word to find out why in the world Matthew Templin, carpenter, needed an attorney.

She did pick up the pages—and slid them into a desk drawer. Another client awaited her in the living room.

Lucinda crossed the office and pushed open the inner door. Parthina Carr, a faded replica of her cousin Gertie, raised her head and smiled. She was wispy rather than thin, with colorless eyes and hair, but her smile was as warm as her cousin's.

"Thank you for your patience with me, Miss Bell. You're terribly kind. Now then, you won't give up on my case?"

"Of course not. It will just take more letters. At least they're responding, and rather quickly."

"That's further than I've gotten before."

"People tend to take notice when they receive letters from lawyers. They don't want to go to court over something like denying a widow her pension. It makes them look bad, and politicians don't like to be made to look bad."

Mrs. Carr chuckled. "Isn't that the truth? They only want to make others look bad." Her face clouded. "They won't do anything like that to me, will they?"

"No ma'am. No one wants to torment a widow that way." Lucinda grimaced. "Ignoring her is quite different from public ridicule. But they won't ignore me."

She hoped. Female lawyers often got ignored as not being truly in the profession like men. Still, she would fight as hard as she needed to. This woman's story was tragic. With her husband dead in a tunnel-building project through no fault of his own, Mrs. Carr was left without any means of support and two children to bring up. Gertie helped where she could. So did other relatives. But most of them didn't have a great deal of money either, the economy not being in the best of conditions that year. Mrs. Carr needed and deserved the pension owed her as the widow of a man injured or killed on the job. Lucinda would make certain Mrs. Carr received that pension.

"I'll work on it today," Lucinda said. "Would you like to stay here longer, or return to Gertie's?"

"I'll be on my way to Gertie's. Looks like snow out there."

Indeed, beyond the window Lucinda hadn't glanced through in hours, snow plummeted in slanting ribbons of white. She stopped herself the second before a groan escaped from her lips. "And windy, I'm afraid. Would you like me to walk with you?"

She didn't want to. She wanted to read Matt's paperwork. If she went to Gertie's, she would stay for the warmth of the kitchen fire, the hot food and coffee Gertie would set before her, the companionship, and Lucinda would get nothing done. At the same time, Mrs. Carr appeared so frail, though she couldn't be more than a dozen years older than Lucinda, that she didn't want the older woman walking down potentially slippery sidewalks.

But Mrs. Carr shook her head. "I'll be all right. I have walking boots on."

But not warm walking boots.

Lucinda glanced to the armoire, where her own sturdy boots resided. "I'll come anyway." She smiled. "You know what Proverbs says about one holding the other up."

"You're right in that." Mrs. Carr laughed and began to tug on her coat, also shockingly shabby.

Lucinda hastened to change into her boots, pin on a felt hat, and wrap up in her warm wool coat and scarf. Seeing that Mrs. Carr donned no scarf, Lucinda took a second knitted strip out of the armoire and gave it to her. "You don't want to risk getting sick."

"No ma'am." Mrs. Carr ducked her head as she wound the muffler around her neck. "About your fee. . . You are spending quite a lot of time on me."

"Never mind about that. Let's get your pension straight."

"I can pay you as soon as you do, but if we lose. . ."

"The Lord will provide. He has so far, and I don't see why He'll stop."

"True. True. For all we may have gone without other things these past two years, my children and I have had food and shelter."

They stepped out of the office door into slanting, stinging pelts of snow and icy rain. Lucinda closed the door and locked it, then turned, slipped on the icy treads. Her right foot shot out over the edge of the step. Laughing, she grabbed the railing and steadied herself. "Yes, I am most certainly going with you."

Slowly, they descended to the sidewalk. They held one another's arms and, slipping and sliding, heads bent against the buffeting wind, walked the two blocks to Gertie's café.

It was still open, with several men, some with their wives, crowded around the tables drinking coffee and eating something savory smelling. Warmth enveloped the room, and Lucinda spread out her arms as though the entire chamber were a fire.

In a way, it was. It was the fire of community and friendship, the closest thing to a home she had. Except she wasn't quite a member yet. The conversation didn't stop at her entrance as it had her first time there. A handful of people glanced up and smiled; two women she'd helped with minor legal issues raised hands of acknowledgment. Still, no one invited her to join their table for conversation. She was still too much of an oddity. She was not a housewife or even a lady seeking a husband. She was more educated than most of these people, and she came from a good family in the South. Yet with the mayor and his wife rejecting her for their gatherings, no one quite knew where Lucinda fit into the scheme of things.

Gertie pushed through the swinging door from the kitchen carrying an enormous teapot, and, of all people, Matt came behind her holding two coffeepots. They both bypassed everyone calling for more coffee or tea. Smiles warm and welcoming, they headed straight for Lucinda and Mrs. Carr.

"Lucinda." Matt set the coffeepots on a table and clasped her gloved hands. "I'm glad you came early. I'm glad. You don't need to be in those rooms eating cold food in this weather."

Suddenly, she didn't care that no one in the room invited her to their table. Matt held her hands in his, warmth seeping through her gloves to her frozen fingers, warmth running up her arms, into her cheeks, into her heart.

Oh no. It couldn't have happened to her. Yet as she gazed into his brown eyes, she accepted that it had.

She'd fallen for him—hard.

She drew her hands free. Still the warmth lingered. The glow inside her continued to burn. "I, um, couldn't let Mrs. Carr walk down here alone. I didn't intend to stay."

"But now?" His gaze traveled over her face, intense, questioning.

She licked cold and dry lips. "I can't imagine wanting to leave."

"Lucinda." His soft utterance of her name caressed her ears. "Will you sit down? I can get you some coffee. Gertie is busy taking care of Mrs. Carr's children, so I offered to help."

"Then I'll help, too."

He arched a brow. "Miss Lucinda Bell of Middleburg, Virginia, will help serve tables?"

"No one is more a servant of people than a lawyer, Mr. Templin." She picked up one of the coffeepots and began to circle the room, jetting arcs of the dark, rich brew into cups with the expertise she'd learned as part of her hostess training as a girl growing up with a father who often entertained clients and other important people in the community. Customers did stop talking now. Their gazes followed her, eyes wide, a few jaws dropped. Did they think she was some kind of snob, above helping Gertie, who had been kindness itself to her? Or did it stem from her being a lawyer and a lady one at that?

Whatever the answers, people's voices dropped after she passed, returning to the kitchen to replace the empty pot with a full one, pausing to fill more cups, even accepting someone's payment before he braved the storm. She didn't catch the remarks until one older gentleman whose hearing was obviously impaired and voice louder than he intended said, "Never thought I'd see a lawyer giving anything to anyone. All I ever thought was that they took out of others' pockets."

The room fell silent. Slowly, Lucinda set her pot on a table and faced the man, her voice pitched a little louder so he'd be sure to hear her. "Mr. Kingswell, you own the green grocer, don't you?"

"Yes, of course I do," he snapped. "What of it?"

"Do you give your groceries away?"

"Of course I don't."

"Then why, after I have spent six years of training, should I give my goods away just because they come from my knowledge and my brain?" Smiling sweetly, she proceeded to fill more cups.

A few people laughed and teased the old man about being bested by a female.

Mr. Kingswell bellowed out, "Because you're a woman. It ain't right."

Lucinda didn't need to respond. Half a dozen women jumped in saying a woman could charge for what she produced in work as much as a man.

"It's even in Proverbs," Gertie declared. "A woman sells what she makes in the marketplace. Miss Bell's marketplace happens to be people's legal needs."

"Then tell her to do some good instead of encouraging our women to have their own wills," one man called out.

Lucinda overfilled the next cup. Hand shaking, Lucinda dropped her pot onto the table and fled into the kitchen. She yanked open the back door, but a blast of wind, laden with more ice than snow now, slammed into her face, reminding her she wore neither coat nor hat. No matter, she could get home two blocks without them.

A hand fell on her shoulder, holding her in place with firm gentleness. The door was pushed out of her hold, the bar dropped into place.

"Why are you running away from us and into that?" Matt steered her toward the stove's heat. "You'll be a block of ice before you reach your rooms, if you even get that far and don't fall down and break something on the way."

"Would anyone come to my rescue if I did?" The instant she said the words, she wanted to pull them back inside. "That was childish. I'm sorry."

"You should be. You know I would." He turned her so her back was to the blazing stove and she faced him. "Are you letting them scare you off? The lady who moved hundreds of miles from home to a strange town so she could answer the calling of the Lord?"

"Perhaps I was wrong in that. Perhaps *I* wanted to be a lawyer and the Lord doesn't want me to be one at all. People here don't like me."

"The women like you. Their husbands are a little afraid of you."

"Me? But I'm so—so—"

"Sweet. Kind. Strong." He rested his hand on her cheek and lowered his voice. "Pretty."

"Pretty useless as a lawyer." She stared down at the toes of her boots peeking from beneath the hem of her serge skirt. If she looked at him, saw the same tenderness in his eyes as she heard in his voice, felt in his hand, she might weep. Worse than weep, throw herself against his chest and sob. It was such a solid-looking chest. She shook her head to try to clear that thought, noting as she did so that her hair was coming loose. "I can't even afford to live someplace where I can cook a pot of hot soup on a cold night."

"But God's given you neighbors to rely on when you need that hot soup, hasn't He?"

"I've never had to ask for anything in my life."

"Including the Lord?"

She sank her teeth into her lower lip.

He nudged her chin up with gentle pressure from his thumb. "You've had everything handed to you, haven't you? A fine education, admittance to law school in spite of being a female, and then things got harder."

"I'm sure I'm supposed to practice law, but if people here don't like me, they won't come to me."

"Sure you're supposed to practice, but why do you think you should be wholly independent in doing so? Let others help you."

"How?"

Almost absently, his thumb stroked across her lower lip, and he smiled. "Don't be so secretive about walking out with me. Go to church with just me and dinner at the hotel after." He raised his other hand to her face. "Go to the Christmas ball with me."

"I. . . How. . . ?" The right question eluded her. Blood roared through her ears. Her heart raced. She raised her hands to push him away but clung to his lapels. *You can't. Not here. Not now.* Surely she said those words, yet no sound emerged.

And then she couldn't talk, for his lips covered hers. His scent of fresh-cut wood and fresh air filled her senses. The floor must have vanished from beneath her feet, for surely she floated on air, with only his hands on her face and her fingers gripping his coat keeping her from banging her head on the ceiling beams.

"Ahem."

The thunderclap of someone clearing her throat brought the floor slamming into Lucinda's boot heels. She would have leaped backward if Matt hadn't held her in place.

"The stove is behind you," he murmured, then looked past her shoulder and smiled. "Are we in your way, Gertie?"

Only Gertie. Good.

Except she stood with the door to the café wide open and half a dozen lingering patrons able to see straight into the kitchen.

Not good.

Gertie was grinning though. "About time."

"About time for what?" Lucinda asked.

That broke the paralysis of the coffee-drinking audience. They burst into laughter. A couple of men called encouragement to Matt.

Lucinda ducked beneath his arm and darted to the counter out of sight of the dining room doorway. She needed the chill away from the stove to cool her heated cheeks, steady her charging heart.

Matthew Templin had just kissed her. She had just let Matthew Templin kiss her. She had welcomed it, perhaps even invited it. Goodness, what was she thinking?

The same thing she'd been thinking when he met her at the door—that she'd fallen for him, that she might even go so far as to say she loved him.

This. Would. Not. Do. She was supposed to practice law, not enter into a courtship with. . . Well, with a highly respected artisan in the town, but one whose parentage was in serious question, thus making him the ridicule of many, scorned by the sort of people she wanted, she needed, as clients, if she was to succeed.

She grabbed her coat and hat off of a stool where they'd been drying. "I must go. I have work to do."

"You can't go out there," Gertie and Matt protested.

Gertie closed the door to the café. "Don't run away from this, child. It's nothing to be ashamed of if you care for him."

"I do. Of course I do. That is—" She made herself face them. "I've never kissed anyone in my life. I need some time to hink."

"Ah, I understand." Gertie strode forward and hugged Lucinda. "Then go home and think, but I'm sending some soup with you and Matthew to ensure your rooms are warm enough."

"Yes ma'am."

"And behave yourself, young man." Gertie punched Matt on the arm, picked up a pot of coffee, and left the kitchen.

Matt took the coat from Lucinda's hands and held it out for her to slide her arms into the sleeves. "I'd apologize except I don't think I need to."

"No, you don't. I didn't object."

"You didn't seem to." He began to shrug into his own coat. "I've been in love with you since you were at my house with the Floyd sisters and you cuddled Purrcilla on your shoulder."

"Don't tell me that."

"What, that I love you?" He rested his hands on her shoulders. "It's not mutual?"

"No. Yes. I mean—" She laid her head against his chest. "I'm so confused."

"I understand." His arms closed around her, so wonderfully strong, sheltering, a shelter from the storm outside and the one within her.

How simple life would be if she were simply a girl from the town, perhaps someone serving in Gertie's café to make her living instead of someone every bit a professional as any male attorney. If only she didn't believe she was supposed to practice law rather than be a wife.

If only love hadn't crept up on her and conquered her heart.

"Let me get that soup." Gertie poked her head around the edge of the door.

Matt let Lucinda go, and Gertie entered the kitchen. "You're going to stay here for the night, aren't you, Matthew? You can't be going back home in this."

"I wouldn't do that to my horse."

Gertie ladled soup into a jar, wrapped it in a towel, then tucked it into a pail. "That should keep it from getting too cold on the way to your place. Now you come straight back, Matthew."

"Yes ma'am. Lucie?" He offered her his arm.

She took it, clung to it as they entered an ice-coated world. He was sure-footed and sturdy. She slipped and slid, but remained upright clinging to his arm.

Two are better than one. . . .

Beyond commenting about the weather, they said little on their way down the two blocks. When they reached her steps, Matt said he'd bring salt by in the morning. He walked behind her, steadying her up each icy tread.

"I won't come in, but I'll wait in the event your rooms aren't warm." He kissed her cheek. "Good night, my love."

"Good night." She unlocked her door and entered her office.

She didn't know if the radiators were working or not. That kiss on the cheek had warmed her enough.

Still, she reheated the soup over her spirit lamp; then, unable to settle with ice pellets pinging against the windows and wind whining around the corners of the building, she sat at her desk and opened the drawer to take out some work.

She found the papers Matt had delivered earlier. Even before she began to read them, her stomach dropped with a sickening jolt. She couldn't represent him legally and walk out with him at the same time. It wasn't illegal; it was just unethical and lawyers frowned on that kind of behavior. It was another mark against females practicing the law. She must make a choice between representing him and continuing a relationship with him.

With her cheek and her lips still feeling the imprint of his kiss, she opened the packet of papers and began to read. The first one was a birth certificate.

Her heart dropped to the bottom of her belly along with her stomach. The further she read the documents, the more her organs seemed to desert her body altogether.

If she represented Matthew, which he certainly needed, she couldn't help John Paul, which he certainly needed, as their claims were in direct opposition to one another, but both centered on the Woodcocks fortune. Or, more accurately, the Daggett fortune.

Both men laid a claim to it.

Thirteen

The next day dawned to sunshine turning the world into a crystal palace complete with glistening trees and shimmering roofs. It would all melt soon with that kind of sunshine, but Lucinda stood before her office window and gazed into the glorious brightness feeling like Sleeping Beauty the day after the prince awakened her.

"Is this why You brought me here, Lord? So I could meet him?"

He wasn't the sort her father expected her to marry. He thought another lawyer, his partner's son, for example, would be an excellent match. She liked Philip Long well enough, but he spent more time on the tennis court or golf course than practicing law. Matt. . . Well, Matt was as solid in his mind and spirit as he was in his form. Who cared that he was a carpenter and not a professional man. He was an artist at his work, and he loved animals. He talked to the Lord more than he talked to a fellow sportsman, and he looked at her like she was the most precious thing on the earth. With all those qualities, his parentage didn't matter to her.

It mattered to him, though, and when he arrived, she must tell him she couldn't help.

He arrived bright and early, with Mrs. Carr in tow.

"Gertie said we need a chaperone," he told Lucinda.

"Probably good advice, except. . ." Lucinda glanced from Mrs. Carr to Matt. "The nature of my business, I really can't have another person around I'm not paying, and, well, the coffers don't run that deep yet."

"They will." He touched her cheek and smiled, and it was

nearly as good as a kiss.

Her insides jellied, Lucinda opened the door to her living quarters. "Why don't you wait in here, Mrs. Carr. That way you won't see any clients or hear anything, and we will still be looked after. I have a few novels you can read. Help yourself to tea or coffee." Realizing she was talking too much, she shrugged. "Make yourself comfortable."

"I will be, Miss Bell. I have my needlework." She held up a tapestry bag nearly as big as a carpetbag. "And I can watch the street. Watching people is forever entertaining."

"Thank you." Lucinda closed the door and turned to Matt. Their eyes met, held, urging her to run to him, see if last night was a mere dream.

"We, um, have a chaperone," she managed to say.

"I suppose this is why." He closed the distance between them in three long strides and kissed her quickly, lightly.

No, the previous night was not a dream. Even that brief contact sent her head spinning, her knees weakening.

"Should I get started on your vestibule?" he asked.

"My—? Oh yes. No, I need to talk to you first." She made herself walk to the desk and open the drawer. Her fingers fumbled at the packet of papers he'd brought her. She retrieved them at last and held them out to him. "I can't help you, Matthew. I wish— Don't look at me like that."

His face had fallen as though she had slapped him. "I have no case?"

"I think you have a grand case. I think you're likely to win. But I can't help you with it for two reasons."

"Which are?" The chilled atmosphere in the chamber had nothing to do with the temperature but everything to do with his tone of voice in those two words.

Lucinda hugged herself. "I can't tell you exactly."

"Why not?" The ice outside could take refuge from the sun in her office.

Lucinda held out her hands to him. "Matt, I can't tell you because it involves another client of mine and I'm not allowed to say anything or represent someone who might be in direct conflict with you. Does that make sense?"

"Not particularly, but I guess you can't tell me."

"No, I can't."

"All right, then." A slight thawing. "That's one reason. What's the other?"

"You and me. That is—" Her cheeks heated. "I can't represent you if we—if you still want to court me."

"Still want to? Of course I still want to." He strode forward and clasped her hands in his. "I've wanted to court you practically since I met you, but you're a lady, educated and refined. I never would have considered courting you if I hadn't found those papers, thought there was hope. I just couldn't think what to do with them. I didn't want to give them to you straightaway, and I— Lucie, if I can't prove my claim, I am always going to be fatherless for reasons people here gossip about despite my mother's change of heart."

"And you think I care about that? I didn't look at those papers until I got home last night, if that tells you anything."

"You may not care, but I do. I don't want to bring you down. You need clients with money, not the sort who are paying you in eggs and roasted chickens."

Lucinda smiled. "I appreciate the eggs and roasted chickens."

"They don't pay the rent. They don't get you out of these awful rooms and into something better." His fingers tightened on hers. "They don't get you what you're used to having."

"I'm getting used to having this." She pulled one hand free and swept her arm out to encompass her office and room. "It's worth it to do what I love."

"It's not a home." He turned away from her, paced to the back window, stood with his hands in his pockets and his shoulders hunched and head bowed, then returned to her. "Lucie, I was praying about what to do about my being attracted to a lady like you, and then I found them. If I'm still only the son of the town's reformed fallen woman, I'm not good enough for you."

"Matthew, that's absurd. You are God's son, His beloved son. An earthly father doesn't matter." Her throat closed before she could say more in protest.

He shook his head. "Not absurd at all. It's fact, my dear. People like the Howards will never come to you."

"They go to Stagpole anyway." She blinked to keep the tears behind her eyelids. "And I have the Floyd sisters."

"Who everyone thinks are eccentric at best. Yes, their money gets them invited everywhere, but no one listens to them."

"And Samantha Howard—" She stopped.

Not good to mention his former love, whom he had given up for a parcel of land, the price her father was willing to pay to get rid of him. Because he wasn't good enough for his precious daughter, the artisan son of an unmarried woman.

Except he wasn't unless those papers were forged. He needed an investigator, a detective, to find out the truth.

"My father isn't going to come after you for courting me," she added.

"But will he be happy about it?"

"If I love you, he won't care. Not unless—" She drew her lower lip between her teeth.

Matt raised a brow.

Lucinda sighed. "Unless I stop practicing law. I had an inheritance from my grandmother that paid for my education, but Daddy doesn't want me to waste it."

"And you'll waste it lowering yourself to my level."

"Matthew."

"Lucinda, it's true and you know it. You've been here long enough. Even the Floyd sisters don't invite me to dinner parties."

"You." She jabbed her finger at his chest. "Why did you even court me if this is how you feel?"

"Because I thought you could help me prove my identity."

"You thought—" Lucinda grabbed for the back of her desk chair behind her. "You thought I'd help you if you courted me?"

"No, Lucie—"

"You thought you could pay me with kisses instead of chickens, did you?"

"Lucinda, no, I only meant—"

She marched over to the door and flung it open to a blast of wind not yet warmed by the sun. "I think you need to leave. I have work to do."

"Lucinda, stop and listen to me." His tone was firm, his face resolute. "Please," he added like an afterthought.

Certain she was going to burst into tears at any moment, Lucinda didn't budge. The wind could account for any excess moisture in her eyes.

Matt didn't move, but someone headed up the steps, a man Lucinda had known existed since before her arrival in Loveland, a man whom she had seen on the street but who had never deigned to speak to her.

"Mr. Stagpole," she said with admirable calm, "to what do I owe this honor?"

Stagpole entered the office and removed his silk top hat to reveal a shock of beautiful silver-white hair still thick and wavy despite his probably sixty or more years. "Good day, Miss Bell. I need a word with you." He glanced at Matt. "A private word."

"Of course." Lucinda smiled, though her insides quaked. "My

carpenter is just leaving. It's really too cold for him to be building me a vestibule, don't you think? Thank you for coming, Mr. Templin."

"You're welcome, Miss Bell." He stepped over the threshold, then turned back. "I'll return when the atmosphere is warmer."

The look in his eyes warned her he didn't mean the outside temperature.

Inclining her head graciously, she closed the door in his face, then gave Mr. Stagpole her attention. "How may I help you? Feel free to sit."

He was looking around the small, shabby office, from her chairs, to her scarred desk, to the fine shelves full of books. He pulled one from the shelves. "I understand you attended the University of Michigan for law school."

"Yes sir. They're quite open to admitting women."

"Provincials," he muttered, then elevated his nose. "I read into the law. I didn't attend school. We didn't attend school back then. Reading was good enough."

"I expect it was, but nowadays, we have to compete with people going to law school, if we don't have your vast experience."

She wanted to gag on her flattering words, even if they were true.

"There's a woman in the capital—that's Washington City— who learned law from her husband and is now teaching other women the law. There's even talk of opening up a law school for women in Washington."

"Humph," Stagpole snorted. "Good idea, keep 'em separate from competing with men."

Lucinda bit down on her tongue until it hurt.

Stagpole slid the heavy tome back onto its shelf and faced Lucinda. "Enough chitchat, girl. I have serious business to discuss with you."

"Of course." Lucinda gave him a brittle smile and sat down behind her desk.

He might choose to tower over her if he wished to intimidate her with his greater size and louder voice, but seated, she could hide her shaking hands. "What is it?"

"John Paul Daggett. You're representing him, are you not?"

"You know I can't tell you."

"Don't go all prim on me, missy. I know you are." He placed his palms on her desk and leaned over it until his face was close enough for her to count his nose hairs and she could smell cigar on his breath. "Don't do it if you know what's good for you."

His breath was turning her stomach. His words went further, raising bile in her throat. She couldn't move away or he would take it as her backing down. She remained stiff and steady in her chair, meeting his eyes full on. "Mr. Stagpole, are you threatening me?"

"I don't need to be that crude, Miss Bell." He leaned a bit closer. "If you continue to help the boy, it won't be good for your career."

"That's utterly fascinating, Mr. Stagpole." Lucinda pushed back her chair and rose. "Now, if you've no further business, I have someone waiting for me."

Stagpole straightened like someone had pulled a string at the back of his neck. "I didn't realize you weren't alone. You should have told me."

Lucinda smiled. "You should have asked." She stalked to the inner door and pulled it open. "Good day, Mr. Stagpole."

His face darkening, he swiveled on his heel and marched out of her office.

Lucinda reached one of her dining chairs before her knees gave way.

"What is it?" Mrs. Carr asked. "You look unwell."

"I think I am." Her breakfast toast and coffee felt more than a little unsettled in her stomach. "I think I'll close the office and lie down for a while."

"Shall I make you some tea?" Mrs. Carr began to gather up a beautifully embroidered handkerchief, needles, and colorful threads. "I don't mind at all."

"No thank you. I'll get some later. Thank you for coming. That was an excellent notion of Gertie's."

"But Mr. Templin is gone." Mrs. Carr's pale eyes tightened at the corners. "I thought he was staying to work."

"It's too cold." Lucinda rose and headed into the office to signal she wasn't going to talk about Matt. "I'll send some telegrams if the telegraph wires aren't down from the storm."

"Thank you. Thank you so much." Mrs. Carr glided past Lucinda and reached for the handle on the outside door.

Her own hand on the edge of the desk, Lucinda exclaimed, "Wait. Please wait." She yanked open the drawer and removed Daggett's file. "Will you please take this down to Gertie? Please ask Gertie to put the other one in a safe place."

New locks or not, someone had broken into her office before. Nothing stopped them from trying again and succeeding with more case files this time. The file was the work she had done on behalf of John Paul Daggett.

Mrs. Carr looked puzzled, but accepted the file and slipped it into her enormous bag. "It'll be safe with Gertie and me."

Safer than in Lucinda's office.

"I know. Thank you." Lucinda closed and locked the door behind Mrs. Carr, then drew the curtains across all three windows. In the twilight gloom, she undressed to her chemise and petticoat and wrapped herself in a quilt upon the sofa that served as her bed. She wouldn't sleep. She couldn't sleep. Her mind raced around and around like a carousel horse with a broken gear sending it spinning out of control. *Matthew. Stagpole. Matthew. Stagpole.* Thoughts of Matt turned her heart into one giant ache. Thoughts of Stagpole left her tense with the desire to strike something or someone.

"How dare he." She beat her fist against her already-abused sofa. "How dare he and Mayor Woodcocks threaten me like that."

If she had been slow with her work for John Paul before, she would be no longer. She would accelerate her work on his case, get a hearing before the end of the year. Before Christmas. And she had a lot of work to do for Mrs. Carr. Between the two of those and the little assignments that came to her, she would be busy enough to forget about Matthew Templin.

But of course she couldn't. He had left his mark on her office with his shelves and door and his locks and his chairs. He had left his mark on her heart.

"How dare he use me like that. Protest all he likes, it doesn't change what it is." This time her desk took the force of her fist, but only once. It hurt her knuckles too much.

She sucked on a bruised finger and stared out the window. From her desk, she could see nothing but the chimney on the building across the street, and a patch of leaden sky. More rain or snow if the temperature dropped. The latter was likely near the end of November in this unforgiving climate.

For the first time in her adult life, she had let herself care for a man beyond friendship. An unlikely man at that. She had let him kiss her because she was convinced he cared. But he'd done so after giving her the papers saying he was, in all likelihood, Mrs. Woodcocks's son by a former husband, a husband before John Paul's father, Paul Daggett. The question was: Why had Mrs. Woodcocks given up that son, and how much of her money, if any, was Matthew entitled to?

He needed to find out for his sake. She simply couldn't do it for him and help John Paul, too.

She concentrated on those two major cases over the next few days through weather that couldn't decide to be autumn clinging or winter begun. She wrote letters and she sent telegrams. She went to church on Sunday, arriving just before the service started and leaving immediately upon its conclusion to avoid talking to Matt.

She saw him there, talking to Gertie and two rather pretty girls who waited at the tea shop. She saw the Howards and Woodcocks, too. Only Samantha raised a hand in greeting.

And she didn't slip out quite fast enough, not before hearing someone whisper behind her back what her mother had seen happening in the café kitchen the night of the storm.

Cheeks burning despite the frigid wind from the north, Lucinda walked as quickly as she could without running, and hid herself in her office. She would never recover from the shame of kissing a man who had only done so to persuade her to help him.

"I'd have helped you anyway if not for John Paul." She proved that to herself by reading up on inheritance laws.

Matthew's staying away from her proved to her that she was right. When she said she couldn't help him, he stayed away. A lady lawyer was more than he could manage in his life.

If this is how it is, would you give it up for him? she asked herself on the way to the post office on Monday morning. *What do you love more—him or the law?*

But should she have to give it up just to win him? That didn't seem right. If he didn't want her as a lawyer, then did he want her at all?

And this is my calling, she reminded herself.

She arrived at the post office and mailed the final papers to get a hearing for John Paul.

"You got a package," the postmistress told her. "Was going to send it down to you, but you may as well take it."

"Yes, and the rest of my mail, if there is any."

There was—an envelope from the Commonwealth of Massachusetts that could only have to do with Mrs. Carr's pension. Lucinda could scarcely wait to get back to her office to read it. Surely this time they would say the pension was granted. Lucinda didn't really want to go up to Boston to argue before a judge.

She knew what the parcel was—two ball gowns from her clothes press at home. She had told her father's housekeeper which ones would suit for a ball in a Massachusetts winter. Except she wouldn't go now.

At her office again, she set the letters on the desk, then carried the ball gowns into the back room—and found her door there ajar with snow-laden wind making a mess of the floor.

The lock had been broken.

Fourteen

Slipping and sliding in the fresh snow, and once landing on her hands and knees in the middle of the sidewalk, Lucinda raced to Gertie's café. She knew she was likely to encounter Matthew there, but she needed help replacing the lock.

For the time being, she had pushed the chair Matthew had made for her in front of the rear door. It wouldn't hold back a determined thief for long, but probably long enough for someone to notice him trying to intrude.

In the event Matthew was at the café, Lucinda entered through the kitchen door. Gertie stood at the stove flipping an omelet with effortless skill. She glanced up at the blast of cold air rushing through the warm room, and gave Lucinda a tight-lipped smile.

"He isn't here," she said.

"I need someone who can change a lock." Lucinda clasped her hands, removed her gloves, and clasped her hands again. "Someone's broken into my office again."

The omelet shot past the waiting plate and landed on the floor.

"Girl, you shouldn't surprise me like that. Now Ted Johnson is going to have to wait longer, and he's already impatient."

"I'm sorry. I'll clean it up." Lucinda grabbed up a spatula and began to lift pieces of egg and mushroom and onion into the slop pail for the pigs. "Doesn't Mr. Johnson own the hardware store?"

"He does." Gertie beat at a bowl of eggs.

"Then do you think he could come fix my lock?"

"I think Matthew would do a better job in the event the door is busted."

"But Matthew isn't here." Lucinda sounded as frosty as the day.

"I expect him in about—ah." Once again, Gertie glanced toward the door swinging open to wind and feathery snow.

He stomped snow from his boots, removed his coat, then faced the room and Lucinda on her knees cleaning up spilled omelet. His eyes met hers, and her mouth went dry. Her heart must have stopped beating, for she couldn't breathe, couldn't move, could only stare at a clump of snow sliding from the crown of his unprotected head and long to jump up and brush it away before it plopped onto his nose.

He raised his hand and brushed it away himself. "Good morning, Miss Bell." His tone matched the snow. "What brings you here to clean Gertie's floor?"

"She had a break-in," Gertie said. "Startled me into dropping—"

"When? Where?" The coldness melted away and he closed the distance between them and crouched before her. "Lucie, what happened?"

"The. . .back door." Her voice was a mere whisper. "I was at the post office."

"Did they take anything?" he pressed.

She shook her head. "But they rifled my desk."

"You need to tell the constable," Gertie said.

"Yes, you do, but if nothing's been taken, they'll put it down to high jinks." Matt reached out for her hands. "I'll clean that up. Were you here looking for me?"

"No, I—" But of course she was. The way she clung to his hands as he assisted her to her feet told her so. The way she wanted to lean against him and have his arms close around her told her so. "I need someone to fix my lock."

"And?" He gave her a half smile.

She ducked her head. "Not to be alone even in the daylight."

"Ah." He nudged her chin up with his fingertips. "Otherwise you'd have gone straight to the constable."

"I do need my door fixed." There, she'd found her voice.

"And you know I'll fix it for you." He caressed her cheek. "Lucie, I've missed you. I want to talk to you."

Vaguely, Lucinda registered that she was alone with Matt. Gertie had taken the omelet and left the kitchen. Lucinda should leave, too, to avoid this dialogue.

"You know where to find me and haven't looked." She made her voice crisp.

His lips tightened at the corners. "I can't come to your office, Lucie—you know that. Not now. I tried to see you after church, but you left like you were being chased by a swarm of bees. Avoiding me, I presume."

"I'm not going to give up my calling so you can be comfortable not having money or a family name."

"I never asked you to." He smoothed a strand of her hair behind her ear. "I wouldn't ask you to."

"But you wouldn't consider letting me know how you feel about me until you thought I'd help you make your claim."

"As if you didn't already know how I feel about you."

"And yourself. Matt." She touched his cheek, smooth shaven and still cold, then stepped out of arm's reach. "God doesn't care who you are or what you do. It's where your heart lies that matters."

"I always believed that." He sighed. "Or at least told myself that. Jesus accepts me as I am, so what else matters? But it clashes with your calling, doesn't it?"

"Even if it didn't, Matt, your claim could drag through the courts for years. Would you make me wait for you that long? I'm nearly twenty-five, you know, quite, quite old to be single."

"If only I thought there was a speck of truth in my claim—"

Gertie pushed through the door, nodded at them, then grabbed up the coffeepot and left.

"You need a detective. I'm sure you can find one in Boston," Lucinda said. "A lawyer can find one for you. If you need help finding one. . ."

"I've already done so. I took the train up a week ago Thursday."

Stupid of her to feel a twist of jealousy that she hadn't known. She had sent him away.

"What did he say?" she asked.

Matt smiled. "She said the papers look authentic and she'll take care of it."

"She?" Lucinda laughed. "You went to a lady lawyer?"

"There are a surprising number of lady lawyers in Massachusetts. I thought I'd honor you that way."

"Oh Matt." She loved him all over again. Her heart beat against her ribs as though trying to break out and reach him.

He smiled at her. "And speaking of lady lawyers, why would someone break into the office of one in broad daylight?"

"Because I'm always there at night and they want something."

"What?"

"I can't say."

John Paul's papers of course. Nothing else in her office would interest anyone in town enough for them to take the risk of being caught. And with the Stagpole house the only one with a view of her back door, she could guess who had sent the perpetrator.

"Did they get anything?" Matt asked.

Lucinda shook her head. "They've been hidden somewhere since Roger Stagpole—" She pressed her fingers to her lips.

Matt pulled them away. "What did he want that day?"

"I can't—"

"Don't tell me you can't say. It had to be serious enough for you to hide some of your work."

"It's work he doesn't want me to do. That's all I can say."

"Lucinda." Matt curved his hands around her shoulders. "Did he threaten you in any way?"

"Not. . .exactly."

"Then you're not going back there."

"I have to. It's my livelihood."

"Then you'll have someone with you at all times and you'll not go back at night."

"So where do I go?"

"Here of course." Gertie had apparently returned without their notice. "I was going to tell you that the minute you told me you had a break-in in broad daylight."

"But who can stay with me during the day?" Lucinda drew away from Matt and crossed her arms. "I can't afford to pay—"

"You can't afford *not* to pay for someone," Matt broke in.

"My cousin will come while her children are in school," Gertie said. "She'll feel like she's earning her fees that way. Then you'll come back here and if you want to earn your pay, you can help me with the breakfast crowd in the morning."

"But—" Lucinda bowed her head in surrender.

She couldn't fight them. They would win in the end because they were right. She shouldn't be alone even during the day if Roger Stagpole was so determined to break the law in favor of his client.

She could report him, but he hadn't done anything she could prove.

"All right," she said. "Let me get my things."

"I'll send someone for Parthina," Gertie said. "You go sit in the dining room and have some coffee while Matt fixes your lock." She nodded to her own door. "My new door can wait."

So that was why Gertie had known Matt was about to arrive—she'd planned for him to work on her door.

A glance showed it had too much of a gap at the top hinge, as though it had warped from the heat inside the kitchen.

Matt agreed, picked up his gloves, and left on a blast of cold air. Gertie took Lucinda's arm and guided her into the café, nearly empty now in midmorning. And Lucinda sat like an obedient child, her life taken over by others.

"I'm not serving You this way, Lord." She rested her elbows on the table in a wholly unladylike fashion and propped her chin in her hands. "Or maybe I wish I weren't."

That stung, the possibility that she no longer felt certain she was serving God in her work. Or perhaps she never had. She'd determined to be a lawyer from childhood because Daddy didn't have a son to follow in his footsteps. Yet the opposition had always been there, not from him, but from her having to go nearly a thousand miles to attend school, and then hundreds more to practice. She looked at those as challenges to overcome like those faced by women who wanted to be doctors or ship captains or journalists. She never looked at it as the Lord trying to tell her to go elsewhere. She wanted this, but did He want this for her? She never questioned it until Matt came along and she found her heart torn between her love of the law and her love for a man. She never took into account her love for the Lord and wanting to serve Him.

Show me what to do, she prayed in silence. *I suddenly don't feel so certain I'm on the right path.*

She received no immediate answers. Parthina Carr arrived, brushing snow from her threadbare coat and with Lucinda's scarf wound around her head and neck. Guilt stabbed her to see the older woman so poorly dressed for the weather. But Mrs. Carr smiled cheerfully.

"So happy to be of use, my dear. Makes me feel like I'm not abusing your kindness."

"But you never were. I think—"

Lucinda remembered the letter from the Commonwealth and pulled it from her bag. It could have something to do with Mrs. Carr's case.

But it didn't. It had to do with John Paul's. It was a hearing date set for two weeks' time, the Tuesday after the Christmas festival.

A good excuse not to go. She would need to prepare then travel up to Boston.

Stomach a little queasy in anticipation of her first court appearance as a member of the bar, she slipped the papers back into her bag, apologized for reading them in front of Mrs. Carr, and rose to don her own coat and hat.

Outside, the snow was beginning to pile up thick enough not to be slippery. It deadened sound as though they walked on pavement made of spun sugar. Carriages passed like ghostly shadows, their wheels and the clop of hooves muffled.

"It's beautiful, isn't it?" Mrs. Carr said.

"It's cold." Lucinda hugged herself for warmth. "But yes, it is beautiful. Rather makes the world clean."

As she wished to make her heart clean from going her own way if it was not the Lord's way, too. " 'Purge me with hyssop, and I shall be clean: wash me, and I shall be whiter than snow,' " she quoted from the fifty-first Psalm.

"Indeed. That's what snow reminds me of." Mrs. Carr took Lucinda's arm, and they strode in companionable silence through the pristine snow.

The sound of hammering broke the stillness. Lucinda entered her front door, and the banging grew louder. Matt at work on her rear door. She couldn't avoid him. She needed her luggage from the storage room and a box to give Mrs. Carr what food she had left in the icebox. When she stepped into the room, nearly as cold as the outside, he smiled at her, and she wondered why she would want to avoid him. She could not, must not, let her work come between them. Except now she was in too deep to quit. She had a hearing scheduled and others pending. She had clients depending on her assistance, even if her fees would come in the form of eggs and roasted chickens.

"If you pack your things up," Matt greeted her, "I'll haul them down in my wagon."

"Thank you." She glanced around. "I need a box. Ah." She snatched up the box with her ball gowns inside. She didn't need to take those to Gertie's.

She went into the living room and laid the gowns on the sofa, two treasures from another life. One was green velvet with falls of creamy lace, and the other a deep red satin. She'd felt so pretty wearing those, a far cry from her usual serge or linen, depending on the season. Ah well, another time would come.

She hastened to pack up clothes for a few days plus her files and the food in the icebox. She would take her files back to Gertie's with her and leave the rest for Matt.

When she descended the steps, Mrs. Carr behind her, she caught sight of someone standing at the bottom of the steps. He darted out of sight before she was halfway down. Watching her or thinking of coming to see her? She hoped the former. She feared the latter.

But she'd be safe at Gertie's. Even she admitted that she liked the idea of being in rooms with other people near.

Matt came by for lunch, and Gertie seated them in a corner. "Talk to her, Matthew."

"You told her?"

"I told her I said everything wrong." Matt took her hand beneath the table. "Lucie, I didn't court you so you'd help me. I had the courage to court you because of those papers, but I didn't have the courage to ask for your help until I knew you better. Please believe me. I know how it looked, and it just wasn't so."

She didn't want it to be so. She let her silence on the matter serve as acquiescence, then let him change the subject to another book. The time passed too quickly, and he rose to go.

He rested his hand on her hair for a moment. "Take care of yourself."

She didn't need to. Gertie took care of her, feeding her far too much, making sure her room was warm, concluding with, "I'm praying for you, child. You look so troubled."

"I'm confused." Lucinda blinked away a sudden rush of tears. "I'm torn between my heart and my work."

"You shouldn't be. He can either take you as you are or not at all."

"He needs to take himself as he is."

Gertie sighed and nodded. "He never cared much about his background until he formed an attachment to Samantha Howard. I warned him, but you can't tell a young man not to fall in love with the prettiest girl in town."

"Especially when she returns that interest." Lucinda hesitated a moment, then asked, "Do you think she cares for him still?"

"Cares for, yes, but not as you're thinking. Never you worry yourself about that. You've enough else on your plate." Bidding Lucinda good night, Gertie left.

Too much on her plate indeed. Lucinda went to sleep counting everything that had gone, was going, and could go wrong, rather than counting sheep.

She woke to the smell of wood smoke and sweat and the feel of someone's hand over her mouth. "Where are the papers?" a voice rasped near her ear.

Fifteen

Matt woke to the low rumble of Growler's voice. He dropped his hand over the side of the bed to rest on the mongrel's head. "What is it, boy?"

Beside his head on the pillow, Purrcilla stirred, and he raised his other hand to calm the feline, as the click of a gun being cocked ricocheted off the walls of the room like a thunderclap in the snowy silence.

"Don't you or your animals move," a voice rasped from the doorway, " 'cause I'll shoot one of them first."

Matt said nothing. He listened for sounds to give away whether or not this man was alone. He let his eyes adjust to the light filtering through the curtains from moonlit snow, and tried to locate the intruder's exact whereabouts. He kept his hands on his animals, though both struggled beneath his hold.

"Good." A floorboard creaked and a shadow moved across the room. "Just tell me where the papers are, and I'll go peaceably on my way."

"The. . .papers?" Matt stared at the tall, still shadow. "What papers?"

Surely not his documents? But of course they were. The mayor and his wife had found them missing and guessed he'd found them.

"Don't play stupid, Templin. I know you have them 'cause the lady lawyer doesn't have 'em."

The lady lawyer. They thought he'd take them to Lucinda of course.

Matt's insides turned to a mass of twisted icicles. "How do you know?"

The shadow chuckled. "Been through her office. Been to Gert—"

Matt sprang up, releasing Purrcilla and Growler. "Did you hurt her? If you've hurt her—"

"Stay put." Light flared. The gun exploded. With a thud and shower of plaster dust and fragments, the bullet hit the ceiling. "Next one goes into that dog."

Growler, poor cowardly mutt, lay flat on his belly half under the bed. Purrcilla had disappeared.

Matt swung his legs over the side of the bed. His feet touched braided rug, then furry dog. He stood, nudging the latter all the way under the bed. "If you've hurt her, you'd better shoot me, not a helpless animal, or you won't be safe anywhere."

"I don't need your heroics. I need those papers."

"I don't have any papers." Matt made himself smile. "Unless you mean the ones I left with a lawyer and detective in Boston."

The man said something foul, then growled, "You're lying. You gave them to your lady friend, you—" Moonlight flashed on the gun barrel.

Matt dove for the floor. The gun reported. Glass shattered. Cold air swirled into the room. Matt slid from the bed, grabbed a book, and flung it at the gun just as it exploded again. The book struck the weapon. More plaster fell.

Matt grabbed more books, flung them hard and fast. The gunman's shadow moved, darted to one side. Books thudded to the floor. The gun flashed, exploded, again, again.

One more book. Matt followed the muzzle flashes and aimed with care. A thud, a grunt. A yowl.

Purrcilla streaked past Matt in one direction, the intruder in another. Something crashed in the kitchen; then the back door slammed.

"You can come out now, Growler." Matt found a lamp

surprisingly undamaged and lit the wick. By the light, he surveyed the mess of his bedroom as he found street clothes and yanked them on. The window was broken, curtains billowing into the chamber. Books lay everywhere, one or two sadly damaged. And Growler only poked his nose from beneath the bed.

Matt drew him out. "Come on, boy, it's safe now." He carried the dog out of the room and closed the door. Repairs could wait.

In the kitchen, he found his settee beside the stove overturned and with a leg broken. One of his first projects from years ago and not well made at all. He shoved the piece aside and studied the door. The lock was intact. The man hadn't entered that way.

A stream of cold air flowing from the parlor showed Matt an open window he'd neglected to lock. He didn't know he needed to there outside of town.

He closed and locked it now, not that it mattered with the bedroom open to the elements. He would have to get more glass. But a little snow on his floor concerned him little then. He needed to get to town, to Lucinda.

He couldn't take the horse. It wasn't trained for riding, and the wagon would never plow through the snow. He could walk just as fast or faster. Still too slow tramping through the fluffy whiteness. Too far from his lady. He normally walked to town in forty-five minutes. It took him the better part of two hours. Snow-caked and freezing, he tramped through the pristine streets of Loveland with its mayor who was anything but pure, and began to pound on Gertie's back door. It opened immediately to reveal Gertie behind a shotgun.

"It's you." She lowered the muzzle. "What're you doing here?"

"Is Lucie all right?"

"Of course she is. She just looks like a nor'easter would blow her away." Gertie stepped back. "But how'd you know to come?"

"I got a visitor." Matt stamped snow from his boots and

stepped into the kitchen. Warmth surrounded him like a blanket, and the sight of Lucinda perched on a stool at the counter with her hands wrapped around a cup of coffee dissolved the ice in his middle.

"Are you all right?" He shed his wet coat and wrapped his arms around her.

She tucked her head against his shoulder and trembled. "I will be. It was hours ago, but I'm still shaking."

"What happened?" Matt released her and perched on another stool. "Can you tell me what happened?"

Gertie handed him a cup of coffee. He took it with one hand and covered Lucinda's hand with the other.

She stared at their entwined fingers. "I woke up with his hand over my mouth and him demanding papers. I thought he meant the ones for J—" She pressed her other hand to her lips for a moment, then continued, "For someone else. But if he came to you, too—" She turned her big blue eyes upon him. "Matt, your claim just might be true."

"Or they thought you sent me up to Boston for this other client of yours." His fingers tightened on hers. "Lucinda, this has to do with Stagpole's threat, not me. It has to do with this client putting you in danger."

"What's this?" Gertie asked from the worktable, where she was rolling out piecrust. "What's this about threats?"

"He didn't threaten me," Lucinda began.

"Lucinda, you know you think he did." Matt frowned at her. "Then your office was broken into, and now this." He took the plunge. "You may need to give up this client for your own—"

"I will not." She narrowed her eyes at him. "I cannot. It would be wrong of me. There's a hearing set already with me to represent him. In Boston in two weeks."

"You can't go."

"I beg your pardon?" She surged to her feet, yanking her hand free so she could cross her arms in front of her. "I have to go. It's my duty."

"You can't travel all the way up to Boston alone with someone threatening you."

"I can't stay here and prejudice the state against my client."

"If the judge knew about the break-in—"

"It's not his concern. We can tell the constable here, but who will we accuse? I can't give him the name of my client. Unless, of course, this has to do with your potential claim, and you want to reveal that much."

"And have the mayor's wife sue me for slander if there's nothing to it?" Matt winced as though one of the intruder's bullets had hit him in the gut. "But Lucie, he had a gun."

"And so do I," Gertie said. "And Lucinda won't be going anywhere without someone to guard her, including up to Boston. I'll close the café and go with her."

"Truly, this isn't necessary." Despite her protests, she stopped shaking, and her face relaxed. She returned to her stool. "You need to be careful, Matt. If he broke into your house. . . What about your animals?"

"They're all right. Purrcilla got stepped on, but she's all right. Growler is scared out of a year's growth of dog hair, but I left him snoring by the stove."

"Poor dog."

"Poor Lucie." He touched her cheek, so smooth, too smooth to be in contact with his rough fingers.

Yet she turned her face into his palm and rested it there.

His heart flipped over a few times in his chest. "Lucie, I—" No, this wasn't the time or place. He rose. "I think it might be wise of me to stay here in town until this hearing. I told him I took papers up to Boston, so whether he wants mine or those of this client of yours, he may leave you alone. Until we get something resolved, I want to stay nearby."

"You can't do that," Lucinda protested. "It's too expensive."

"He could stay in your rooms," Gertie offered, crimping the edges of pie shells filled with apples, cinnamon, and sugar. "Keep anyone from rifling through your things again."

"I'll have to get the animals, and it'll take me awhile to get the horse and wagon into town, but if you don't care, Lucie—"

"I don't care, but Matt, that sofa isn't nearly long enough for you."

"I'll bring a bedroll." He stood looking down at her, having a thousand things he wanted to say, unable to get any past his lips.

He settled for kissing her hand, took the keys she retrieved for him, and returned to the snow and cold.

It took him until well past daylight to pack up his things in the wagon, gather up the cat and dog, and secure his house with some boards over the windows. Then he drove into town, left his things in Lucinda's storage room, put up the horse and wagon in the livery, and climbed the steps to Lucinda's office, Purrcilla in his arms, Growler following on a leash. Even the outer room carried her scent, something light and pure and sweet like vanilla. He set Purrcilla down, opened the door to her living quarters, and stopped, staring at the fancy dresses spread across the sofa.

His head and his heart filled with the image of her wearing one of those, the green velvet one, spinning around the Howards' ballroom floor with him. Just the two of them together then, always, forever.

The image shifted back to the night before, the notion of a man with a pistol breaking into Lucinda's room, and he knew he'd been a fool. Too easily, he could have lost her the night before. The man had nearly shot him. He might have shot her. She refused to give up her client, and he admired her for her dedication to her work, important work someone had to do in a world full of men and women who were dishonest and cruel without God's saving grace. If the only people who came to her for help were those who could pay in eggs and roasted chickens, then why should he let that come between them? He could support a wife now. And he could keep her safer from the occasional madman, if she were with him all the time.

"Lucinda Bell," he said aloud, "if you'll have me as I am, a mere carpenter who doesn't know who my earthly father is, then I would like to spend my life with you."

Smiling, he held the sleeve of the green velvet dress to his cheek. "I'll ask her when she's wearing this."

Sixteen

Never being alone seemed too much like going back to childhood, when her mother or a nursemaid followed Lucinda wherever she roamed, which had usually been walking with the dogs in the mountains or curled up in the library with a book. What changed was either Gertie, Mrs. Carr, or Matt accompanied her to her office, to church on Sunday, and on the errands she ran like visiting the post office or telegraph office.

During the week, she saw a few clients, wrote more letters for Mrs. Carr's pension, and prepared for John Paul's hearing. From everything she could find on Massachusetts law, he could be emancipated with good cause. His testimony of being cuffed about the head and once receiving a black eye from his stepfather and the statements showing a shocking amount of his money gone, even accounting for the financial panic that year, were more than enough evidence to set the youth free. Once she accomplished that, however, she intended to set up a trust for his money so he couldn't fritter it away on the riotous living of an independent youth at college.

This was more than enough evidence for her to think the man who had broken into both Gertie's and Matt's homes was after the paperwork she had on John Paul's case, paperwork she had sent home with Mrs. Carr. In the event the Woodcocks figured that out, Lucinda retrieved it and mailed it to her father's friend in Boston with an explanation. It would be there when she needed it for the hearing.

But the man may have wanted Matt's documents. She couldn't deny that possibility. That meant they likely held validity.

So did that account for his attentiveness? He was attentive. More than guarding her, he talked to her. They spent time in the library poring over favorite books and introducing one another to new ones. They talked of philosophy and religion and scripture. They walked in the snow, and on Saturday they and Mrs. Carr's children played a game of tag with snowballs.

Her heart filled to bursting. Beyond the apprehension of what the Woodcocks would try to do next lay a deeper, more important fear that this would all vanish once the possibility of danger to her passed.

Then one night, while Gertie sat knitting in the far corner of her parlor, Matt picked up the Bible from a table and flipped it open. "I've been reading this. It's from the eighth chapter of Romans. I've read it before, but it's just coming home to me that even if I never know who my real father is, I have my heavenly Father."

Lucinda glowed with the joy of his new understanding. Her hopes rose that he would stop letting his background interfere with his loving her completely.

But Sunday morning, when she walked into church with Matt and Gertie, the "ladies" of Loveland flared their nostrils and turned their backs on her. Matt's arm tensed under Lucinda's hand, and he pulled a little away from her, not more than an inch or two, but the gesture wasn't lost on her.

"Remember what you read last night," she whispered as they slid into the pew.

"I do. And what about you? I haven't been thinking about how not having enough business to make all your schooling worth the effort will frustrate you in the future."

"Matt—" She couldn't protest with enough sincerity to continue, for until that moment, she had believed her alliance with him wouldn't matter. These women shouldn't care.

Shouldn't and what they did were two different things. They shouldn't, but they did scorn him and now her for letting him court her.

"I'm still going to the ball with you," she finished instead.

Samantha came to the office one day to make certain of that. "Let me see your dresses."

"They're not here. I'm staying at Gertie's now."

"So I heard." Samantha tilted her head and smiled. "And Matthew is staying here in town to be near you more often. Is this good?"

"Except for those ladies who snub me for associating so closely with him." Lucinda rubbed her tired eyes. "Samantha, I am wondering if something is wrong with me that I'd let my work be more important than my love for him."

"A good question to ask." Samantha settled onto one of the two visitor chairs for which Mrs. Carr was sewing cushions. "I thought keeping Daddy's money was more important than him, though I think you two suit better than we did. He's kind of bookish for an artisan."

"I was always considered bookish for a proper lady." Lucinda rolled the edge of a paper on which she'd been taking notes. "I always read the law it seems like. With Daddy and Granddaddy lawyers, the books were everywhere."

"But who's more important? Will you treat him like I did and find something else more important? And you are coming to the ball with him, are you not?"

"I am."

And the Monday after, she would travel up to Boston for John Paul's hearing. After that, she would tell Matt that, if it was what lay between them, she would finish up her open cases and give up practice.

Oddly, the notion didn't hurt as much as she thought it would.

She had done it, practiced law, proven she could. If she won Mrs. Carr's pension for her and John Paul's independence for him, even her short time of practice was worth the effort. As for her education. . . Well, education was never wasted when it taught one how to learn for oneself.

"Don't hurt him." Samantha's face softened. "He's been hurt enough in his life."

"I don't intend to," Lucinda reassured her. "Now let's go back to Gertie's and see my dresses."

They did so. Samantha preferred the green velvet for the time of year. "And it will look so pretty with your hair. Do you have ribbons? Flowers to decorate? What about jewelry?"

"I have pearls," Lucinda said. "They'll do. And I'll buy some ribbon."

"I wish I could spend more time with you, but—" Samantha sighed. "You may as well know, she's decided you're a poor influence on me and would rather I not spend too much time in your company."

"I. . .see." Mrs. Howard may as well have doused her with ice water and rocks. This must be how Matt felt when people rejected him.

"No, I don't think you do." Samantha smoothed the fall of lace on the bodice of the green dress. "It's not because you're a lawyer. Mother isn't against females getting an education. If she hadn't gotten sick, I might have gone to Vassar or Wellesley. But she's afraid if I'm around Matthew too much, it'll stir up those old feelings."

Lucinda smiled. "Did you tell her he's spoken for?"

"I did, but she thinks a first love is the strongest." Samantha laughed. "So you should be jealous of me."

"I'm only jealous of how pretty you are."

They argued playfully over who was prettier; then Samantha

excused herself, Lucinda returned to work, and the week sped by, racing to the ball on Saturday and her debut in court the following Tuesday.

On Friday, she received a special delivery notice delivered by a courier. When she broke the seals, she found news inside so exquisite she cheered aloud.

"What is it?" Mrs. Carr popped out from the other room, needlework still in hand.

"We won." Lucinda ran across the room and embraced the older woman. "We—ouch!" She'd gotten stuck with Mrs. Carr's needle.

"So sorry." Mrs. Carr disengaged herself and inspected her embroidery for specks of blood. "What did you win?"

"Not me, us." Lucinda waved the letter in the air. "You're getting your pension."

"Praise God for bringing you here." Mrs. Carr began to cry. "My boys will have Christmas for the first time in two years. How can I ever thank you?"

"You just have." Lucinda wiped tears from her own eyes, joy for Parthina Carr, pain for herself.

How could she stop work that got these kinds of results?

How could she live without the man she loved knowing she could have kept him?

But it shouldn't matter to him, Lord.

She struggled with herself the rest of the day and too much of the night. She determined to enjoy herself at the party and spent the day helping Gertie serve breakfast to the workingmen crowd, then washing and curling her hair. Gertie pinned it up for her, winding the blue velvet ribbon through the curls, then hooked the dozens of buttons up the back of the dress. The dress fit fairly well, though seemed fractionally loose in the waist. Lucinda wound a satin ribbon around her middle to disguise the looseness and pinned the front with a pearl brooch.

"She looks like a princess," one of Parthina Carr's boys declared.

"If that boy doesn't propose to you tonight," Gertie declared, "I'll skin him alive."

When Matt arrived, as elegant as any man others would call a gentleman in black suit and snowy shirt, Lucinda nearly proposed herself. She could quite get used to seeing that face every morning. She had gotten used to seeing it every day.

And his eyes. When he looked at her, his eyes melted like chocolate on a hot stove. "Lucie." He clasped her hands as though he would never let her go.

She didn't want him to let her go. She did so they could don wraps against the cold, clear night, walk to the rented carriage over frozen snow and mud, and drive to the far end of town and the Howards' residence.

Lights blazed along the drive, lanterns hanging from trees reflecting off of the snow. A tree hung with cranberry chains, candles, and silver paper shone in a front bay window, and from the front door spilled the sweet strains of music and the muted roar of an excited crowd.

This was no ball for only the wealthy in town. Anyone who could afford a ticket could attend. The money supported Mrs. Woodcocks's favorite charity, a nearby orphanage. The Howards graciously opened their home and ballroom for the occasion.

"I feel a little like Cinderella," Lucinda admitted, "transformed into a princess for the night."

"You are a princess every night." Assisting her from the carriage, Matt paused to kiss her hand. "I just hope some Prince Charming doesn't come along and sweep you off your feet."

"He won't. I brought him with me."

Laughing, they entered the house, presented their tickets to the footman at the door, and followed the line of attendees up the steps to the ballroom. They paused in the doorway, taking in the sight of everyone from a local farmer dancing with one of the Floyd sisters, to Roger Stagpole dancing with the librarian. Chandeliers cast a yellow glow over best dresses and decorations in green and gold.

"I most definitely feel like Cinderella," Lucinda said. "The kingdom is celebrating—something."

"I think we can celebrate something." Matt slipped his arm around her waist and drew her into the spinning crowd.

Lucinda's feet barely touched the floor. Nor did they stop for the next hour. Others invited her to dance, men from the businesses in town, who'd gotten to know her at Gertie's. They guided her expertly, or they trampled her toes. Whatever their skill, they were polite, kind, even friendly. She was becoming part of the community, finding a home in this lovely little town. No matter that the mayor had ill intentions toward her and would dislike her even more after Tuesday's hearing, even if she lost.

Matthew rescued her after an hour, giving her a cup of mulled cider. "I almost wish it were cold," he admitted. "It's warm in here."

"And it's cold outside." Lucinda tilted her head to smile up at him sideways. "Any place that's a compromise?"

"There's a musicians' gallery to this ballroom. It's really too small for more than a quartet, so it never gets used for this ball, but I know how to get up there. I rebuilt the stairway after it suffered some water damage when the roof leaked a few years ago." He offered her his arm. "Shall I take you?"

"Please do. We'll be alone without being alone."

"You're such a proper lady." He covered her hand with his. "It's one of the many things I love about you."

Loved about her. He'd said it. Lucinda's heart skipped a beat.

Her feet wanted to skip along the corridor, around the corner to a narrow, dark passage, and through a door one would miss in the paneling if one didn't know to look for it. A little light filtered from above, illuminating the staircase so narrow the lace-trimmed ruffles on her gown brushed the walls. The staircase led to a balcony above the ballroom, where a carved wooden screen allowed light through and sound out. But if she and Matt spoke softly, no one would know they were up there.

"This is lovely." Lucinda pressed her face to the screen and watched the dancers. "It's like a flower garden with all the colorful dresses. That red one is beautiful."

"You're the beautiful one here." Matt took her hand in both of his. "I saw your dress in your room and imagined you wearing it here with me." His fingers tightened. "So I waited until tonight. I want—that is—I know a lot of people won't approve—one of them may even be your father. But I'd be honored if you—if you'd, um—" He swallowed.

Lucinda wanted to cry, "Yes, of course I'll marry you," so he didn't have to suffer any longer. But she didn't want to hurt his pride; he had to get the words out himself.

"I don't know if I can do this knowing what it means for your practice," he said in a rush.

Lucinda brushed his hair back from his face, allowing her fingers to linger in the soft waves for just a moment longer than necessary. "I have already decided that if necessary, I'll give up my practice rather than have my work come between us."

"Lucie." His face twisted. "I never thought you'd. . . I don't expect you to. . . Then you must really love me."

"I must." She smiled at him.

"Then the answer is yes?" His face shone.

Lucinda laughed. "You haven't asked the question—"

For question and answer, he drew her against him and

kissed her, and she kissed him back. Below them, music rose and fell, laughter and cheers broke out like shooting stars across a night sky.

And footfalls pounded up the gallery steps.

Matt pulled away, his body tense. Lucinda turned as a footman ran up to them. "Mr. Templin. Been looking all over for you. Miss Howard said you might be here."

"What is it?" Matt asked, an edge to his voice.

"Gertie. She needs you. There's been an accident."

"Has there? What sort of accident?"

Lucinda stared at him. "You don't believe it?"

"I'm being careful about trusting him." Matt fixed his gaze on the young man. "Well?"

"I—I don't know, sir. John, he's the footman at the door, he said as how a little boy came running up and asking for you."

"Parthina Carr's boy," Lucinda cried. "Matt, what do you think it could be?"

"I don't know, but I'd better go find out." He scowled down at her. "You stay here. Go back to the ballroom and don't leave until I get back."

"I'll come with you."

"No, don't." He brushed his knuckles along her cheekbone, then turned and followed the footman to the stairwell.

Lucinda started to follow, but suddenly the door closed in her face. She gasped, reached for the knob.

And a hand closed over her mouth. An arm encircled her waist, and someone murmured in her ear, "You're coming with us."

Seventeen

Gertie's house was peaceful. The café lay in darkness. Parthina Carr opened the back door to his knock, and her face registered shock to see him.

"What's wrong?" she asked.

"What's wrong here?" Matt returned.

"Why, nothing. We're having some hot chocolate and knitting."

"You didn't send your boy to the Howards' to fetch me?"

Mrs. Carr stared at him, mouth agape. "I'd never do that at night."

Heart in his throat, and without another word, Matt spun on his heel and sprinted back along Main Street toward the Howards' faster than he had left. Still too long, too far. At least half an hour passed before he reached the mansion. His hair was disheveled, his bow tie askew. If they didn't let him in—

He confronted the footman at the door. "Who told you to send me away?"

The man looked blank. "Told me what?"

"To fetch me for an emergency."

"Don't know what you're talking about."

Matt looked into the man's eyes and believed him.

"Is your name John?" he asked.

"No sir, it's Tim. You should know that. We went to school together."

Matt did remember then. Tim hadn't teased him about his lack of a father, and he'd called him sir.

Matt took a calming breath. Everything might be fine here. "I need to find my—my fiancée." There, he'd said the word, and it tasted sweet. "I left in a hurry. Can you help me?"

"I can't leave here, but I'll ring for a maid."

He rang a bell on a nearby table. Moments later, a maid appeared, and Matt made his request. "And I'll look in the ballroom."

She wasn't in the ballroom. He climbed to the empty musicians' gallery and peered through the screen. Nowhere did her crown of golden curls bob above a green velvet dress. He waited for a whole dance set to conclude, wasting precious time, and she was nowhere around.

Nor did the maid find her. She met Matt outside the ballroom. "I searched all the withdrawing rooms for ladies, sir, and no one's seen her."

"There must be four hundred people here. Someone has to have seen her. The servants? Did you ask them?"

"Not yet." The girl began to twist her apron.

"I'll ask them if you'll show me where to find them." She took him to the places where footmen and maids waited to see to guests' needs. In an upstairs corridor, a tiny girl, no older than fifteen or so, squeaked out, "I seen a young lady who'd fainted. She was wearing a green dress."

"Where did you see her, Peggy?" the other maid asked.

"Who was with her?" Matt added.

The child ducked her head. "A gentleman was carrying her. I was thinking maybe she'd drunk some spirits. People do sneak them in here, you know."

Fainted or rendered unconscious? Likely the latter.

"Where'd they go?" Matt demanded.

"Um, out, um, out to the carriages."

And Tim hadn't mentioned it.

Matt pivoted toward the steps.

"They went by way of the door closest to the stable yard," the little maid called out to him.

He paused. "Where is that?"

"I'll show you." The first maid, her face alight with curiosity, led the way through a maze of passages, down a back staircase, and out into the night. Too easily someone could slip Lucinda away without being noticed as anything other than a concerned gentleman helping a faint female into fresh air. Matt wouldn't have thought anything of it himself with another woman, but with Lucinda, he doubted anything could make her faint. And someone had threatened her and him recently. The hearing for someone important was in three days. Apparently, they wanted to stop her. It had nothing to do with him or his potential claim.

A burden he didn't know he was carrying slipped away. He wasn't responsible for her abduction. No matter how things worked out for him, he hadn't placed her in danger.

But he would get her out of it.

He charged into the stable. "Who's left here in the past half an hour?"

A crowd of grooms and coachmen turned toward him, their faces blank.

"No one, sir," a groom said.

"No one?" Matt glanced back at the line of carriages, the paddock of horses beyond. "You're sure?"

"Do you think we wouldn't notice someone taking a horse and carriage?" an old coachman demanded.

"No, it's just that. . . I'm looking for someone."

"Sweetheart leave you?" one man jeered. "Find out—"

Matt didn't wait for the taunting remark. He knew it all too well, and it didn't hurt him. Finding Lucie was so much more important than word battles with the ignorant. His heavenly Father loved him. As much as he would have liked to have known something about his earthly sire, he wasn't less of a person because he didn't.

He felt like less of a person without Lucie. She was part of him. He felt her absence from his presence. He had to find her, but she had disappeared once her kidnappers had taken her from the house.

If they didn't take a horse or carriage, then they had to have carried her to somewhere nearby.

After leaving the stable, Matt began to walk around the house, seeking clues, searching for ideas. The snow wasn't fresh. Many feet had trampled it during the week until, beneath the glow of the lanterns, it resembled nothing more than wave-pounded sand.

Close to the house anyway. As he moved farther afield, taking one of the lanterns with him, he saw that fewer and fewer human feet marred the whiteness. At last, when he paused to empty snow from his shoes, he saw them—two sets of footprints leading into the trees on one side of the Howards' land. He pushed his sodden shoe back onto his foot and headed into the trees.

They threatened to hurt Matt if she wasn't quiet. Considering one man had broken into his house and used his gun, Lucinda believed them and kept her mouth shut all the way down the back stairs and through the freezing night. She also wanted to remain conscious, so she didn't want to risk one of the men knocking her out before she learned where she was going.

She didn't need to ask why, not with the hearing in three days. That led her to the *who*—Mayor Woodcocks and possibly his wife. They had ordered her abducted from the ball in order to keep her from the hearing.

"You won't win," she said through chattering teeth.

They had dumped her in an outbuilding only a short walk through the woods from the Howards' house. Possibly the Wood-cockses' land. There, with only a thin blanket to stave off the cold, she huddled on a stone floor certain they didn't have to kill her. She would die from freezing long before morning.

If she didn't get herself out.

She would get herself out. Hearing nothing of her abductors nearby, she began to crawl around the room on her knees, one hand straight out in front of her to feel obstacles and another hand in front of her face to protect her from colliding with anything in the dark.

She encountered nothing except a shelf of clay pots, some still filled with earth. If any gardening tools had been there, they had been removed so as not to provide her with a weapon. At least not a good weapon. But a thrown pot, or one brought right down on someone's head, would work well if one didn't get grabbed while trying to apply the blow.

The lock on the door was stout. The panels didn't even tremble when she kicked them as hard as she could. If she had a small, sharp object, she could perhaps unscrew the hinges. But she didn't have anything so accommodating on her person. One generally didn't need a small sharp object at a ball except for hair pins, which weren't as useful for picking locks as heroines in books seemed to manage. Lucinda discovered that after ruining three pins poking and prodding at the tumblers inside the door lock to no avail. All she accomplished was to send her hair tumbling over her shoulders. The cloak of it was welcome. She could barely feel her fingers and toes.

If she didn't get out of there, she would die.

Her kidnappers might come back. Matt might find her. She could huddle in her thin blanket and ball gown and pray for that kind of assistance. Or she could pray to save herself, for immediate help.

She chose the latter, then began to circuit the shed again. Again, all she found was the shelf. A nail? She groped to the back of the shelf to find what held it in place. Yes, some kind of nail, something too big for her purposes. Shaking from the cold, she slumped against the shelf—

And it crashed to the floor. Clumps of dirt, splinters of wood, and shards of broken pottery scattered before her, over her, around her.

Broken shards of pottery.

Hope rising, she fumbled on the floor for the right size of broken clay vessel. Several large chunks sliced through her silk gloves and into fingers so numb from cold she didn't feel the pain. Unable to find anything small enough, she wrapped a larger piece in one of her gloves and smashed it against the stone floor until it cracked and fragmented into smaller bits.

Shaking so hard she could hardly hold her makeshift tool, she groped her way back to the door and began to work on the hinges. If they were rusted shut, she would never get anywhere.

If she didn't stop trembling, she would never get anywhere. She dropped her tool twice before she got one screw out. Her shard broke on the second screw, and she had to make another piece. Again and again she lost or broke her fragile instrument. But finally, the door groaned, sagged, and gaped with only its lock holding it in the frame.

A cold, damp wind rushed in upon her. It felt as sweet as the purest summer day. It was freedom.

She stumbled into the snow on feet she couldn't feel. She must get away, find her way back to the Howards'. If she could find her way, remember the path through the trees, not encounter anyone. Ahead of her, she saw lights. The house of whoever owned the shed. She went in the opposite direction.

And ran into the man striding around the corner of the outbuilding.

He grabbed her arms. "How'd you get out? Never mind that.

Those fools never should have put you in the gardening shed."

Mayor Woodcocks. Lucinda went limp. She couldn't even speak through stiff lips and chattering teeth.

"I wanted you held, not dead," he growled. "You'll have to come inside now, but if you scream, I'll tie you up in the shed and let you turn into a block of ice."

At that moment, Lucinda only cared about the notion of inside, a fire, a radiator, warmth. Like a docile lamb, she allowed Woodcocks to drag her to a french door off of a terrace and shove her over the threshold and onto a thick wool rug. A fire blazed on the hearth beyond two wing-backed chairs, and she half walked, half crawled toward the heat, thanking the Lord. She might be a captive still, but she would thaw out.

"The men are holding your gentleman friend," Woodcocks said as he locked the door behind him and drew the curtains. "If you misbehave, he's dead."

"Not quite yet," Matt said, rising from the depths of one of the wing-backed chairs.

Eighteen

Matt drew Lucinda to his side with his left arm. In his right hand, he held the poker. "Good evening, Mayor. Thank you for bringing my lady in from the cold, though perhaps you should tell us why you've taken us away from the ball."

"I think you know." Woodcocks slipped behind his desk and reached for a drawer handle.

"Down." Matt spun Lucinda toward one of the chairs and lunged across the room.

The poker struck Woodcocks's arm as he brought a pistol from the drawer and fired. The bullet whined past Matt's ear and thudded into the paneling. Matt grabbed the man's wrist and twisted it behind him. He yelled and kicked, but the gun flew out of reach. Matt hooked his foot around the mayor's ankle and they crashed to the floor.

Bigger, younger, stronger, Matt held the man down. "You—will —not—hurt—my—lady."

Woodcocks heaved and coughed. "Can't breathe."

"She will go to that hearing and win," Matt continued.

"Your stepson deserves his freedom," added Lucinda.

"Can't. . . let. . .him," Woodcocks wheezed. "Not. . .his. . . money either."

Matt started. The momentary distraction was all Woodcocks needed. He heaved up, knocking Matt off of him enough to twist and reach the gun. He aimed it over his shoulder. Even at that awkward angle, the range was close enough he would kill if he pulled the trigger.

"No," Lucinda cried from above them. "Mayor, please. I–I'll delay the hearing if you drop the gun."

"Get out of the line of fire," Matt commanded.

"Not good enough," Woodcocks said. "Drop John Paul's case."

"I can't. It'll discredit me as an attorney. I'll never be able to prac—" She broke off, and her hand rested on Matt's shoulder. "All right. All right. I won't go to the hearing." She was sobbing.

"I'll write a letter right now," Lucinda continued.

"Get away," Matt said. "This won't stop Woodcocks. John Paul will just get another lawyer."

"I can stop him from getting another lawyer." Woodcocks cocked the gun.

"Lucie, move." Matt hurled them both backward.

The gun blasted. Searing pain scored across Matt's upper arm.

Woodcocks rolled to his feet and stood over them, the muzzle of the pistol shifting from one to the other. "You two are going to disappear tonight. Lost in the snow and frozen to death, I think, while out on a tryst." He drew back the hammer. "Which first?"

The library door flew open, banged against the wall. "Vincent, no." Mrs. Woodcocks hurtled across the room, crimson satin skirts swishing and swirling around her. She flung herself against her husband as the gun exploded, and she slumped to the ground.

"You shot her," Lucinda cried.

With a roar like a wounded bull, the mayor ran for the french doors and into the night.

"Matt, she's wounded," Lucinda said.

She quite possibly was dead. Blood running down his arm, Matt pushed himself up and reached for Mrs. Woodcocks. "Ma'am, how badly are you hurt?"

"All right." She opened her eyes. "Just a scratch." She gave him a half smile. "He never could hit a target."

"Why did you do such a thing?" Lucinda kneeled beside the

older woman and pressed her hand, then a fold of her skirt on the wound across her shoulder. "He could have killed you."

"He was going to kill you." She didn't speak to Lucinda; she spoke to Matt. Her gaze held his. "You know why."

"I do." Matt pressed his handkerchief to his own wound. "I found the papers."

"I put them there for you to find. I was tired of the lies. Tired of the way Vincent was wasting money meant for my sons, making me hide the truth about you."

"I want to know why, ma'am, but we both need help now. It can wait."

"Both? Matt?" Lucinda glanced at him, followed his hand to his bleeding arm. Her face paled.

"If you faint on me," he said, "I won't marry you."

She smiled. "Then I'd better not faint."

Lucinda filed the paperwork to postpone the hearing for John Paul's emancipation as a minor wishing to be independent. With his stepfather captured and in jail awaiting trial for kidnapping and attempted murder, his claim wasn't quite so urgent. It could wait until his mother recovered from a wound that proved more serious than a scratch.

Matt, too, was put to bed in one of the Woodcockses' rooms, and Lucinda stayed with the Howards so she could be close at hand. Three days after the Christmas ball, they all gathered in the parlor with coffee and cakes, no one touching the latter, and Mrs. Woodcocks told her story.

"We were out west on the silver mines in Nevada. My husband—he was Matthew, too—and my son died in a mine explosion. There I was, a widow with a fair bit of money, not safe as a woman alone in a mining camp. So I headed back east to my family." Infinite sadness clouded the woman's eyes. "I was overcome with grief and illness, and collapsed in Davenport, Iowa. A gentleman, Paul Daggett, came to my aid, and I married him to make it all decent." She wiped tears from her cheeks.

"You needn't tell us now," Matt said, "not if it upsets you too much."

She shook her head. "You have a right to know now. Daggett was a riverman and died in an explosion three years later. And there I was a widow again, but this time with my new baby. I came east and started my life over. Vincent courted me, but I didn't truly like him. He had a mean streak and no money. I figured he wanted mine. He was ambitious. So I turned him down."

"And he forced you somehow?" John Paul spoke up for the first time. "He's like that."

"Yes, son, he forced me." Mrs. Woodcocks sighed. "He presented me with you, Matt. Do you remember?"

"I do. I was eight or so and didn't know why I was being paraded in front of this grand lady. Then taken away again. As far as I knew, I was the son of a woman who had an unsavory past. It's all I remembered—the years after the cave-in."

"You had survived that explosion and a woman with a poor reputation had found you and taken care of you. Woodcocks had done his work. He found her and found you and discovered that my first husband had lived awhile after the accident. Long enough that when I married Paul Daggett, I wasn't yet a widow."

Everyone gasped.

She smiled sadly. "Yes, it is shocking. It would have made me a pariah in society, amongst anyone, if not outright made me a criminal."

"Not likely," Lucinda said, her heart squeezing. "You didn't know."

"I take comfort in that, but it didn't stop Vincent from blackmailing me all these years. He brought Matthew here to remind me of what he could disclose about me. He made sure you had enough, Matthew, as I would have protested less, but he made sure you weren't accepted fully in this town because he didn't want anyone to believe you if the truth came out."

John Paul rose. His face was white, his hands shaking. "This means that I—I'm a—a—you and my father weren't married."

"That's a legal matter that will take awhile to straighten out," Lucinda said.

"No one needs to know," Matt said. "I'm legitimate in the eyes of the Lord. We can leave this story between us."

At that moment, Lucinda thought she would fall in love with this man all over again every day of her life. She reached for his hand. "You are so wonderful."

"I'm trying to deserve you." He raised her hand to his lips.

"But the money," Mrs. Woodcocks protested, "what Vincent has left of it, belongs to you."

"I don't need it," Matt said. "I have my work and my house and my land and my Lucie, who will keep practicing law as long as she wants."

"Good." Mrs. Woodcocks leaned toward Lucinda. "This town needs an honest lawyer. Stagpole has been helping Vincent all these years, and he'll go down with him."

"Are you saying I—I get to stay who I am?" John Paul asked. Everyone laughed.

"Yes—" A look of wonder crossed Matt's face. "I just realized. You're my brother." He rose and embraced the younger man, slapping him on the back. "We can't tell anyone for M—Mother's sake, but we know, and that's what matters."

"I think I'll make Miss Lucinda my project," Mrs. Woodcocks said. "The charities could use an honest lawyer to make sure all the donations and legal papers are in order. With Roger about to be arrested, will you take that on, my dear?"

"Um, yes ma'am." Lucinda gulped.

It was work she could do and still be a wife and, hopefully in the not-too-distant future, a mother.

"It's the least I can do to make up for how I've treated you." Mrs. Woodcocks sighed. "I was frightened though. Roger Stagpole was wasting the money, and I needed to get it away from him before it was all gone. Matthew was doing well for himself, but John Paul wasn't raised to have any skills. He needs it. So Roger told me to help run you out of town. But you're a special young woman. You don't give up, do you?"

"Not giving up is why I'm here." Lucinda gazed at Matt, talking to John Paul across the room. "And I can't imagine wanting to be anywhere else."

Mrs. Woodcocks nodded, then excused herself to go to her room to rest. She asked John Paul to lend her support up the steps, leaving Lucinda and Matthew alone.

They faced one another from across the room. "I love you," they said together, then laughed.

Matt closed the distance between them and kneeled before her. "Will you still marry me, knowing I've given up a fortune and complete respectability?"

"I'm not sure I'd have married you if you hadn't given it up." Lucinda leaned forward and kissed him. "Are you all right with me still taking on cases?"

"As long as they don't put you in danger." He shook his head. "I can't believe the mayor was after both of us for both things."

"Yes, to stop me from getting to the hearing and to get your birth certificate back."

They sat in silence, gazing into one another's eyes for several moments. Then Lucinda smoothed her hand over his brow. "You look tired. You should rest."

"In a moment." He captured her hand in his. "How soon

will you marry me?"

"The hearing is now the week after the new year, and John Paul will certainly win now. So after that?"

"That long?"

She smiled at him. "I'd like my father to be here so you can ask him officially."

Matt drew his brows together. "Any chance he'll say no?"

"I already have his permission. The rest is a mere formality." She laughed at Matt's surprise. "Telegrams are wonderful."

She hadn't thought that when she'd received hers from Belva Lockwood and Trudy Perry, but now, with her father's telegraphed response folded into her skirt pocket, she liked the swift communication.

"What did he say?" Matthew asked.

"That if you'll still let me practice, keep you."

Matt laughed.

Lucinda didn't. She touched his face with her scarred fingertips. "I'd marry you even if you said you wanted me to stop."

"I know." He pressed her hand against his cheek with his fingers. "How did I deserve such love?"

"It's a gift. All forms of love are a gift from the Lord. Since He is our perfect Father, we have the most perfect of inheritances."

"Eakes has a charming way of making her novels come to life without being over the top," writes Romantic times of bestselling, award-winning author LAURIE ALICE EAKES. Since she lay in bed as a child telling herself stories, she has fulfilled her dream of becoming a published author, with two dozen books in print.

She lives in Texas with her husband and sundry pets. She loves watching old movies with her husband in the winter, and going for long walks along Galveston beaches in the summer. When she isn't writing, she considers that housework is a time to work out plot points, and visiting museums is a recreational activity.

A Love so Tender

by Tracey V. Bateman

The floor of the old gazebo groaned beneath booted feet, and Aimee guessed, without turning, that Greg had followed her. He knew her too well. Knew exactly where she'd go to cry. Oh, why didn't he also know that she just wanted to get away? To hide from her humiliation.

A warm hand cupped her shoulder, and she turned. "Don't cry, Aimes."

Despite her breaking heart, Aimee Riley couldn't help but feel compassion for Gregory. His gentle voice consoled her with obvious misery at being the one to cause her pain.

"Is there no chance, Greg?" She despised herself for being weak enough to even ask.

His gaze searched hers, pleading for understanding. "I've always loved you. You know that. But as a member of my family. A cousin. Not in a romantic way. It wouldn't be fair for me to give you hope of marriage."

Stung by his frank assessment of their relationship, Aimee lifted her chin, mustering her dignity. "There'd be no shame in a marriage between us. Everyone knows we're not related by blood." She knew before she opened her mouth that the blunt reminder would hurt him. He winced, and she regretted speaking. "I'm sorry, Greg. Uncle Andy loves you just as though you were a natural son. Of course you belong in this family."

He smiled gently, forgiveness shining from his eyes. "I know you didn't mean to be hurtful. I only wish I didn't have to cause you pain."

"Is there. . .someone else?"

It wasn't fair to force the admission from him. Aimee knew that. And when he averted his gaze, she wished she'd never been so forward as to ask. Especially since she already knew the answer. Cynthia Roland had set her cap for Greg, and he didn't seem to mind. The entire town of Hobbs, Oregon, was abuzz with speculation as to just when young Pastor Greg would muster his nerve and request the honor of courting the fair lady.

"Aimee. . ."

"I know, Greg." Her heavy tone admitted the defeat washing over her. She slumped against the gazebo railing, not caring how unladylike it appeared. "Cynthia is a lovely girl. And there doesn't seem to be a malicious bone in her body. I'm sure she'll make a wonderful minister's wife."

Greg chuckled and took Aimee's hands. "Let's not jump the gun. I haven't even asked to court her yet."

"Then you'd best get moving. If I'm not mistaken, Adam Trent has been making eyes at her, too."

A frown furrowed his brow. "He has? Uh. . .do you think Cynthia might be enjoying the attention?"

Aimee shrugged. "I'm sure she favors you, but a girl can't wait forever, Greg."

And yet that's just what she'd done. She had grown to the old-maidish age of twenty-six while waiting for Gregory to realize he loved her. Now the truth was upon her. He would never love her the way a man loves a woman. He'd never look at her with the same lovesick expression that appeared on his face whenever Cynthia entered a room.

With sickening clarity, Aimee knew she'd wasted her youth on a futile pursuit. Now Greg would move on, and she had nowhere to go. No man to love her and, at her age, no prospects.

But one thing was certain. She would not sit by and observe Gregory's courtship and pretend to smile while another woman claimed his heart. Somehow, someway, she had to leave the Riley farm and find a new life for herself.

One

A imee gathered a deep breath and prayed for a steady hand as she reached up and grasped the brass doorknocker. She gave three sharp raps, waited a moment, and was just about to knock again when she heard footsteps approaching from within, then the turning of a doorknob.

"Why, Aimee!" her aunt greeted her and, to Aimee's relief, showed only joy at seeing her again. "What on earth are you doing? No one told us you were coming."

"No one knows. I—I just. . .left, Auntie." Exhaustion and grief suddenly overcame her. She threw herself into Aunt Rosemary's arms and finally let loose the tears she'd been stifling since beginning her adventure.

"There, there." Rosemary patted her head as though she were a child. When Aimee's tears were spent, her aunt took her by the shoulders and held her at arm's length. She studied Aimee's face, concern marring her own smooth features. "Now what is this all about?"

"M—may I come in? It's starting to drizzle again."

"Of course." Rosemary's cheeks bloomed. "I declare. My manners flew right out the window from the shock of seeing you, of all people, on my doorstep."

The still-attractive middle-aged woman led the way into a plain but tidy parlor. "Now sit down and make yourself comfortable while I go fix us a nice pot of tea. Are you hungry? I was just going to set out some cookies for the children."

Aimee's stomach grumbled in anticipation. "I don't want to be any trouble."

"Nonsense. I'll be back in a jiffy."

Aimee removed her shawl and sank into the wing chair next to the fireplace. The crackling fire brought a welcome heat to her chilled bones. She rested against the cushion, staring at the fire, and allowed her mind to drift over the past fifteen hours. While her family slept, Aimee had lain awake, considering her dismal future. Finally, just before dawn, she'd grabbed her reticule, saddled her horse, and galloped the five miles into Hobbs to catch the morning stage. So impulsive was her decision, she'd left without even bothering to pack a bag.

The exhilaration of getting away from home, of doing something unexpected and riding toward a new life, had carried her for about the first half of the stage ride between Hobbs and Oregon City. But her bravado crumpled with each mile. At every stop along the way, she'd expected to find her pa or one of her brothers waiting to take her home. Foolishly, she'd even hoped that maybe Gregory would realize he couldn't live without her and would come after her himself.

Warmth flooded her cheeks at her folly. Greg was probably relieved that she'd gone. At least now he could court Cynthia without the whole town reminding him that Aimee loved him. And the nosy folks in the little settlement would do it, too. Poor Greg would be miserable, and so would Aimee and most likely Cynthia. This way was better for everyone involved.

The townsfolk would realize why she left and would discuss it for quite some time, but that couldn't be helped. She'd done what she had to do. And anyone with a lick of sense would know she was right.

Rosemary entered the room, her slightly plump cheeks lifting with her smile. "These gingersnaps are fresh from the oven, so eat them while they're warm." She set down the plate of cookies and offered Aimee a steaming cup of tea. "All right, now. Time to confess. Why are you here all by yourself? Are you running away?"

Aimee had to laugh. "I'm a grown woman, Auntie. I do not have to run away from home like a naughty child."

The fine lines at the corners of Rosemary's eyes crinkled. "And yet here you are with no bags and without sending word of your arrival."

Expelling a sigh, Aimee gave a nod of concession. "You're right. I ran away," she admitted glumly.

"Want to talk about it?" The older woman covered Aimee's hand with hers, her eyes filled with compassion.

"I'm so humiliated." Aimee groaned, setting her cup and saucer on the table next to her chair. "I practically threw myself at him."

"Greg?"

"Who else? He's always known that I love him. Everyone does. I'm no good at hiding how I feel."

"Honesty is an endearing quality, Aimee."

Aimee gave a very unappealing snort. "Ask Greg how endearing it is. The poor man felt like an utter cad for being forced to break my heart."

"I'm sure Gregory will be fine. His wisdom and love for the Lord are two of the reasons your uncle Hank felt he could leave the congregation of Hobbs in Greg's hands."

Aimee's heart nearly burst with her pride in Gregory, and for a moment she pushed her wretched existence to the background. "Oh Aunt Rosemary, he's such a wonderful pastor. The church has grown by five families since Greg took over." Her eyes widened. "Not that Uncle Hank was doing anything wrong. Our town is just growing, and Greg has implemented a new outreach program."

Rosemary laughed. "Don't apologize. Hank knew he was outstaying the Lord's calling over the past several years. Our marriage and this orphanage brought him to the next phase of what God has called him—us—to do."

Aimee lifted her cup and saucer and sipped the warm tea. It felt heavenly going down. "How many children are living here now?"

"We are nearly at capacity. We have twelve children, ranging in age from two years old to thirteen. So many of the other homes are overfilled. We don't advertise our presence, but we don't turn anyone away either. We just figure God will bring the ones that He intends for us. A dozen little ones is quite a challenge though."

Aimee's heart pounded in her ears as she broached the topic she'd been practicing for the past several hours. "Auntie, do you need some help?"

Two thin lines appeared between Rosemary's eyebrows. "What do you mean? Are you thinking of leaving home for good, Aimee?"

"Yes ma'am." Tears burned her eyes. "I can't stand by and watch Gregory fall in love with another woman."

"I thought I heard voices." Uncle Hank's baritone fairly echoed off the walls as he made his presence known with all the grace of a charging bull. "Aimee honey, what are you doing here?"

Rosemary glanced up at her husband of six months and beamed. "I think we have the answer to our prayers, darling."

"What prayers are those?" he asked, planting a kiss first on his wife's cheek and then on Aimee's.

"For the right person to help out. Aimee would like to stay here and help with the children and the house."

Confusion mingled with joy in her uncle's freckled face. "Really, Aimes? What's your pa going to say about that?"

Why did she continually have to remind her family of her age when she'd rather never bring it up? "I'm a grown woman, Uncle Hank. I'm ready to leave home."

He gave a whoop and gathered Aimee into a bear hug. "This is wonderful! Not only did God send us just the right person to help—she's part of the family, so she already knows all our faults. And she loves us anyway." He released her and waggled his brows.

"At least I hope she does."

Aimee laughed and fought to catch her breath. "To be sure. Faults and all."

"Well then, Aimee, our dear niece, it appears as though you're going to be the first one in the family to hear our news." Uncle Hank beamed as he walked to his wife and gathered her against his side with one long arm.

Rosemary grew pink and ducked her head.

Aimee gasped. "Uncle Hank! Are you two. . . ? Auntie? A baby?"

Joy radiated from the couple. "Can you believe it? I'm going to be a mother! At my age."

"And a wonderful mother you'll be, darling." Uncle Hank gave her shoulder a squeeze.

Aimee glided forward and hugged them both. "Grams will be so thrilled."

A loud crash came from the other room, followed by the squeals of children's voices. Almost instantly a round-faced little girl with long black braids, who must have been around six or seven, skidded into the room. "Jeremy conked his head on the table." Her voice squealed. "He might be dead."

"He ain't dead," a boy's voice called. "Just a mite befuddled. Hoo boy, that's gonna be some goose egg."

Rosemary glanced ruefully at Hank. "I'll go see about that."

Aimee stepped forward. "Let me help. I may as well start earning my keep."

"I'll help Rosemary deal with the children," Uncle Hank said firmly. "This is your first night here. I don't want them scaring you away so soon."

Aimee laughed at the expression of mock fear on his face.

"Yes," Rosemary said. "Finish your tea. There will be plenty for you to do tomorrow. First we need to take care of whatever mess the children have made, then herd them to bed with a Bible reading and prayers. In the morning we'll send a telegram to your parents, letting them know you're fine."

Uncle Hank gave Aimee a look of reprimand. "You didn't tell them you were coming?"

Aunt Rosemary—bless her—patted Uncle Hank on the arm and headed him toward the door. "Aimee has her own reasons. All we need to be concerned with is that God sent her to us in our time of need."

Still looking unconvinced, Uncle Hank nevertheless allowed himself to be led from the room. Aimee smiled, breathing a prayer of thanksgiving before biting into a gingersnap.

For a fraction of a moment, doubt invaded her heart, threatening to dispel the joy of her newfound home. In her mind's eye, she saw herself aging year by year as new children entered and left the orphanage. Old Auntie Aimee. White haired and thick waisted. Taking care of children who weren't hers. No husband. Only years of growing old by this very fire. Was that to be her destiny?

Oh Lord. I don't mean to sound ungrateful. But surely this isn't Your plan for the rest of my life. Is it?

A knocking at the door interrupted her thoughts. Fighting her rising panic, Aimee rushed across the parlor, into the foyer, and reached for the front doorknob. A matronly woman stood on the porch, holding a baby in her arms.

"Have you room for one more?" she asked. The weariness in her voice struck a compassionate chord in Aimee.

"Won't you come in?"

She gave a vigorous shake of her head. "No time. I got to be on the next train to Seattle." She peered closer. "Please say you got room for the lad."

"Why, I'm not sure if we do or not." Aimee peeked into the

blanket and saw the baby's chubby face. A toothless grin snared her heart. She smiled back and the baby cooed. "Where is the child's mother?"

"Dead. Gave birth three months ago. Barely got a glimpse of him before she slipped into glory."

Pity clutched Aimee's heart. How sad to bear such a perfect child and never get to hold the baby in your arms. "And the father?"

"Gone. Went back east to take care of family business before his wife's time came. I'm not sure where. Said he'd be back. That was six months ago. The poor man doesn't know about his wife. He'll be coming back expecting to find her."

"Can't you keep the babe for a little longer? Perhaps the father is on his way home as we speak." The thought of a man arriving home to find his wife dead and his child missing nearly broke Aimee's heart.

"Wish I could." Tears pooled in the elderly woman's eyes. "My boardinghouse burned to the ground last night." A sob caught in her throat. "We barely escaped with our lives. I spent most of the day trying to find a home for little Georgie, but none of the foundling institutions have the staff to care for a newborn." She looked down at the infant in her arms, and her face softened with love. "He's such a good baby. I'll miss him dreadfully. But I can't take care of him anymore. It'll be all I can do to take care of myself. I—I came close to leaving him on the doorstep, just so's you couldn't refuse to take him in like the others did. But I couldn't bear the thought of leaving him like that. Without knowing he'd be well cared for." She stared frankly into Aimee's face. "I can tell you're decent. Do you know God?"

"Yes ma'am. I'm a Christian woman."

Mist-filled eyes implored Aimee. "Take him, miss. You're my last hope. I don't know what else I can do."

The baby started to whimper. Aimee's heart lurched. She didn't even know the policies of the house. How did Uncle Hank decide which children to take in? She didn't know, but somehow this infant's presence the same night she arrived seemed like a sign to Aimee. She couldn't turn her back on a baby who had nowhere else to go. Then she remembered Auntie Rosemary saying they didn't turn any children away.

With a reassuring smile, she lifted the newborn from the woman's arms. "You say his name is Georgie?"

"That's what his mama said she was going to call her child if she had a boy. I've been calling him that out of respect for her wishes, but I suppose you can name him whatever you want."

"Georgie is a perfect name for a perfect little baby." As if sensing her reaction, the baby nestled against her, evoking feelings Aimee had never known. Feelings she could only guess were maternal in nature. She looked at the angelic face, and her heart staked its claim. Georgie was hers. God had given him to her. And no one was taking him away.

Rex Donnelly stared in horror at the charred remains of the boardinghouse where he'd left his Anna less than a year before. When he'd stopped receiving her letters, he'd known something was terribly wrong. *Oh Lord. Did she die in the blaze that took this house?*

"Looking for Mrs. Carlton?"

Rex turned at the sound of the female voice. An elderly woman stood on the walk in front of the house next door.

"Yes ma'am. Do you know where she is?"

She shook her head. "Left the day after the fire."

"Do you know anything about my wife, Anna Donnelly? She was a boarder here. She was going to have a child when I left."

The woman clucked her toothless gums. "Poor dear didn't

make it through the birth of her baby. So many of them don't, you know."

Rex felt his breath leave him as though he'd been punched in the stomach. "Are you sure?"

"Of course. I helped with the birth. She was a brave little thing. She kept saying, 'Poor Rex. My poor Rex.' That you?"

Rex's legs refused to hold him up another second. He sank to the ground, heedless of the expensive suit he wore. His Anna—dead. And thinking of him as she died. Why had he stayed in New York so long? How could he have allowed Mother to convince him his father needed him more than his own wife?

He sat with his arms slung across his bent knees and stared at the remains of the house. Imagining his wife calling for him. Bearing their child.

He'd almost forgotten the old woman standing just a few feet away until she spoke. "For such a frail young lady, she gave birth to a strapping little fellow. Squawked like all get-out until we got him some warm milk. Then you should have seen him gobble it up. Fat as a little mouse, he was."

Rex's mind buzzed with confusion as he tried to process the information. "Y–you say my son lived?"

"Sure did. That little wife of yours wanted him named Georgie, so that's what Mrs. Carlton called him. The foolish old woman spoiled the little lad rotten if you ask me. Held him any time he made a peep. You can't raise a child that way, I told her. But did she appreciate my advice? No, she did not. Never mind that I raised ten young 'uns, and she never even had one of her own."

Georgie. After Rex's father, George Donnelly. Renewed love for his wife surged through Rex. Had she named their son after his grandfather to let Rex know she forgave him for leaving? "Do you happen to know where Mrs. Carlton is now?"

The woman's smile faded to a frown. "Now I can't say that I

do. I came home after helping my daughter during her confinement, and the house had burned to the ground. Ain't seen hide nor hair of Mrs. Carlton since. I think she has a sister somewhere up north. In Washington, maybe. I can't remember for sure."

"Did she take my son with her?"

"I expect so. She was quite attached to the little fellow."

Rex stood and dusted off his trousers. "How long has it been since the fire?"

She frowned, and her eyes took on a faraway look. "Well, my memory isn't as pert as it once was. But I'd say at least two—no, closer to three months."

"Thank you for your help. If you should see Mrs. Carlton or hear from her, please ask her to get in touch with me. My name is Rex Donnelly. I'm staying at the Grand Hotel. I'll be there until my law office and home are built. After that it shouldn't be too difficult for her to find me."

"The Grand Hotel, eh? That's pretty highbrow. I guess I can remember that well enough."

Rex thanked her again. He dismissed his cabbie and headed down the street on foot, his heart squeezed in the painful reality that he'd left his young bride to bear their child and die alone.

Anger burned within him for succumbing to his mother's manipulation. When he'd returned home to try to persuade Father to invest in a western law office, he'd discovered the man ill, with a short time to live according to the doctors. He'd tried to tell his mother about Anna, but she refused to listen.

The wagon train west was to be his last adventure before settling down and taking his place in the law firm in New York. Donnelly, Donnelly, and Donnelly. Father, Uncle, and Rex. Mother had convinced him that telling Father he wanted to stay out west would only hasten his death, and she forbade him to speak of it—or of Anna.

He'd stayed east much longer than he ever expected. When Father died, he did so without the knowledge that he was going to be a grandfather. He would have been so proud of his namesake.

Against his mother's wishes, Rex had taken his inheritance and left New York for good, praying that Anna would forgive him for leaving her alone for almost a year.

Tears streamed unchecked down his cheeks, but he didn't care. His sweet Anna was gone. He should have been at her side. Now his son was being raised by a stranger. Without a father to teach him the things a boy needed to learn to grow to be a man.

Determination stood like a statue in his chest. His hands balled into fists of resolve. He would find his son. Would hire every detective from here to Seattle if he had to. He wouldn't stop looking until Georgie was home where he belonged.

Two

Six years later, 1881

Aimee sat on the creek bank and watched Georgie splashing about in the water with Bandit, the oversized brown-and-black pup that had shown up on the orphanage doorstep three months ago. Georgie had claimed him at first sight, and Aimee hadn't had the heart to say no.

She laughed at the pair's antics. How the boy loved his grandparents' farm. Leaving the city every few months for a week-long visit did wonders for them both. And judging from Bandit's joyous barks, the mutt wholeheartedly agreed.

"That Georgie is quite a boy, isn't he?"

Aimee's heart nearly stopped at the sound of Gregory's voice. She turned and smiled. "He sure is."

"You've done remarkably well raising him so far."

A flush of pleasure rose to her cheeks. "Thank you, Greg. How is Cynthia?" she asked for want of anything else to say.

His face clouded. Greg had been ready to marry her years ago, but Cynthia seemed intent on stringing him along. Aimee had to fight ill feelings toward the woman. Cynthia's reasons for not marrying Gregory baffled Aimee as much as everyone else in town. Though several years younger than Aimee, Cynthia was still considered an old maid, and one would think she'd jump at the chance to marry a man as wonderful as Greg.

"She decided to return to Chicago with her ma and pa. They never have quite been able to make a go of the farm, and Cynthia's ma finally had her fill of the West."

"You're joking! Going back with her parents?" Indignation

shot through Aimee. "Is she daft?"

Dropping down beside her, Greg let out a chuckle. "Most folks think I'm the one who's daft for waiting all these years."

Aimee understood waiting. She understood longing for someone who didn't share her love. Reaching across the grassy bank, she covered his hand with hers. "You're not daft, Greg. Just in love."

A soft breeze caught a loose strand of hair and tickled her neck. She shivered. Greg looked into her eyes, his expression intent. Aimee swallowed hard as he turned his hand over and laced his fingers with hers. "I've been thinking about something, Aimes."

"Y–you have?" *Oh God, please let this be what I hope it is.*

"We get along okay, don't we?"

"We always have," she agreed.

"What if. . ." He glanced back at the creek, where Georgie's giggles rang like bells in the warm summer air. "What would you think about just going ahead and getting married? I mean you and me."

Waves of joy poured over Aimee. "Are you sure, Greg?"

He squeezed her fingers. "I've been thinking about it a lot since Cynthia turned me down the last time."

Aimee's joy gave way to a sinking feeling. A woman didn't want to hear about another woman's rejection when the man of her dreams proposed.

Greg must have recognized her expression because sorrow filled his eyes. "I'm sorry, Aimes. But I have to be honest. I'll always carry some affection for Cynthia."

The admission pierced through Aimee like an arrowhead. "Are you sure you want me to marry you?"

"It's time for me to settle down with a wife and begin raising a family. I thought that woman would be Cynthia, but she's made it perfectly clear I'm not what she's looking for."

"Why did she waste the last six years leading you on?"

He sent her a rueful grin. "Why indeed?"

"Ma! Watch me swim."

Aimee turned her attention toward her growing son. He splashed about, barely making progress.

"Did you see me?" he called with six-year-old pride.

"I did, honey. Good job." Aimee considered him for a moment. She could teach him to read and write, to dress properly and say his prayers. But what about the things a boy needed a father to teach him? Farming, fishing, hunting, building a home. She supposed her uncles and brothers would step in and take up the slack in regards to his training. But was it fair to Georgie not to have a father of his own? Especially when there was a wonderful man right here waiting for her to make a decision? Her hesitancy only proved she was about as touched in the head as Cynthia.

As usual, Greg seemed to sense her thoughts. "The boy needs a father. I'm offering him one. I'd be a good husband, Aimee."

"I have no doubt of that, Greg. Truly. May I have a little time to think it over?" The thought of being second choice didn't sit well with Aimee. Would she always lie in Greg's arms at night and wonder if he was thinking of another woman?

"Oh, there's another reason I came out today." Greg reached inside his shirt pocket. "You received a telegram from Oregon City."

Aimee frowned, accepting the envelope. "I hope everything's okay at the orphanage." She slid her thumbnail along the seal and pulled out the telegram. She'd read only half of it when her hands started to tremble, her head began to swim, and she fought for air.

"Aimee, what is it?" From a distance she heard Gregory's question. She felt the telegram slip through her fingers. His deep voice read the wretched words.

Georgie's Father Came. *Stop*. Is on His Way to the Farm. *Stop*. Arrives Sometime Today. *Stop*. So Sorry. *Stop*. Love, Uncle Hank

Aimee's throat constricted, and she nearly choked on a sob. "Why? Why did Uncle Hank tell him where Georgie is?"

Greg gathered her into his arms. "Because it was the right thing to do," he said softly.

Aimee sobbed against his shoulder. "How could it be? Georgie doesn't know his father. Where has he been for the past six years?"

Gregory didn't respond. And no response was necessary. Aimee pulled away and jumped to her feet. "I'm taking Georgie and getting out of here. No one is stealing him from me. Do you hear me? No one."

"Aimee..."

Ignoring him, Aimee turned to the creek. "Time to get out of the water, Georgie."

"Aw, Ma. We just got in."

"Obey me at once, young man, or I'll march you straight to the woodshed."

"Yes ma'am," he said glumly. He slogged out of the creek, followed by an equally drenched puppy. Obviously not ready to end the game any more than his little master, Bandit grabbed onto Georgie's sleeve and tried to pull him back to the creek. "No, Bandit," Georgie admonished, jerking away. The puppy barked and grabbed hold again.

"Stop that right now, Bandit," Georgie said firmly. "Or I'll march you straight to the woodshed."

Despite the seriousness of the situation, Aimee couldn't keep from laughing. She sobered instantly. They had to hurry before the man claiming to be Georgie's father showed up to take her son away.

From his hired mount a hundred yards away, Rex surveyed the large ranch-style home in front of him. He felt a measure of relief to know his child's adopted mother was presumably raising his son well. Her aunt and uncle, who ran the orphanage, had seemed agreeable enough. The children in their home were well cared for, smiling, apparently lacking no essentials. He'd seen no signs of neglect or abuse. Indeed, they had appeared to be one big, happy family.

He still felt uneasy about the couple's refusal to accept his rather large donation. He squirmed a little at the memory of the suspicion in the woman's eyes, as though he were trying to buy his son. But that wasn't the case. He'd simply wanted to thank them for caring for the boy.

The door opened, and a young woman stepped onto the porch. Rex frowned as a child followed, then an older man carrying two bulging carpetbags. Indignation exploded in his chest. The couple at the orphanage must have telegraphed ahead and warned the woman of his visit. It was obvious she meant to take his son and run away.

He nudged his mount to a trot and reached the house before the woman could descend the steps and climb into the waiting buggy.

"Stop!" he commanded. He reined in his horse and dismounted in one fluid motion. "Where do you think you're going?"

Fury reddened her heart-shaped face. "None of your business."

The lad looked at the woman, and surprise lit his blue eyes. Eyes that exactly matched Rex's own. Rex caught his breath. He couldn't even respond to the woman's anger. He could only look in wonder at his son. Flesh of his flesh.

He took a tentative step forward. The woman put a protective arm around the boy's shoulders. Paying her no heed, Rex continued his advance and climbed the stairs to the porch. He knelt before the boy, feeling his throat tighten.

The lad offered a pudgy hand. "My name's Georgie. What's yours?"

"Rex," he replied, his voice hoarse with emotion. As much as he wanted to declare himself as the boy's father, he knew that wouldn't be fair to all concerned.

"Did you come to visit my grandpappy?"

"Um. . ."

The man standing on the porch, presumably the boy's "grand-pappy," stepped forward. "Good to meet you, Rex. I'm Michael Riley. Would you like to come in?"

Rex stood and accepted the proffered hand, but hesitated to leave the porch. He wasn't about to give the lady an opportunity to run away with his son. And from the gleam in her enormous, molasses-brown eyes, he suspected that was exactly what she had planned.

She fixed him with an icy glare before turning her attention to the boy. "Georgie, why don't you go into the kitchen and see if Grammy has a cookie for you?"

"We're not leaving on our trip?" Georgie's innocent question brought a blush to the woman's cheeks. "I thought we had to hurry."

The woman cleared her throat. "There's no need to rush now. Please do as I say."

He grinned. "Come on, Bandit. We get to stay longer."

Rex watched his son and canine companion disappear inside.

"Shall we?" Mr. Riley asked, gesturing toward the door.

"Pa!" With a look of outrage, the woman blocked the door-way. "You aren't really going to let him come inside, are you?"

"I most certainly am." He gave the young woman a look of reprimand.

Wordlessly, she preceded them into the house. Mr. Riley led Rex to the dining room table.

An older woman breezed into the room from behind swinging doors. "Georgie told me we have company."

From the tender expression on Mr. Riley's face, it was apparent this woman was the object of his affection. "Star, this is Mr. Donnelly. Rex, this is my wife. We own this farm."

Mrs. Riley took Rex's hand in hers. Her violet eyes indicated a wary acceptance. "I'll bring some coffee and cake."

Michael Riley touched his wife's shoulder. "Thank you, darling. And then join us, will you?"

"None for me, Ma," the younger woman said in a belligerent tone. "I have no appetite."

When Mrs. Riley had left the room, Mr. Riley broke the moment of awkward silence. "This is my daughter, Aimee. She's raised Georgie since he was left at the orphanage six years ago."

Rex hesitated a moment, then glanced from Mr. Riley to his daughter. "I'm Georgie's father."

"He's my son." She glared at him, and despite his irritation, Rex couldn't help but admire her spirit.

"I have no wish to fight you on this, Miss Riley. But I will if you push me to it."

"How do I know you're telling the truth?"

"Why on earth would I lie about such a thing? If I wanted to adopt a child, the orphanages are filled with suitable children. I want my own flesh and blood. I've searched for six long years to find him."

"How can you be so sure Georgie's your son? Lots of children have blue eyes like yours."

A sense of satisfaction filled Rex. So even the child's adopted mother had noticed how much Georgie resembled him.

He reached into his pocket and pulled out two documents. "This is a letter drawn up by a friend of mine, an attorney whom I trust. Mrs. Carlton dictated it and added her mark."

"Mrs. Carlton?"

"The woman who ran the boardinghouse in Oregon City where my late wife and I lived. She's the one who brought Georgie to you after her home was destroyed by fire."

The look of recognition in her eyes indicated his words rang true with her. "Let me see that." Miss Riley snatched the document from his hands. Her lips trembled as she read the words on the page.

> To whom it may concern,
>
> I, Sarah Carlton, do solemnly swear that a boy child, one George Donnelly, was handed over by me to the Riley Home for Orphans. The child's mother died giving birth in her husband's absence. His pa, Rex Donnelly, has returned to find his child. I hope this letter will set to rights what I did that day.
>
> Sincerely,
>
> Sarah Carlton X

Miss Riley glanced up. "What's the other one?" she asked hoarsely, her eyes scanning the second document he held.

"A court document naming me the child's legal father."

"But. . .no one gave me a chance to fight this. How can the court just grant you guardianship without hearing my side?"

For the first time, Rex felt a hint of tenderness toward this woman as her beautiful eyes filled with tears, her rosy, full lips clutched between her teeth. He knew the pain of loss. Of longing to hold his child in his arms. He couldn't do anything about her pain, but he could sympathize. "I'm sorry, Miss Riley. I appreciate all you've done for my boy. But you'll find everything is in order. I'll be taking my son with me back to Oregon City."

Her eyes narrowed. "If you've lived in Oregon City all these years, why is it that you are only just now finding Georgie?"

Smarting from the implication that he had an ulterior motive for finding his son, Rex held up a silencing hand. "Let me assure you, Miss Riley, I have been actively searching for Georgie since I learned of his existence a little over five years ago. The lady next door to where the boardinghouse once stood remembered only that Mrs. Carlton had a sister who lived up north. We assumed she had taken my son with her. When I finally located her, she told me where to find the child. Does that satisfy your suspicion?"

She reddened and gave him a curt nod.

Mr. Riley leaned forward. "When will you be leaving with Georgie, Mr. Donnelly?"

"As soon as possible. I suppose we should call him in here and tell him the truth."

A gasp exploded from Miss Riley's lungs. "You can't do that so soon. He doesn't even know you."

"Then the sooner we get acquainted, the better."

Mrs. Riley entered, carrying a tray of coffee and slices of cake. "I thought you might be hungry after that trip," she said, smiling.

"Thank you, ma'am. I admit that I am a bit hollow."

"Have you a place to stay, Mr. Donnelly?" she asked, setting a cup of coffee in front of him along with a small plate holding a slice of crumb cake.

"No ma'am. I suppose there is a hotel in town?"

"Only a few rooms above the saloon."

"Not exactly what I had hoped for. Is there a boardinghouse where I could stay for a night?"

"Only Mrs. Barker's, but she's full up."

Mrs. Riley smiled at him, genuine warmth filling her violet-colored eyes. "You're welcome to stay here."

Surprise nearly caused him to choke on a bite of the delicious cake. "I couldn't ask you to do that, particularly under the circumstances."

"Nonsense. We can't have Georgie's father living over the saloon. And besides, this way our little fellow can get to know you before you tell him the truth."

So there was a motive behind her kind offer. But it wasn't a malicious motive, merely concern for the child she considered to be her grandson.

Miss Riley sat red faced, her eyes sparking anger. "Ma! Are you honestly asking this man to be our guest? He's stealing my son!"

"Aimee, please don't overreact."

She stormed to her feet, nearly knocking her chair backward. "Overreact? Do you honestly expect me to sit at the table with him during meals?"

"I certainly do. For your son's sake if for no other reason."

Rex refrained from reminding them that Georgie was his son, not Miss Riley's. No sense in stirring the fire under an already boiling pot. The girl's ma showed a lot of common sense. Not that Miss Riley had inherited any of it, but Rex could respect the unspoken request not to yank Georgie from a loving family without easing his son into some sort of a relationship. He would grant that request, as long as Miss Riley behaved herself.

He caught her hostile gaze, surprised at his own calm. "If you've a mind to listen, here is what I propose, Miss Riley."

Three

This was what Rex was proposing? That he stay for a whole week at the farm and get to know Georgie before taking him away? Aimee looked up from her laundry bucket, her blood boiling.

Watching Rex romp in the barnyard with Georgie and Bandit, she felt the weight of betrayal heavy in her soul. How could her parents have welcomed that man into their home? By allowing him to waltz in and take over her son, they had effectively thwarted any chance she had of running off with Georgie. If they had made him go into town to those rooms over the saloon, she would have been long gone by now.

Aimee slammed one of her pa's soggy work shirts against the washboard and scrubbed with fury, ignoring the droplets of soapy water that splashed onto her face. How was Rex's plan supposed to benefit her? At the end of the week, she'd still be absent her wonderful little boy.

Tears burned her eyes. As diligently as she tried to keep them at bay, the hot tears seemed to come anytime they pleased. During the past twenty-four hours, she'd prayed over and over that God would change Rex's mind. Make him see how much Georgie loved her. So far God hadn't seen fit to answer. Or if He had, the answer was a resounding no.

Still, she couldn't hate Rex. He obviously loved Georgie. He showed amazing patience and had even said prayers with Georgie the night before. Aimee had stood outside the door and listened, so she knew the man had a relationship with God. There was really nothing about him to object to other than the fact that he was slinking into her life and stealing her son.

She took out her aggression on Pa's work shirt, twisting and twisting the fabric until not one single drop of liquid escaped.

When the entire mound had been washed and rinsed, she took the pile of clean clothes to the rope clothesline stretched between two posts next to the house. Laundry was the one chore she could do without, but she'd volunteered this time so she could keep an eye on Mr. Donnelly and Georgie.

"Ma, look! Mr. Donnelly taught Bandit how to fetch."

"Well, rah rah for Mr. Donnelly," she muttered under her breath, but forced a smile and called, "That's good, honey. Mr. Donnelly must have quite a way with dogs." She lowered her voice again. "Seeing as how he *is* one."

Rex chuckled as though he knew exactly what she was thinking. Aimee bristled. The man possessed far too much self-assurance for her liking. "Georgie, it's time to get cleaned up for supper."

"Aw, Ma! Can't Bandit fetch one more time?"

"Listen to your mother." Rex ruffled Georgie's hair.

The boy beamed. "Yes sir." He bounded inside without one more word of complaint.

Rex headed toward Aimee. Pretending not to pay attention, Aimee noticed his long-legged stride. From the corner of her eye, she admired the way he held his head straight and confident, his shoulders broad and squared. Why had he never remarried? She frowned at her line of thinking and turned back to the shirt she'd just tossed over the line.

"If you hang the shirt like that, it's never going to get dry."

"What?" Aimee glared at him.

His eyes twinkled in amusement. He motioned toward the clothesline. "The sleeve is twisted."

"Don't presume to tell me how to hang laundry!" Aimee knew

he was right, but she would not give him the satisfaction of acknowledging it. While he looked on, she twisted every sleeve in the basket and hung all the shirts that way. When she finished, she gave him a "so there" nod and snatched up the basket. "And another thing," she said over her shoulder. "I do not need you to tell my son to obey me."

He reached her in a flash and fell into step, matching her stride for stride. "Really? From the looks of things, *my* son was obviously being disobedient. It seems as though someone needs to get him in hand before it's too late to train him properly."

"He was only showing his initial displeasure. He always does that before doing as he's told." Aimee winced at the admission. What kind of a mother allowed her child one opportunity to disobey?

"I stand corrected," he said, sarcasm dripping from his lips. "I'll be sure to keep your method in mind while I'm teaching him to obey."

Aimee stopped short. Rex turned, his brow raised as he waited for her to speak. "Mr. Donnelly. Y–you wouldn't hurt him, would you?"

His expression gentled. "No, Miss Riley. I give you my word that my methods, while probably not as lenient as those you've employed, will not be designed to break his spirit or harm him beyond the swift, brief pain of a spanking."

Unable to speak around the lump in her throat, Aimee jerked away and stepped past him. Rex reached out, his warm hand curling around her upper arm. She despised the way her heart leapt in her throat at his nearness.

"Please unhand me, Mr. Donnelly. I am engaged to be married, and I'm sure my fiancé would not appreciate the idea of a man grabbing his future wife."

A scowl marred his otherwise perfect features. "No offense

intended, Miss Riley. My desire was only to assure you once more that your—my—son will be safe with me. I care about his happiness."

A dreaded sob caught in Aimee's throat. "If you care about his happiness, how can you consider taking him from the only mother he's ever known?"

His eyes clouded. "I assure you, it isn't an easy decision. But Georgie is very young. While he may always hold a tender spot in his heart for you, he will soon adjust to his new life."

A tender spot? Oh, the ache was almost more than she could bear. Would her son forget all about his mother in such a short time?

"Miss Riley, I know this isn't fair to you." He reached forward and grasped a loose curl, almost as though the act came naturally. . .instinctively. Aimee drew in her breath as he tucked it behind her ear and continued, oblivious to the fact that her heart was pounding in her ears. "If it were possible for us to come to a satisfactory arrangement for visitation, I would consider it, but I see no way to accommodate us both."

Hope rose inside her. "Oh Mr. Donnelly. I would allow you to see Georgie any time you wish."

His lips curved into a rueful smile. "I was speaking of visitation for you, Miss Riley, not me. Haven't I made it clear that my son will be going back to Oregon City with me at the end of the week?"

"Perfectly." Aimee lifted her chin. "I just thought perhaps, after seeing my son's devotion to this family, you might care more about him than your own selfish desire to tuck him away in your fancy house. I suspect you'll have him attended by servants, and if he sees his father for ten minutes a day, he'll be lucky."

Rex's brow rose and red crept into his face. With satisfaction, Aimee knew she'd voiced his intentions precisely. But her victory was short lived as she imagined Georgie in such a situation.

"Mr. Donnelly, surely you can see that's no life for a child."

"Indeed? That was precisely my childhood and I think I turned out all right."

Seeing that he wasn't going to budge, Aimee looked him square in the eye and glared. "That, sir, is a matter of opinion."

Rex watched Aimee across the table. She pushed her food around on her plate, but bites were few and far between. His heart truly did go out to the young woman. The soulful brown eyes nearly did him in with every glance. Especially when quick tears sprang, and she lowered her lashes in an attempt to hide the enormous pools. He admired her for that. Under other circumstances, the mere fact that she wasn't using tears to manipulate him would have induced him to give in to her desires. But some things were acceptable to give a woman because of tears, and some weren't. This was an example of the latter.

Simple deduction. Rex was the boy's father. Therefore the boy belonged with him. During his short time at the Riley farm, he had grown to appreciate this hard-working family. They were respected in their community, well-off financially, for country folks; and he was truly grateful that Georgie had spent the last six years in the bosom of the Riley family. But God had seen fit to return his son to him, and that was that.

His gaze shifted back to Aimee, and he found her glaring at him. Her anger toward him made him uncomfortable. His pleasing personality had won him more cases than his knowledge of the law, and he was unaccustomed to downright hostility. Especially from a young woman. As a matter of fact, the opposite usually proved true.

If the society column of the *Oregon City Spectator* were to be believed, he was the most eligible bachelor in the state. Women usually found him to be quite a charming fellow, if he said so himself. How disconcerting that Miss Riley despised him. Of course she had mentioned a fiancé. One who would not take kindly to his hands on the fair young woman. Rex couldn't blame him. But where was the lucky man? It had been three days, and Rex hadn't seen evidence of a fiancé. That seemed odd. Rex knew one thing for certain. If he were going to marry a woman as beautiful and spirited as Aimee Riley, he wouldn't let her out of his sight. Wouldn't take a chance that some other man would come along and snatch her heart away.

Aimee glanced up once more, her eyes narrowed in contempt. "Since you seem unable to refrain from staring at me, Mr. Donnelly, I am afraid I'll have to remove myself from your relentless gaze." She shot to her feet with a huff.

"Relentless gaze?"

Miss Hannah, Aimee's grandmother, laughed and patted Rex on the shoulder. "Don't mind our Aimee. She's always been a little too outspoken for her own good."

"Much too outspoken." Mrs. Riley pursed her lips in displeasure. "Aimee, I insist you sit back down and apologize to our guest." She stared at her daughter until the young woman sat as she'd been told.

"I apologize, Mr. Donnelly."

"Oh, now, Star. Don't be too hard on her." Miss Hannah took a sip of milk. "I remember how much you adored that very thing about her nature when you first came to live with us."

"What one might consider adorable in a five-year-old is not so precious in a grown woman who should know better."

"Aimee isn't your daughter, ma'am?" Rex wished he could suck the words back in as Aimee and Star both blinked in surprise. "Forgive me, please. That is none of my business. You both have such striking features. It just never occurred to me that you didn't share the same blood."

Aimee's cheeks bloomed pink.

Mrs. Riley smiled. "I married Aimee's father when she was a little older than Georgie. She's mine in all the ways that matter."

Her knowing gaze met his, and Rex shifted in his seat. Her meaning was clear. Georgie was part of this family whether related by blood or not.

"So you think our Aimee's striking, do you?" The plump Miss Hannah gave him a little punch in the arm.

"Grammy!"

"Well, he said it," the old woman replied with a sniff. "A man ought to be able to back up his words."

"Yes ma'am. I find Miss Riley uncommonly beautiful. And I understand her fiancé does, as well."

Sudden, tense silence thickened the air with almost tangible presence. What had he said wrong?

"Fiancé?" Mr. Riley studied his daughter's red face. "Is there something you'd like to share with us, Aimee?"

"I—I meant to tell you, but everything got so out of hand with Mr. Donnelly coming."

"You're getting married, Aimee?" Mrs. Riley asked softly.

Twisting a napkin between her fingers, Aimee tossed Rex a disdainful look as though she wished he were that cloth square and she were twisting him. "Greg proposed down by the creek the day Mr. Donnelly showed up."

Rex studied her carefully. She didn't appear to be a woman joyously proclaiming the news of her recent betrothal. As a matter of fact, she seemed almost reluctant to admit it.

"Greg?" Mr. Riley placed his fork on his plate. "Our Greg, honey?"

Miss Hannah spoke up. "What a question. Do you know another Greg, Michael? Now what's this all about, Aimee? What about Cynthia? I thought they were getting married."

"She and her parents are moving back to Chicago soon."

"She's leaving Greg?"

Rex was having trouble keeping up with the conversation.

Aimee cleared her throat; her eyes shifted downward to the napkin in her hands. "She never really agreed to marry him. And Greg realizes she never will, so he asked me."

Indignation clutched at Rex's breast. How could a man make a woman feel as though she were second choice? And why would this beautiful creature even consider such an arrangement?

He opened his mouth, but snapped it shut instantly. What right did he have to interfere in such affairs? In a few days, he would be gone and would never see them again. Rising, he glanced around the table. "If you'll excuse me. This is a private family matter that I'm sure Miss Riley would prefer not to discuss in front of a stranger." He glanced at his wide-eyed son, who seemed to be taking it all in. "How about we play fetch with Bandit before dark?"

"Yes sir." Georgie hopped up, but looked back at Aimee. "If you marry Pastor Gregory, does that mean I'll have a pa?"

Out of the mouths of babes. . .

A strangled sob left Aimee. She shot from her chair and ran from the room.

Georgie's face clouded. "I'm sorry," he whispered, his little lips beginning to tremble.

Rex crouched down and took his son by the shoulders. "You didn't do anything wrong, son. Women who are getting married often have outbursts like that."

"Ma's not mad at me?"

"Nope. I promise."

A slow grin spread across his face. "Can we go play fetch now?"

"Yes." He placed his hand on his son's shoulder and walked him to the door.

The little boy's shoulders rose and fell with a sigh. "It sure will be nice to have a pa."

Swallowing around a sudden lump in his throat, it was all Rex could do not to snatch the child up in his arms and tell him the truth. But he had agreed to let Aimee be there so they could tell him together. Tonight wasn't a good time, but tomorrow he would insist upon sharing the news with Georgie.

He tried to keep his mind focused on the rousing game of fetch, but thoughts of Aimee wandered uninvited through his mind, distracting him.

He turned at the creak of the door opening. The thump, thump, thumping of a cane followed as Miss Hannah stepped onto the porch. "Let the boy play by himself for a while. I'd like to have a word with you."

"Yes ma'am." He tossed the stick once more, and both Georgie and Bandit ran after it. In a few strides, he reached the porch, then leaned against the railing.

Miss Hannah made her way to the rocking chair in the corner of the long porch and sat heavily. "So what do you think of our Aimee marrying a man who is obviously in love with another woman?"

Again Rex bristled at the thought, but he controlled his answer like any good lawyer. "I don't guess I have a right or a reason to feel anything about it."

"Ah, but I didn't ask how you felt. I asked what you think."

"Is there a difference?"

"Very much so. Sometimes following the heart goes against good common sense. Aimee, for instance. She's been in love with Greg from the day my son, Andy, married Greg's mother and arrived in the valley. That was so long ago, it wouldn't even occur to her that she doesn't need to be second choice for any man."

"That's certainly true." He tossed a stick into the bushes next to the steps. "I suppose her devotion to this Greg is why she never married before now? I'm sure she's had plenty of offers."

The elderly woman stopped rocking. She shook her head with regret. "All the men around here knew it was useless to try to come courting. She had tunnel vision all through her childhood. Could only see Gregory. We thought she had finally given up on him when she left home six years ago. It seemed as though she transferred her love for Greg into a motherly love for Georgie."

"It's obvious my son's been well tended. I am grateful to her for that."

"I'm annoyed at that grandson of mine for coming back here and throwing her a bone just because he got jilted by the love of his life. It's not fair to Aimee. She's still young enough to find true love."

She gazed at him so intently, Rex suddenly realized Miss Hannah was implying he should romance the young woman. He had to admit the idea had merit. But the circumstances were too bizarre. Besides, for better or worse, the girl was getting married.

"I'm sure Aimee knows what's right for her, ma'am. Far be it from me to interfere with matters of the heart."

Her features scrunched in displeasure. "You're making a mistake to discount Aimee as a possible bride. I've seen the spark between you two. And don't deny it."

With a short laugh, he shook his head. "More like a stick of dynamite. Believe me, it's not romantic attraction sparking between us. She has only disdain for me—as expected, given the circumstances."

A snort filled the air. "Let me tell you something. You don't get to be my age without a little bit of understanding of human emotions. And I say the two of you have enough sparks between you for a Fourth of July celebration. And speaking of that, I hope you'll join us tomorrow for the Independence Day picnic after church."

"Yes ma'am," he replied, relieved to shift the topic of conversation.

She nodded. "Good. You be sure to bid on the lunch box with the big, blue gingham bow." She winked at him.

"Bid?"

"Haven't you ever been to a box social?"

"This is the first I've ever heard of one. What is it?"

"The young ladies fix box lunches, and the men bid on them—and the honor of eating the dinner with the girl who made it. This year the proceeds are going to the orphanage in Oregon City." She gave a pointed glance. "I should think you would have a vested interest in this particular charity."

"You're right about that." He grinned. "So you say I should bid on your box? Does that mean I get to eat lunch with you?"

She braced herself with her cane and rose. "Now be sure and bid on that box with the blue gingham bow. You won't be disappointed." She winked at him and thumped into the house.

Longing filled Rex's heart as he watched her go. How could he deny his son this wonderful family? Weren't they everything he had wished for as a child?

Four

Aimee fumed as the bid rose higher and higher on her basket—the one containing thick roast beef sandwiches, apple dumplings, and potatoes fried to just the right crispiness—all of Greg's favorites.

Gregory seemed a little lost. As auctioneer, he wasn't allowed to bid, so he'd worked it out with his little brother, Billy, to bid, and Greg would pay him back the price of the basket. But this—this Rex wouldn't stop bidding on her basket.

It was as though he knew which one belonged to her and he was bidding on it just to make her mad. And it was working. She was furious. Wasn't it enough that he would be stealing her son in a couple of days? Did he also have to deny her the small pleasure of eating her picnic lunch with the man she loved?

"Twenty-five dollars!" Rex called out. A collective gasp filled the room.

Gregory sputtered. "Twenty-five dollars. That's—um—quite generous. I'm sure no one will be able to compete against that."

Aimee's heart sank as Greg sent her a look of apology. Twenty-five dollars was as much as he made in a month. She couldn't expect him to spend his entire salary just for the pleasure of sharing lunch with her. But...Rex?

Stomping forward, she stood in front of Rex while he reached for the basket with a sheepish grin on his face.

"Looks like I won your grandmother's box," he said triumphantly.

"G–Grammy?"

"Yep. The one with the big, blue gingham bow. She told me so last night."

"Why, that's cheating! No one is supposed to know who made what boxes. I've half a mind to turn you in."

Amusement tugged at his lips as he perused her face. "Indeed? To whom? Surely box social rules do not fall under the sheriff's jurisdiction." He glanced over her shoulder and held up the basket with a big grin. Aimee turned to find Grammy grinning, as well, and clasping her hands together in the victory sign. "If you'll excuse me, Miss Riley, my dinner guest is waiting."

"By all means, Mr. Donnelly. Enjoy your meal."

"Thanks. I will."

Folding her arms across her chest, Aimee watched with grim satisfaction, waiting as he strode right up to Grammy. She stood by as Grammy pointed around him—straight at her. Grammy had set them up. But why? How could she betray Greg, her own grandson? Rex turned slowly, his face flushed. He shuffled back to where Aimee stood. The discomfiture in his expression was all the reward Aimee needed.

"Serves you right for being such a show-off," she said with a smug sniff. "Twenty-five dollars, indeed. Now poor Greg is going to have to go hungry."

"Oh, I wouldn't be so sure about that."

"What do you mean?"

Aimee turned in the direction he indicated. Her mouth went dry. Greg leaned against the wall, holding a red-ribboned box, and Cynthia stood in front of him. Smiling, talking. Tapping him on the shoulder, flirting. And Greg was lapping it up like a thirsty dog. Aimee's stomach knotted. Greg took Cynthia's hand. Aimee held her breath as he brought it up to his mouth and pressed a kiss on her knuckles. Cynthia's face softened. The face of a woman in love.

"Aimee?"

She barely heard Rex's voice through the rush in her ears.

"Aimee. . ." He grabbed her hand and tugged.

Woodenly, she followed. Rex led her to an empty space behind a large, leafy tree. He spread his jacket on the ground and motioned toward it. "Please do me the honor."

"Thank you," she whispered. "Why are you being so nice to me?"

"Because you need a little niceness right now." He sat across from her. "I take it that was Cynthia?"

"How do you know about her?"

"Last night at dinner, you mentioned that Greg proposed to you after she jilted him."

Heat suffused Aimee's cheeks. "Yes, that's Cynthia," she said dully. "Greg's loved her for years."

Rex reached up and thumbed away a tear from her face. The tender gesture tugged at Aimee's heart, and more tears flowed.

He clicked his tongue, admonishing her as though she were a child. Aimee found it strangely comforting. "Why would you agree to settle for a man who can't love you with all his heart? You're much too special for that."

"I—I hoped Greg would learn to love me that way." But she knew now that would never happen. "He's an honorable man, Rex. He's always been good to me. I can't fault him for loving someone else. He was willing to marry me, be a father to Georgie." For a brief moment, Aimee had lived her dream. "How could everything crumble in just minutes?" she asked, more to the wind than Rex.

"I'm truly sorry, Aimee."

"If you take my son, I'll be left with nothing." Was it unfair to appeal to him this way?

Thankfully, Rex didn't seem to hold it against her. Instead, he moved forward slightly. He stuffed his handkerchief into her hand and gathered her to him with strong arms. He held her while she sobbed. Aimee didn't protest.

Suddenly two long legs appeared next to their picnic spot. Aimee's heart raced even before she looked up. Greg's eyes flashed in unspoken anger. She thrilled to the way his jaw twitched. He was jealous!

"Aimee," Greg said stiffly, "may I have a word with you?"

Indignation clutched Rex's chest. The preacher clearly wasn't good enough for a woman with Aimee's earthy spirit. She deserved someone who would fight an army of men to ensure no other man would ever hold her in his arms. That's what he'd do if Aimee belonged to him.

The expression on her face as she slipped her dainty hand inside Gregory's and allowed herself to be hauled to her feet plainly bespoke her devotion and absolute forgiveness of the man who, only moments earlier, had humiliated her with another woman in a roomful of family and friends.

It made Rex sick. Obviously, she didn't have even half the intelligence or self-respect Rex had given her credit for having.

He hopped to his feet. "You two stay here and talk," he said to his former dinner companion. "My compliments."

"What about your basket?" Aimee asked, her gorgeous brown eyes filled with concern.

Despite his resolve that Aimee was a sentimental fool destined to a fate of unhappiness, he couldn't help the softening in his heart. He smiled, glanced at her fiancé, who glared a warning, and reached out to cup her silky smooth cheek. She blushed and averted her gaze. Rex released her. "I'll be fine."

He left them standing together and refused to look back.

Rex walked along the dusty street. The entire town had been transformed into a sort of fair. Apple bobbing, target shooting, log-rolling contests. There were booths where ladies were selling pies, cider, hats, anything to make a few dollars to send to the orphanage where his son had been taken.

What might Georgie's fate have been if Aimee hadn't fallen

in love with the boy? Everyone knew there were good orphanages and bad ones. His heart lifted with thanksgiving every time he imagined the horror scenario his son had escaped. God had been watching over Georgie from his birth.

"Mr. Donnelly!"

Rex looked about, searching for the person who had called out to him.

"Over here!"

Rex grinned when he spied Miss Hannah. He had a few words to say to her anyway. He strode over to a crudely constructed table and sat on the bench beside her. "So I should bid on the basket with the large gingham bow, eh?"

She clamped her lips together, and her eyes spoke volumes of merriment.

"I sincerely hope you intend to ask the Lord's forgiveness for that little deception. Your granddaughter was furious, and I don't think her fiancé is extremely happy either."

Miss Hannah gave a dismissive wave. "Gregory isn't right for Aimee. And he knows it. He's just getting desperate to settle down."

"That's not fair to Aimee. She should marry a man who loves her."

Miss Hannah glanced sharply at him. "Or at the very least a man who knows he's on his way to loving her."

Rex recognized a trap when he heard one. He leaned back, a mock grin twisting his lips. "Is that what the whole basket-bidding hoax was all about? You're matchmaking between Aimee and me?"

"You could both do worse." Not even a hint of an apology. Rex had to admire her spirit. It was easy to see where Aimee had gotten so much spunk.

"But the lovely Aimee is engaged to be married. Besides, I've only known her for a few days, and believe me, she's not interested in getting to know me better."

Miss Hannah gave a snort only a woman of her advanced age could expel and still be considered a lady. "She will come around. Besides, engagements aren't marriages."

"They might as well be." His mind conjured up the uncomfortable memory of Gregory kissing Cynthia's hand and carrying her basket. The preacher was apparently confused as to which woman he was engaged to.

A heavy sigh escaped the plump woman. "I happen to know that Cynthia Roland has decided not to move back to Chicago with her parents after all. You can no doubt figure out the implication of that."

"Gregory would jilt Aimee?" Fresh anger burned Rex. "What kind of a preacher is he?"

"Don't you go bringing God into matters of the heart, young man. My grandson is a godly man with a strong calling. He needs a wife. When Cynthia refused him, he turned to the one woman he knew loved him unconditionally. One with a son who needed a father."

"He has a father."

"Yes. And he needs a mother, too."

"I thought we were discussing Greg and Aimee."

She gave him a knowing grin. "We were. Now we're discussing you and Georgie and Aimee."

"I don't understand."

"Greg will be asking Aimee to let him out of his proposal. And, of course, she'll agree."

"And why should this concern me, Miss Hannah? I'll be leaving here in two days with my son, and it's unlikely I'll ever see Aimee again."

Her eyes flashed. "Just like that? You would take a boy from his mother?"

"His mother's dead. I am his father."

"Aimee's the only mother he's ever known. He loves this family. Do you honestly believe he'll be happy without us?"

The optimism he'd expressed earlier in the week was waning, and he no longer felt certain that the boy would settle into a life with nannies. Still, how could he possibly agree to the ludicrous suggestion Miss Hannah seemed to be implying?

"I don't know, ma'am. How does a parent ever know what is truly the right choice?"

She patted his hand. "There are some things that shouldn't require a lot of consideration. Taking a boy away from a good mother is one of those things."

"What about keeping a boy from a good father?"

"Whether you're a good father or not remains to be seen, doesn't it?"

Defenses raised, Rex laced his fingers in front of him. "I will be a good father to Georgie. He'll never lack for anything."

"Except a mother's love."

"I imagine I'll marry again someday." Here they were back to the topic of marriage. He pressed on before she could suggest Aimee would make an exceptional wife. "When I'm good and ready and when I fall in love."

"Looks like you might have to get good and ready in a hurry."

With an exasperated sigh, Rex opened his mouth to reiterate his position about Aimee when he noticed the old lady was looking past him, a frown marring her weathered features. Rex turned to see a woman speeding down the street on horseback, wearing a blue dress. "Is that. . . ?"

"Aimee. Yes."

"Where's she going?"

"Looks like she's headed for home."

Concern filled Rex. He imagined the conversation she'd just endured with her so-called fiancé.

Coming to a sudden decision, he shoved up from the bench. "I'm going after her before she breaks her neck, riding like that."

"I'd appreciate it."

"You'll keep an eye on Georgie?"

"Of course. Aimee wouldn't have left like that without knowing Georgie would make it home safely. The boy is with Michael at the pig-judging contest. No safer place to be than with his grandpa."

Rex didn't bother to argue the point that perhaps the safest place for a boy was actually with his father. But then Michael Riley was probably the closest thing Georgie had to a father prior to Rex's presence at the farm.

As he strode to the hitching post where his rented mount stood tethered with a feedbag attached to his ears, he considered Miss Hannah's words. This family loved Georgie. How could he take the boy away?

He mounted and took off down the road at breakneck speed. By the time he caught up to the girl, she had reached the creek and tethered her mare to the gazebo. He dismounted and joined her as she stared out across the rippling water. Tears streaked her dusty cheeks. She looked adorable.

And Rex knew what he had to do.

Five

Why couldn't he just leave her alone? Aimee leaned against the rail of the gazebo, resting on her elbows. She stared into the setting sun and didn't bother hiding her belligerence. How could Rex possess the audacity to come after her when anyone could plainly see she wanted to be left alone?

"What do you want, Rex?" she asked without looking up.

"To make sure you get home safely."

Despite her broken heart, Aimee still had her pride. She lifted her chin. "I've been riding since I was five years old. I think I know how to handle my horse. Besides, as you can plainly see, I am home. Practically."

"Okay, so maybe I just didn't want you to have to be alone at a time like this."

"That's sweet of you, but it's really not your place to worry about me."

He imitated her stance and rested on his elbows. "Your grandmother was worried. She sort of asked me to come after you."

Resentment rose in Aimee. "When will my family realize I'm grown up? Lands! I'm thirty-two years...old." Dread clawed at her. Bad enough she was so old, but to admit her age to a man? She was as bad as Grammy. Pretty soon she'd be old and crotchety, with no manners and no sense of propriety to hold her tongue. Heaven forbid she ever belched in public, but if she continued on this track, she'd be doing it in no time.

Rex chuckled at her discomfiture. "If it makes you feel any better, I'm thirty-five."

Aimee gave an undignified snort. "It doesn't matter how old men are. Besides, you've been married before, so everyone knows that someone wanted to marry you. You know what I am."

He gave her shoulder a playful nudge. "Beautiful? Smart? Spunky? A good mother?"

Spinster. Old maid. Long in the tooth.

It wasn't that Aimee didn't appreciate his attempts to lift her spirits. She did. But who really cared? "What difference does it make if I'm beautiful, smart, or spunky? I'm still unmarried. And as far as being a good mother goes, you of all people know how much good *that* does me. You're taking away my child."

Suddenly very weary, she turned from the glaring sun and leaned her backside against the gazebo. She wrapped her arm around the white column and didn't bother resisting the melancholy tears rising to the surface. "When my pa built the new house a few years ago, he asked Uncle Andy to build this gazebo for Ma so she could come here at the end of the day and enjoy the beauty of the sun setting on the water."

Rex straightened and stood watching her, his hands stuffed inside his trouser pockets. Aimee nodded toward two rocking chairs in the center of the gazebo. "My uncle Andy built those. Ma and Pa come out here together often in the spring when the wildflowers are in bloom and the geese are coming back from their flight south." She released a sigh and met Rex's gaze. "Isn't that a lovely thing for a man and wife to do? I've always wanted the sort of relationship they have. Always imagined that Gregory would be standing right about where you are now and would ask me to marry him at sunset. Wouldn't that be a gorgeous picture?"

"Any picture with you in it would be gorgeous, Aimee. Don't you know that?"

Rex stepped forward and took hold of her hand. By the time a protest formed on her lips, the warmth of his touch had enveloped her, and she no longer cared to tell him to mind his manners. Human comfort felt too good. Even his.

Rex swallowed hard. "Aimee, I've been thinking about something your grammy said."

Sensing he didn't need or desire a response, Aimee remained silent and waited for him to explain. While she waited, she studied his profile. A square jawline and straight nose along with perfectly set eyes beneath a well-proportioned brow gave him the appearance of an aristocrat. Even with a hint of a shadow along his jaw, this man was as handsome as any Aimee had ever seen. Perhaps even the most handsome.

"Your grammy told me it isn't fair to Georgie to just rip him from you. After all, you've been his mother since he was born."

Aimee gave him a rueful glance. "I believe I mentioned the same thing. More than once, as a matter of fact."

His gaze intensified. "That was before I got to know you. Now that I know you and my son, I'm convinced he wouldn't be happy apart from you."

Aimee's heart leapt. Was Rex about to propose a marriage of sorts? Her palms dampened. Her mind began to work furiously. Was it worth it to marry a man she didn't love just to be with her son day in and day out? A resounding *yes* echoed through her skull. She held her breath. *Oh Rex. Just say it.*

"I propose you come live with us in Oregon City."

"Oh Rex, yes. Anything to be with Georgie."

"Are you sure?"

"Absolutely."

"There is the matter of your pay of course. But be assured, anything I offer is generously above your salary at the orphanage, I'm sure."

Aimee gaped. "Y–you want to pay me?"

He chuckled. "I could hardly expect you to be the boy's nanny free of charge."

The gazebo floor began to spin like a merry-go-round, and Aimee's feet weren't quite steady beneath her. She swayed, felt herself falling.

Rex caught her just in time. His strong arms surrounded her, and he led her to one of the rocking chairs. As in a dreadful dream, Aimee felt him lower her into the chair. "Are you all right? Should I get you to a doctor?"

Shaking her head, Aimee tried to open her eyes. "No doctor. I'll be fine. Just. . .let me sit here and catch my breath a minute."

"What happened?"

"I thought. . ." Heat scorched her cheeks.

"You thought what?"

"Never mind."

"Oh dear. You believed I was going to propose, didn't you? I'm sorry. You are a lovely young woman and any man would be honored to marry you."

"Except for Gregory, of course, and apparently you." Bitterness dripped from her tongue, but she couldn't care less. How much disappointment and humiliation must a woman endure in one day?

"Be reasonable, Aimee." He spoke with a controlled edge to his voice. "We hardly know each other."

"You hardly know Georgie, either, and yet you want to take him away."

"You know that's different." He took her shoulders between his hands.

Aimee met his gaze. "Not to Georgie, it isn't. You're nobody to him."

"Don't. . ." His eyes flashed and his voice warned, but Aimee was past caring. Let him hurt as badly as she. A nanny! As though

Rex were Pharaoh's daughter, offering her the chance to nurse little Moses. Her own son! But Aimee couldn't be satisfied with just being a nurse. That wasn't good enough. She had to be Georgie's mother.

"I'm the one he loves." She pounded Rex's chest, sobbing as she spoke. "I'm the one who stays up with him all night when he's sick. I feed him, sew his clothes. Who are you? You're just. . ."

"Aimee. . ."

Ignoring the warning tone and the gentle nudge she felt in the pit of her stomach, she spat out the words almost before her brain registered them. "You might as well have died along with his mother, for all he knows."

Horror widened his eyes. He tightened his grip. "Are you so bitter about where life has taken you that you could be so cruel? Do you think you're the only one who has ever suffered loss?"

"What difference does that make?" Aimee didn't want to hear about anyone else's pain. He didn't know what it was like to be her. Unwanted. Unloved. Alone.

"You had your say. Now it's my turn." He kept her firmly grasped in his clutches and stepped closer. She could feel the warmth of his breath on her face. "Aimee Riley, you're the biggest kind of fool. What sort of woman wastes away her youth on a man who clearly will never love her?"

"It wasn't a waste. I thought someday he'd—"

"No you didn't. In your heart you knew he'd never love you the way a man loves a woman."

"I don't know what you mean." Her knees were beginning to weaken at his closeness.

"Yes you do. You're a passionate woman. Too passionate for that man."

"Don't you dare disparage Gregory's good name."

"Disparage? I pity him. How sad to have the adoration and

devotion of a woman like you and not have the gumption to love you back. He deserves to have a pale flower like Cynthia at his side. It serves him right." He leaned closer.

Aimee gasped. "Rex Donnelly, don't you dare kiss me."

He smirked. "You're not very good at reading men, Miss Riley. To tell you the truth, kissing you was the last thing on my mind. But now that you mention it. . ." His gaze shifted downward until it found her lips. He lowered his head until only immeasurable distance remained between them. "Have you ever been kissed, Miss Riley?" His silky question, whispered almost against her lips, sent a shiver down her spine.

Unable to speak, barely able to breathe, Aimee shook her head.

He winced and pulled back. "Then I will not take advantage of you and steal your first kiss."

Disappointment curdled in Aimee's stomach like sour milk. "I–it's a good thing for you that you turned me loose. My pa would have—"

"What? Forced me to marry you?" He gave her a sardonic smile and mounted his horse, tipping his hat. "I'm sorry to disappoint you."

Aimee sputtered as she watched him ride away.

Rex willed his heart to stop racing as he galloped toward the farmhouse. He'd come so close to asking her to marry him. Why, at the last minute, had he cowered? Miss Hannah made a lot of sense. Aimee was Georgie's mother in every way that mattered. The boy would be miserable apart from her. But he would be miserable apart from his son. Marriage to Aimee made all the sense in the world.

Though Aimee had never given him an answer to his pitiful proposal, Rex knew instinctively she wouldn't agree to such an arrangement. And really, it hadn't been a fair offer.

Still, he couldn't quite convince himself to turn back and ask her to marry him. Perhaps he was a selfish boor, but when he married again, he wanted to be in love. And Aimee had spoken of wanting the same kind of relationship her parents had. The sort of loving devotion that caused two people to hold hands or walk arm in arm, as he'd seen Aimee's parents do several times, even after twenty years of marriage.

He tethered his horse to the rail in front of the house, then started to climb the steps to the porch. Bandit came yelping from across the yard, nearly knocking Rex over in his canine exuberance. "Hey boy, what are you up to?" Bandit wagged his tail, his entire fat body shaking with excitement. Rex ruffled the dog's fur. "It's nice that someone's happy to see me," he said dryly. "Even if you are just a mutt."

After sending Bandit on his way, Rex strode into the house and toward the bedroom the Rileys had graciously offered him during his stay. He peeled off his boots and stretched fully clothed onto the bed.

Georgie's image sprang to his mind, and he smiled. How odd that three days could so change a man's perspective. How could he have ever known the depth of love one person could feel for another? Could Aimee possibly love a child she hadn't carried in her womb the way he loved the boy—his flesh and blood? Rex knew the answer to that question. Aimee loved Georgie with as much devotion as any mother who had borne her own child.

His heart clenched with emotion, and for the first time he wasn't sure if he was doing the right thing.

Six

By the time Aimee roused herself and made it back to the house, the sun had fully set. Still, there was no sign that her family had arrived home yet. But she hadn't expected it. The Independence Day celebration wouldn't end without a few fireworks being set off, and the display was probably just beginning.

The house was completely dark when she stepped inside. Had Rex rejoined the celebration? Hunger gnawed at her stomach, but the thought of building a fire on such a hot night didn't appeal to her. She did, however, need to see her way around the cabin.

After lighting the lamp above the stove, she grabbed some cheese from the cold box and buttered two slices of bread. That, together with a glass of fresh milk, provided her supper.

She was just giving in to an indulgence, slicing a fresh apple pie that Ma had deemed unfit to sell at the celebration, when Rex appeared. Aimee's heart jumped at the sight of him, his shirt slightly disheveled as though he'd been sleeping in his clothes, his dark hair ruffled, giving him a look of vulnerability that belied his royal features.

"Glad you made it back okay." His sleep-husky voice made her knees weak. "I had planned to come back for you."

"I told you I am fully capable of taking care of myself." She stabbed at the slice of pie with her fork.

"Are you pretending that's my heart?" Rex drawled.

"What heart?" Aimee muttered.

"I heard that."

Aimee shrugged. "Are you hungry?" Holding a grudge was no

reason for allowing a guest to starve.

"Famished."

"We have bread, cheese, milk, and pie." If that wasn't good enough, he could just go hungry.

"Sounds perfect."

"Fine. Sit down and I'll get some for you."

"Thank you" came the meek reply. "About earlier. . ."

"I do not wish to discuss it." Glad he could see only her back, Aimee fought the heat rising to her cheeks.

"Perhaps you don't, but I want to apologize for being so forward." His voice had grown thick with. . .something. "You're quite beautiful, and being alone with you. . ."

Aimee heard the scrape of a chair against the wooden floor. "I'll be outside," he said. "I don't think we should be alone in the house."

She turned. "B–but what about your dinner?"

"I'll eat it out there." He stomped across the floor and slammed the door behind him.

Aimee released a breath. How could there be this attraction between them? Her dreams of Gregory had only consisted of wanting to spend her life with him. She'd dreamed of children and working by his side, but never of passionate kisses. Her heart had not raced at his closeness as it did every time Rex came near. What did that mean?

Her hands trembled a little as she carried his sandwich and a glass of milk to the porch. A jolt shot through her when his fingers touched hers as he took his meal.

"Sit over there or go in the house," he ordered.

"Well, you don't have to growl!"

"You don't seem to realize how easily you could be compromised in a situation like this. What is your family thinking by not sending someone home to chaperone?"

Aimee jerked her chin. "My family trusts me. They know I am a decent woman."

"That may be, but they hardly know me. How do they know what sort of man I am?"

His candid question sent a shudder of fear down Aimee's spine. She snatched the rifle next to the door. "You'd better not try anything with me, mister."

"Relax and put that thing down. I'm not going after you." He took a bite and followed it with a gulp of milk. "The most I would have done was steal that kiss. And in our present circumstances, that would be enough to compromise you."

Aimee leaned the rifle back against the side of the house. "Heaven forbid you should compromise me and then be forced into marriage." Bitterness loosened her tongue.

"I could think of worse things than being married to a beautiful woman," he said, a wry grin tugging at the corners of his lips. "But I married the love of my life. If I marry again, I'll do so because I'm in love again."

"I understand." *I just wish I knew why I seem to be so unlovable.*

"You never gave me an answer earlier."

The abrupt change in topic gave Aimee a start. The truth was that all she had thought about after he'd left the gazebo was his offer to hire her on as Georgie's nanny.

"Part of my heart says it's a good idea," she began, carefully choosing her words. "But the other part of me knows it would be harmful to Georgie for me to live as his nanny but not be his mother anymore. It would be too confusing for a child his age."

A heavy sigh escaped Rex. But the shadows covered him, preventing her from seeing the expression on his face. "I thought you might not agree to it. I guess it was a bad idea."

"I wouldn't say that. It was a well-intentioned idea that wasn't given much thought."

"I stand corrected. Look, none of this is my fault, you know. Any more than it's yours."

Aimee frowned into the darkness. "You chose not to be with your wife when she gave birth to Georgie. If you had been there, you could have raised him from birth."

Rex grimaced. "I had no choice. Shortly after I found out my wife was pregnant, I went back east to inform my parents."

"Why couldn't you have written to them?"

"Though you may have difficulty believing this, I was once an irresponsible young man." He spoke in a self-mocking tone.

Aimee couldn't help but smile. "A fault of youth, not character, I'm sure."

"You're too kind." He shifted forward in his chair, and the shadows receded, the moonlight drawing attention to his handsome face. Warmth circled in Aimee's stomach.

He nodded as though oblivious to her reaction. "I had the best education. . .Harvard, in fact. After I graduated, I joined Father in the firm, as expected, and spent several years bored to distraction with the ridiculous cases he allowed me to negotiate. I suppose I was a bit spoiled."

Aimee rocked in Grammy's chair, remaining silent while he continued.

"One night my friends and I attended a Wild West show. We met a man who had been a real scout for numerous wagon trains. His tales of adventure touched a desire I had for excitement. Much to the chagrin of my parents, I always had a bit of a wild nature."

"Another fault of youth."

A shrug lifted his broad shoulders. "Perhaps. But I was ready to throw away my education, my years of experience as a lawyer, and head west to be a farmer like your pa."

"A noble profession."

"True, but not the one my parents had worked so hard to create for their only son. My father was a lawyer. My uncle is a lawyer. Their father started the firm in New York. How could I grow up to be anything other than a lawyer? You can imagine their reaction when I told them the news."

"That you were coming west?"

He nodded. "My mother cried and pretended to faint, and my father yelled and lamented ever raising such a wooden-headed fool. By the time the dust settled, they had agreed to finance a wagon train adventure west, provided I promised to return home afterward and re-establish my place in the firm."

"And you met your wife on the trail." Aimee pressed her fingers to her throat as longing rose inside her. For love. For a man of her own. "She must have been very beautiful to make you give up everything just to marry her."

"She wasn't beautiful in the same sense that you are. Her face was plain, but her spirit was gentle. And she brought out a thoughtful side of me I hadn't previously known existed. I wanted to please her. To make her laugh. To be a man worthy of her." His voice caught in his throat. "I took a train back east a month after we arrived in Oregon City. I settled her in, found a midwife to tend to her and a doctor as backup in case something happened. But it wasn't enough."

"You did all you could," Aimee soothed, ashamed of herself for the envy she experienced as Rex spoke of the woman he loved.

"I was anxious to get back to New York—even though I was certain I would be disinherited—and get back to my wife. When I arrived home, Father was ill, and the doctors didn't give him much hope. I had to stay and watch over his interests in the firm. I wrote to Anna every day. I was frantic when I stopped receiving letters from her."

"The woman at the boardinghouse didn't contact you to let

you know your wife had died?"

"Mrs. Carlton couldn't read or write."

Pity tore at Aimee's heart. She no longer burned with resentment against Rex. The man had moved heaven and earth to find Georgie. How could she deny him his son?

"I understand why you wouldn't want to enter into a marriage that is anything less than the one you had with your wife." Her eyes misted. "I admire you for holding out when marriage to me would be easier."

He gave a laugh. "From what I've seen of your feisty character, I doubt marriage to you would be easy. Adventurous is the word I'd use."

Though it was little consolation, Aimee knew he was paying her a compliment. Too bad his adventurous nature had fled with his youth.

Her lips curved into a grin. "Rex, I think you've waited long enough for the joy of being a father. If Georgie is awake when they get back, let's tell him tonight."

Georgie's face glowed with a joy that Rex hadn't dared hope for when Aimee gave him the news. "I have a pa?" he asked with loud exuberance.

"You sure do," Aimee said, her voice thick with unshed tears. "Mr. Donnelly has been looking for you ever since you were just a teeny-weeny baby."

"And you didn't know he wanted me?" Georgie frowned as though trying to figure out a puzzle.

"I didn't know where to find him."

Georgie turned a shy gaze on Rex. "Are you coming to live with us at the orphanage when Ma and me go back next week?"

Aimee sniffled and turned away abruptly, obviously leaving it to Rex to explain the rest.

Rex patted his knee, and Georgie climbed into his lap. "The law says that a boy belongs with the parents God gave him."

"Ma always says that God knew we were both alone, so He gave us to each other."

His wide, innocent eyes seared a hole through Rex's heart. "Georgie, God sent you to Aimee because He knew I was trying to find you. And He knew she would take better care of you than anyone else in the whole world."

The boy beamed. "She makes the best apple pancakes ever. Don'tcha, Ma?"

"After Grandma." Her voice trembled as she fought to keep from revealing her emotional state to the boy. Rex appreciated her efforts. But Georgie's frown convinced him that the child knew something was going on. He climbed down from Rex's lap and walked over to Aimee. He slipped a pudgy hand into hers. "What's wrong, Ma?"

When she turned to face him, there was no more hiding the tears. She knelt before him on the floor and gathered him into her arms. "Georgie, I love you so much."

"I love you, too." His voice quivered.

She pulled back and brushed a lock of hair from his forehead. "Your pa is right about God sending you to me. But I thought God gave you to me forever. Now I know that He only wanted me to take care of you for a little while, until your pa could find you and take you to live with him."

Georgie frowned. "God's taking me back?" Anger flashed in his eyes. "He can't do that!"

Aimee gasped. "Georgie, sweetie, you must never be disrespectful when speaking about God. He can do whatever He wants because He is God."

"Y—you don't want me anymore?"

Aimee's tears flowed unchecked. "Of course I want you.

Forever and ever. And if I had my choice, we would never be apart. But there's a judge who says you must go and live with your pa."

Georgie kicked at the floor with his booted toes. Then he whirled around and faced Rex with fury. "I don't care what nobody says. I'm not leaving my ma!"

"Georgie," Rex said, trying to keep his voice steady, "I'm sorry this is happening to you, but I'm afraid you have no choice."

"No! You can't make me. Bandit will tear you up like a wolf. I'll—I'll run away. I hate you." The child beelined for the door and slammed it shut behind him.

Rex caught Aimee's gaze. "That could have gone better."

"I'm sorry, Rex. I couldn't help the tears. I tried not to cry."

"I'm not blaming you." Releasing a heavy sigh, he stuffed his hands into his pockets. "Should I go after him?"

"I'll go." From the kitchen door, Mr. Riley's voice echoed through the room.

"Georgie will listen to Pa," Aimee said softly. "They're very close."

Rex sat at the dining room table for what seemed like an eternity. Aimee sat across from him in silence, as though sensing his need to be alone with his thoughts. When Mr. Riley returned, he carried a sleeping Georgie in his arms.

Rex looked up, trying to read the man's face. Mr. Riley nodded. "He'll be fine. Just be patient and kind until he settles in."

Anxiety clutched at Rex as he watched the man walk down the hallway and take Georgie to his room. Patient he could be, and kind. But how could he soothe the gnawing feeling that what he was about to do was all wrong?

Seven

A imee flopped onto her bed and tossed aside the telegram she'd just received from Uncle Hank and Aunt Rosemary. The children at the orphanage were asking about her. When was she coming back? They loved her and missed her.

Veiled behind the polite urgency, Aimee knew her aunt and uncle were asking the question, "Are you coming back at all?" They needed her. Desperately.

Over the past six years, the orphanage had grown in capacity. They'd built onto the house, adding four new bedrooms, each of which held four children, sometimes as many as six.

Now a mother of twin redheaded boys, Rosemary relied on Aimee's help more than ever. Aimee's trips to the farm nearly did her poor aunt in.

Aimee glanced at the telegram. How could she answer when she had no idea whether or not she was coming back? She loved the children. And though she missed the city and her aunt and uncle, how could she live just blocks away from Georgie and not rush to his side, begging Rex to allow her to see her son?

It had been three days since Rex left with her son. Her body ached from very little food or sleep, and her eyes were red and puffy from hours upon hours of weeping. Rex had taken Georgie while the little boy slept, in the wee hours of the morning. He'd rented a wagon to take them home rather than deal with temper tantrums on the stage.

She couldn't blame him, but she wondered how Georgie had felt when he woke up in a swaying wagon with a man he'd only met days before. He hadn't even been given the opportunity to kiss his mommy good-bye. It was all too much for such a little boy. Too much for his mother.

Tears welled up again. If only she could have held him once more. But Rex had been firm. Not unkind, but resolute. Feeling a fresh wave of sobs coming on, Aimee buried her face in a fluffy feather pillow and gave in to the tears.

"Aimee Riley, I have had just about enough of your moping about!"

Aimee's head shot up at the sound of her ma's voice. The usually mild-mannered Star Riley stood in the doorway.

"Ma?"

Her violet eyes snapped as she stalked into the bedroom with purpose. "That boy needs his mother. What are you going to do about it?"

"There's nothing I can do, Ma. The law is on Rex's side. No judge would give Georgie to me when his own father wants him."

"I'm not talking about the law. I'm talking about the heart and what's right. Now that boy is part of this family. Do you think I would have let anyone waltz in and take you away from me? No sirree. I would have fought like a she-wolf to keep my girl."

Aimee bristled under the criticism but kept a respectful tone. "That's different. You and Pa were married."

"True. But you and Georgie have six years of shared love and memories together." Ma leaned forward. "And don't underestimate Rex's feelings. That man lit up like a Roman candle every time you walked in the room. He's smitten."

"He doesn't want to marry me." Aimee retrieved her hankie from her sleeve and blew her nose. "He wants to marry for true love."

"Who says he should marry for anything less? But if you hide away here, he'll never have the chance to know you, honey. You have to get back to Oregon City and keep yourself in that man's mind."

"I can't make him fall in love with me," Aimee said glumly. *If I had the ability to change anyone's feelings, Gregory wouldn't be mooning all over Cynthia right now. Of course, that wouldn't help me get my son back.*

"Aimee Riley, you have to get up and fight. Show Rex Donnelly how much he and Georgie need you."

"I don't know. . . ."

"All right, then, you leave me no choice. Just remember, I'm doing this for your own good."

Aimee frowned at her ma. "Doing what?"

"I'm tossing you out."

Laughter formed and died on Aimee's lips almost simultaneously. Staring into Ma's stony face, Aimee's jaw dropped as disbelief rushed over her. "Are you serious?"

"Yes, I am. Get your things packed and be ready to leave on the afternoon stage. You have commitments to Aunt Rosemary and Uncle Hank, and they need you. Whether or not you use that time to fight for your son is up to you."

Indignation shot through her. "Why, Pa won't stand for it!"

"That's the spirit. Remember that feeling when it comes time to fight for your son."

In the face of her ma's unrelenting demeanor, Aimee began to panic. "Grammy!" she hollered. "I need you!"

"Don't even bother. Grammy is the one who suggested it, and Pa agrees. As a matter of fact, he's waiting to drive you into Hobbs to catch the stage."

Betrayal, that's what this was. Plain and simple. They were all Judases. But even as the tears stung her eyes, a strange sense of relief flooded her now that she had no choice. The agony of indecision had been lifted.

Slowly, she rose and started to pack her belongings.

"Mr. Donnelly, I must have a word with you," the woman standing before Rex said tersely.

Rex looked up from his desk and heaved a sigh. Nine words he'd come to hate over the past three weeks. He had a swinging door when it came to nannies for Georgie. Miss Long was the sixth in a line of bewildered and frustrated women.

"Where is my son?"

"He is in the waiting area, hopefully behaving himself."

Alarm shot through Rex at the thought of the damage Georgie could do in the amount of time it would take Miss Long to draw her pay and leave his office. The boy had transformed from the enchanting son who had captured his heart into a child he didn't recognize.

Georgie refused to take a bath without bodily force, he deliberately tracked in dirt and mud, and he smeared his food on the table at every meal. In essence, he drove his nannies daft until they had no choice but to leave a position paying twice what they would make serving a family with well-behaved children. And no amount of threatening, reasoning, or begging could induce the child to amend his ways. He'd made his demands perfectly clear: He wanted his mother.

"What can I do for you, Miss Long?" As if he didn't already know. "I'm very busy."

"Yes sir. You usually are. And that's what I've come to discuss with you."

Rex perked up; perhaps this wasn't the usual resignation. "Is there something you'd like to say?"

"I'm quitting."

Rex scowled. "I understand," he said grimly. Reaching into his jacket pocket, he pulled out a few bills and handed them over.

"This should more than compensate you for your time."

Shamelessly, she counted the bills, then scrutinized him with steely eyes. "I'm going to tell you something for your own good, Mr. Donnelly."

The old spinster couldn't just quit. No, she had to remind him what a failure he was. For the sake of politeness, he dropped his pencil onto the tablet in front of him and leaned back in his chair, motioning toward a leather wingback on the other side of the desk. "If you're going to list my parental shortcomings, at least have the courtesy to sit at eye level."

She gave him a tight smile and lowered herself into the seat as though she were a queen granting favors to one of her subjects.

"What can I do for you?"

"You're a good man, Mr. Donnelly. One doesn't dispute that. But when you take a child to raise, you must spend time with that child. The boy is lonely."

"I am spending as much time with him as possible. Running a law office is a lot of work. Particularly when I'm doing it alone."

"Raising a child is also a lot of work. Imagine how happy the child would be if you spent as much time playing with him, teaching him, loving him as you do nurturing your business."

"Believe me, there is nothing I'd rather do than make a career of caring for my son. Unfortunately, life doesn't work that way."

"Perhaps you are right. But surely a few minutes of your attention each day to let the boy know his father loves him isn't too much to ask."

Her words made a lot of sense, and he conceded to feeling the same things. But how could he find the time? "Miss Long, thank you for your candor. I believe I'll take the rest of the day off. Perhaps my son would enjoy a walk in the park."

Miss Long's face broke into a smile. She handed him the bills he'd paid her. "I believe payday is still a week from now."

"I don't understand."

"You're a fine man. I can see you are trying. I've decided to give you another chance. An unruly child I can tame; an uncaring parent is beyond my limitations."

Relief shifted through him, and it was all he could do not to scramble across the desk and kiss her weathered cheek in gratitude. Knowing that wouldn't be appreciated, he simply offered her his hand. "I can't express my gratitude. You'll find a nice bonus in your pay envelope next week."

She stood and briefly shook his hand, then smoothed down her skirt as though embarrassed that she'd touched him. "That will not be necessary. The agreed-upon salary is more than generous."

Shaking his head in amazement, Rex watched her leave his office. He straightened the papers on his desk and walked across the room.

In the lobby, his secretary glanced up in surprise. "Sir?" Wilson said. "Mr. Crighton from Crighton and Shiveley is here to speak to you."

Rex grimaced. How could he have forgotten this important meeting? Mr. Crighton was an old friend of Father's. He'd left New York ten years earlier and had made quite a name for himself in Oregon City. Now he wanted to discuss a merger. Rex glanced toward the waiting room. The stern-looking man sat next to Georgie. "What is my son still doing here?"

"Your nanny said he was to stay," Wilson said, "because you're taking him to the park."

How could he have forgotten in only a few minutes? Panic swelled. He'd have to postpone the outing for a couple of hours. But Georgie could hardly be expected to wait that long. "Has she already left?"

"Yes sir. She said to tell you she will not be back until it's time to get Georgie ready for bed." A slightly amused grin tweaked the corners of Wilson's lips. "She told Georgie you and he were going to the park, so there's no getting out of it, sir."

"I don't want to 'get out of it.'" *What of Mr. Crighton?*

Wilson shrugged.

Rex stepped across to the waiting area. To his relief, Mr. Crighton's eyes were crinkled with merriment over something Georgie was telling him.

"Hello, Mr. Crighton. I see you've met my son, Georgie."

"Yes, I have. I think you may have a future attorney on your hands. The boy is quite the debater."

Dread formed a knot in Rex's stomach. "Oh?" He swallowed hard.

"Get that worried look off your face, Donnelly. I find your son delightful. He just informed me that he thinks children—not old men like me—should be judges, because it seems old men don't know what a boy wants."

"I see." Rex glowered at Georgie, who gave him a deliberately innocent look. The boy was only six? He seemed much too wise to be so young. "In regards to what?"

"I'm surprised you have to ask." The thick-waisted attorney stood and stuck out his arm to Georgie. The boy hopped off the chair and accepted the meaty hand. Crighton chuckled. "It was a pleasure meeting you. And it just so happens that Judge Crawford is a friend of mine."

Hope lit Georgie's blue eyes. "He is?" His glance shifted from Crighton to Rex and back.

Mr. Crighton sent the boy a broad wink. "He is. I'll discuss your plight with him and see what I can do."

"Thank you, sir."

Rex scowled. "I suppose I'm going to get your bill for representing my son."

Throwing back his head and revealing a thick neck, Mr.

Crighton howled. "You just might."

"Wilson," Crighton called across the room, "reschedule my appointment with Mr. Donnelly. He has something much more important to do than to talk merger with me."

A light glowed through Rex. "Thank you, sir."

"Don't thank me. I have three sons of my own who barely know me and couldn't care less if I live or die. I only wish I'd taken off a few days to take them to the park when they were little."

Georgie tugged at Crighton's coat. "Do you want to go to the park with us?"

The boy's wide eyes nearly begged the man to say yes. Rex shifted uncomfortably. Who could blame Georgie? He barely knew Rex, and they'd seen very little of each other in the past three weeks.

Mr. Crighton smiled at the boy and ruffled his mop of hair. "Another time."

Georgie's disappointment was more than evident in his drooping chin as Mr. Crighton left the office.

"Well Georgie, shall we go?"

The boy shrugged and wordlessly walked to the door. He stopped and turned, his face red with anger. "I want to go home."

"You mean instead of to the park? I guess we could play soldiers or something."

"Not your home. Me and Bandit want to go home to the orphanage."

"But your m—I mean, Miss Riley isn't there."

"She'll come if she knows I'm there."

"Georgie. . ." Rex crouched down before his son and met him at eye level. "How about if you go visit your friends there?"

The boy's eyes lit up with hope. "You mean it?"

Rex nodded. Maybe he was doing something right after all. Since Aimee had stayed at the farm, he wouldn't have to worry about Georgie throwing too big of a temper tantrum when it was time to leave. "We can go right now if you want."

Georgie's face split with the first smile Rex had received since bringing his son home. A light heart guided Rex to a cab and remained with him while Georgie chattered incessantly about the children at the orphanage. Children who were like brothers and sisters to him. His light heart continued while he paid the cabbie, walked to the door of the orphanage, and watched while Georgie burst inside without knocking.

"Auntie Rose!" he shouted. "I'm home!"

"Georgie!" A plump woman bustled into the room. She grabbed him up and squeezed. "It's so good to see you. Aimee! Come quick. Georgie's here!"

As in a nightmare, Rex watched while Aimee ran into the room.

"Oh, thank You, Lord," she gasped and opened her arms.

"Ma!"

Rex swallowed hard past a lump in his throat. Before him, wrapped in each other's arms, stood the perfect picture of a mother and son.

Georgie would never forgive him when it was time to leave the orphanage.

What had he done?

Eight

Georgie's chubby arms nearly strangled Aimee, but she welcomed the sweet pain—reveled in the soft warmth of his little body, the scent of his hair. She looked over his shoulder to thank Rex for bringing the child, then understanding dawned. From the scowl on Rex's face, he was anything but glad to see her.

Georgie pulled away, his face shining. "Father brought me to play with the children." He turned his smile on Rex. "You see? I told you she'd come to the orphanage if I did."

"So you did, son."

Aimee could see Rex was doing his best to show a lighthearted demeanor—and that he was struggling immensely to accomplish the task. She stood with a sigh. Obviously he hadn't seen the light and brought Georgie back to her, as she'd hoped. "Georgie, the children are in the kitchen having lunch. Would you care to join them?"

"Yes ma'am." He dashed toward the kitchen, then came to an abrupt stop and wheeled about. "Will you come, too?"

"I'll be there in a minute. I'd like to talk to your father first. And Georgie, please walk to the kitchen. Remember, we do not run in the house."

The lad continued at a more restrained pace.

Aimee turned back to Rex, surprised to see a look of bemusement on his face.

"What is it, Mr. Donnelly?" Funny how she'd called him Rex numerous times at home, had cried in his arms and even almost kissed him, but she now found it difficult to call him by his given name.

Once Georgie disappeared through the kitchen door, Rex turned his focus back on her. He shrugged. "I find it amusing how quickly he obeyed you. After my boasting that I'd be better at disciplining him, the boy has been a challenge for his nannies."

"Nannies? How many does he have?"

"Oh, only one at a time. It's just that they come and go rather quickly." He gave a self-mocking grin. "When you're not around, he's quite a little terror. You sure you won't reconsider the job? I pay quite well."

Aimee bristled. "First of all, let me assure you my son is not, nor could he possibly ever be, a 'terror.' Secondly, I am his mother, not his nanny. I sincerely hope that one day you'll understand that you can't just rip a child away from everything he holds dear."

"I won't debate you on the second point, but I can say with great conviction that the boy is most definitely unruly and, in fact, quite destructive."

"Well, that is no doubt your fault. What did you expect when you callously uprooted him with no regard to how he might feel about the matter?"

"I didn't uproot him callously, no matter what you might think. I knew how difficult it would be for him to leave you and your family. But children do not know what's in their own best interests. That's what parents are for. To make the right decisions."

"The right decisions? You don't even know Georgie. How can you say what's best for him?"

Rex narrowed his gaze, anger flashing from sapphire-blue eyes. "I am his father. Like it or not, Aimee, the child belongs to me. I loved his mother, and she would have wanted me to raise our son."

"Perhaps," Aimee said, despising the tears just behind her eyes, burning, threatening to spill over any second. "But don't you think a mother would understand the longings of another woman? After all, what might have become of Georgie if I hadn't taken him in to raise as my own?"

Rex slapped his thigh in frustration.

Aimee jumped, but he didn't seem to notice her reaction to his sudden movement.

"I don't know what more you expect of me! I've offered you a position whereby you are allowed to raise him, see to his needs, give him the love he desperately needs from a mother." He stared at her for a moment, then gave a reflective nod. "But then, that's not really fair to you, is it?"

The tears burst through and spilled over as she shook her head. "More important, it isn't fair to him. To have his mother not really be his mother. Nor is it fair to you, Mr. Donnelly."

"Please, call me Rex," he said softly, fishing his handkerchief from his pocket. He stepped forward and handed it to her.

"Thank you."

"Why isn't it fair to me?" he asked.

Heat warmed her cheeks, and she averted her gaze to her boots. "You may decide to remarry someday. When you take a new wife, you'll have no need of me or any other nanny. His new stepmother would provide his care."

"Just for the record," he drawled, "I have no immediate plans for marriage. And if I did, I would never throw you out. You would always have your place with Georgie."

She smiled at his naivete. Did he really think a new bride would allow a child's foster mother to remain in the home as competition for her stepchild's affection? And possibly her husband's? But of course, she couldn't be so bold as to suggest his possible future wife would be a jealous shrew (though she couldn't imagine the fantasy bride to be anything but). She decided to take another, just as viable, route to the same conclusion. "Do you believe Georgie would ever give another woman a chance to mother him with me in his life? It wouldn't be fair to your wife. So you see, it's just a bad idea for everyone concerned."

He raked a hand through his hair. "I suppose you're right." He stared at her, his eyes narrowing. "How long have you been back at the orphanage?"

"Two weeks."

He raised a brow. "And you haven't attempted contact with Georgie?"

"I've watched him playing in his yard several times. But no, I have not tried to contact him. I love him too much to put him through the separation again."

He didn't react to the fact that she obviously knew where Georgie lived and had been watching him. "So perhaps I've done more harm than good by bringing him here."

"I don't know, Rex."

"But what do you think? As the one who has raised him so far?"

"I feel a slower withdrawal would be better. Less traumatic."

He nodded slowly. "Perhaps I should bring him around a few times a week and allow him to play with his friends. And see you of course."

Joy rose on a tide of hope. She clenched her hands together and forced herself to remain calm. "Whatever you think best."

A wry grin twisted his perfect lips. "How generous of you."

She shrugged, irritated by his mockery. "You already know what I think. I'd keep him here indefinitely if it were up to me."

He moved closer, lowering his voice. "If I allow these visits, you realize they're only for a short time, right? I will be introducing him to children who move in my circles as well. He will begin school next fall with children of privilege. I will provide him with lessons to teach him to be a gentleman. This arrangement and his association with orphaned children will only be temporary."

Aimee didn't trust herself to speak. If she did, she'd tell him that Georgie would never be a snob. That he had been taught that all men were created equal. Just because he now had a father of circumstance didn't mean he would abandon those values. She had a year to reinforce those ideals, and she had every intention of getting started as soon as possible.

Rex's expression softened, and he reached forward, fingering a lock of her hair that had come loose. "You're a very pretty woman, Aimee Riley. If I dared, I'd try to claim that kiss after all."

Indignation filled her. "Don't you dare." As she jerked away, pain shot through her temple. "Ow!"

"Your hair's woven around my finger. Don't move." He uncurled the lock and let her go. "Such beautiful hair. It's a shame to keep it up."

Aimee gave a sniff. "It's so unruly I can barely get a comb through it. If I leave it down, it turns into something resembling a rag mop. Not a pretty image, is it?"

He chuckled. "I guess not."

Awkward silence fell between them. "Would you like to sit down awhile, Rex?"

"I don't think so. I'll be back to get Georgie at five."

Disappointment shifted through her. "You don't want to stay? The children play baseball and blind man's bluff after lunch. It's quite entertaining."

"I have work to do."

Aimee followed him down the hallway.

At the door he paused and turned, a pensive expression softening his features. "Life is never as easy as we'd like it to be, is it?"

"Sometimes we make it harder than it has to be."

His face hardened. "For instance?"

"For instance, how foolish for a woman to hold on for fifteen years hoping a man will fall in love with her, when she knows he never will."

His lips curled into a heart-stopping smile. "I'd venture to say you're also referring to the hardships I make for myself."

She gave him a frank look. "I guess so."

"Please, speak freely."

"All right. You complain that Georgie is unruly and unhappy, yet instead of allowing yourself time to really get to know him or play with him as you did at the farm, you run off and work at every opportunity."

"Have you been watching me as well?"

Her face blazed at her slip of the tongue. "I can't help but notice that Georgie is always with other people."

"I have to work, Aimee."

"Not as much as you do." Aimee paused, gathering a breath to muster courage. She looked him square in the eye. "Do you know what I think?"

He quirked an eyebrow. "No, but I'm sure you're about to tell me."

"I think you're exactly the kind of father yours was. The kind you resented. And now you're doing the same thing to Georgie—ignoring him, letting others raise him. He needs his father!"

Anger burned in Rex's eyes, and the muscle in his jaw flinched. "Oh? And I thought all he needed was his mother." He slammed through the door and stalked down the walk.

Self-righteous, sanctimonious, know-it-all, interfering woman!

And absolutely right.

He hated to admit being wrong. But in this case he had no choice. He was raising the boy exactly like his father had raised him. But not for the reasons Aimee supposed. Mostly because the child hated him. Things would be different if Georgie begged him to stay home, laughed with glee when he was present the way he did with Aimee. If he said even just a few endearing words, Rex would move heaven and earth to spend as much time as possible with his son. But Georgie resented Rex's presence. He showed indifference and sometimes downright hostility any time Rex suggested reading a book or playing catch. Even hide-and-seek held no appeal.

In short, the child wanted nothing to do with his father, regardless of Miss Long's opinion, Mr. Crighton's admonishment, or Aimee's insistence. Rex despised the idea of Georgie growing up lonely. But the boy was giving him no choice. This boycott could not be tolerated. The most Rex would allow was a more gradual withdrawal from the people of Georgie's past. But as soon as the school term began next year, all that would be behind him. His son would have to accept the inevitable.

"Father!"

Georgie? Rex frowned. Surely not. He turned and swallowed hard. Georgie was running down the walk toward him. "What's wrong, son?"

The boy glared at him, his eyes accusing. "Where are you going? I thought we were spending the day here."

Rex's heart leapt in his throat. "I thought you'd like to spend some time alone with your friends."

"Don't you want to play baseball?"

"I. . ." For the first time in a very long time, he didn't have a reply to an outright question. "Do you want me to?"

"Sure. We could use another man. The girls are whipping us."

A grin began deep inside Rex's heart and quickly spread to his face as he slipped his arm about his son's shoulders. "We can't have that, can we?"

"No sir. They always win."

"Think they'll let a grown-up play?"

He shrugged. "We let Ma play sometimes, but she can't hit the ball. She can catch pretty good though."

As Rex reentered the house, he realized Georgie had just spoken more words to him in the last couple of minutes than he'd spoken in three weeks. Not only that, but his son wanted him to play baseball with him. He knew one thing for certain: He was going to do everything short of cheating or hurting someone to make sure the girls lost this game.

Nine

The days grew shorter as late summer turned into a gloriously refreshing autumn. And Aimee's sorrow had turned to joy. Her son was back in her arms. For now, anyway, and she refused to think about what might happen when Rex decided Georgie was ready for the final break.

The apple harvest was upon them, and the children nearly buzzed with excitement as six wagons lined the street in front of their home.

The yearly trip out of town to Haley's apple orchard was the highlight of the fall season. Mr. Haley gave the children all the leftover apples, the ones that had fallen and even some still on the trees. Anything the orphanage was willing to haul away. The man even gave them the use of several wagons and a driver for each. They would make an all-day event of it, complete with a picnic lunch.

"Is Pa here yet?" Georgie's repeated question was beginning to get on Aimee's nerves.

"For the tenth time, Georgie, he'll be here in a few minutes."

"How many is a few?"

She smiled. It was a fair question.

"I'm not sure. More than two, less than sixty."

Georgie kicked at the floor with his boot. "Aw, he's not coming. I bet he forgot."

"I'm sure that's not the case, Georgie."

Aimee sighed. The truth of the matter was that she, too, was beginning to wonder if he'd ever show up. Georgie had stayed at the orphanage last night to experience the excitement of the preparations for today. Rex had promised to arrive by ten, but it was already ten thirty and there was no sign of him. The horses were getting antsy and so were the children. And quite frankly, so was Aimee.

"What do you think we should do?" Uncle Hank entered the room, his jerky steps an indication of his impatience.

"I suppose if Rex shows up and we're not here, he'll just come out to the orchard."

"Do you agree we should go ahead and leave, then?"

"I think so." She said, glancing at Georgie. His brow furrowed.

"I'm sorry, Georgie. I'm sure he'll be along later. Something must have kept him."

Georgie shrugged. "I don't care, anyway."

Aimee wanted to shake Rex! How could he disappoint his son this way?

They piled the children into the wagons and slowly headed through the streets. The bustle of getting all the children situated had left Aimee flustered, and she was glad to be sitting next to the driver of her wagon. She gathered in a deep, cleansing breath when they left the city behind.

The wagons jostled over rutted roads and grassy fields until finally coming to a stop at the orchard. Row after row of sweet-smelling trees lined the fields. The children tumbled out of the wagons. Excited chatter filled the air.

Aimee looked around, searching for Georgie among the little people milling about grabbing baskets, crates, and burlap bags from the wagons. Her heartbeat picked up.

"Auntie Rose, have you seen Georgie?"

Her aunt shook her head. "Didn't he ride with you?"

"I thought he was with you."

"It'll be all right. Hank! Have you seen Georgie?"

"Didn't he ride with Aimes?"

Panic began to gnaw a hole in Aimee's gut. Where was he? He must have been left behind.

"I'll go back for him," Uncle Hank offered.

Aimee placed a restraining hand on his arm. "I'll go." She climbed into the closest wagon. "Pray, Uncle Hank!"

Rex eyed the clock once more. His stomach sank. The wagons must have gone by now. This meeting was lasting forever. Mr. Crighton sat before him along with the other partners. Papers had to be gone over, signed, everything made official for the merger to take place. Mr. Shiveley's long-winded speech about expectations and the best way to work together had droned on and on until Rex had to fight the urge to jump up and ask the man to sit down and shut up.

He hoped Aimee and Georgie would understand. Rex had no choice but to stay and finish the merger. Business was business. Regardless of what he preferred to be doing.

He tapped his finger on the table and waited for the last of the men to sign the papers. Finally, Mr. Crighton glanced up and smiled. "I think that concludes things. Congratulations. And gentlemen, welcome to the law offices of Crighton, Shiveley, and Donnelly."

Rex stood. He offered a general nod. "I'm delighted to have the opportunity to work with such a distinguished group. But if you'll excuse me, I have to be somewhere."

Mr. Crighton shook Rex's hand. "Taking my advice and spending time with that little fellow of yours?"

"Yes sir. I'm late, to tell you the truth."

"Then by all means, don't let me keep you." Crighton chuckled. "Tell Georgie I'm still working on his case."

Rex sent him a wry grin. "Sure will."

Fifteen minutes later, his heart sank as stared at the two-story Victorian home that served as an orphanage. By the lack of activity, he realized the group had left without him. With a defeated sigh, he climbed out of the cab and paid the driver.

"Shall I wait, sir?"

"No thanks. I'll walk."

Dejectedly, Rex strode up to the porch and sat, wishing for all he was worth that he'd arrived thirty minutes sooner. Suddenly he felt just as he had when he was a child, watching the schoolyard children play and run while he was forced to endure tutors and eventually a private boy's academy. Alone while everyone else had fun. He had been looking forward to orchard day with more anticipation than he had realized. Now, where excitement had once danced lay a heavy lump of disappointment.

He stood, stuffing his hands into his pockets, and trudged down the steps, wishing that he'd postponed the meeting.

"Father!"

Sucking in a cold breath, Rex whipped around in time to brace himself as Georgie flung into his arms. "I knew you'd come. I just knew it!"

Rex grabbed him in a tight hold. "I was sure you'd gone. I'm so glad I didn't miss you."

He held the boy at arm's length and looked him in the eye, smiling at the way Georgie beamed at him. Because of him. His heart thrilled at the realization that his very presence had caused his son's present happiness.

After the immediate surge of joy, Rex glanced about. "Where is everyone?"

Georgie averted his gaze to the ground. "They left."

"They left you all alone?"

He nodded. "I wanted to wait for you."

"Your mother agreed to that?"

Georgie nodded. "She said once you got here you would ride out to the orchard and catch up with the wagons."

Rex had never felt such indignation amid rising fear of what might have come of leaving a six-year-old boy alone.

What if the meeting had gone on for another two hours? What if he'd decided it was too late and had simply gone home? Georgie would have been left with no one to fix him lunch.

"Come on, Georgie. Let's go rent a horse and we'll ride out and join your mother."

He had plenty to say to Aimee.

Anger burned in Rex as Georgie slumped against him in the wagon, lulled to sleep by the swaying horse. When he saw a wagon coming toward him and recognized the driver, he reined in the mare.

Aimee halted her wagon next to his. "Thank goodness you found him," she said in breathless relief. "I was so worried."

"There would have been no cause for worry if you hadn't left him alone in the first place."

Her jaw dropped, and hurt flashed in her eyes, followed by a glint of anger. "How dare you criticize me?" She jerked the reins around the brake and jumped down, her petticoats flashing.

Rex turned his head to avoid allowing his focus to linger on her calf. When he turned back, she was standing next to his wagon, determination in her stance. "Give me Georgie. I'll put him in the wagon."

Stubbornness shot through him. "He's fine where he is. Perhaps I can protect him better than you can."

"You? You can't even be on time after you promised me—" She gathered a deep breath and began again. "—after you promised Georgie that you would be here to ride with him to the orchard." She reached up. "Give him to me."

"Maybe I didn't make it on time, but at least I thought he was safely with his mother. Not left alone to fend for himself. You are entirely too permissive with my son, Aimee."

A gasp left her, and she dropped her arms to her side. "You mean you think I left him on purpose?" Her voice squeaked.

He narrowed his gaze, trying to gauge the level of sincerity in her question. "Didn't you?"

"Of course not! What kind of mother do you think I am?"

Sickening reality formed a knot in Rex's stomach. Georgie had looked him in the eye and told him a bold-faced lie without even flinching a muscle.

Aimee's face blanched. "You mean he told you I left him on purpose?"

Rex nodded, his back teeth clenched so tightly he didn't trust himself to speak.

"I can't believe..." She glanced at Georgie, and her face twisted into a scowl. "All right, young man. I know you're not really asleep. Open your eyes this instant and be prepared to explain."

Aimee wanted to shake the child for causing such an unnecessary upset between her and Rex. Georgie opened his eyes slowly, his trepidation evident in the wide blue pools.

"What do you have to say for yourself?" she demanded.

He turned his gaze to his pudgy fingers.

"Look at me," Aimee said. "If you can tell a bold lie, you can at least have the gumption to face the truth once you're caught."

"I just wanted my pa to come with us."

Rex's arm tightened around the boy. Aimee bristled, knowing Georgie's admission had softened his father's outrage considerably. She needed to separate them quickly if Georgie was going to be properly disciplined for this infraction. She huffed. *And Rex accuses me of being too permissive.*

"Come down here."

This time Rex made no objection as she reached for Georgie and pulled him from the wagon. She grunted beneath the child's weight and set him on his feet.

"Why did you sneak off without getting in one of the wagons? I was frantic." A sob caught in her throat. "Sweetheart, I thought I'd lost you. I was very, very afraid."

"I'm sorry, Ma," he mumbled. "I was afraid Pa might not know where the orchard is."

It didn't escape Aimee's notice that for the second time Georgie had called Rex "Pa" rather than "Father." One look at Rex, and she realized that he, too, understood the implications. Georgie was finally settling into the relationship. Disappointment edged through Aimee's stomach. There would be no turning back now. The boy loved this man. Even if Rex decided to give Georgie back to her, the poor thing would be devastated. *Oh Lord. What is the answer?*

Rex dismounted and stood beside Aimee. "Georgie, don't you know that it's wrong to lie?"

Aimee fumed. Of course the child knew he wasn't supposed to lie. Did Rex think she had completely shirked her duty as a mother?

The child's lip trembled. "I'm sorry," he said, tears thick in his voice.

"All right," Aimee said, "you're forgiven. But remember, lying is wrong." She glanced at Rex. "May he ride with me?"

"Wait a minute. That's it?"

Aimee blinked. "What do you mean?"

"What about his punishment?"

Anxiety bit through Aimee. Was Rex going to beat Georgie? He'd promised not to harm him.

"He feels bad for lying. Is there a reason for further punishment?"

"Of course there is." Rex hunkered down and met Georgie at eye level. "Do you understand that what you did was wrong?"

Georgie nodded as large tears rolled down his cheeks.

Aimee's heart melted. "You see? He's suffered enough."

Rex whipped around and glared her to silence. He returned his attention to Georgie. "Do you understand that when you do something wrong, you have to be punished?"

"Yes sir." Georgie's voice quaked, and he looked miserable.

"All right. For your punishment, you will not be allowed to play at the orphanage for a month."

Aimee gasped. Not come to the orphanage? Didn't Rex realize that by meting out such a punishment, he was also punishing her?

As if sensing her thoughts, Rex turned and captured her gaze. He gathered a deep breath. "Your mother will come to our house for visits during that time."

Worry edged through Aimee, and she nibbled her lip. She had purposely avoided visiting at Rex's house. She didn't want to grow accustomed to a feeling of camaraderie between herself and Rex. Not in his home. How could she keep herself from wanting to belong there if she ate meals there, tucked her son into bed there, sipped tea in the sitting room? A shudder crawled down her spine. How on earth would she guard her heart?

Ten

Frustration swelled inside Rex as he stared down at a furious Aimee. The woman irritated him to no end.

Pacing the hallway outside Georgie's bedroom, she glared, her brown eyes flashing to almost black in the flicker of lamplight above her head. "I don't see why you're being so stubborn about this," she fairly exploded. "Three weeks is long enough punishment when a holiday is at stake. He should be allowed to come home for Thanksgiving."

The woman just didn't know when to stop. Rex knew he'd have to be firm. "First of all, need I remind you that this is his home? Secondly, I said one month and I meant one month."

"You—you're just. . .mean." She whipped around, stomping furiously down the steps toward the front door.

He caught her just before she could scurry away into the night. "Where do you think you're going?" he demanded, pulling her back inside.

"Home!"

"Just like that? In the dark all by yourself?"

"It's preferable to one more second in your company!"

"Be that as it may, you are not going out in the dark alone." Reaching above her, he pushed the door shut. "It's cold outside, and you don't even have your shawl. You'll get sick."

"For all you'd care."

He glared down at her and pointed his index finger. "Wait here. I mean it." He rang the bell for his driver. Almost instantly, Mr. Marlow appeared. "Yes sir?"

"The carriage, please. Miss Riley is ready to go home."

Marlow nodded. "I'll bring it around directly."

"Thank you."

Marlow was an efficient and conscientious employee. Rex had hired him just after purchasing his own horses and carriage. He figured Aimee would be more comfortable this way than riding in hired cabs. Now he wondered why he'd ever bothered to consider her comfort. She was much too spoiled in the first place.

He glanced sternly at her, as though she were a petulant child. "I will escort you home like a gentleman."

She gave an incredibly unpleasing snort, but clamped her lips together, obviously refusing to speak to him.

"Well, isn't that characteristic of you?" With grim satisfaction, Rex noted the way her eyes flickered with curiosity.

"What's that supposed to mean?" she asked.

"Oh, just that your behavior is all too predictable."

"It is not."

"Yes it is. I could have predicted that you'd stop speaking to me and pout like a child all the way home. You do that any time you don't get your way."

Her eyebrows drew together, and her cheeks turned a beguiling pink. "I most certainly do not pout."

"Well, we won't belabor the point."

She silently fumed until Marlow rang the bell, signaling the carriage was ready. Aimee deliberately ignored Rex's offered hand of assistance and instead struggled with her skirts in an undignified climb into the leather seat.

"You could always have Thanksgiving with us, you know," he suggested.

She cocked an eyebrow at him. "Aren't you afraid that having his mother with him will make him too happy? We wouldn't want to undo any of that punishment, now, would we?"

Rex rolled his eyes. The woman was just gunning for a fight.

He'd made a legitimate offering of peace. Compromise. So why the argument?

He shrugged. "It's your choice."

Aimee clasped her hands in her lap and turned her gaze toward him. "I suppose you're generous to offer, feeling as strongly as you do about Georgie's punishment." The fury on her face softened in the moonlight streaming through the carriage windows. "Thank you. I accept."

Her head rested against the side of the carriage, and she stared out into the street.

"It's starting to rain again," she mused softly.

"Yes."

"I've always loved the rain. As a little girl I would stay awake and listen to the raindrops outside above my head. I would imagine there were angels tiptoeing on the roof."

Rex scarcely breathed as she spoke, giving him a rare glimpse into her thoughts. "I didn't know angels tiptoed."

Aimee grinned. "Of course they do."

"Then what are their wings for?"

Aimee stuck out her tongue. "Don't try to sully my childhood memories."

A chuckle rumbled in Rex's chest. "Sorry."

"Rex, why can't you relent just this once and allow Georgie his holiday with us? I'm sure you'll have a nice dinner at your house, but Georgie will want to be with all of his friends."

Bitter disappointment slammed into Rex's gut. He'd been a fool not to realize she was only being civil as a means to an end. "Woman! I said what I meant and I meant what I said. Now let it go."

A gasp escaped her milky-white throat. "Don't call me 'woman' like that, as if. . ."

His curiosity was piqued. "As if what?"

She jerked her chin toward the window. "Never mind."

A shrug lifted his shoulders. "Suit yourself."

She sighed. "As if I were your woman. Sometimes I think we act like a married couple. I think it confuses Georgie."

Her quiet reflection disarmed Rex. He moved across to sit next to her in the seat. "It confuses me, too, Aimes."

She turned to him, placing a gloved hand on his cheek. "This must be as difficult for you as it is for me. I can imagine how you feel. Loving your son and not wanting to take him away from the mother he loves, and yet. . ." She let the sentence hang in the air as Marlow halted the carriage in front of the orphanage. "I do understand you sticking to your guns about the punishment." Her lips trembled. "You are the better parent."

He covered her hand with his. "That's not true, honey. I'm stronger in the area of discipline. But you're stronger in other areas. That must be why God designed families to have two parents. Where one is weak, the other is strong."

"Perhaps," she said softly, reaching for the door.

Rex placed his hand over hers on the handle. "Let me, Aimee."

She slipped her fingers from his. Rex was keenly aware of their close proximity. He pressed his forehead to hers and cupped her head. "Do you think there is any hope for us?"

"W–what do you mean?"

Rex pulled back and studied her. Her eyes remained closed, as though she couldn't quite face him. Her lips, full and slightly parted, beckoned to him. He resisted with difficulty.

Was he falling in love with her, or did his affection stem solely from a desire to keep the woman Georgie looked to as his mother in their lives?

She opened her eyes and stared for a moment as though reading his thoughts. A sad smile curved her lips. "Good night, Rex."

Moving back, he opened the door and climbed out in front of

her. This time, she accepted his help.

"Will you have Thanksgiving dinner with Georgie and me?"

"That would be wonderful."

"I give the servants all holidays off, so I can't promise much of a meal."

Aimee laughed, the rich sound filling the night and lifting Rex's spirits. "How about if you supply the food and I come over early on Thanksgiving and do the cooking?"

"Sounds like a good idea." Rex grinned.

It wasn't until he left her at the door that he realized the implications of having her in his home, cooking a meal for him, and sharing the holiday with their son. Was he ready for this? Was she?

Aimee opened the oven door and smiled in satisfaction at the golden-brown turkey. A lovely fragrance wafted throughout the kitchen. She inhaled deeply, glad that she was adept in the kitchen.

"Smells wonderful in here."

Rex's sudden presence in the room and his compliment caused a rush of heat to flood Aimee's cheeks, and she was glad for the warmth of the oven to mask her flush.

"Here, let me get that." Rex reached forward and took the two towels from her. "Step back so you don't get burned."

A smile tugged at Aimee's lips as Rex pulled the turkey from the oven and set it atop the stove. He turned to her, and his boyish grin bespoke pride in his accomplishment. He looked so much like Georgie at that moment that Aimee nearly lost her breath.

"Thank you, Rex," she said.

"Shall I call Georgie to the dinner table?"

"Do you mind if we eat in the kitchen rather than the dining room?" Eating at the enormous table in a large, open room seemed much too impersonal for a holiday meal with only three participants.

He shrugged. "Why not?"

Aimee watched him leave. Then she set about carrying the food to the table. By the time Rex returned with Georgie, the kitchen table was laden with holiday fare.

Georgie's eyes grew large. "Are all the children coming?" he asked.

Aimee drew her lip between her teeth. "I suppose I made too much."

"Cook will be making turkey pie for a week," Rex said with a short laugh.

He nodded at Georgie. Aimee frowned at the look that passed between them. She was even more perplexed when Georgie walked around the table and pulled out her chair.

"This is for you, Ma," he said, pride shining in his eyes.

Aimee glanced up at Rex. He sent her a wink. "He's learning to be a gentleman."

"I see." She smiled at Georgie and took the seat he offered. "Thank you," she said. "You did that just right."

Pride swelled in her chest as she watched her son fairly strut to his own seat.

"Let's say the blessing," Rex suggested.

They bowed their heads, and Rex prayed over the meal. After the "amen," he looked up. "Shall I carve the turkey?"

"Not yet," Georgie said. "First we have to say what we're thankful for."

"Oh. Is that what you do at the orphanage?" he asked.

Aimee smiled as Georgie nodded his blond head. "Yes. We start with the youngest. So that's me."

"Definitely you," Rex said. "Go ahead."

"I'm thankful for my dog, Bandit. And for Ma and the orphanage." He hesitated and looked at Aimee as though asking permission.

She nodded and winked.

Georgie turned his gaze to Rex. "And I'm thankful to have a pa."

Rex swallowed hard, and Aimee knew he was fighting back tears. Her own emotions were rising to the surface, so she could well imagine how he felt.

Rex cleared his throat. "You next," he said, casting his gaze upon her.

"Well, I'm thankful that I'm having Thanksgiving dinner with my son. I'm thankful for a wonderful family and for all the children at the orphanage." She paused and turned her gaze on Rex. As he returned her stare, his jaw tightened. "I'm thankful that God allowed Georgie's father to find him so that Georgie can have the pa he has always wanted."

The knot of tension in his jaw relaxed, and tenderness filled Rex's eyes. "And I am thankful for my son, Georgie."

Georgie squirmed and beamed.

"I'm also thankful that my son has had a mother like Aimee to love him all those years when I couldn't be around."

Somehow, the joy Aimee had felt at all the words of thanks diminished. Rex's gratitude had been expressed in past tense. Aimee had the uncomfortable feeling that he might be telling her that Georgie's time with her was coming to an end.

Eleven

"But we always have Christmas at the orphanage," Georgie argued with his father. "Ma and Auntie Rosemary bake apple turnovers and make new shirts. And everyone gets a new pair of boots." Georgie grinned. "Shiny new."

Rex looked at his son across the breakfast table and knew he needed to tread carefully. If his Georgie had been raised with him, as he should have been, the child would have been accustomed to dozens of toys, covered in gold and silver packages with red bows. Whatever he desired. It nearly broke his heart to see his son so excited over a new pair of boots. "Do you get any toys?"

"Oh sure! One year I got a fishing pole. Once I even got a jackknife, but I hardly ever use it. Uncle Hank bought me a Bible last year, but that's not really a toy."

"Wouldn't you like to have a Christmas with a dozen packages under the tree, all for you?" Rex inwardly groaned at his attempt at manipulation.

Georgie's eyes flickered with interest, then he frowned. "Ma's making apple flapjacks for breakfast this Christmas."

"I know, son." For the third time, Rex attempted to reason with the boy, who couldn't seem to get it through his head that he would spend Christmas with Rex and not Aimee at the orphanage. "But we talked about this, remember? Grandmother is coming tomorrow. She's been looking forward to meeting you. I've already invited her to spend Christmas with us."

"Ma wouldn't care if she comes, too. She always says the more the merrier."

Rex could well imagine Aimee being so generous. But the

thought of Mother spending a day with a group of orphaned children. . .

He cleared his throat to avoid giving in to the sudden desire to laugh out loud. Mother wouldn't appreciate his amusement at the thought of her discomfiture. Besides, he needed to stay firm. "Grandmother would prefer to spend Christmas at our house."

"Are you sure?"

"Completely."

A frown creased Georgie's brow, then his face brightened—evidence of a formulated plan. "I could spend the day after Christmas with her."

"I'm sorry, Georgie. But you and I are going to spend Christmas at home with your grandmother Donnelly."

"But—"

"No more arguing. This decision is final." He didn't mean to sound cross, but the boy simply wouldn't listen. He came by his stubbornness honestly, so Rex couldn't really fault him for it. Still, he had to learn not to push. Aimee loved him to distraction, but she was sorely lacking in matters of discipline.

Georgie finished his breakfast in glum silence. Then he pushed back his plate and glanced up with soulful eyes. "May I be excused?"

"You may." Rex wished there was more to say. He also wished Mother hadn't telegraphed to inform them she was coming for the holidays. But he couldn't very well tell her not to come. She had every right to meet her only grandchild—the namesake of her late husband. And Georgie needed to meet her, too.

When Georgie said his prayers that night, he asked God to let Santa Claus know where he'd be spending his Christmas. Rex's heart went out to the lad. He didn't like to disappoint him. But sooner or later, Georgie was going to have to realize that he didn't belong at the orphanage with Aimee.

"I can't believe she did it again." Aimee stared in disbelief as Gregory sat in the armchair across from the fireplace, his head down. His fingers raked through his hair, which he'd allowed to grow to shoulder length as he'd worn it in his youth. "Cynthia clearly doesn't deserve you, Greg."

"I know. But I love her." His shoulders shook as he sobbed.

Aimee knelt before him and gathered him close. How could you possibly? she wanted to ask. Why love someone who constantly breaks your heart?

But she knew matters of the heart couldn't be explained in simple statements, so she let her cousin cry out his frustration and heartbreak.

When he composed himself, Greg took her hands in his. She looked into his red but still handsome face, and her heart began to race. She knew, before he formulated the words, what he was getting ready to say. "Marry me tonight, Aimee. We'll go east for a honeymoon, and when we get back home, we can continue to build up the congregation in Hobbs."

"Greg. . ."

"Please don't turn me down, my dear friend. You're all I have. I'm tired of being alone."

"What a touching proposal." A deep voice from the doorway alerted their attention. When she saw Rex, Aimee gasped and pushed to her feet. "Do say yes, Aimee. I don't see how you could resist."

"Who let you in?" Gregory grumbled.

With a dark scowl, Rex strode into the room. He looked down at Greg, his lips curled in contempt. "The lovely Cynthia jilted you again, I take it."

Aimee gasped, fury shaking her like a twister through a tree.

"How dare you come in here and insult my guest!"

With a hard glint, Rex leaned closer to her. "I'm talking to Greg. You stay out of it."

Gregory stood. "Here, now. You've no call to speak to Miss Riley in such a manner!"

Anger burned so brightly in Rex's eyes, Aimee feared he might send Gregory to the ground with a large-fisted punch in the nose.

Instead, he stood his ground, towering over Greg. "Do you honestly believe you have the right to tell anyone how to properly treat this woman? That's laughable."

Greg's face grew red.

Aimee felt heat rising in her own cheeks. "Oh Rex, why can't you just mind your own business?"

Rex turned on her. "I could, but I choose not to. Besides, you are my business, and watching you eat your heart out over this imbecile is intolerable."

"Oh." She stepped back as all intelligent thought left her.

Rex didn't seem to notice as he turned his attention back to his prey. "How comforting it must be to you, knowing that a beautiful woman is waiting in the wings just in case the one you love doesn't return your affection."

Gregory nodded, shame washing over his face. "You're right. It's not fair to Aimee." He turned to her.

Aimee fought against a sudden rise of tears.

"Aimee. . ."

She knew that regretful tone well. Too well. He was rescinding the proposal—again. Humiliation and anger created a battle inside her. "Get out," she said through gritted teeth. "Both of you!"

"Aimee?" Greg's brows went up.

Rex laughed. He pressed a kiss to Aimee's forehead. "That's the spirit." He turned to Gregory. "Well, friend. Looks like neither of us is welcome here. How would you like to go see Georgie? You can stay at my house as long as you need to."

"Actually, I think I'd rather go home. Can you drop me at the train station?"

Rex nodded, and they headed toward the door.

Aimee moved forward quickly. "Wait, Rex. Where is Georgie? You didn't bring him?"

"He stayed home to have a French lesson."

"I see. Then. . .why did you drop by?" *Other than to destroy any hope I'll ever have of getting married.*

"Oh, yes." He fished in his jacket pocket and retrieved an envelope. "Mother is giving a dinner party and would like to invite all of my friends."

"When is it?"

"Tonight. Short notice, I know. I was supposed to deliver the invitation yesterday, but I got detained at the office until late."

Aimee gaped. "I—I couldn't possibly—"

"Of course you can. You must. Georgie will be crushed if you don't come."

"But I have nothing appropriate to wear." It was true. Her wardrobe had been sadly lacking over the past few years. Running an orphanage hardly lent itself to the need for formal gowns.

"You have nothing appropriate to wear to what?" Rosemary entered the room, her cheeks glowing, hands red and wrinkled from standing over the hot laundry tub. "Nice to see you, Rex. I see you've met Greg again." She said it with a "poor Greg" tone that made Aimee cringe in embarrassment for him.

"Good afternoon, Miss Rosemary." Obviously recognizing an ally, Rex forged ahead. "I've invited Aimee to a dinner party Mother is giving at my house."

"A dinner party? How delightful. You should go, Aimee. An evening out will do you a world of good."

"As I was explaining to Rex," Aimee said pointedly, trying to gain her own support from her aunt, "I have nothing to wear and not enough time to prepare something."

Clearly unable or unwilling to read Aimee's lack of desire to attend the function, Rosemary gave a dismissive wave. "Nonsense. A garment came through in the donation barrel just last week that I think will be perfect. Have you forgotten that I owned my own dress shop before I married your uncle? I can whip just about any gown into something suitable for any occasion."

A wicked sense of glee rose inside Aimee. Perhaps he had won, but the cost would be a great deal of worry on his part. "Oh, do you mean the bright purple taffeta gown?" She glanced at her aunt, her eyes uncommonly wide in an effort to induce the woman to play along. Indeed there had been a purple taffeta. They'd immediately cut it down for doll clothes.

Aunt Rosemary's lips twitched with amusement. "Are you thinking what I'm thinking?"

"I think so. A couple of nice big bows at the shoulders would just be lovely." She glanced back at the men, maintaining her innocent expression with effort. Greg's expression held amusement. Aimee warmed to the familiar feeling that they understood each other. They always had. Even as youths growing up together, they had been a team. Only Aimee had fallen in love, and Gregory had not.

"Purple bows?" Rex's frown said it all.

Aimee enjoyed his horrified tone immensely. "Don't you like purple, Rex?"

"Well, yes, I do, but—"

"Perfect. Now, you men run along. What time shall I be there, Rex?"

"I'll be around to escort you at seven."

"Why, don't be silly. You can't leave your own party. Uncle Hank can drive me over in the wagon."

"It's my mother's party, not mine, and I wouldn't have asked you to come if I hadn't intended to escort you myself."

"All right."

At the door, she smiled fondly at Greg. "I'm sorry about Cynthia, Greg."

He shrugged and planted a kiss on her cheek. "Serves me right. Perhaps God doesn't plan for me to marry."

Pain clenched Aimee's heart. Rex frowned, and Aimee feared he might start in on Greg again. She touched his arm. His bicep twitched and he turned to her. His expression softened as he covered her hand and nodded. Aimee swallowed hard. How could she be so aware of Rex's presence when Greg was in the same room? What on earth was wrong with her?

She slipped her hand away from Rex's warmth.

Rex turned to Greg. "Shall we go?"

Greg glanced from Rex to Aimee, his eyes cloudy with question. Aimee looked away. How could she tell Greg that she had feelings for Rex? Feelings she couldn't understand. They were...different somehow than those she experienced for Greg.

"I'll see you tonight," Rex said, tipping his black felt hat.

Aimee nodded, willing her heart to settle down.

Rex allowed Greg to precede him into the carriage, then climbed in.

"What do you say we start over?" He extended his hand.

Greg gave him a twisted grin and accepted the gesture of friendship. "I never wanted to hurt Aimee, you know."

"And yet you do it so well...and so often." Rex grimaced. So much for starting over.

"You're right of course. Aimee and I have always been a pair. I was her escort for parties and dances until Cynthia came along. I suppose she had a right to expect we'd marry someday."

"Women generally do begin to get ideas after a while."

"Is she getting ideas about you, Rex?"

Alarm shot through Rex at the blunt question. "Why would she?"

"You're escorting her to the dinner party tonight. And let's face it, you weren't very happy about my proposal. I'd say you were downright jealous."

If this man weren't a preacher... He gave a short laugh. "I think highly of Miss Riley, but only in the sense that she's been a good mother to my son."

Gregory nodded, though Rex could see the doubt lurking in his eyes. "Has it occurred to you that you are going to hurt her much more than I ever could?"

"What are you getting at?"

"We both know this arrangement with Georgie isn't going to last much longer. It can't. When you take that boy away from Aimee, she'll have nothing left to hope for."

"She's a beautiful woman. I expect she'll marry."

"When? She's already past thirty years of age."

Rex narrowed his gaze. "What are you suggesting?"

A shrug lifted his shoulders, and he shifted with the jostling of the carriage. "I saw something between the two of you."

"I admit there is a genuine affection."

"It's more than that." Greg gave him a frank assessment. "I think you're falling in love with her."

"I think you need to stick with preaching because you're not much good at matters of the heart."

Greg gave a self-mocking grin. "While it's dismally obvious that I am a failure in my own attempts at finding love, I'm surprisingly accurate when it comes to pegging other couples. And I'd say you and Aimee could be headed for something lasting if you would give it a chance."

Twelve

After a frenzied lunch, Aimee and Aunt Rosemary shooed the children who didn't attend school out to play while they worked on alterations. In the yard, Uncle Hank roared, and the childish screams of delighted terror nearly sent Aimee through the roof.

Rosemary grinned. "The bear game. That's a relief. It's a mite louder than the horse game, but at least he'll be able to walk straight in the morning. The horse game always has him doubled over with back pain for a few days."

Aimee laughed, her heart light and airy. The thought of putting on a pretty new gown and going to a dinner party lifted her spirits higher than she'd had any idea it would. She slipped out of the pinned garment so that Rosemary could begin sewing, then put on a rose-colored dressing gown. A knock sounded at the door.

She sent her aunt a pleading look.

Rosemary shook her head, cradling the new garment in her arms. "You'll have to get it, Aimee. If I move right now, all the pins will fall out."

Clutching her dressing gown modestly at the neck, Aimee walked to the door, praying whoever was on the other side wouldn't let it be known that she wasn't dressed at this time of day.

She opened the door a crack—just enough to peek outside. A gangly, blond-headed boy stood on the porch holding a large box.

"Good day, ma'am." His toothy grin covered a great deal of his face. "Got a delivery for ya."

"You must have the wrong address," she said.

He double-checked the ticket and glanced at the number

above the doorframe. "Number 111; this is the right place. Miss Riley?"

Aimee frowned. "I'm Miss Riley, but there's a mistake. I didn't order anything."

"I was told to deliver this box and not to take no for an answer."

Suspicion clouded Aimee's mind. "Who told you to deliver it?"

He hesitated.

"It's all right. You won't get into trouble. I won't tell."

"Mr. Donnelly."

Indignation shot through Aimee. "Well, you can just take it back to Mr. Donnelly."

Misery showed on the poor boy's face. "If I do, I'll lose my tip. I was going to buy my ma a whole chicken to cook. And some carrots and potatoes to go along with it. Think you could take the box and give it to him yourself?"

Aimee felt shame clear down to her bare toes. "Of course I'll take it. Wait here one minute and I'll fetch my bag."

"No thank you, ma'am. Mr. Donnelly said the money he gave me was to cover anything you might try to give me."

"Well then, it'll have to be our little secret, won't it?" She flashed him a grin, which he returned. Aimee hurried to her room, but when she returned, the boy had gone. She smiled. A youth with integrity. He'd go far in life with those ethics.

"Who was it, Aimee?" Rosemary called from the parlor.

Aimee carried the box into the room. "A delivery boy brought this. From Rex." She lifted the card, read it, and laughed.

Rosemary gave her a bemused smile. "What?"

"It says, 'I lied. I hate purple.'"

"Oh my. Maybe we shouldn't have fibbed to him, even in jest."

"We didn't exactly fib. Everything we said was true. We just sort of implied the dress we would be fixing for me was the purple taffeta." She tossed the box onto the sofa. "Clearly Rex is afraid

I'll be dressed inappropriately and doesn't want me to embarrass him in front of his mother."

Rosemary expelled an exasperated breath. "Or maybe he simply doesn't want you to be embarrassed in a roomful of socialites. You always think the worst. Especially about Rex." She nodded at the box. "Aren't you going to open it?"

Aimee planted her hands on her hips. "No. I'm not going to wear it, so there's no point."

Rosemary nodded. "I understand. But let's at least look at it. It must have come from a fancy shop." She cut her gaze to the box. "Aren't you even a little curious?"

Aimee grinned. "All right." She opened the lid and lifted a light blue gown from the box.

Rosemary drew in a breath. "Oh my. You have to wear it, Aimee. Rex obviously has feelings for you."

"How did you draw that conclusion?"

"A man doesn't buy a gown this exquisite for someone he doesn't intend to marry."

"Marry!" The idea was ludicrous. Still, Aimee's pulse quickened at her aunt's words. "Th–that's ridiculous." She fingered the lovely blue silk gown.

It didn't matter. A woman couldn't accept such an intimate gift from a man unless they were married or at the very least betrothed. That wasn't the case with Rex. He'd made it perfectly clear before they'd left her pa's farm that he wasn't interested in marrying her. This gown was only a way to save himself embarrassment.

Resolutely, she stuffed the gown back into the box and replaced the lid.

"Mercy, Aimes, you should wear the gown. It's the prettiest thing you've ever owned."

"It isn't fitting. Besides, the one you're working on is lovely as well."

"Not like that one."

"Nonsense," Aimee said stubbornly. "This one is just as lovely. Lovelier, in fact."

"You're lying again." Rosemary shook her head. "Rex isn't going to be very happy if you throw his gift back in his face."

With a shrug, Aimee forced herself to walk away from the box containing the most gorgeous gown she'd ever seen. "I couldn't care less. Really."

Aunt Rosemary gave her a dubious glance, but continued to work on the green gown. A gown that, only a few minutes ago, had made Aimee happy. Now she felt as though Christmas morning had arrived—only she'd gotten a lump of coal in her stocking instead of a nice, juicy orange.

She eyed the box longingly. Could she? No. A girl had her pride. Rex could get angry all he wanted. She didn't need him to buy her appropriate clothing. The green gown might not be as stylish or expensive as the one he'd sent over, but it was respectable and fitting for a dinner party. Rex would simply have to accept it.

Rex stood at the bottom of the steps as Aimee appeared on the landing. He studied her with a combination of relief and irritation. Relief that she wasn't wearing a purple gown with large bows sewn on the shoulders. Irritation because. . .visions of her wearing the blue gown had driven him all day.

Her shoulders squared as she descended the steps. Even in an outdated, remade gown of deep green, she took his breath away.

He smiled, and a wave of relief washed over her features. Clearly she had thought he would berate her for not wearing the dress he'd chosen for her. And if she'd decided to wear the atrocious gown she'd described earlier—more than likely as a way to horrify him—he might have insisted she march back upstairs and change. But how could a man argue with perfection?

His gaze moved over her, and his pulse quickened. A loose, upswept hairstyle showed off her mane of blond curls. Tendrils escaped, by accident or design he wasn't sure, but Rex stood mesmerized by the silken threads that brushed against her milky neck. At the base of her throat, he could just make out the pulsing of her heart.

The sight ignited his sympathy. She must be nervous about the dinner party.

He reached for her hand and led her down the last two steps. "You look lovely."

"Thank you. I'll have the other gown returned in the morning."

Rex shook his head with determination. "You'll do no such thing. It was a gift."

"A gift I cannot accept, Rex." She walked to the pegs on the wall and removed a cape that matched the gown she wore.

Rex followed her until he stood just behind her. "Here," he said softly, nearly reeling from the scent of her hair. "Allow me."

Slowly, Aimee relinquished the cape. Rex settled the wrap in place. He tightened his fingers on her slim, rounded shoulders, his forefinger testing the soft skin at the side of her neck. "Keep the gown. Wear it for me some other time."

At her sharp intake of breath, he swallowed with difficulty. She nodded and leaned back ever so slightly. Rex pulled her closer against him, closing his eyes as he took in the full effect of her scented hair.

"You're beautiful," he whispered against her ear.

"Rex, I—" Her breathy answer revealed that she, too, felt the connection between them. Something had changed in their relationship.

His mind weighed the possibilities. Aimee wasn't like the women who moved in his circles. Young girls who thought nothing of a stolen kiss—and, in fact, tried to finagle one whenever possible. A kiss would mean something to her. She would want a marriage proposal. And she would have the right to expect one.

"Rex, you're hurting my shoulder."

He released her. "I'm sorry," he said, gathering his composure. "I've never seen you so dressed up before. I'm afraid I lost my head for a few minutes."

Her cheeks bloomed with color. "I've never had an occasion to dress up before."

He smiled. "I'll have to be sure those opportunities come your way more often. You're much too lovely to keep yourself hidden away."

Her blush deepened. "Thank you, Rex."

He cleared his throat. "Shall we go?"

"Yes. Just let me tell Rosemary. She and Uncle Hank are overseeing baths. I feel a little guilty leaving them to it."

Rex waited in the foyer for her to return. He was smart enough to admit a couple of things. One, he was falling for Aimee Riley. Two, he could think of just one reason not to pursue a relationship with her, but it was a good one: She and Georgie would both be devastated if things didn't work out.

Did he dare believe that she might be a wonderful gift from God? His second chance at true love? Or was a match between them doomed to failure?

Aimee returned, her shy smile snagging his heart and twisting it with bittersweet pain. Rex offered her his arm. She might be a grown woman, well past the age to marry, but Aimee was an innocent. A farm girl. How likely was it that they'd really have anything in common once they got past the first few kisses?

Of course they had Georgie in common, but was that enough to make a happy marriage for a man and woman born to two different worlds?

"What is it, Rex?" Aimee's soft squeeze on his arm brought him back to the present. He glanced down into her upturned face, deliberately keeping his gaze from her pink mouth. "Nothing. Except I can't imagine there will be very many happy women at the dinner party."

Her brow furrowed. "Why ever not?"

Covering her hand with his, he winked and walked her toward the door. "Because no woman likes to be overshadowed by another. And no one there will be able to hold a candle to you."

She rolled her eyes and nudged him. "Don't be silly."

Rex laughed and led her to the waiting carriage.

Thirteen

Aimee knew she was more than likely squeezing the blood flow from Rex's arm, but he was too much of a gentleman to attempt to remove her stiff fingers. Instead, he smiled and introduced her to the guests one by one.

She greeted face after blurred face until she was certain she had met a couple of people at least twice. But she still hadn't seen Georgie or Rex's mother among the guests. A little dinner party? There had to be fifty people in the room.

Oh, why hadn't she worn the blue silk gown? Her pride always made a fool of her. Most of the ladies were wearing a variation of the dress Rex had purchased. Apparently it was the latest style. A tight bodice and a bustle. Her gown looked like a relic compared to these.

"I should leave," she whispered to Rex.

His eyes narrowed as he glanced down at her. "Are you ill?"

Aimee considered feigning nausea or a headache, but decided against it. "I'm not properly dressed."

"Nonsense. You're the only woman sensible enough not to spend money you don't have to impress someone—my mother, to be precise—just because she happens to be from New York, where fashion is king."

Aimee's heart warmed at his attempt to make her feel better. "This gown is dreadfully outdated. I'm sorry, Rex. I must be embarrassing you. Please make my apologies to your mother and allow me to go home."

A low growl escaped his throat. "Come with me." He clamped his hand over hers to prevent her from fleeing and ushered her out of the room, into a hallway, past the stairs, and into a small room. He shut the door. A dim light glowed in one corner.

Aimee leaned back against the wall, feeling like an utter fool and wishing she'd never agreed to come. "I'm sorry, Rex. This was a mistake."

"Things always have to be just so for you, don't they?"

Aimee blinked. Her jaw dropped.

He continued before she could formulate a response to the sudden attack. "I think you like playing the martyr. It's easier than taking a chance on something real."

Fury burned through Aimee, and she hurried across the room. She was just about to slip out into the hallway when the door slammed shut, cutting off her flight. With a sharp gasp, she spun around, her back pressing into the cold wood. Rex towered above her, resting his hand on the door just over her head.

"How dare you keep me here against my will?" She glowered. "A lawyer should know that's illegal."

"I'll only keep you here long enough to have my say. Then you can leave and never come back for all I care."

Pain jabbed at Aimee's heart like a two-fisted punch. He didn't want to see her anymore? What about Georgie? She stopped fighting and bit back a rush of tears.

"You sat around and wasted your childhood on an idiot, blind to the possibility that some other man might suit you better. You refuse to take care of Georgie unless it's in the capacity of mother, when you could have cared for him day in and day out as his nanny. You're too stubborn to wear my gown, and now that you see yours is a few years out of fashion, you would rather spoil my evening, embarrass my mother, and disappoint Georgie than make the best of a situation you created yourself. At one time I thought your precious Greg was the fool. But now it's clear. You're both pathetic. You deserve each other."

Aimee sputtered. Anger gripped her tongue, preventing a single word in her defense.

"You are an invited guest to dinner, which, I believe, is about to start. Georgie insisted upon attending—something Mother almost had vapors over—and he made certain that his name card was right between his mother and his father."

"He did?" The information chipped away the stony anger cementing her heart.

"Yes, he did. So you have a choice to make. Either swallow your pride and join me for dinner, or go home and don't come back."

"Don't you think that's a little harsh?"

"No. I want Georgie to be raised by someone who will teach him to have a backbone. Stick things out. I don't want him to think he can run away every time life gets a little hard."

"I don't do that!"

"Don't you?"

His challenge was more than she could allow to pass unanswered. He was completely wrong about her character. Loyalty to one's first love wasn't hiding. But the thought of never seeing Georgie again gave her only one choice.

"I'll attend the dinner, Rex."

"Good."

Her ire rose at his smug smile. She ducked under his arm and grabbed the doorknob, glancing pointedly at his restraining hand.

He moved back.

Silently, they returned to the drawing room, where the guests were waiting to be called for dinner. Despite their argument, Rex seemed to sense her nervousness and placed his palm at the small of her back. The warmth of his touch moved through Aimee, and she struggled to remember why he deserved her wrath.

"Ma!" Georgie's voice cut through the air, silencing the room.

Joy filled her at the sight of her son. She had never seen him look so handsome, dressed in a black suit that closely resembled Rex's. The resemblance between father and son was striking.

Aimee crouched and opened her arms. He slammed into her, nearly knocking her over. His tight squeeze took away her breath.

"My, you are getting big and strong, young man."

Georgie pulled back. "Look." He grinned from ear to ear, showing off an empty space where his two front bottom teeth used to sit. Aimee gasped. "You lost two teeth in one day?"

"Nope. Three days apart."

Rex chuckled. "I'm not sure the second one was ready, but Mother gave him a penny for the first one."

"Georgie! Did you pull out your other tooth for money?"

The boy glanced down. "It was loose. But it did hurt an awful lot when it came out."

"The boy will be lucky if he doesn't have a crooked tooth come in now." A white-haired woman dressed in a deep rose-colored dress of shimmering silk glided forward. She held her back straight and her head erect. "Had I known he would do such a thing, I would have given him the second penny in advance and told him to wait until the other tooth came out naturally, the way God intended."

Awestruck by the regal woman, Aimee slowly rose to her full height.

Georgie took a long look at Aimee and let out a low whistle. "Boy, Ma. You sure do look pretty. I never saw you in such a fancy dress."

"Thank you, sweetheart." Heat scorched Aimee's cheeks, and her heart soared at the words of praise.

He beamed at her and slipped his hand into hers. At least she had one ally at the party.

Mrs. Donnelly's gaze swept Aimee. Her lips tightened, and her brow rose with obvious disapproval. "Don't you look lovely, my dear. You must be Aimee."

Aimee sensed the forced politeness, and her heart sank. "Yes ma'am."

"My son and I are in your debt for caring for our Georgie. We'll have him molded into a proper young man in no time."

Georgie glanced up at Aimee, his nose scrunched. "I'm not proper?"

Indignation filled Aimee as she looked into the hurt-clouded eyes of her son. How dare this woman make Georgie feel as though he wasn't good enough for the likes of her. "You're perfect, sweetheart."

Despite her reassurance, doubt covered his face. "Do you want to go to my room with me, Ma?"

"Nothing would give me greater pleasure."

Aimee glared at Rex, then at his mother, and allowed Georgie to escort her from the room.

"Well, Miss Riley is quite the spitfire, isn't she?"

Rex glowered at his mother as she strutted down the hall to the banquet room. "You deliberately baited her. Why?"

Edna Donnelly stopped, her smile frozen on her lips. Palpable silence filled the hall. Then she entered the room full of guests with a grand flourish. She clapped her hands, though the gesture was completely unnecessary. All eyes had turned her way the moment she appeared in the doorway.

"May I have everyone's attention? It's time to move to the dining room."

The guests came to life as conversations resumed and everyone followed the hostess's suggestion. Rex watched them go, maintaining a proper silence rather than embarrass his mother by publicly showing his disapproval of her methods.

When the last guest had disappeared through the door, he

turned back to his mother. "Now, why did you feel the need to behave in such a manner toward Miss Riley?"

Touching her collar, his mother raised her chin. "I don't know what you mean."

"Now that Georgie is with us, we'll make him into a proper young man? You insulted the way she's raised him."

"Why, I did no such thing. How can you even suggest it?"

Obviously she wasn't going to admit to any wrongdoing. That was his mother's way. She was a master at maintaining her innocence under any circumstances.

Rex recognized the futility of belaboring the point. "Excuse me."

"Where are you going?"

"To find my son and his mother."

"His mother?" Her lips turned up in a tight, condescending smile. "Don't you think it's time to end that charade? It's really no good for anyone."

"By 'anyone,' I assume you mean you?"

His mother's expression darkened. "I suggest you watch your tone with me. You may be an adult, but I am still your mother and I deserve your respect."

"You're right. I'm sorry, Mother." He bent and kissed her cheek. "I'm going upstairs to find Aimee and Georgie. Feel free to start dinner without us."

She huffed as he walked away.

He trudged up the steps. So far tonight wasn't going well at all.

"Why can't I spend Christmas at home, Ma?"

When Rex heard Georgie's voice, he stopped in the hall a few feet from the boy's bedroom. He held his breath, his body tense and poised to intervene if Aimee said anything inappropriate to their situation.

Her sweet voice spoke softly. "Honey, I'm sure your father has discussed this with you, hasn't he?"

"Yes" came Georgie's small voice in return.

"What did he say?"

"That *she* wants us to have Christmas here at his house."

Rex closed his eyes. Even after living here for five months, Georgie still didn't consider this house to be his home. The thought squeezed at his heart. He listened closely for Aimee's reply.

"Georgie, you shouldn't refer to your grandmother as 'she.' That's disrespectful, son."

Rex smiled. Despite the way his mother had treated Aimee, she was doing her best to keep things in the right perspective for Georgie.

"My grandmother isn't very nice. Not like Grandma and Grammy. I don't think she likes me very much."

"Why would you say such a thing?"

"I don't know."

"Would she have given you a penny if she didn't like you?"

"I. . .guess not."

"Besides, who could possibly not like you? You are perfect."

Georgie giggled, and Rex decided to take that moment to make his presence known. He strode into the room. "Well, aren't you two going to come downstairs and eat dinner?"

Mother and son fell silent.

"Aren't you hungry, Georgie? It's been awhile since lunch."

"Can't Ma and me stay up here and talk?"

Rex sucked in a breath and tried to stave off a sudden stab of jealousy. Would his son ever want to spend time alone with him?

Aimee breathed a sigh that clearly revealed she'd much rather do as Georgie suggested, but she knew she was the only one who could convince the lad to comply without argument. "Georgie, I am simply famished. Auntie Rose and I worked on this gown all day long, so I haven't had a bite to eat since breakfast. Your pa says I get to sit right next to you, so we can talk while we eat."

Georgie looked down at the floor and kicked at the rug. "Grandmother says only ill-bred children speak with their mouths full."

Rex hid a grin, but Aimee giggled outright and grabbed the boy close for a hug. "Learning to be a gentleman is quite the challenge, isn't it, precious? I tell you what. Let's make sure we only talk between our bites of food, all right? That way your grandmother won't fuss at either one of us."

Georgie nodded, though he still looked doubtful.

"We'd best go downstairs, then."

Georgie headed down the hall. Rex wrapped his fingers lightly around Aimee's arm. "Wait a moment, will you?"

She turned on him, eyes blazing. "Not now," she hissed. "Let me get through this dinner with a little dignity intact."

Fourteen

Aimee sat in gloomy silence during the carriage ride home. The longest ride of her life. What a disaster the night had turned out to be! Rex's mother was a horrible, horrible woman. The epitome of wickedness. Well, perhaps not wicked, but she was still awful. And Rex was awful by association as far as Aimee was concerned.

Watching out the window as houses went by, Aimee refused to acknowledge that she wasn't alone. She raised her chin and pretended not to notice when Rex released a frustrated breath as the carriage jostled through the nearly empty streets. "Look, Aimee, I said I'm sorry. What more do you want me to say?"

"I want you to guarantee me that you will not let your mother decide how my son is raised."

"She won't."

"Have you told her that?" She ventured a glance across the seat, but his face was shadowed in the dark carriage. Only the street lamps provided an occasional glow through the windows.

"Mother will be going home after the new year, so why should I hurt her feelings when nothing she says concerning Georgie will hold once she's gone?"

"Don't be so sure about that. I heard her accepting an invitation to a winter masquerade ball to take place during the month of January." Besides, the woman looked awfully comfortable acting as hostess in her son's home. If she went back to New York before summertime, Aimee would eat her own hat.

But Rex obviously couldn't see past the end of his nose where his mother was concerned, so there was no point in trying to argue the matter.

Aimee could feel his gaze on her, but she refused to look at him.

Finally, he broke the silence. "If you're insinuating my mother is going to stay in Oregon, let me ease your mind. I assure you, she has a full social calendar that she wouldn't give up for all the grandsons in the world."

"I don't think it's her grandson drawing her here. More likely it's her son." Aimee cringed at her bitter tone. "Rex," she said more softly, turning in the seat, "Georgie wasn't raised in finery and with privileged class manners. He's a simple boy with simple friends and a simple mother. He's not very happy the way things are right now. And frankly, I'm surprised you can't see that he isn't adjusting to this new life."

Aimee could feel him tense even across the carriage seat, and she knew she'd offended him.

He cleared his throat. "I'm sorry that you don't approve of Georgie's new station in life, Aimee." His hard-edged tone made her stomach clench with anxiety. "I suppose I could give all my money to the poor and spend the rest of my days behind a plow, barely scratching out a living from the dust of the earth. Do you think that would satisfy you?"

Aimee bristled at his sarcasm. "Is that what you think of farmers? Need I remind you that my pa is a farmer? And a very successful one at that."

"I'm surprised you can abide him if he's so successful."

Aimee wanted to scream. He was deliberately misunderstanding her point. "My worries have nothing to do with success or failure or wealth or poverty. Only that my sweet little boy feels as though he doesn't measure up. Somehow he's gotten the idea that his grandmother dislikes him." Her voice broke. "He has always been secure in the knowledge that as far as his mama is concerned, the sun rises and sets with his wonderful smile. He isn't accustomed to constant criticism. And I can't bear to see him so sad."

"Mother dotes on him. She is just very rigid in her disciplines when it comes to proper social behavior." Rex stretched his arm along the back of the carriage seat and stroked her shoulder.

Aimee's frustration prevented her from the enjoyment she might have felt at the warmth of his touch. She jerked her arm away from his fingers. "And clearly I've failed to train him properly."

"I never said that. Obviously, he's a fairly well-behaved child. He's happy and secure in the world you've created for him. But his manners are not those of other children in his class. That's just the fact of the matter. I'm sorry I upset you, Aimee. But I truly believe we need to find a balance between your permissiveness and Mother's control."

Aimee sniffed. "Then you admit your mother will have a hand in his raising. Even when I'm no longer in his life. Tell me, how long are you going to allow her to run your life? And Georgie's?"

He moved his hand from her shoulder. Cold tension filled the carriage between them. "I don't have to explain myself to you. He's my son. Not yours."

Pain knifed through Aimee at the words. For the first time since they'd come to a compromise about Georgie, Rex had spouted the words he'd obviously been feeling for some time.

The carriage pulled to a stop, and she opened the door before the driver could climb down and help her out. "Aimee, wait," Rex called as she hurried up the walk, fighting back tears.

"Wait a minute," Rex said, catching up. He made no move to physically detain her, but the pleading in his voice stopped her short.

Slowly, she turned. "What more is there to say? You've made your position perfectly clear. There's no room for me in Georgie's life."

"I certainly did not say that," he snapped. "Stop being so theatrical."

Mindless of her gown, she sank onto the cold step, suddenly void of strength. "What's the point anymore?"

Rex sat next to her, his shoulder pressed to hers, providing welcome warmth. "I misspoke out of frustration, Aimee. I shouldn't have been so blunt. I know as far as Georgie is concerned, you are his mother, but. . ." He raked his hand through his hair and heaved a sigh.

"But I'm not his mother, right? And the arrangement is no longer acceptable." Tears flooded her eyes and spilled over. "I can only imagine how confusing all this must be to Georgie. The sooner he understands that I can't be his mother anymore, the sooner he'll be able to adjust to life as the son of a prominent lawyer."

"Now you're just being stubborn." He rubbed his jaw. "Can we wait until after Christmas at least?"

Aimee's heart sank. Deep down, she'd held out hope that Rex might ask her to reconsider. To allow things to continue as they were. To be Georgie's mother. But in her heart, she knew that was impossible. It wasn't fair. Or natural. The confusion was too much for such a little boy.

Swallowing around a lump in her throat, Aimee shoved to her feet. "I'd best get inside."

Rex stood. "I'm sorry you were so uncomfortable tonight."

"It's all right. Your friends were gracious, for the most part. I just didn't belong. And it was more than simply wearing an out-of-fashion gown. Good night, Rex. Thank you for inviting me."

Aimee didn't give him a chance to respond. She hurried up the steps and slipped inside before giving in to the sobs lurking at the bottom of her throat. Avoiding the kitchen, where the light glowed and she knew Rosemary was waiting for a full report, Aimee ran up the stairs to her room. She threw herself across the bed and cried until her tears were spent. Lacking the will to properly ready herself for bed, she remained fully clothed. She lay, staring at the ceiling, until dawn, trying to imagine her life without Georgie. But how did one imagine a sky with no sun, moon, or stars? Earth with no lovely flowers or wiggly puppies?

How, Lord? How do I surrender my child?

Rex sat in the drawing room before a crackling fire, mulling over his conversation with Aimee. Part of him agreed that it was time for her to let go. But he admitted to himself that his motive for agreeing was only because Georgie might give him a chance to be a real father if he didn't have Aimee to fall back on. Shame flooded him at his selfishness.

On the other hand, if Aimee was out of Georgie's life, she was out of his, too. And that didn't sit well with Rex, no matter how much he tried to convince himself that she wasn't a proper fit in this life he'd created. The memory of Georgie's ashen face when he thought he wasn't a "proper" young man made Rex squirm with outrage. All that he'd despised about growing up, he'd reestablished right here in Oregon, and now his son had to live in the same environment.

Did Mother, as Aimee suspected, plan to remain here and take Georgie into her own hands? Hands that were capable, but cold. That's what he remembered. No loving pats, as he'd seen Aimee give Georgie countless times. No soft kisses and murmured assurances of love and acceptance. He closed his eyes and imagined his son and Aimee together. Despite his claim as Georgie's father, did he really have a right to separate those two?

"That was some spectacle you made tonight."

Rex expelled a sigh and opened his eyes as his mother entered the room, as usual, owning the atmosphere. "What spectacle are you referring to, Mother?"

"You know very well what I am referring to, Rex. With that woman. Running after her like some lovesick fool."

"Someone had to follow her. You insulted the woman who was good enough to raise your grandson for six years."

"I did no such thing." She took a seat in the chair across from his before the fire. "You've certainly changed since moving to this rough country. I think you should accept Mr. Crighton's offer to buy you out and come home. You still have a position in your father's firm. One word from me and you'll be senior partner."

"Mother, I thought we agreed that you wouldn't interfere with my business dealings." He smiled, despite his irritation. "Besides, Mr. Crighton didn't offer a buyout. He suggested a merger."

Edna rose to her full height. "I should think you would want my input. Your father always said I had a head for business."

That much was true. Rex looked fondly at his mother. She could be infuriating at times, but Rex knew she had his best interest and that of her grandson at heart. "Your offer is appreciated. But my life is here now. With Georgie."

"That's ridiculous. You must come home and find a suitable mother for your child."

"Are you insulting Aimee again?" Resentment rose in his breast. "Really, Mother, I don't know how you could be so ungrateful."

She rose slowly, and Rex could see her struggle to maintain dignity. "I am most grateful that George is healthy and happy. I firmly believe that your Miss Riley should be generously compensated for her role in his upbringing thus far. But surely you recognize that she mustn't continue to associate with him."

"I'm not sure that I do recognize that. And I would never insult her by suggesting payment to her for loving him and caring for him. And, yes, for being his mother for six years." Rex shifted uncomfortably at the thought that he'd done exactly that by asking her to be Georgie's nanny. Tonight he had accused her of being unreasonable for not accepting the position. He'd done her a grave injustice.

Edna expelled a breath. "As long as she is in his life, acting as his mother, he will never learn that this is his home. Here, with you. Or in New York, should you change your mind about moving back home."

Rex cringed as he recognized his own thoughts over the past few months. He stared into the flames licking the stone inside the fireplace, and suddenly clarity flooded his mind. Time wouldn't change Georgie's heart. He loved Aimee. They were part of each other.

"Mother, I've just come to realize something."

She gave a short nod and a tight smile. "Good. I am glad you've come to your senses."

"I have. Most definitely. Aimee is home to Georgie."

"What was that?"

"Aimee. Georgie will never be happy anywhere unless she's there. She will always be his mother. I could no sooner find a replacement for her than anyone could take your place in my heart."

"Well, I am pleased to hear that you still love your mother. I wonder sometimes that you can simply abandon me to that lonely house now that your father's gone."

"The point is that if Georgie is to have only one parent, it will have to be Aimee."

Edna gasped. "You can't be serious. One does not give up one's child."

"And yet I have been expecting it of Aimee."

"I won't allow it."

Rex stood and crossed the room. He kissed his mother's cheek and engulfed her in an embrace. "It's Christmastime. If God could give His only Child at Christmas, I suppose I can do the same."

Fifteen

Aimee gazed at the seven-foot fir tree standing in the glow of the fireplace. The children had worked hard on the paper chains and painted dough balls that decorated it. A wistful sigh escaped as she remembered previous years. Georgie had always adored decorating the Christmas tree.

Twenty-two children had hung their stockings all over the mantel and the wall and anywhere else they could find. Aimee longed to give them so much more than new pairs of boots. Rosemary had sewn pinafores for the girls and shirts for the boys. Aimee knew the children would be happy and excited to receive those. Each stocking was filled with juicy oranges, a small trinket, and a peppermint stick.

Aimee undressed and stretched out on her bed, the weight of her first Christmas without Georgie in six years pressing down on her, nearly suffocating her with its gloom.

The downstairs clock struck midnight. Tears slipped down her cheeks as she stared at the ceiling. Shadows danced from the branches swaying in the breeze outside her window.

She closed her eyes and evened out her breathing, hoping to find a little sleep before the children arose.

The sound of something tapping on glass pulled her from her near-doze.

Fear gripped her. She froze.

Tap-tap, she heard again—harder this time.

Someone was outside her window, and she knew it wasn't Santa Claus.

The tapping increased. "Aimee!"

Aimee frowned, curiosity replacing fear. She sat up, pulling her coverlet to her neck. "Who is it?"

"Rex. Open the window. This branch won't hold me much longer."

Aimee pushed back the covers and grabbed her dressing gown. She opened the window. "What are you doing here? Why didn't you come to the door?"

"I didn't want to wake the children."

"H–how did you know which window was mine?" Aimee's cheeks burned to be having this conversation with Rex, or any man, outside her bedroom.

"I saw you walk past the window right before you snuffed out your lamp," Rex replied. "Go downstairs and open the door for me."

Aimee nodded. "Be careful climbing down."

A couple of minutes later, she opened the front door. Rex was striding away from the house. "What on earth are you doing?"

"I have your Christmas present in the carriage," he said over his shoulder.

Horror shot through Aimee. She hadn't purchased him a thing! She'd spent every dime on the children. "Rex, you shouldn't have. . ."

Her protest died on her lips as he turned around, carrying a sleeping Georgie in his arms. "*Shhh.* Show me where to lay him."

Scarcely daring to breathe lest the wonderful dream disappear, Aimee led the way upstairs to her room. She hesitated outside the door.

Rex exhaled. "Don't be silly. I'll have to go in there if I'm to put Georgie to bed."

Aimee gathered her courage and allowed him entrance.

"Where?"

She pointed to a privacy curtain across the room. "Georgie's cot is behind that." Aimee scrutinized the room. It didn't even come close to the luxurious bedroom the child had at his father's house. But it was the best they could do once he grew too old to continue sleeping in Aimee's bed.

She wanted an explanation as to why Rex decided to bring Georgie over for Christmas Day. But as she opened her mouth to voice her curiosity, Rex shushed her with a finger to his lips. He motioned with his head for her to go out of the room.

Once they entered the hallway, he closed the door behind them. "Now where do I put Bandit?"

Aimee grinned. "The kitchen. He has a bed by the stove."

Rex fetched the overgrown pup, and Aimee led the way into the kitchen. Bandit circled twice and settled onto his bed of old, ripped-up quilts.

"I guess he's glad to be home, too," Rex said.

"Would you like some coffee?"

He shook his head. "I can't stay. Mother wakes up and checks Georgie's room several times during the night. She'll be frantic if she finds him gone."

"I don't know how to thank you for bringing him home for Christmas. I know what a sacrifice it must have been to even consider it—this being your first Christmas since finding us. . .him."

"This is where he wanted to be." He pointed to the sitting room. "Does Georgie have a stocking over the fireplace and a pair of boots under the tree?" His tone was slightly mocking, but so gentle and filled with pain that Aimee couldn't be angry with him.

She nodded. "And a new shirt."

When they arrived at the front door, Rex reached into his pocket. "I have another gift for you."

"Oh Rex. You shouldn't have. I—I didn't get you—"

"I didn't expect you would." He handed her an envelope. "These are documents," he said in answer to her questioning frown, "stating my desire that Georgie be raised by you."

Aimee's world spun. She blinked, imagining the implications of the words he'd just said. "You mean forever?"

"Yes."

"Surely you don't mean that."

His eyes held the pain of truth. His jaw clenched and unclenched as he struggled against raw emotions.

"Why, Rex?" Aimee clutched the envelope tightly to her breast. "You love Georgie as much as I do. You've every right to raise him. No judge in the country would disagree."

Rex chuckled. "Georgie's been speaking with an attorney to try to get that changed."

"What on earth do you mean?"

"My future partner in the firm. Mr. Crighton. He's taken quite a liking to Georgie and has the child believing he's going to represent him in court to try to convince a judge to let him live with you."

"And you're going into business with this man?"

"It's all in good fun." Only Rex wasn't laughing. As a matter of fact, the pain on his face was palpable.

"Rex, why are you doing this?"

He raked his fingers through his hair. "I finally saw things clearly tonight. Georgie belongs with his mother."

She touched his arm. "What of his father?"

Rex covered her hand with his. "I hope to stay in his life. Perhaps we can maintain some sort of relationship."

"Oh Rex. Of course you will. Georgie loves you very much."

Hope sprang to his eyes, then faded. "I'd better go."

Aimee's heart filled with compassion, and an unexpected desire to comfort him filled her. "Wait. I do have a gift for you."

His brow rose as Aimee stepped forward. Her heart pounded in her ears, and she pushed up on her toes, pressing her lips softly to his. He blinked in surprise.

She smiled at his loss of composure. "My first kiss. My gift to you."

Emotion washed over his face, and before Aimee knew what was happening, he swept her around the waist and pulled her close, cupping her head in one large palm. "And your second," he said an instant before his head descended. Fire ignited in Aimee's belly as his mouth moved over hers. She wrapped her arms around his neck and reveled in feelings she'd never before experienced.

A curious mix of disappointment and relief filled her when he let her go. Silently, she touched her fingers to her lips and stared at the man who had just upended her world. For many years, she had dreamed of kisses, but nothing in her wildest imagination had prepared her for the real thing.

Rex drew a ragged breath. He reached forward and pressed his palm against her cheek for a brief second. Aimee couldn't decipher the expression in his eyes.

"Merry Christmas, Aimee Riley."

Rex leaned back against the carriage seat while Marlow commanded the horses forward. He could still feel Aimee's warmth against him, the sweetness of her kiss. His pulse quickened with the memory. He didn't question why he'd kissed her. It was the only thing he could have done. Her gentle gift had been the match that fired up a long-overdue flame.

The impropriety of kissing her in the middle of the night while she was in her dressing gown struck him. He supposed, in all decency, he should propose. He could imagine her angry response, when she had time to think about it, accusing him of compromising her just so she'd have to marry him and he could keep Georgie. A short, ironic laugh escaped him. Wasn't that exactly what he'd accused her of back at the farm while they were standing in the gazebo?

When he arrived home, the house seemed even quieter than before. He knew the stillness was due to the inactivity of the late hour, but knowing Georgie wasn't there. . .wouldn't be there in the morning. . .left a giant chasm. He walked into the boy's room. The empty place that his son had filled in his heart was void once more.

"Thank heavens you've arrived." Mother's frantic tone caused him to turn around. "I was just about to send for the sheriff."

"There's no need."

"I assume you are aware that Georgie is missing?"

He nodded.

She frowned and stretched her neck to look around. "Did you find him?"

Walking to the bed, Rex picked up Georgie's pillow, still indented from where the child's head had rested only an hour before. "I'm the one who took him."

Mother planted her feet on the carpeted floor. "What on earth is going on?" she demanded. "I insist you tell me at once."

"I've taken Georgie back to Aimee."

"You're allowing him to spend Christmas with those orphans after all? I don't know what to think about you sometimes." Her voice faltered, and she walked across to him. She studied him for a moment, then drew a sharp breath. "It's more than just Christmas, isn't it? What did you do?"

Rex lifted his head and met her gaze. "Georgie needs to be with his mother."

With a groan, she sank down on the bed next to him. "Tell me you didn't give up the child."

Rex gave a short laugh. "Amazing, isn't it? I spent six years frantically searching for him. Hiring the best detectives. And six months after finding my son, I give him up."

Mother shoved up from the bed, shaking her finger at Rex as

though he were a naughty boy. "You go get him back at once! That child is a Donnelly. We do not give up our children."

"No, we simply give them over to the care of nannies until they're old enough to ship off to boarding school. That's not the life I want for Georgie."

Mother's eyes narrowed. "Are you saying I failed in my raising of you? Why, you went to the best schools. Moved in just the right circles. I could kick myself for ever being fool enough to allow your father to pay for this wagon train adventure. If not for that, you never would have married your common little wife who didn't even have the gumption to weather childbirth and raise her own son."

"Mother!" Rex bit back the torrent of words he wanted to say, knowing she deserved his respect regardless of the cruelty spewing from her lips.

"How could you dishonor your father's memory by giving up his namesake?"

"Please try to understand, Mother," he said, suddenly so weary all he wanted to do was lie on Georgie's bed, breathe in the lingering scent of his son, and sleep through Christmas.

"I will never understand," she hissed. She spun on her heel and exited the room.

Giving in to his desire, Rex stretched out on the bed. Tears formed in his eyes, and he made no attempt to prevent them from running down the sides of his head and soaking into Georgie's pillow.

Sixteen

"Ma! I'm here. Jesus heard my prayers!"

Aimee jolted awake as Georgie bounded onto her bed. She smiled. It hadn't been a dream. Her boy was home—for good.

He straddled her belly. "Ma! Wake up."

"I'm awake, Georgie." She laughed and sat up, tumbling him from her stomach.

"Jesus heard my prayers. I came home!" He frowned. "Do you think Santa brought me? Or angels?" His eyes grew wide. "You think Father will be angry when he finds out?"

Aimee smiled at her son's enthusiasm. "Well, I'll tell you a little secret. Your father is the one who brought you."

"He did?"

"Yep, and you were asleep. He carried you right up the stairs and into this very room and laid you very gently on your bed so you wouldn't wake up."

"Do you think. . . ?"

"What, honey?"

"I already wrote to Santa and told him I wasn't living at the orphanage anymore. Miss Long promised to mail my letter to the North Pole. He probably didn't know where to bring my peppermint candy and orange."

Aimee smiled. "I bet he did. Shall we go check?"

Georgie bobbed his head. Then he stopped short. "Where's Bandit?"

"He's here."

As if summoned by Georgie's whim, Bandit's low *woof* drifted up the stairs.

"Bandit! We're home."

Aimee dressed quickly and hurried downstairs, following the excited chatter coming from the sitting room.

Uncle Hank and Aunt Rosemary gave her questioning frowns.

"Rex brought him last night," she whispered. "I'll tell you the rest later."

As they concentrated on the children, Aimee's mind drifted to the night before. The memory of the kiss she and Rex had shared sent a shiver down her spine.

Her heart ached for the misery she had observed in his eyes. She couldn't help but be excited that Georgie was home with her. But what about Rex? How was he doing without Georgie this morning? Had Rex told Georgie that he was letting him live with her from now on?

For a fleeting minute, worry clawed at her. Would Georgie be glad at the news? Or did he prefer living with his father?

"Look at my new shirt, Ma!" He proudly displayed the garment.

Aimee smiled. "It's lovely, Georgie."

During the mayhem of activity that followed, Aimee slipped out and headed for the kitchen to start on Georgie's favorite breakfast: apple pancakes with warm maple syrup. Flapjacks for twenty children and three adults would take awhile. Long enough for her to sort out her thoughts and feelings about the events of the night before.

Could she really take Georgie away from his father? Despite the fact that he'd admitted Georgie was happier with her, was it fair not to give the two of them a chance to be together as father and son?

Rosemary entered the kitchen as the griddle sizzled. "So?"

Aimee shrugged. "Rex brought him last night."

"For Christmas, right?"

"Forever." Even as Aimee said it, she couldn't believe the sacrifice Rex had made. "He—he said Georgie belongs with me."

"Oh Aimee. What made him decide that?"

"I don't know. He just said Georgie wasn't happy."

"Did Georgie seem unhappy to you?" Rosemary began pulling plates from the shelf.

"He misses me. He wanted to spend Christmas here at home."

"True. But it seemed to me that he was beginning to adjust pretty well."

"What are you suggesting? I take him back to Rex?"

"I don't know. I guess not." She grabbed a platter and set it on the counter for Aimee. Her brow furrowed into a troubled frown.

Silently, Aimee slid flapjacks off the griddle, then dropped several more spoonfuls of batter. How could Auntie Rosemary even suggest that Aimee give him up? Even though she didn't come right out and say it, Aimee knew the way her aunt thought.

"I can't take him back, Auntie. I won't. Rex will stay in Georgie's life if I'm the one to raise him, but if Rex raises him, how likely is it that I'll have a place as Georgie's mother?"

"I'm not sure I understand."

Panic swept through her. "Rex's life is filled with parties that important rich people attend. With Rex, Georgie would be raised in a privileged class." Tears formed in her eyes. "Before you know it, he would be moving in those circles himself, and I would become a source of embarrassment."

"What utter nonsense." Rosemary's indignant voice filled the kitchen. "Georgie could never be ashamed of you. He adores you."

Beads of perspiration formed above Aimee's lip. "I know he does now. But I wouldn't fit in with the people his father associates with. Like those at the party the other night." She sighed. "He'd eventually be ashamed."

"I think you're wrong."

Aimee glanced sharply at her aunt. "Why do you think Rex should be the one to raise Georgie?"

Aunt Rosemary hesitated, and Aimee thought she might deny it again. Instead she sent Aimee a look of frank assessment. "A man can teach a boy things a woman can't. You can tell Georgie how to be a gentleman, but Rex can show him by example. Rex is a fine man, and it wouldn't hurt Georgie to learn some of his manners."

Tears formed in Aimee's eyes. "I don't think I could let him go."

Rosemary closed the distance between them and took Aimee into her arms. "I'm sorry. Don't listen to me. What would I know of such things? Besides, Georgie needs you both."

How could he fire someone on Christmas? That would make him the coldest person alive. He would just wait a few days. Leave Miss Long to believe Georgie would be back after the holiday.

"What am I to do for the days until Mr. Georgie's return?" The nanny stood before Rex's wingback chair, her face pinched with worry.

Miss Long was no fool. She had, no doubt, surmised the truth. Either that or she had heard him and Mother discussing the situation. The news had probably spread throughout the household.

"Do you have family you can visit?" he asked.

"No sir, I don't. My parents are dead, and I didn't stay in touch with my brother after he left home. I am quite alone."

"You're more than welcome to stay here until the child returns. Just relax. Help yourself to the library or do some shopping. Whatever you wish." *Just don't ask me about Georgie. Not yet.*

"Thank you." She seemed to understand. "Merry Christmas, Mr. Donnelly."

"Merry Christmas, Miss Long." A thought occurred to him. He stood and strode across the room. "Wait just a moment."

She turned at the door, a puzzled look on her face. "Yes?"

"I forgot to give you this." He reached into his pocket and retrieved his billfold. He pulled out more money than she made in a month as Georgie's nanny. "Your Christmas bonus."

"Bonus? But that isn't necessary." She stared at the money, making no move to take it from his hand.

"Nonsense. Everyone needs a little Christmas gift. Buy yourself a pretty dress."

Did he detect a faint blush on her cheeks? He smiled and pressed the bills into her hand. "You've done a remarkable job with Georgie. I don't know what would have become of us if you hadn't been good enough to stay after all the others left."

A smile lifted her lips. "It has been my pleasure to care for the boy. He's been much better behaved since Aimee came back into his life."

Rex stiffened. "Yes, well, a boy needs his mother."

Miss Long reached forward and gave him a motherly pat on the arm. The first physical contact she'd ever initiated—and behavior that Mother would deem inappropriate to their stations. But the nanny offered no apology. "He needs his father as well. And you are a wonderful father, Mr. Donnelly."

"Let me ask you something, Miss Long. Why do you think Georgie was so unhappy here with me? What did I do wrong?"

Miss Long hesitated a moment. "In my opinion he wasn't unhappy with you at all. At first, yes. But he was adjusting very well. It's not unusual that he would prefer to stay with the children and the mother he's always known."

The news came as a surprise to Rex. He wished he had asked her opinion before signing Georgie over.

Mother glided into the room. "Thank you, Miss Long. You may go. I wish to talk to my son."

"Yes ma'am. Good night, Mr. Donnelly."

"Good night. And thank you."

She nodded and left the room.

"I suppose you told her that you no longer require her services."

"Not yet. I didn't have the heart to sack her on Christmas."

"Admirable."

Rex waited while she sat in the Queen Anne chair across from his. Then he took his own seat. "What did you want to discuss with me, Mother?"

"That woman, Miss Riley. She's rather old to be unmarried. Is there something unnatural about her?"

"Of course not! She's just never found the right man."

"Well, it's obvious you are taken with her. I must warn you, though, do not marry her. She will not fit in with your plans or your lifestyle. There are several suitable ladies whom I have my eye on for you."

"I believe that is my choice, Mother." He arched his eyebrow for emphasis. "And if you're referring to any of the young ladies at the dinner party the other night, let me assure you, not one of them interests me in the slightest." How could they when he couldn't stop thinking of Aimee long enough for thoughts of anyone else to linger?

"I realize, of course, that you'll do as you please. But need I remind you of what happened at the dinner party? That girl was dressed in a completely unsuitable gown. And she made a complete spectacle of herself—and you—by contradicting me in my own home."

Rex gave an inward growl. Perhaps Aimee had been right. Was Mother staking her claim on his home?

"Aimee wore an outdated gown because it was all she had. I invited her at the last minute. So she had to make do with the only gown she owned. I thought she looked lovely."

"Yes, yes. She is a lovely young woman. No one is disputing that. But she is common, son."

Rex's defenses rose. "Mother, I won't have you insulting the woman I—" He swallowed down his near admission. But of course the slip wasn't lost on his mother.

"I see," she said, her lips white with tension. "The woman has clearly been using young George to gain your affection."

Rex laughed. "Don't be ridiculous, Mother. Aimee Riley would never use Georgie to snare me into matrimony."

Mother shook her head. "You are very naive in the ways of women. She's baiting you. Making you long for your son so that you'll propose."

A brief image flashed through Rex's mind. Aimee and Georgie and him in the front yard, a circle of three, laughing. . . playing. . .a family. His fantasy was interrupted when the front bell rang.

Mother shot him a look of annoyance. "Who on earth would be so ill-bred as to arrive uninvited on Christmas Day?"

A moment later, Rex opened the door. A grinning Georgie stood on the front step with Aimee behind him, her face void of color. Her eyes appeared too large and her lips trembled.

"Merry Christmas, Father!" Georgie flung himself into Rex's arms.

Rex lifted the boy into an embrace and held him close, drinking in the scent of his hair until Georgie squirmed to get down. "Go into the drawing room. Grandmother will show you where to find your Christmas gifts."

His big blue eyes grew wide. "I have more presents?"

"Of course."

Rex looked at Aimee as the boy raced off, no doubt to shock his grandmother with his lack of manners. Rex smiled. "I planned to send them over tomorrow. I wanted to get some things for the rest of the children first so they didn't feel left out."

Aimee attempted a smile, but it fell short.

"What are you doing here?" He frowned. "Is everyone all right at the orphanage?"

"I—I. . ." Her lips trembled, and emotional distress played across her face.

"Come into my study for a moment and tell me what's wrong." She nodded and allowed herself to be guided into the study.

Rex closed the door once they were inside. He led her to a sofa. "Why did you bring Georgie back?"

"He. . .he wanted to come home, Rex. He was afraid you'd be all alone on Christmas."

Joy flooded Rex. "He wanted to come home?" He stopped just short of breaking into a foolish grin. "Oh Aimes. Did you tell him that he would be living with you from now on?"

She shook her head. "I didn't get a chance. I planned to wait until bedtime. But after dinner, he just announced that he'd best get home so you wouldn't be lonely for him on Christmas."

Rex peered closer. "Are you letting him spend the night?"

Shaking her head, Aimee snared her bottom lip between her teeth and took a ragged breath. "I'm not taking him, Rex. It's not right. Georgie is your son. He needs to be with you."

"What do you mean? For months you've been trying to get Georgie from me, and now that you have the chance, you're giving him back? That doesn't make sense."

Aimee stared down at her hands. "As much as I love my boy. . ." A sob caught in her throat, cutting off her words mid-sentence. "As much as I love him, there is no good reason to take him away from you. It's not fair to either of you. Georgie can't be deprived of a good education and French lessons and his father's attention just because I'm lonely."

"Oh Aimee." Rex took her hands in his and brought them to his lips. "How can I ever thank you?"

"There is something you could do for me."

"What's that?"

"Offer me the nanny position again."

"But I thought you were completely against doing that."

"I was. And it won't be easy to take care of him without being his mother. But you were right when you said I always have to have things my way in order to be happy. This time I have to do what's best for Georgie. And if that means he lives with you and I become his nanny, then so be it."

Rex stroked his chin, his eyes clouding. "There's just one problem. Miss Long is an exceptional nanny. I couldn't fire her."

Tear flooded Aimee's eyes. "Y–you mean you don't want me?"

Reaching forward, Rex snagged her perpetually loose curl, rubbing it between his thumb and forefinger. "I didn't say that. I just said you can't be Georgie's nanny. I want you to be his mother."

She shook her head. "No, Rex. It's too much for Georgie. It's time to make the break."

Rex swallowed hard. He knew what he wanted to do. Knew what was right. For all of them. "Aimee, I want you to marry me."

A gasp shot into the room from the doorway. Mother stood there, fuming.

"Mother, may we please have some privacy?"

"Fine. Just remember what I said." She slammed the door, and Aimee jumped.

One look at Aimee's ashen face, and Rex knew what her answer would be.

Seventeen

Rex glared at Hank Riley as though the news the man had just given him was his fault. As the reason Aimee hadn't come to see Georgie in a month finally dawned on him, his heart slammed against his chest. "What do you mean she's gone?"

"She left the day after Christmas, Rex," Rosemary said gently. "We assumed you knew. The school board offered her the teacher position for the winter term, and she decided to accept."

Betrayal formed a gash through his heart, slicing like the edge of a knife. "She didn't tell me."

Rosemary moved around her husband and opened the door wider. "Why don't you come in, Rex? Have some coffee with us. We've missed you around here."

"You have?"

Rosemary smiled and took his hat. "Of course. You're part of the family."

Rex stepped across the threshold and followed her into the sitting room.

"How is Georgie?"

Guilt seized him. "He's doing well. But he misses his mother."

"She misses him, too."

"Then why did she leave?" Exasperation flew from his lips. "She could have married me and been his mother forever. I told her that."

"Please sit down." Rosemary motioned toward a flower-printed settee. She sat across from him on the arm of her husband's chair and draped her arm across his shoulders. "I certainly hope that isn't how you proposed."

Hank chuckled at his wife's indignation.

Rex frowned. "What do you mean?"

"Oh Rex. For mercy's sake. No wonder she ran home to her mother. You made her feel like you were sacrificing in order to accommodate Georgie's love for her. Of course she couldn't agree to that."

Rex gaped. "I asked her to marry me because I'm in love with her. Not because Georgie needs a mother. It's a bonus, of course, that she's already his mother, but that's not the reason I proposed."

Rosemary's expression softened. "Then perhaps you should tell her so."

"I did."

A raised eyebrow and a dubious frown answered him.

"Before I brought Georgie back with me in the first place, I told her I wouldn't marry until I was in love."

"Did you tell her you love her?" Rosemary asked softly.

"Well, no. My mother barged in before I had the chance. After that, Aimee wouldn't listen to a word I said."

"That sounds like my stubborn niece." Hank cleared his throat. "If you'd like my opinion, you'd better go after her." He reached across his wife's lap and took her hand, lacing his fingers with hers. "I wasted twenty years because I didn't have the gumption to let this woman know how much I loved her."

"You waited that long?" Rex asked, focusing on Rosemary.

A pretty blush covered her rounded cheeks. "A woman won't run after a man. The Bible says a man who finds a wife finds a good thing. It's in a man's nature to do the pursuing. A woman wants to feel wanted."

Well Aimee was definitely wanted. Rex thought about her until he couldn't get a lick of work accomplished. And Georgie missed her so much, he was sullen and bullheaded, once more returning to the unruly boy he'd been when Rex first brought him home. They both wanted her, but even more so, they needed her.

Without Aimee, their family was incomplete.

Rex pushed to his feet. "I'm going to get her."

"It might not be easy," Rosemary warned.

Rex frowned. "I thought you said. . ."

"Oh, she loves you, and I'm sure she wants to marry you. But she's convinced she doesn't fit into your life."

"Because of the dinner party?"

"Partly, I suppose."

Determination swelled his chest. He wouldn't lose her. Not now. Not ever. If he had to sling her over his shoulder and bring her back bodily to convince her how much he adored her, he would. One thing he knew for certain. . .when he returned to Oregon City, Aimee would be his bride.

Six hours later, Rex stood on the porch of the Riley farmhouse, holding his sleeping son in his arms.

"What on earth?" Mrs. Riley's confusion-clouded eyes lit up when she recognized him. "Oh Rex, come in."

"Thank you, ma'am."

"Bring Georgie back here to Aimee's room."

He deposited his son on the bed and followed Star into the living room. "Is Aimee here?"

"She's in town, hosting the spelling bee."

Disappointment clutched him. "I see."

Aimee's mother smiled and laid a gentle hand on his arm. "They should be finishing up soon. I'm sure she'd appreciate an escort home."

"Really?"

"Of course. Georgie will be fine here. Go on."

Rex didn't need another nudge. The thought of seeing Aimee again and declaring his love for her sent him to the buggy without looking back.

Aimee smiled at the pudgy eight-year-old girl standing before her, trying desperately to remember how to spell the word *chrysanthemum*.

"Take your time," she said to the child. "See the word in your mind. You can do it."

Sarah Cooper closed her eyes and concentrated. Thirty seconds later she correctly spelled the word and moved to the next round. Six words later, she was pinned the winner of Hobbs's spelling bee—the fourth one this year.

With winter so dreary and long, the townsfolk tried to find amusement where they could. Spelling bees, sing-alongs, revival meetings. All had their places in the entertainment of the citizens of Hobbs.

Aimee had settled back into life at the farm fairly easily. She missed the orphanage children and ached for Georgie. And her heart nearly broke every time she thought of Rex. She had to admit to herself, if to no one else, that he'd stolen her heart. The love she had for Rex far overshadowed the feelings she'd had for Gregory. Now when she looked at her cousin, her only emotions were the comfortable love and affection borne of years of knowing someone.

Aimee congratulated the parents of the newest spelling bee winner and headed toward the door for a breath of air. She noticed Greg across the room. Her gaze caught his as he sensed her perusal and looked away from the young lady who held his attention.

Aimee smiled. Cynthia might have left him bruised, but it appeared Miss Thayer, whose father was a new merchant in town, might be just the salve to ease the pain. Aimee's heart lifted in joy for him as she noted the rapt expression on the girl's sweet face.

"Excuse me."

Aimee looked away from Greg and into the face of Jonas Clay, a young widower with three children and a large farm. He and his wife, Millie, had grown up in Hobbs along with Aimee and Greg. The warmth of friendship enveloped her. There was something nice about the familiar.

"Good evening, Jonas."

"May I escort you outside, Aimes?"

"Thank you. It's getting awfully stuffy in here."

"Yeah, hot as summer."

When they reached the hitching post, Aimee turned and smiled at her old school chum. "Lorna did well in the spelling bee."

He beamed with pride for his young daughter, who had made it three rounds against children much older than she. "Her ma was a good speller. Taught her everything she knew." His expression crashed.

In a rush of sympathy, Aimee took his hand. "I'm sorry, Jonas. Millie was a good friend to everyone. She's surely going to be missed by all."

He tightened his grip on her hand. "It's been two months, and I can't seem to get her out of my head."

"That's to be expected. After all, you loved her."

"Why couldn't it have been me?" His face screwed up, and Aimee could see he was fighting hard to keep tears at bay. "My girls need a ma more than they need a pa. If it had to be one of us, why couldn't it have been me?"

"Oh Jonas. How would Millie have taken care of them? Your children needed you both, but life doesn't work out the way we want sometimes. We just have to accept what happens and make the best of things. Find happiness as it comes." She squeezed his hand. "That's what Millie would have wanted for you."

"You think so?"

Aimee nodded. "I know so."

"I've been thinking." He locked his gaze to hers. "Aimes..."

Dread flowed through Aimee. She sensed what was coming. "Jonas, don't say it."

But he rushed ahead anyway. "I need a wife. You're not married. We've known each other since we were in school together."

"We're not in love, Jonas."

He grinned at her. "Don't you think we're both a little old to be holding out for romance?" He laced his fingers with hers. "We would get along fine. You know we would. My girls like you."

He made a lot of sense. "I don't know, Jonas. Is it crazy to think that a man might actually fall in love with me someday?"

The dubious expression on his face made her cheeks burn. "Isn't it possible that I might fall in love with you? Right now I'm still grieving over my Millie, but there's a lot to be said for sharing a life with someone. I can see us moving past our friendly feelings and ending up with something deeper. In the meantime, I wouldn't ask anything of you besides the regular cooking and cleaning and caring for my girls. Later, maybe..."

Heat seared Aimee's cheeks. "I don't know, Jonas. Maybe I want more than to 'end up with something deeper.' I just don't think—"

He touched his fingers to her lips. "Don't say anything just yet. Think about it. Pray about it. And tell me in a week or so." He lifted her hand to his lips. "Please, Aimee."

Aimee's heart ached as she watched him walk away. The answer was already clear in her heart. As fond of Jonas as she was, she couldn't marry him. Her heart was taken. Owned by Rex Donnelly. Now and forever.

How could she have been so foolish as to walk out of his life? Her son's life? They needed her. She needed them.

Even in the dark, Rex recognized Aimee standing next to a tall man in the moonlight. Jealousy burned like fire in his blood, and it was all he could do to stay put and not rush forward, demanding an explanation. But he hung back. Perhaps Hank and Rosemary had been wrong. Perhaps the reason she'd turned down his proposal was because she didn't love him after all.

He watched as her companion left her standing alone. Aimee rubbed her arms and leaned back against the hitching post.

Still stinging from the sight of another man holding her hand, Rex stepped back. What was the point? A branch crackled beneath his feet, and Aimee's head jerked up.

Aimee's heart pounded furiously against her chest. She wanted to run as fast as she could to the schoolhouse. . .to safety.

"Who's there?" she said hoarsely.

She held her breath as a man stepped out of the shadows.

"It's me," a familiar voice called.

"Rex!" she breathed. Warmth flowed over her, chasing away the icy chill of the January night. "What are you doing here?"

"I brought Georgie to see you."

Excitement mingled with disappointment. Excitement that she'd see her boy again. Disappointment that Rex wasn't coming after her because he missed her and couldn't live without her.

"Where is he?" Why was he staring at her with such intensity? She matched his gaze and tried to focus as he stepped close.

He gave a short laugh. "He's at the farm with your parents. I've come to take you home."

"Oh Rex. Can we go right away? I'm aching to see him."

"Do you need to say good night to anyone?"

Aimee frowned. "No. Why would I?"

"I saw you holding hands with a man. I thought he might be your beau."

Aimee's heartbeat quickened to the sadness evident in his tone. "Jonas is a good friend. His wife passed away a couple of months ago. He wants me to marry him."

All expression fled from Rex's face. "You can't."

"You're right. I can't marry a man I don't love. . .or one who doesn't love me." She gave him a pointed look. "May we go home now so I can see my son?"

Relief crossed his features. Smiling, Rex took her hand. "My buggy is over there."

"How's Georgie been?"

"Lonely." The warmth in his voice nearly took her breath away. "We both have been."

"So have I, Rex. So lonely."

He stopped beside the buggy and turned her to face him. "Aimee, when I say I've come to take you home, I don't mean to the farm. I mean to my home."

Aimee drew in a cool breath as he stepped forward, cupping her face in his hands. "W–what are you saying?"

"You know exactly what I'm saying." His throat practically growled the words. "I'm marrying you, Aimee Riley. So don't give me any reasons why you shouldn't marry me. Don't tell me you don't love me, because I can see it in your eyes. I can see it in the pulse at the base of your neck. You love me as much as I love you."

Aimee's mind spun with the force of his words. Did he realize that he'd just told her he loved her? Could it be true? In her wildest dreams, Rex had admitted the words over and over, but when the reality of daylight shone through, Aimee had never quite been able to make herself believe he might actually love her.

"Say something," he commanded.

"I–I'm not sure what to say."

"Tell me you love me, too." He pressed a soft, quick kiss to her lips, still holding her cheeks between his palms.

Aimee breathed out a sigh. "I do love you, Rex. But what about—"

"There are no buts." He kissed her again. "You love me. That's all I need to know."

"Your mother. . ."

"I put her on a train back to New York the day after New Year's. She won't be around to insult you."

"What about the things she said about me? She's right. I didn't fit in at the dinner party."

He pressed his forehead against hers. "Honey, I don't invite socialites to my home. That was solely my mother's doing. I like the simplicity of just going to work and coming home every day. And maybe an occasional outing to the theater with my wife."

Aimee's stomach curled as his voice took on a deep, husky tone. The way he said "my wife" filled her with longing. She lifted her arms and clasped them around his neck. "Oh Rex. It sounds lovely. Are you sure?"

His arms moved from her face to catch her around the waist. He pulled her close. "More sure than I've ever been about anything in my life. Marry me." Without waiting for an answer, he crushed her to him, covering her lips with his in a kiss that left her breathless and pushed away any lingering doubt.

Aimee thrilled to his embrace. When he pulled away, she smiled. "Yes, Rex. I'll marry you."

"Before we go back to Oregon City?"

"The sooner the better."

He kissed her again, this time gently, his lips moving over hers with tenderness that caused tears to form in her eyes.

"Are you crying?" He frowned as his gaze captured hers.

"Tears of joy."

He took her hand and pulled her to the buggy. "Let's go tell our son the news."

Aimee nodded, her heart filled with joy and thanksgiving. As they rode shoulder to shoulder toward her parents' farm, she